SPEAKEASY

Daniel E. Speer

PublishAmerica
Baltimore

© 2013 by Daniel E. Speer.
All rights reserved. No part of this book may be reproduced, stored in a retrieval system or transmitted in any form or by any means without the prior written permission of the publishers, except by a reviewer who may quote brief passages in a review to be printed in a newspaper, magazine or journal.

First printing

All characters in this book are fictitious, and any resemblance to real persons, living or dead, is coincidental.

PublishAmerica has allowed this work to remain exactly as the author intended, verbatim, without editorial input.

Softcover 9781627723831
PUBLISHED BY PUBLISHAMERICA, LLLP
www.publishamerica.com
Baltimore

Printed in the United States of America

PREFACE

The 1950's era was one of growing pangs; treading new waters; pushing the envelope to the breaking point and beyond; trying new things and spreading your wings. The daring became more daring and the meek were swallowed up and passed by for being too passive with no outward desire for change. The adventurous became bold while their behavior, although brazen, had an aura of dread lingering nearby to ward off the overzealous urge to throw caution to the wind.

This story takes place during that time and is about how a young and naive teenager is coerced into assisting with a known gang of thieves. Within just a few years, he caused the death of one person, angered many more and somehow avoided joining the growing list of people wanted by the FBI. In the end, he's hung out to dry by the people he worked for and sets out to repay those that used him for their selfish gain.

CHAPTER 1

My name is Adam Dwayne Cooper. I go by "A.D". Everyone calls me that except my mom and dad (Marvin and Nell Cooper) and my oldest brother (and one of my former teachers, Mrs. Sumner), they call me Adam. I didn't have a life of leisure while growing up. I was the youngest of three boys (just a year apart), all who had to work at an early age to assist with the family bills and livelihood. My dad was a long-haul trucker that was seldom home and my mom only worked in the fields as a young girl. Her work around the house took most of her time, so an outside job was not even considered. She washed and ironed, cleaned the house, made the beds, cooked the meals, washed the dishes, and even mowed the lawn when she couldn't get one of us to do it. Any of us would do it for a dollar, but she refused to pay us for working on our own place. Every week, she ran errands to pay bills, do the grocery shopping and run us around to various events. She loved to dress up for church on Sunday and took pride in having her three boys along side her on the pew. My dad never went to church, even when he was home from his truck trips.

My first job was in the pepper fields, just a few miles from our home in Henley. I was only ten years old. The farmer offered the summer work for 50 cents a bushel basket. The farm was divided into four fields that were mostly flat and expansive, and the picking of the crop was staggered in order for the peppers to ripen. One field was planted with bell peppers that were picked later in the year, but it was too close to school starting and our mom wouldn't let us pick them. That was fine with me.

We walked to the Community Center in town where an old blue bus would pick us up and drop us off at the main house and work shed of the farm. Everyone would pick up their baskets and walk to the fields assigned for the day. Sometimes it was over a ten minute walk to the spot where we started. The older kids would sometimes bully the younger ones in route. One particular girl, Daisy, would usually end up crying before we arrived at the picking spot. She was older than me but obviously more fragile with her feelings and I felt sorry for her, but never crossed the line drawn by the older boys.

It would take a good picker about a half hour or more of stooping, selecting and picking peppers to fill a basket. Everyone was assigned a number of long rows (usually eight) and you would walk up one row and down the next, picking only the ripe peppers as you went. In the bright sunlight, you could barely make out the end of the row...it was a long way away. Once the basket was filled, you walked to the low-boy trailer that was in the middle of the field and emptied your basket into a larger basket to be inspected by a farm hand. The owner preferred you walk around the row to the trailer rather than walk over the plants for fear of breaking stems or crushing peppers, but most everyone walked over the tops of the plants anyway. The farm hand would remove peppers that were unfit for processing, like rotten ones, unripe ones, and deformed ones, and empty the remaining good ones into a large bin. He marked down on a pad the name of the picker and the quantity of baskets under it, then handed the basket back to you for refilling. The picker got docked a whole basket if the ranch hand found too many culls to throw out. I had more than my share of those. The man inspecting the baskets was called Hank by the owner, but when one of the pickers called him that, he told them that his name was George. I never could figure that out and rather than stir up something that I didn't want any part of, I just didn't speak to him at all. Many times I didn't finish my assigned rows and had to have help from those that did.

I thought I worked hard, but was dismayed to discover that I ranked at the bottom of the list when compared to the other twenty plus pickers. A few of the pickers (my age) would pick 10-12 baskets a day. I managed to pick 8 one time. Most days I averaged 6. One other kid, probably 10 or 11 was almost as bad as me in his numbers. He got yelled at a lot from his older siblings and would just sit down and not pick for hours. He did a lot better when no one was hassling him.

I figured out that I was more in tune to things in the morning hours because I could only fill two and sometimes three baskets in the afternoon. That girl that the older kids picked on could out do me every day. My oldest brother, Mark, and other brother, Cecil, also worked in the fields that year and they both out did me without a problem. They both bragged about it with gusto, calling me a sissy and lazy, but never bothered me during the day like that other boy. Mark did about 15 baskets a day and Cecil averaged at least 12. The day started at 7 a.m., lunch at 11 a.m. and work stopped at 4 p.m. What took me the most time was the walk to the trailer to empty my basket. Being shorter than most of the others, I did walk around the row rather than step over, plus I found too many things to do on the way there and on the way back. Like pick up rocks that were interesting to look at, or fiddle with the leaky faucet handle on the water spigot. I didn't mind standing in line to empty my basket, except for the scorching heat.

The boss would yell cuss words at us when he caught us goofing off. One of the older boys said the man used to be a drill sergeant in the Army. I remember trying to repeat one of the words one time at home when Mark made me mad, but Dad promptly stopped me and warned me never to let him hear me say it again.

"That's not a good word, Adam. Don't you ever let me hear you say it again or I'll make you wish you hadn't," he warned.

I can remember the exact word with clarity, and have since learned it's meaning, but have never said it again to anyone.

Due to me and Mark always arguing, the boss separated us by half of the field's length so that we wouldn't be close to one another. Why he didn't do that with that other kid was a mystery. I often felt sorry for him because his two brothers and sister yelled at him a lot. Sometime during the day I think everyone in the field got hit by a pepper. I got hit several times with one from someone a few rows over, but I could never pinpoint who did the throwing. I thought at first that it was Mark, but he surely couldn't throw a pepper from that far away and be accurate enough to strike. I didn't dare retaliate without possibly hitting the wrong person and getting in trouble. Often times, the peppers would fly during the bus ride back to town, too. The driver caught one of the older boys one time and made him get out and walk home. He tried to blame it on another person, but was seen in the act. We weren't too far from town when it happened, anyway, so it wasn't a long walk. That boy never returned the next day or the next. Someone said he got another job somewhere and wouldn't be back.

I remember it well; especially the blazing sun and no shade. Have you ever tried to seek shade in a pepper patch? I made a lot of trips to the outhouse. Not to use it every time, but there was some shade there, cast by the outhouse itself, and that water spigot was just a few feet away. I didn't dare linger too long, though, because someone would tell on you if you did and the boss would dock you a whole basket.

I come down with a stomach ache the last week of picking and only worked two days. Mom allowed me to stay home and take care of my stomach. She instructed Mark to pick up my paycheck. I worked for almost six weeks and made $120.00. Mark and Cecil made almost twice as much as me. Mom took all of it. Mark argued with her for a bit, but he lost and he had to forfeit all of his pay as well. She did buy some clothes for each of us, though; each of us got a brand new coat for winter wear. I did decide that picking peppers was hard work and not the thing that I wanted to do with my life.

I tried bucking hay the summer I turned twelve, but that too was way too difficult for a small person like me. The rancher questioned if I could do the work when he hired me and I convinced him that I could. I started out bucking the bales onto the trailer, but couldn't physically do it, so the rancher put me on the trailer to straighten bales as they were hoisted up. That too was harder than I bargained for, so I quit after only three days. I decided right then that hard work for little pay was not the life that I wanted to lead. Something, somewhere, had to be better than working this hard for a living.

"I don't want to do that kind of work again," I acknowledged to no one in particular.

I wasn't afraid of work, just not capable of doing work that called for strength. After I matured a bit and put on some weight, the jobs for those with bulk and strength were unavailable, it seemed, so I looked for work that would utilize my mind more than my body.

I was raised in poverty, but didn't know it. Shucks, I had food, clothing, shelter, and very strict parents. We lived like everyone else around these parts, so we considered the rich folks the ones that had nice yards and shiny automobiles. If you were really well off, then you could afford to have your lawn mowed and taken care of and your car washed and waxed regularly. Mark mowed lawns of the rich one summer and made real good money. Mom took most of that too, but did let Mark have some pocket change to spend on candy or whatever at the local mercantile. That was another reason to not seek work of any kind...Mom would take every bit of it. I have no idea what I would have spent money on; junk most likely, but still, having a little change in your pocket would make a fella feel good, I think.

One of those rich folks lived just a little ways behind us. At least most of the people in Henley considered them rich. Mark never mowed their lawn because they had a crew come in every week and work all day long on the lawn, trees, bushes, shrubs, and flower beds. They had a really nice house that was as long as a football field it seemed...well, maybe not that long, but it took up a lot of space. It had trees and shrubs all around it and large evergreens down one entire side of the place. They didn't have any young kids our age. Occasionally, a pretty blonde lady would visit. She always arrived in a big black car, driven by a chauffer. She never stayed in the house long, though, before she got back in the chauffer-driven limo and rode away. My mom said she was a daughter of the family and an only child. They had two really nice, fancy cars and a three car garage. I never did see a third car that belonged to them. Their names were Charles and Barbara Parker. It was rumored throughout the area that they were former movie stars.

Our food was usually cold cereal or oatmeal for breakfast. We often had peanut butter and jelly sandwiches (and once in a while we had tuna fish sandwiches) or soup and crackers for lunch. Mom would cook up a pot of beans about once a month and we ate beans and cornbread for what seemed like every night for weeks on end. Every now and then, we got corned beef hash for supper and once in a blue moon, we were served scrambled eggs and toast. Mark would ask permission to fish at the pot holes once in awhile and bring back a small bass or two that Mom would fry up. Our meals weren't fancy, but they sustained us. We knew better than to complain because either Mom or Dad would tan our hides with a switch or a belt. I vowed many times to someday do better than my parents. I knew I would probably never be rich like the Parkers, but I figured I could do better than what I had.

Our little four-roomed house (with an upstairs room) sat at the end of Porter Road. Porter road was a dead end road with a vacant lot next to our house that my dad used to park his truck when he brought it home. The front room was large and the arch that led to the table and kitchen was at one end with the hall at the other that led to the bathroom and my parent's bedroom. The landlord had converted the attic into a bedroom and built a set of stairs at the end of the front room. I and my brothers slept upstairs. I slept with Cecil at one end of the attic and Mark slept alone at the other. Mom built two shelving areas for our clothes. She made them out of wood planks across cinder blocks. They worked just as good as anyone's chest of drawers. We sure could have used a window or two, especially in the summer when it was in the mid 90's for days on end. The temperature upstairs on those days reached over the hundred mark, I'm sure. Mark refused to sleep upstairs a lot of the time during the summer and took a blanket outdoors on the grass and slept under the stars.

We almost froze to death in the winter months until Dad bought a used wood stove to put in the front room. Prior to that, the only heat source was from an oil floor furnace in the hall. Heat rises, but it sure didn't do a lot of rising in that house. I can remember seeing my breath on many a morning when I woke up to go to school. It was not unusual to be wrapped up in a blanket while eating breakfast before getting dressed and leaving the house. I swear it was warmer outside on occasion than in that cold house. Mark either stole or borrowed an electric heater one time and just about set the house on fire with it. It didn't work too well and the cord was frayed a little, and although Cecil tried to tell him it was dangerous, he plugged it in anyway to a light socket extension and the sparks flew, knocking the power out in the entire upstairs. Mark changed the fuse that blew and got rid of the heater. I don't think my parents ever knew about that little ditty.

There was a small lumber mill up near Crestview that we got log ends from and split and stacked for our use. I can remember a lot of slivers being stuck in my hands and fingers from handling that wood. Mark almost chopped off his foot while splitting wood one time. Lucky for him he had shoes on or he certainly would have lost a toe, probably. The wood was also a source of fighting and arguing on whose turn it was to carry it in.

During the school year, we pretty much fended for ourselves on many days, because Mom would want to sleep in. She would get us up, though, and once our feet were on the floor, she would return to the warmth of her covers. Sometimes we ate breakfast and sometimes we didn't, depending on what there was to eat. If the milk was spoiled, we would refrain from cold cereal and maybe eat a slice of bread; or toast it in the oven and eat it with some jam. Once we had finished, we would grab our lunch sacks and head for the bus stop at the main road to catch a ride to school. Mark was late for the bus a lot of the time because he would primp in the bathroom too long. I can remember a lot of mornings seeing him sprint for the waiting bus.

"One of these days, I'm not waiting for you, Mark," the bus driver would chastise.

"Go on without me, then. I don't care," Mark would reply as he plopped down in a seat.

Mom was usually home when we returned and had the house cleaned, the clothes washed and often a snack for us. She sometimes went to the store and restocked the cupboards with food. She wasn't a lazy sort, just slow getting started on the day. She stayed up late at night many times, reading or crocheting. One thing we could always depend on was her fixing our sack lunches before she went to bed. They consisted of peanut butter sandwiches most times (with jam on occasion), and a cookie; sometimes home made and other times store bought. I begged for a lunch box one year, because a lot of the other kids had one, but was told that paper sacks would be my carrying case as long as I lived under her roof. We were really good about bringing home our lunch sacks every day. If you were careful, a paper sack would last an entire week or more.

The summer months were like a totally different time and place in comparison to school time. Mom would sometimes want to go berry picking or get an early start on cleaning or something and get us up to help. We didn't get to sleep in much during our summer vacation. She encouraged us to look for work saying that the family could use the extra money. Once we found work of any kind, she was diligent in getting us up to go, making our breakfast and challenging us to do a good day's work. Not all of us were lucky enough to find work every summer.

I was small in stature early on but by the time I was a teenager, I looked much older and had grown to 5' 7" tall. I know that our old house is probably gone now, but I suspect there were marks on the door jamb to prove our growth spurts. My brothers were always bigger and stronger than me, but by the spring the year I turned 15, they never bothered to pick on me anymore because I could hold my own when fighting them. Mark graduated that spring and Cecil drowned that summer at the pot holes.

The set of pot holes was about a half mile southeast from the house and consisted of 11 holes that underground springs filled with water. They weren't very big in size, maybe thirty or forty feet across with small streams connecting them and most of them were only about ten feet deep. Large cattails, small trees, and clumps of bushes surrounded most of them and a small patch of dirt and rock every so often was used to enter and exit the water. One hole was larger than the others and deeper too, so it was where we did most of our swimming.

One time Cecil sneaked off to do some skinny dipping at the pot holes with the neighbor girl and she said once he dove in and just never came up. She waited around for him for close to a half hour thinking he was trying to play a trick on her again and come up behind her and scare her, but it never happened. She ran back to the house and told my mom. The authorities looked for his body and found it in a clump of cattails near the bank of one of the holes. The funeral service and burial for him was the following week and Mark got to go to the funeral but I had to stay home. Our neighbor lady, Mrs. Gibson, stayed with me while the others attended the service. Mom was able to contact my dad, who was trucking somewhere out west, and he flew home for the funeral. Mom had to drive over to the airport at Clarkston to pick him up.

"You're still too young to be going to funerals. Wait till you understand what they are all about, and then you can go," Mom said to me.

She continued to lecture us on swimming in the pot holes without supervision.

"You just never know what might happen there," she would say.

She had always forbidden us swimming in them, but fishing was okay. Naturally, being boys, we challenged her authority at every turn. I never ventured that way again, but I know Mark did a time or two. Him being older and thinking that he was wiser prompted him to disobey Mom's orders whenever he liked. He was that way his entire life, thinking that rules and regulations were meant for others, not him. I don't think he felt like he was above the law, just didn't think they were written to include him. That was Mark; always considering himself just as good as most people and better than many.

I remember mom making us go to church with her every Sunday. Cecil always wanted to go to Sunday school and wanted to walk to the church, but Mom insisted he wait for the rest of us and we all sit together. She allowed me and Cecil to go with Mrs. Gibson a few times and we attended her Sunday school class. We were instructed to find Mom immediately afterwards, though, and sit together for the main church service. Mrs. Gibson lived on our street and walked everywhere she went. She was a widow lady and said to be wealthy, although she never looked or acted the part. The few times I encountered her over the years, I never asked her about Mr. Gibson or how much money she had.

The little Methodist church was only a short ride for us and many a Sunday was spent there. I never had a Bible to call my own, but Mom's was big enough for everyone. I could barely carry its weight, although I tried a lot thinking I was relieving my mom of the burden. The preacher, Pastor Snow, was an old man (in his sixties I was told) that not once in all the times I attended his church, opened his Bible. He quoted a lot of scripture from memory during his sermons, though. Who knows if they were correct? Cecil was one of several that walked down front during an altar call one Sunday and Mark made fun of him, saying he was just doing it to get attention and did it because everyone else was doing it. I never questioned his move, figuring he must have had a reason.

I didn't get pushed around at Mountain View county school due to my size and most kids respected me for what I was, rather than who I was. Mountain View was one of four county schools that housed all of the kids in the valley through the eighth grade. Pawnee Falls had one named Gilmore; MacAfee had one named John Adams Elementary; and Woodsboro, (the largest of the small towns), had the fourth county school named McKinley and the one high school. Woodsboro High School provided the higher education for those in the area that decided to attend a higher level of school. A lot of kids dropped out of school after the eighth grade to help in the fields or assist at home while others joined the Army or a branch of the armed services. Mark knew one girl that quit school after the eighth grade and got married. I sure thought that was a risk. Mom cautioned the three of us constantly about not making that mistake. Mark graduated from Woodsboro High. He never even considered going on to college, but started looking for work instead.

How Mountain View got its name was always a mystery to everyone, because there isn't a mountain within a hundred miles in any direction. Our state is known for its flat land and many jokes have been told saying that you can see Lake Crimson on a clear day (It's the state's largest lake that is well over 200 miles away). Perhaps the most satisfying tale suggests that the founder of the town was wishing for the view of a mountain when it was founded. Another tale says that the founder was delusional and saw mountains in his mind.

The city of Clarkston was in Clarkston County, thirty minutes east, and it not only had a county school and a high school, but also had the only junior college for miles around. The closest four-year college was in Albany, about an hours drive south of Henley. Albany was one of the largest cities around our part of the country.

I was always smarter than most of the kids my age and also smarter than a lot of kids older than me. I never understood why or how, but I was able to grasp things quicker than most and apply myself better than others. I was smarter than Mark and a lot smarter, book wise, than my mom and dad, who neither one had a high school education. I sometimes wish that I had finished high school, but as things worked out, it just wasn't meant to be. My teachers always marveled at my ability to learn and use the things that I learned so quickly. They all told me that I would do well in whatever it was that I decided to do. My teachers liked me and that made me feel wanted and important; especially, Mrs. Sumner.

"You be sure and make a good decision on where you intend to end up in life, Adam, or you may find yourself somewhere you don't want to be," she once told me.

That certainly didn't make any sense to me. I guess she meant jail or somewhere bad. I liked her a lot. She was really young to be a teacher, I thought, and real pretty. I never met her husband, but seen him pick her up after school one time. I felt like I was liked more at school than at home due to there never being a lot of love shown in my family. It seemed that we were always angry. We yelled at one another a lot and seemed to never get along. The disputes were not earth shattering, but trivial. Mostly arguments over who did what last; like wash dishes, carry out the trash, haul wood, mow the lawn, or whose turn it was to use the phone. We had a party line that some lady was constantly on making it difficult to make a call. Mark would argue with her a lot in an attempt to dissuade her from using the phone so much. It didn't seem to do any good. We argued a lot over what radio program we were going to listen to during the evening. Mom usually settled that argument by turning the radio off all together.

All three of us boys wrestled and fought over the stupidest things you could imagine. Even when we were playing games we usually ended up fighting or arguing over something.

It was usually over a rule that got changed or ignored for a better advantage by someone. It seemed that I was always the one ending up on the dirty end of the stick. We loved to play basketball in the driveway and shoot at the wire hoop Dad put up over the door of the garage. It was the steel band from a nail keg he picked up at the hardware store. The games were usually H-O-R-S-E or variations of it. The basketball was one we got for Christmas one year. It was leather and amazingly stayed firm all the time. We often played outside at night in the summer time and got as many of the neighbor kids involved as we could. It was usually a game of hide-and-seek when that happened. It too usually ended up with a fight over some stupid thing.

Cecil had a knack for getting under Mark's skin whether we were playing a game or just sitting around. He would make some wise-cracked comment or strike up an argument on something he said. Once the comment was made, the fight was usually on. Mark would throw something at him or hit him in the arm or leg in protest. Cecil lost part of a finger during one of those little skirmishes. Mark bit it off. He was mad a Cecil because Cecil called him a liar over something he said he did. Mark took exception and told him to apologize. Cecil refused and they wrestled for a bit before Cecil came up screaming like he'd been shot and holding up a bloody hand. Cecil may have gotten the worst end of things, but Mark got the whipping of his life. I didn't look, but I bet he had blisters on his butt from the spanking that Dad gave him. He wasn't able to sit down for several days without wincing from pain. Cecil lost the tip of his little finger on his left hand. Nothing major in the way of losses, but still, that's pretty bad when you think about it. He wore a bandage on his hand for weeks before it finally healed. I have since accounted all the arguing and yelling to my dad, though, because he was never happy with how things were when he was home.

He and Mom would argue a lot, it seemed. I never really understood why they yelled at one another, but it became so common place that us boys stayed out of it.

My dad used to smoke cigarettes, but stopped doing so when he had a horrible coughing spree one time while inhaling a cigar. It was given to him by a friend who had just became a father and passed out cigars to his buddies in celebration. I remember the cigar lying on the window sill in the kitchen and wondering what it tasted like. Mark convinced Dad to smoke it by his constant whining about wanting to try it. Dad gathered all of us on the front porch and lit the thing. He got it going real good and passed it to Mark who took a puff and immediately started hacking. Mark passed it to Cecil and trying to be manly about it, he held the smoke in for a bit and when his eyes started watering, let it out and walked away coughing like you never heard before. I refused to take the thing and Dad took another puff and drew it deep into his lungs. He began to cough like never before and so harshly, that we all begin to get concerned if he was going to be able to get his breath back. Dad made all us swear that day that we would never ever smoke.

"And I swear that I'm quitting too," he stated, and took out his pack of cigarettes and crushed them in his hand.

My dad was a long-haul trucker so he wasn't home very often. When he was home, he would always act the leader of the family and tell us what to do. He decided all disputes, whether it was right or not. What he said was the law. I can remember being cuffed up beside the head on many occasions for not acknowledging his orders or forgetting to say *"Sir"*. He wasn't in the Armed Services due to a bad leg that he broke when he fell off a horse as a kid. The *"Yes Sir"* was just showing respect for your elders, he said.

Dad was the youngest of three boys in his family. I never did meet any of my uncles; grandma or grandpa, either. He only referred to them on occasion and anytime any of us asked about them, he was quick to squelch the topic and change the subject. I do remember one of them being named Dwayne, though, and I have always felt that I was named after him. He did mention that one on them was killed in the war; Uncle Bobby, I think, but I'm not sure. As far as aunts and cousins are concerned, I figure I will never find out about either. Kids at school don't talk much about their grandparents or families either, so it didn't bother me. I just hope I don't wind up in the same boat.

Dad was killed in a trucking accident in New Mexico the fall after Cecil's death. He was hauling a truck load of sugar beets. The full details of the accident were never revealed to us boys, but according to Dad's driving partner, Wilbur, it was gruesome. The truck rammed into the back of another truck and then went under it, was all we were told. Wilbur was not hurt in the accident but died several years later from a heart attack.

"I told Marvin it was my turn to drive, but he insisted on driving to the next stop even though he was so tired he could barely keep his eyes open," Wilbur told my mom at the funeral.

We all came to the conclusion that Dad had fallen asleep at the wheel.

The whole area around our place consisted of small towns and large farm land. Field crops were dominant in the valley with peppers, potatoes, soy beans, and sugar beets being the main ones. A few smaller farms were scattered across the county growing corn, hay or grain. Corn was grown over many acres elsewhere in the state. I was told in school that corn was the state's number one crop. A dairy farm was just up the road a piece toward Crestview. We got our milk from there once in a while. I didn't know of any other dairy farms anywhere around. A cattle ranch was located way out toward St. Lawrence in Ferry County. A rich man named Bishop owned it. My dad hauled a load of grain to his place on several occasions.

When we weren't working at one of the big farms during the summer, we would sometimes walk down to another set of pot holes outside of Jasper. There was a high knoll there where you could actually see the town of Clarkston some twenty plus miles away. Those holes had some really good bass fishing. It wasn't unusual for Mark to jump in and swim around once in a while. The hardest part of those times was not letting Mom find out. If she caught him, or suspected him of swimming there, the belt would be lashing out and leaving welts on his backsides for sure. I can remember Mark borrowing my shirt one time because his was wet. Momma stopped us just inside the front door and quizzed us as to where we had been. Mark lied to her and told her that Jimmy Johnson threw water on him and got his shirt wet so he took mine. I got in trouble for exposing my skin to the hot sun and risking getting burnt. Mark never bothered telling her the truth. I looked at him for support and he just shrugged his shoulders and walked away.

Penn Ridge bordered the north portion of the valley and the Mudd River divided the farm land like a snake crawling through the grass. The river dug deep crevices out of the landscape in several places, causing huge canyons. Small towns dotted the landscape in Northwest Blaine County like spots on a dappled horse. The larger cities in the area were miles away in all directions. I had not visited any of them. Mark went with Dad one time on a truck haul and saw a lot of the area from the cab. Few people in our neighborhood had ever made the trip to the bigger cities. Besides the Penn-Crest Railroad crossing the valley, section roads and county roads divided the land that my dad said looked from the air like someone free handed a big checkerboard.

We all missed our dad, but Mom took Dad's death the hardest. When she returned from the funeral (which I and Mark were forbidden to attend) she was never the same as before. She constantly wore a frown on her brow, never smiled and always seemed sad. She stopped going to church, so we didn't go either. After about six months, she started staying in her bedroom more and more. She wouldn't come out of her room for days on end at times. She ate in the bedroom when she ate anything. We fended for ourselves, mostly on peanut butter and jelly sandwiches. I tried my hand at cooking several times. The prepared meal wasn't bad, but I decided I wasn't cut out to be a cook. I think I used every pot and pan in the kitchen. I tried my best to keep the house picked up and clean. I swept the floor regularly and tried to mop it a few times. Mark helped on occasion, but most times, it was only me doing the work. Mark drove the car to the small towns around looking for work. He was gone a lot, it seemed. I washed clothes in the old ringer washer that sat on the screened-in back porch. The washer was given to us by someone. I swapped out the bedding with clean sheets and pillow cases regularly; even Mom's when I could get her up. One time I did it when she was in the bathroom after convincing her that taking a good hot bath would make her feel better. She bought my suggestion and while she was bathing, I changed out her bedding. Mom always ironed our clothes, but I didn't. Wrinkles don't look so bad once you've worn the thing for a while.

By Mom not eating, she was wasting away to nothing. Mark said it was depression from losing both Dad and Cecil. Pastor Snow dropped by a few times to talk to her, but she wouldn't speak with him. She wouldn't even come out of the bedroom when Dale the insurance man stopped by to get her weekly payment. They used to talk for hours on end at times. Now, one of us would knock on the bedroom door and tell her who was here and she would direct us to the dresser where an envelope was placed. We handed Dale the envelope and he would give us a small receipt in exchange. I looked at the receipt once and noticed that it was for $1.40. He always asked about her.

"Your mom still not feeling up to snuff?" Dale would ask.

Then one night after Mark and I had gone to bed, we heard a ruckus outside that made us both get up and check it out. We heard yelling and cursing coming from the back of the house. We investigated and found Mom standing in the back yard yelling at the neighbor's house across the back fence.

"What's she doing, Mark?" I asked.

"I think she's lost her marbles. Mom wouldn't say those words if her mouth was full of them. I can't see anyone that she's yelling at, so she must be seeing whoever in her mind. She could be sleep walking too, I expect," Mark guessed.

"Let's get her back inside, then, okay?" I suggested. "If she's sleep walking, maybe we can steer her back inside without waking her."

"Okay, but if she wakes up we may have hell to pay. You just don't know how she will react," Mark cautioned.

Mom wasn't sleep walking, but for some reason she didn't know who we were and began to slap at Mark first and then me when we tried to return her to the house. We were successful in our attempt and she was soon back to sleep, but mumbled for a few minutes before doing so. We had to laugh at her comments, though. She was very unhappy about someone in her mind re-roofing the garage without telling anyone. That's what she was yelling about and cursing whoever it was.

"She's loonier than a coot, I'm telling you," Mark commented afterwards.

Mark got fed up with being the *Man of the House* and took off to be on his own when he was just a month away from being 19. He loaded up the old '50 gray Plymouth with all of his stuff and left without so much as a word. Mom never drove the car any more and I guess Mark figured it was his for the taking. I always envied him because now I had to be the Man of the House and didn't want to be. I figured some day it would be my turn to leave and I wouldn't hesitate. The sooner the better was all right with me. We got a letter from Mark about two months later. I ripped it open to read what my arrogant brother had to say and found out that he was living in St. Lawrence and working with a construction company that helps build the new highways. I had heard about the new roads crisscrossing America, and wondered if I would ever be able to drive on one of them. I couldn't imagine two and three lanes going the same direction. That sounds dangerous and a bit frightening to me, but maybe they know what they're doing. Mark said his job was driving a road grader. I couldn't imagine Mark driving a road grader, but I was happy that he found something to do with his life.

That old car had a memory or two tied to it. The time Mark drove it into the creek has to be near the top of the list. Us boys rode along with Mom one time while she visited one of her friends over in Mountain View. We were told to stay in the car while she took a pot of beans inside to the lady. The Tennyson Creek flowed past the lady's house to the side of her driveway.

Mom left the car running while she ran inside. Mark was not tall enough to see over the steering wheel without a few catalogs under him, but he got the car in gear somehow and while turning the steering wheel as though he was driving, steered the car forward right into the creek. Water started coming in around the front doors and running to the back seat where Cecil and I sat. We screamed like girls and got all panicky. Cecil bailed out of the car like it was on fire and sat out side on the creek bank watching the water flow in and around the car. I stayed curled up on the seat and watched the water rise to about the midway point. Fortunately for him and us I guess, the man two houses over had a tractor that was used to pull the car out of the ditch. What was going to be just a quick errand turned out to be a whole afternoon event. I can remember Mom scolding Mark though and telling him how lucky he was that his dad wasn't home. I can't remember when it was that Mark finally learned to drive.

Another time with that old gray car was when a rock came right through the windshield while we were driving home from a trip to see Dad's new truck. It was parked in a field over near Jasper and he was so proud of it and insisted that the whole family have a look at it. Dad was driving and, like always, us boys were in the back seat sitting on our hands. That was how Dad made us sit when he was driving. Once in a while, Cecil would stand up behind him and look over his left shoulder. I guess Dad was either psychic or could feel Cecil's breath on the back of his neck, because every time Cecil stood there, Dad would know it.

"Are you boys sitting down like I told you?" he would say.

Cecil would quickly plop back down on the seat like no one's business.

On our return home that time, Dad was following a large dump truck with dual wheels on the back. He mentioned to Mom that he could see what appeared to be a rock stuck between the tires.

"That could be a dangerous situation if it came loose," he observed.

He hadn't much more than got the words out of his mouth when it did let go and came right into our car through the windshield on Mom's side. She screamed to the top of her lungs and everyone got all excited. By the time Dad pulled over and stopped the car, Mom had passed out. Glass had scattered all over her dress and in the front seat. No one was injured, but I can remember seeing that big hole in the right windshield. It was fixed the very next time I got in the car. I don't know how Dad got it fixed so quickly, but it was done in less than a week, I bet. He went back out on the road soon after that little episode in his brand new truck.

My clothing was mostly hand-me-downs from my brothers. When Dad was alive, Mom would often make my shirts and bed clothes. She insisted I wear the pajamas she made for me. My brothers never had to wear pj's at all. They were allowed to wear just their skivvies to bed. Cecil swiped a pair of my flannel pj's from the shelf one bitterly cold winter night just for more warmth, but I think that was the only time. I told on him and he got a whipping. Everything Mom made was all hand sewn with needle and thread because she didn't have a sewing machine. I once saw her pulling threads from an old tattered table cloth that she had found and winding the thread around a folded over piece of heavy paper. She would sometimes get a sack full of material from a lady that worked at the five and dime store in town. Every now and then, a few patterns would show up with the sack of material. Also in the sack would be a few magazines and an occasional paperback novel. I cherished those like gold. When Mom sewed, I would read. I read a few of those magazines from cover to cover over and over again. I wished for the good old days many times over since Mom became a recluse. The magazines were used to make a fire one time when we were out of wood, so the idea of re-reading any of them was out of the question.

I would wear my new shirts with pride, even though the style was out of date. Button-up style shirts were made as pull-overs because she didn't have buttons and couldn't afford them. I didn't know or care. My jeans had patches on the knees and other than a pair of old overalls and two pair of wool dress slacks (which I wore to church), most of my pants were short; cut-off or torn off right below the knee. I would cinch up all of my pants with a belt that was way too big for me.

"I can have someone cut that belt off for you if you think it would look better, Adam," Mom said one time.

"It's fine, really," I would counter while fingering its lengthy end.

I wore some of Dad's old clothes (the better ones) after he died and it made me feel closer to him somehow. I can remember rolling up the pant legs of the overalls a few times to keep them from dragging the ground.

Every once in a while, Mom would talk to me about important things that I might come across during my rise into adulthood. She would preface each one with…*'when you get older, you'll find'*…I actually looked forward to those conversations because I usually learned something from them. I remember when I was seven years old, she told me that Santa Claus was not real and the Tooth Fairy was just a made up story. Those realizations were a little more devastating than discovering that there wasn't an Easter Bunny.

We didn't talk much about the difference between boys and girls, but she always cautioned me on how I treated females, young and old.

"Always respect women of any age and never ever hit a girl in the stomach. That's where babies are made and you just never know if God is in the process of making one, so never hit a girl in the stomach," she warned.

"I promise Mom," I replied.

"You be sure and love the girl you get pregnant, too, understand?" she told me as if it were an unpardonable sin.

"Oh, Mom; that's embarrassing," I remember replying.

"Your dad will tell you about the Birds and Bees some day. But, meanwhile, you be sure and keep your hormones in check", she stated.

I had no idea what she was talking about, but didn't dare ask. My dad never did have that talk she spoke of.

My dad was never open about his family or his upbringing. Most of the information obtained as to his background was from our mother. He was raised on a dirt farm in the mid-west and ran away at the age of fourteen due to not wanting to be beat up anymore. He got a job topping trees for some outfit and during that job, fell from a tall tree and broke his shoulder, hip and pelvis. It took over three years to finally heal to the point that he could walk upright and work for a living. That's when he got the job helping at Mom's place. He walked with a limp ever since his accident, but it never interfered with his work. He was hired by the trucking firm right after we moved to Henley and worked for them right up to the day he died. Mom said he spoke of a sister a few times, but Mom never met her nor did any of us. Her name was Lilly, she thought, but couldn't be real sure.

Another of our talks was about her family, whom I never met either. She and Dad ran away together to get married and she abandoned her family. I had a Grandma and Grandpa Caldwell somewhere out there (a grandma and grandpa Cooper, too, I think) but I had no idea where Pimberton was other than somewhere way east of here. My mom didn't talk about her family much. She said once that she missed her mom, but knew that making contact with her would be a big mistake, so never did. She told me that she lost her older sister during a twister when she was just twelve years old. She refused to go to the storm cellar and instead, hid in the outhouse during the storm and when it was all over, both her sister and the outhouse were gone. Her body was later found in a field five miles away.

"My daddy was a cruel man, Adam, and you have to promise me that when you have kids someday, that you will treat them like the most important thing in your life. You hear what I'm saying?" she told me.

"Okay, Momma, I promise," I told her without really knowing what I was saying. "What did Grandpa Caldwell do to you?" I asked.

"He used to pull my hair for no reason just to hear me scream. He wanted to show his dominance over my sister and me so he branded us with a branding iron. I was eight years old and your Aunt Harriett was ten. I would show you the scar, but it's in a place you don't need to see. He locked me in the storm cellar for three days one time because I burned the cornbread. Mom finally let me out while he was visiting with the neighbor. He did a lot of things that I can't tell you about," she concluded with her voice trailing off.

"When did you get the courage to run away?" I asked.

"The time he kicked me in the stomach with the toe of his shoe while I was sleeping", she said. "My bed was a pallet on the floor and I didn't hear him call me to wake up, so he kicked me awake. I bled internally for a few days before your daddy took pity on me and hauled me to a doctor in a town further north called Winston. Your daddy was helping in the fields of our farm at the time and saw me throw up blood, so took me to the doctor. I never returned home." She spoke with a hurt in her voice.

It took her over a year to heal, she said, and had two miscarriages during that time. Then she got pregnant with Mark when she was just 17 and she and Dad found their way to Henley by way of the Whitney Bus line. Cecil was born in a house not too far away from where we lived and I was born in the hospital in Woodsboro. After hearing some of Mom's stories, I have always felt that she should have left that horrible home life long before she did, but not being there or knowing the circumstances, I never talked about it.

Speaking of shoes; my shoes were usually a pair that I had obtained from the local Salvation Army Thrift Store. I had socks, but preferred not to wear any. I remember one particular pair of shoes that I wore for everything; a pair of penny loafers. I loved those shoes and have since owned numerous pairs of them. A person I disliked immensely died because of a comment about a pair of those shoes when I was just 18 years of age.

CHAPTER 2

That's right; I was responsible for another human being dying when I was only 18 because he ticked me off.

You see, at the age of 15 I became a very rebellious teenager. I quit liking school; mainly, because Mrs. Sumner left for another job, so I didn't bother to go often. I quit altogether the following year. I despised my older brother leaving me to nursemaid my reclusive mother and being alone all of the time…so I got up the nerve at the ripe old age of 17 and left home for a better life. My older *'know-it-all'* brother, Mark, left home when he was almost 19 to work, so I figured it was my turn. I joined up with a 24-year-old delinquent named Frank Epperson that I thought was a pretty cool cat. I met him one day when I had walked off the job at the feed store.

I was tired of doing all of the chores at the house by myself and wanted a job away from home where I could make some money and get out of the rut I was feeling, so I applied at the feed store. The owner, Mr. Carson got word to me by way of Dale, the insurance salesman, and asked me to start the next week. I was offered 50 cents an hour, four hours a day, four days a week. I started in the bulk feed barn, stocking the bags used for bulk feed and helping the farmers and ranchers load their purchases. One day I got two sizes of feed bags mixed together and you would have thought the world had come to an end the way Mr. Carson reacted. It would have taken all of ten minutes to straighten them out, but he made me remove all six sizes and stock them all back again in the correct alignment. I argued with him for a few minutes trying to get him to realize that I could do it a lot quicker by just straightening the two sizes I goofed on rather than the entire rack, but he insisted, so I did what he asked. It took me most of my four hour shift to accomplish, but I finished. From that day on, he treated me like an idiot. He even called me stupid in front of a friend of his and a customer.

"That's not very nice, Mr. Carson. Please don't call me that," I requested.

"What are you going to do about it, Cooper; quit?" he replied. "If you do, I won't pay you a dime," he added, laughing.

So I quit, anyway. I walked off the job and went to the filling station for a soda pop. On the way out, I walked through the main store and took 20 dollars out of the cash drawer. That was the very first time I had ever stolen anything. But I figured I had it coming. Maybe not the entire amount in wages, but the remaining was for taking his guff. I met Frank at the station. He was having his car filled up with gas and struck up a conversation with me while waiting. He was dressed in a suit with a skinny tie. It looked funny to me, but I didn't laugh at him. He invited me to join him at Virgil's Stop 'N Go for a bite and talk business. I asked what it was and he simply said if I was interested and joined him, he would tell me.

The *business* he wanted to discuss was he needed a partner and the way he described it, I got more intrigued with every word. Not once did he say anything about breaking the law or anything bad. He told me he was a salesman of a product made for cars and trucks...Newkirk Seat Covers. He showed me a brochure of the item and while I was looking at it, he stated that he needed someone to go ahead of him and pave the way for him to go behind and cinch the deal. Heck, in the mood I was in, I would have joined him if he was a traveling preacher. The juicy hamburger I was devouring was enticing enough. He would train me, he said, and together we would make a lot of money. I was impressed with the way he handled himself with confidence and figured he could train me to be just like that.

I always looked older than I really was, and Frank thought I was near 20 and I never told him different. I lied to him during the whole meeting; about my age, my independence, my schooling, everything. When it came time to pay up, he impressed me again with the wad of cash he took out of his pocket. He invited me to move in with him and I agreed to do so. He told me to meet him back at Virgil's at five o'clock and we would become partners. I had no idea at the time that he was looking for a partner in crime. I slipped into my house and grabbed several items that I thought I would need and stuffed them in a large paper sack. Before I headed back to the drive-in to meet up with Frank, I knocked on my mom's bedroom door in anticipation of telling her goodbye and she angrily yelled out for me to leave her alone, so that is what I did; I left her alone.

"Moving out of here won't bother me. I should have done it a long time ago," I thought to myself as I walked out the front door and slammed it for emphasis.

I met Frank at the appointed time. I don't think he had left the place after our meeting. I jumped into his car and we traveled out of town and headed down the road toward his place in Hardee. I knew of the town, but had never set foot in it. It had a big grassy square in the center of town with a statue of a man in the middle.

"Who's that?" I asked.

"Some guy named Stickles I was told. He was supposedly some great Civil War hero. Waste of time and money if you ask me," Frank replied.

"Did he live here or something?" I asked.

"Beats me, probably; in this county, anyways, I think," Frank guessed.

When we got through town, we turned down a side street and pulled into the driveway of a huge stone house. As we sat in the car, Frank confessed that he had snowed me and that what he was really after was a partner to help with his chosen profession…*robbing people and places of their money.*

"Think you can deal with that?" He asked after explaining what he proposed.

"I think so. How do we do it?" I asked.

He was a slick talker and the way he described it, it didn't sound all that bad or difficult, so I told him okay and joined him in a life of crime. I never told him I was just 17 and was leaving home for the first time. I didn't consider myself a snot-nosed kid, and certainly hoped Frank didn't.

"I noticed that you haven't started shaving yet. What are you waiting for, Christmas?" Frank teased.

"An old man once told me that once you start shaving, you can't ever stop, so I figure to wait as long as possible. Does it bother you?" I told Frank.

"Not in the least. As long as you're smart like that, we should get along just fine," Frank commented.

I knew that I wasn't stupid and had a good head on my shoulders, so figured that assisting him in robbing people and places couldn't be all that hard. I was doing my own snow-job from that moment on.

"One thing I can't do is drive. Is that going to be a problem?" I asked.

"Not at all, my friend. I can teach you if you like," he offered.

"That would be nice of you," I said.

"Once you got it down, you can take the test and get your license," he stated.

It wasn't long after that statement that I spent some time behind the wheel and with the teaching of Frank; I was driving like a pro. It came so easily. I actually enjoyed it. The trips up and down Mudd River Road got easier and easier to do. I ventured out on to the State Route a few times and enjoyed that feeling even more. Frank's car was fast and handled really well. I liked driving it and driving in general. The fact that I had never gotten a license was beside the point. I was a little scared of that task and kept making excuses for not doing it every time it came up.

Frank had heard my story and why I was hooking up with him, so he thought it necessary to tell me his story, I guess. He said he was mostly raised in a foster home with four other boys and he hated it. He was only six years old when he was put in it and didn't leave until he was a teenager. There was a girl in the home for a brief time, but she got adopted quickly. The boys ranged in age from 5 to 11. None of them wanted to be there and every one of them tried at various times to escape. He ran away several times, but was caught each time and the county sheriff kept returning him. He left for two days one time, but discovered that he left without his pocket knife, so returned to get it. He sneaked into the home and got it and was on his way back out of town when he was caught by a night time security guard at the boat docks. The guard hauled him to the police station and they promptly proceeded to return him. He tried a few more times, but got caught each time. Then, when he was 14 he got away for good and made his way to the Blaine County area.

During his years in the foster home, he did a lot of bad things, like kill dogs, set fires, rob people, and destroy property. He was let off each time he got caught and was punished by having to scrub floors or paint fences, but was most proud of the fact that he hadn't spent one night in juvenile hall. One of the fires he set was his own house, killing his parents and baby sister. The fire was totally by accident…

…One summer night, late in the evening, he and another boy from the home went out an open window and played around the neighborhood for a while before venturing out into the town's other neighborhoods. They wound up in his old stomping grounds and began playing with a book of matches. They were in the back of his old house near several paper sacks full of dried weeds and grasses that his mother used for flower arrangements. Frank said they heard some dogs barking and then a really loud noise from close by. That frightened them, so they quickly ran off. He swears to this day that he blew out the match he had just lit, but the match didn't go out and the fire ignited the sacks and within minutes the house was engulfed in flames. He and his friend looked back at the rising flames and knew that they had started it, but rather than return to put it out or notify the occupants of the home, they ran for their lives.

"Never play with matches, Sport. I'm not kidding," he said matter-of-factly.

"You were responsible for your own mom and dad's death?" I asked.

"Yeah. And my baby sister," he said. "But let me finish."

As he continued his story, he said he was never accused of the fire and no one ever asked him about it. He and the boy he was with made it back into the foster home without being seen. He told me that when he ran away the last time, (almost a year later) he took a small jewelry box from his foster mom, thinking it had stuff in it that would be worth money. When he got alone and opened it, he discovered mostly junk and one lone ring with a stone in it. The man at the pawn shop in a nearby town gave him five dollars for it. He dumped the box and everything else in a trash can; except a fancy leather luggage tag with a lighthouse on it and a small chain attached that he kept for some reason.

"I put the tag on a suitcase in my room. I like lighthouses and it serves as a reminder of things," he said.

He was able to get to a town up the road a ways and con an old lady at the bus station into acting as his guardian and traveled with her to her destination and then further by himself until the guise caught up with him. He was forced to get off the bus in a town in Tennessee and the local cops were notified, but before they could get to where he was being held, he got free and ran away. He hitched rides with trucks for the most part because the drivers seemed to understand his plight and never asked a lot of questions. He wondered the land for a few years, staying here and there, begging for food some of the time and stealing it at others. He made it all the way to New York he said, but he didn't like the people or the weather, so headed west. He worked a few odd jobs in various places in his travels and when he got to this area he decided to try things on his own and started his life of crime. His excuse was that he had to eat regularly. I couldn't fault him there. He resorted to small thefts at first because they were quick and less dangerous.

He told me it was really great to have me as a partner. I sort of got the idea that some of what he told was exaggerated. I'm sure he meant to portray himself as tough and under control. He said that the past few years of his life has been very successful and he has been very happy. I never asked how he got put in the foster home and away from his parents, but figured there was a darn good reason.

Frank lived in an old silver-colored trailer behind Old Lady Jenkins' place just a few hundred feet west of town on Second Street. Frank said Mrs. Jenkins was in her 80's and terribly hard of hearing. The trailer had a bedroom at one end, the kitchen and dining area in the middle and a living room at the other. The bathroom was off the hall toward the bedroom. The main door was in the small living room that opened out into the driveway. It had a screen door on it, so the main door was open most of the time during the day when we were home. The back door (which was hardly ever used) was a door into Frank's bedroom. I was told that the bedroom was off limits to me. I wondered why, but didn't ask. A big picture of a white lighthouse (with red stripes) was hanging over the couch and a tall brass lighthouse was on the shelf next to the door. Frank assigned a hall closet to me to put my stuff in and said I could sleep on the couch. Blankets and a pillow were in the closet for me to use. Frank went over some basic house rules with me and welcomed me to my new home. It was sure better than my old house.

"It's not a lot of room, but we'll make it work. We share the grocery buying and you can feel free to cook whatever you want to eat, just make sure you clean up after yourself. I like to stay neat and clean. I won't live in a pig pen," he warned.

"I'm not much of a cook. What is it that you like to eat?" I asked.

"Don't worry about me. I'll eat just about anything. I'll leave a list of things on the counter to buy. Nothing extravagant, though. If you need some extra cash, just ask," Frank instructed.

Mrs. Jenkins lived alone and you hardly ever seen her. I didn't meet her right away, but seen her numerous times; mostly in her yard messing around in the flower beds. We usually just waved at one another. I hollered at her on occasion, but she either didn't hear me or ignored me. Her house was really old and apparently she was born in it and has lived in it all her life. Her father was supposedly a young up-and-coming officer in WWI. The house was a stately, two-story, stone construction with two large columns at the corners and rather than totally face the street, the high porch and front door sat at a 45-degree angle facing the street and the driveway. It looked like someone had cut off one corner of a square.

The front of the property was fronted by two huge sycamore trees that reached more than 60 feet in the air and had leaves that were twice the size of my hand. A twisted-wire fence circled the yard and a high rose trellis bridged the driveway. In the spring, beautiful primroses literally engulfed it. Two big willows were planted on either side of the driveway at the back of the rose trellis and the branches hung down so far they touched the ground and partially hid the trailer from the street as well as the car when we drove it up close to the trailer. The trailer set sideways to the driveway, right behind the two big willow trees.

The house sat on a quarter acre of ground on the corner of Second Street and Juniper. Frank said he thought the house was used as a school house a long time ago. He had been invited in on several occasions and thought the house was probably haunted. He felt it was damp and cold and put an eerie feeling inside you.

"It just gives me the creeps, I'm telling you!" Frank commented one time.

An old black man named Jefferson lived next door and he delivered groceries and medicine to Mrs. Jenkins regularly and when he would see one of us he would just nod or tip his ever-present fedora. The man's grandson, Willy, lived with him and mowed Mrs. Jenkins' yard in the summer time and raked the leaves in the fall. Raking leaves in that yard was a huge job.

A good sized open field was next to the trailer and was once used as a garden spot, but now was a big field of mostly weeds and clover with two towering sunflowers growing close to the trailer. A large scrub oak tree grew wildly right in the middle of the field and a small filbert tree was next to the fence on the far side of the field next to Mr. Jefferson's house. The wire fence at the back of the property was sagging from rotted fence posts and weeds were growing almost as tall as the fence. There was a corn field on the other side of the fence and it was being tended to by a farmer with a very loud tractor. It woke me several times in the early morning when he was apparently getting a head start on a hot day of farming.

About once a month, sometimes more often, a young lady driving a big long, dark blue Cadillac would stop in to visit the old lady and check on her for an hour or so, then leave. I hadn't met her, but noticed that she always wore full, flowing skirts and had some really nice looking legs. The line up the back of her hose was as straight as an arrow. Frank admired her breasts more and said she was a niece from Albany. I never questioned that. Our comings and goings didn't seem to disturb anyone around, let alone Mrs. Jenkins.

Our first job together was a local mom and pop store in the small town of Classic, population 112. Classic was eleven miles southeast of Hardee at the junction of St. Paul and Cottage Roads. The store was at the corner with the caution light. Supposedly, Frank had canvassed the place and scoped it out for what he described as a *"boat load of cash"*. I was nervous and scared at the same time. The caper took all of fifteen minutes and yielded a whooping $21.00. I guess Frank was figuring on a toy boat. The back door that Frank tried to jimmy open was already unlocked and all we had to do was turn the knob and walk in. My faith and belief in Frank began to wane almost immediately. In the next few months, I took over the directing of our jobs and Frank followed my lead.

"I trust you and you seem to have a feel for this stuff already, so you can direct the jobs from here on out," Frank told me.

By mid-summer, we had robbed nine different stores and gas stations in a radius of 30 miles and reaped about $320 and change. Frank kept most of it and paid me like a wage from the take. It wasn't a whole lot, but it was more money than I had ever seen and it meant I could eat like normal people and wear clothes that fit.

Frank had a rack of ties (I counted fourteen) and he insisted I wear one during our jobs. The brownish-orange one was my favorite. The robberies were all night-time capers. We would case the places for a few days before hand and break-in at night after places closed. The latest we ever worked was around midnight one time at a clothing store that had remained open late for some kind of birthday or anniversary sale or something like that.

I relied heavily on Frank's knowledge of the area and began making notes of my own about each heist. I kept a log of sorts about each job and the details surrounding it—dates, times, places, amount, etc. I could never keep track of the amount at each heist because Frank would often times take the stash before I had a chance to see it, then dole out some of it to me later as he saw fit. That amount I wrote down in the log.

"Have you ever been suspected of robbing these places or come close to being caught, Frank?" I asked him

"Not once, Sport. I have always been real careful," he stated.

We didn't have guns, nor did we need them. We both had flashlights with us on every job. Frank carried a crowbar and I carried a small canvas bag to put the cash in when it was called for. There were usually coins in the offing and every now and then, there would be some checks in the mix, but those we left behind. One time, there were four rolls of quarters in the money box and we took them. The small amounts we were getting fit nicely in our pockets so the bag usually stayed in the car. It was amazing to me how little we had to use the crowbar to gain entry to places as well. The gas stations were notorious for leaving a door or window open or unlocked. The grocery stores and mercantiles were more security conscious than anyone. I can't recall any of those being left open. It was common for folk to leave doors unlocked at their homes, but businesses not so much, I thought. We found a number of businesses that locked their doors but left a window open or unlocked. I would crawl through the window and open the door for Frank to enter. We always used the door to leave. Frank and I worked well together and made a good team. I was having fun, actually.

The nervousness was still there each time, but more of an air of excitement.

My favorite job was gas stations. Every station we hit reaped a fair amount of money that was usually just lying in the cash drawer or under it. Only a couple of them had their cash hidden. It took a little longer to rob those because we had to hunt for the stash, but we normally found it in with the oil filters or lying in the tool box. We got grease and oil on our clothes a few times, but after robbing those places, we walked away with a little more pride in our step.

Small groceries and variety stores were more difficult. Entry was gained fairly easily, but the money was usually hidden in some small area of the store and the robberies became like hide and seek adventures. It took a lot more time, but only once did we not find the stash. The only thing we took from that caper was a jar of lemon drops and a hand full of chocolate bars. My flashlight was not working very well on that job, so I took a couple of batteries as well. We found money stashed behind cans on the shelf, under barrels, in the chest freezer, and once under a lamp shade that silhouetted the money from the light bulb being used as a night light. It's a wonder that the paper bag the cash was in wasn't set on fire from the heat of the light bulb.

"They'll try hiding money in the strangest places sometimes," Frank commented.

One particular job was not only strange, but got a little testy as well.

Frank wanted to rob the furniture store in MacAfee. He had visited the town one time a few months back and overheard a conversation at a café that got his interest. Apparently the people talking were employees of the store and were concerned that the owners didn't deposit their money but once a month and kept it in a stuffed pillow until that time. We cased the place a few times during the day time and one time was in the store at closing and actually witnessed the clerk putting money inside a throw pillow. We naturally looked away when we were noticed and promptly left the premises. We returned that night after midnight and looked for a way in. All of the doors were locked and the ground level windows were solid glass, but a window above the back door gable looked like it was partly opened, so I climbed up to it to investigate. It was open about an inch, but I couldn't open it any further, so tried to pry it open with a board I found. The board broke and the piece that I was prying up on went through the pane, shattering it into small pieces.

"Quiet, A.D., or you'll wake up the guard dog," Frank whispered up to me.

"Sorry. There better not be a guard dog or you're going in on your own," I whispered back down.

I carefully slipped through the broken window and stepped on to the landing of the upstairs area. At first I thought it was a living quarters, but quickly found out that it was a storage area. I quietly maneuvered my way around some boxes and went down the stairs to the front to let Frank in. He eased through the front door and quietly closed it behind him. Then after turning to walk toward the area of the throw pillow, he let out a scream that sounded like someone being murdered.

"What on earth are you screaming about?" I asked a little perturbed.

"Look!" Frank whispered with hardly any breath.

I looked at where he was pointing and there on a chair cushion was a large stuffed dog staring up at me.

It's just a stuffed animal, Frank," I chastised. "You scared the devil out of me."

"That thing scared me, I'll tell you!" He exclaimed.

We found the throw pillow on a sofa near the counter and just like we figured, it was stuffed with money. I grabbed a pillow from a nearby bed display and took the pillow case off and used it for the money. We made a good haul on that caper and Frank gave me two fifty dollar bills. I used the pillow case on my own pillow after that.

"Have you ever robbed a house or a person, Frank?" I asked one day.

"Not much there in my way of thinking, Sport. Why, do you have someone in mind?" he asked.

"No, I guess not, just wondering is all," I stated.

Actually, I was thinking of someone! Mrs. Gipson, the old lady on our street in Henley that took us to church now and then. Mark said that she was rich. He had seen her several times with a wad of cash in her purse or pocket. Rumor had it that she carried lots money in her bloomers and had a fortune hidden in her house. I also thought of the Parker house, but figured those people were more likely to use a bank for their large sums of money. Either one would be interesting to find out for sure, but I backed off from mentioning it to Frank for fear that he may not cotton to robbing a place that was occupied, like a house.

Although I had learned to drive, I chose to ride shotgun and let Frank be the wheel man. We would drive his '54 Robin Egg Blue Ford Deluxe through the streets of the little towns while I scoped out the various stores and businesses that might hold something dear, like money. Within the first year, we were hitting larger places like furniture stores and appliance stores for much bigger hauls.

We became known as the ***"Cloverleaf Bandits"*** due to the county sheriff in Woodsboro finding my 24-inch clover chain at the scene of the second job in his town in a week. Woodsboro was just a few miles up the road from Hardee and probably three times the size. All of the towns around us relied on the Blaine County Sheriff Department out of Woodsboro to police their area. The department only had the sheriff and seven deputies and they had a big job protecting twenty-some small towns in a thirty-mile radius.

Blaine County was bordered by Penn Ridge Road on the north with Mavis County on the other side of it; County Line Road on the west with Ferry County further west; State Road 1212 on the south with Tennyson County south of there; and Lynnfield Road on the east with Clarkston County and the city of Clarkston in that direction. The only towns with a cop were Pawnee Falls and MacAfee. They had one policeman each and the cop in MacAfee was also the Mayor. The closest city with a police force was Clarkston. Very seldom would anyone see a state trooper on any of our local roads.

I learned to make the clover chains at home one summer between jobs. I think I was only about eight. A really good looking gal by the name of Mary Jo taught me and my brother Cecil how to make them. She lived just down the road from our house. She was older than us by a year or so, but sort of cottoned to me more than Cecil and I prided myself in that fact.

I called her my girlfriend and I stole my first kiss from her when I was eight. The three of us walked to school together a lot in the spring of the year and often would walk home together. I saw Mary Jo in her underwear one summer night and have thought about it a few times. Cecil and I were walking home from a Cub Scout meeting and when we passed Mary Jo's house, she was crossing in front of an opened window in nothing but her bra and panties. Cecil whistled at her and she dropped to the floor like she'd been shot.

"Wow! Can you believe that, Cecil?" I whispered in amazement.

"I've seen it before. She strips down to her underwear out at the pot holes too," he bragged.

Mary Jo was the girl that was with Cecil the day he drowned.

Making a clover chain is a pretty simple task, really, and you can make them as long in length as you want. (Or until you run out of clover stems.) Having a field full of them right next to the trailer makes them easy to obtain. The one I dropped in that store at Woodsboro became a trademark after finding out what the sheriff called us. I dropped that one by accident, but I made it a point to put one at the scene of each of our robberies after that. I had to make a lot of them and store them for when colder times were present so that they could still be our trademark year around. I stored them in the freezer compartment of Frank's refrigerator.

Hardee was not all that big, but bigger then Henley. The big square in the middle of the street divided Main Street north and south with First Street dividing it east and west. It had a good-sized mercantile/variety store named Bratts on the south corner of the square and a service station right next door. Across the street and south a little bit was a small grocery store and one of two taverns. A hardware store was after that with a barber shop/beauty salon attached to it. A good-sized parking lot separated the tavern from the hardware store. Back across the street and next to the service station was an attorney's office that shared space with the US Land Office. Next came a combination insurance office and realty office with a vacant lot next to it and then came Second Street. I learned later that the town also had a café; a doctor's office; a dentist office; a department store (with the best popcorn anywhere in the county); a hamburger joint; a small Assembly of God church; a small assembly hall that hosted local events and weddings; and a shoe store. The owner of the shoe store was also a cobbler and made saddles, reins and halters for horses. The department store had a little of everything, including a soda fountain. Frank bought his clothes there and I purchased a small table to sit my alarm clock on. The bus station was inside the hardware store, as was the liquor store. Hardee never had a post office, but a high flag pole sporting the United States flag stood at the north end of the square. The area's main post office was in Woodsboro, as was the closest library and the only used car lot around. Woodsboro had the only movie theater around too. I often wondered if the Parker's were ever shown on the big screen. If a person was in need of a new car, expensive jewelry, or large appliances, they would need to go to Albany, Middleton, or Clarkston to shop. Frank cautioned me on being seen a lot in town for some reason. I figured us being thieves had a lot to do with it.

CHAPTER 3

I never once (in the early days) thought about us getting caught for what we were doing. It was more like a game than anything else, because it was fun and I was reaping some decent cash and not having to work very hard for it. Choosing the smaller towns in the area to rob from meant familiarity and we soon established a comfort zone. Frank coached me on the ills of becoming too comfortable with what you were doing saying that a person can become over-confident and take unnecessary risks. When that happens, the chances of being caught increase substantially. So, at Frank's suggestion, we began to branch out for larger prizes and the bigger towns. His thinking was that the larger jobs would keep us more focused and more on our toes and prevent getting callus or over confident. I thought just the opposite in that we were taking bigger risks and increasing the chances of being caught, but bowed to the more experienced and knowledgeable authority.

Churches are scattered all over the place in the area. Some are larger than others and some are just little holes-in-the-wall places. Every town in Blaine County has at least two churches and some towns as many as a dozen. There is always a bazaar, a tent meeting, or a fund raising event happening somewhere involving a church. I got wind of such one day that sounded really interesting.

At the barber shop, I overheard a few men discussing the building of a new church, or at least a building associated with one. I listened more intently from across the room and got the gist of most of what they were saying. Apparently, a large group of men were meeting somewhere nearby to collect a goodly sum of money for a building fund. I scooted further down in my chair and stuck my nose deeper into the magazine I was looking at and tried to listen in on their conversation. The barber was involved in the talk and I noticed in the mirror that the three men looked over my direction frequently and then their voices dipped in volume by a bunch. They obviously didn't want me to hear what they were saying.

"Next," the barber called.

I took the chair and got my hair cut with little said. The other two men had left the place and another man had entered to await his turn. The barber acknowledged the new customer and diligently worked on my hair until I nodded that I was satisfied. I paid my fee and left the building to return home thinking about what I had heard. I asked Frank about the whole thing and he hadn't heard anything, but admitted that he kept a low profile around town and wasn't privy to a lot of what was going on.

"I would advise you to do the same, Sport. We certainly don't need anyone checking us out," Frank warned.

"Not to worry, Frank. I'm careful," I assured him.

Several weeks later I was visiting the local mercantile store and overheard two middle-aged gentlemen discussing the building fund meeting being held right there in Hardee. Thinking they may be the same two I overheard at the barbershop, I ducked down an aisle adjacent to them and walked silently up to be even with them.

"Are you going to the meeting Friday night?" one asked the other one.

"I plan to. Bert said to bring my cash, all $250 of it," the other replied.

"If all of us bring that or more, we should be able to nail this whole thing down in short order. It will be nice to have our own place," the first one stated.

"It sure will. Is the meeting in the same place as before?" the other man asked.

"No, it's been moved to the back room at the Land Office," the first one reminded.

"Same time?" the other one asked.

"Yeah, 7 o'clock," the first one confirmed. "If you drive over, you can park at the Mudd River Tavern, I'm told."

I left the store with the idea of asking Frank about it.

"Hey Frank, remember me telling you about that building fund thing, well it's happening this Friday night at the Land Office," I related.

I told him about me hearing the men talking at the mercantile.

"No kidding?" Frank asked.

"I can't swear by it, but that's what I heard. What do you make of it?" I asked.

"Could be. I think I know that Bert guy you heard about. He runs the Land Office. Makes sense to hold the meeting at your own place, I guess," Frank stated. "What did these guys look like?" he asked.

"I couldn't see there faces, Frank. I was in the other aisle. I could just hear them. They were both at the counter when I left the building and they didn't see me, either," I told him.

"Are you thinking of robbing the meeting?" Frank asked.

"Yeah, I am!" I sort of grinned when I said it.

"I thought we were looking into robbing places in a different area due to that over-confident issue we talked about," Frank questioned.

"We will, and this is different, don't you think?" I questioned back.

"Yeah, I suppose. Are you confident it can be done?" Frank asked.

"Not totally, but I'd like to look in to it. Okay?" I asked.

"Sure, but be careful," Frank cautioned.

"I can't do it by myself, Frank. You would have to help," I told him.

"There is a lot of money to be had, it sounds like," Frank mused.

"I'm guessing so, if what they indicated is true," I agreed.

Speakeasy

"Okay. Plan it out and let's take a look at it. It just may be the start of those better jobs we want to do," Frank said.

I worked hard at it for several days. I walked up to the Land Office and tried to look uninterested while looking around for access to the back room. I asked a few questions of the lady in the lawyer's office and discovered that Frank was right in the guy that runs the Land Office being this Bert fella. She volunteered more information than I asked for by revealing that the KOC often held their meetings in his office.

"KOC? What's that?" I asked.

"Knights of Columbus," she stated matter-of-factly.

"Oh," I said, not knowing who she meant because I had never heard of them.

"My husband is attending a business meeting there Friday night," she continued. "It's a special one, too, because he has to take $250 to donate to the building fund," she practically bragged.

"I don't understand," I posed.

"Oh, I'm sorry. The KOC want to build their own place so they won't have to meet in strange places all the time. My husband is the chairman of the building committee and he says this meeting is key to settling on a final place to build," she stated.

"Are there a lot of men attending? How long does the meeting last, usually? My friend might be interested in going if it's not too long," I lied.

"Oh, if he's not a member already, he won't be able to. It's for members only. The meeting will last about two hours or so, I would imagine. There should be near 20 or so of them there. My husband is usually home by 10," she volunteered.

"You must live a ways for it to take that long to get home," I questioned.

"Oh, not far. George, that's my husband, will stop off at the tavern with a few of the others before he heads home. It's sort of a ritual after their meetings," she blushed.

I thanked her for the information and left to resume my planning. I figured if the meeting lasted until about 9, we should be able to confront the Chairman of the committee when he emerges from the building, barring any unforeseen problems, and take all of the cash involved. If George was donating $250, and the rest of the men did likewise, the haul could be upwards to a few thousand dollars.

I caught Frank up on my progress and asked him what he thought of my plan.

"Great. How do you propose to do it; just ask him for it?" Frank asked with a smile.

"If he isn't by himself when he leaves, it may be safer to do it wherever he stops afterwards, don't you think?" I asked.

"I knew you had a good head on your shoulders for this kind of thing, Sport," Frank praised my thinking.

We got real lucky in the end. The Chairman left the premises after the meeting with another guy driving a station wagon. He was carrying a small cash box under his arm. We followed them and they stopped at the Mudd River Tavern.

"They could have walked across the street, don't you think?" I asked. "There were probably ten or so more that did."

"I suppose, but maybe they didn't want to carry the cash box there," Frank replied.

The men parked and walked into the tavern. I slowly pulled into the parking lot and parked in the shadows next to their car.

"Grab that flashlight out of the glove compartment and check out the inside of their car, Sport. They didn't have anything in their hands when they went in that I could see," Frank whispered.

I did so and shined the beam into the car. On the floor of the passenger side sat the cash box we saw being carried out of the Land Office.

"I see it Frank. It's right here. The car door's locked, though," I whispered.

"Maybe we can jimmy it open. Get the crow bar out of the trunk and try it," Frank suggested.

"No need, Frank. The back door is unlocked. Did you notice if the dome light came on when they got out?" I asked.

"No I didn't. Go ahead and unlock the front door and open it. Be quick and maybe no one will notice if they are looking this way," Frank stated softly.

We got away with out being caught and relished in the glee of obtaining a great sum of cash without so much as a yawn.

The boys that went inside the tavern will be kicking themselves for a long time for being so careless. Frank gave me $200 of the take. Of course I never found out what the total take was.

Our sights were raised and our reach broadened to bigger and better things. The planning of the heist of the cash box was a stepping stone to those new heights and the prize in the cash box whetted the appetite for more, much more!

The town of Clarkston was big enough to have two banks. Morgan National was the largest and most popular and catered to most of the businesses and business people in the area. Its large columns of granite appeared to rise forever. The 16 stone steps to the tall wooden front doors were wide and inviting. I could just imagine the ones running the bank acting all high and mighty with neckties on the men and fancy dresses on the ladies. Maybe someday we could take that bank down a notch or two. But, the little Clarkston County Bank on the next block over held the intrigue of small town America and seemed ripe for the taking. It had only six steps to its front door. It, in contrast to Morgan National, catered to most of the farmers in the area and many of the farm workers. I was told one time that the salsa plant, Siete Mares, Inc. (Seven Seas) encouraged their workers to bank at Clarkston County Bank for that very reason. We decided to rob the little Clarkston County Bank before taking on the Big Boys of Morgan.

I visited Clarkston County Bank several times by entering and looking around each time. It was not running at a real hectic pace, but comfortably busy. There were no staunchly-tied men in fancy suits and the two women tellers were dressed in simple dresses and very friendly.

"I think we can take it, Frank. It would be a lot easier than Morgan National, I bet," I said, trying to convince him.

"Be sure and plan it good, then. We don't want it to be our last job, you know," he replied.

On one visit (pretending to be someone looking for a good bank) I struck up a conversation with a young male customer, and he told me I would not be disappointed in choosing Clarkston County. He looked at me as though he thought I was a little young to be banking on my own, but didn't say anything, just went on with his business. I noticed that the two lady tellers were not real careful about their counting out the money to the customers. As far as correctness was concerned, they were probably okay; at least no one was bickering about being short-changed, but the lackadaisical way they handled the money and their position was unprofessional in my way of thinking. Of course I had nothing to compare it to, it was just a feeling I had. The young and cute one wore glasses and looked like she was about 14. The other one was quite a bit older and pretty heavy. One time the young one actually dropped several coins and stooped to pick them up. She had to walk away from her position to track one down and when she did, I noticed that she left an unguarded, wide open money drawer. Obviously, the older teller noticed it too.

"Brenda, don't leave your money drawer open like that," the heavy teller called out in a loud whisper.

"Oh, shoot. I keep forgetting," Brenda said apologetically.

She returned to the counter with the retrieved coins and began counting out change to the customer.

"Jumpy little things, aren't they?" She laughed when she returned.

The customer agreed and laughed right along with her. The whole atmosphere was one of friendliness and carefree banking. Heck, I could have reached right through the bars and grabbed what was in the drawer without her seeing me. I decided at that point that we should do a day-time job and forget about trying to break in after closing. The whole situation was out of our expertise, anyway. Neither of us had ever robbed a bank; neither of us knew how to do a safe-cracking; and neither of us had ever broken into a bank before. All of that was overwhelming enough, let alone trying to do it at night, so I figured a note to a teller would have to do the trick.

I practiced for hours that night on writing a note that was readable and to the point. I reworded the note a number of times, but after several attempts, I stayed with this:

"This is a hold-up...give me all the money in your drawer."

I printed it at the top of lined notebook paper in dark letters and tore it off, folding it and putting it in my back pocket. I rehearsed getting it out and presenting it to the teller. I personally thought I did pretty well and I picked the time and day that the job would be pulled off. I told Frank that it had to be a Friday because that is when everyone brought their pay envelopes in to deposit or to cash.

"And due to that fact, the bank will have more money on hand to make all of the payday transactions," I went on.

"Pretty smart thinking, Sport," Frank commented.

I also figured the early part of the day, not too long after opening; say 10:30 would be the perfect time to do the job. On two of my visits, I noticed that the bank was not real busy during that time of day, whereas later in the afternoon would coincide with customers cashing their payroll checks before the bank closed.

I had done quite a bit of reading in my short life, just not many newspapers; and I certainly hadn't listened to a lot of news reports. We had a radio at home, but it was mostly used for listening to Soap Opera's, *"The Lone Ranger", Gunsmoke,* or *"Sky King"*. The local newspaper, <u>The Blaine Gazette</u>, published in Woodsboro, had picked up on the little jobs being done around the area and began to catalog them into a continuing story line. I bought my very first ever newspaper at the local mercantile and read about the saga of the '*Cloverleaf Bandits*'. The reporter did a little embellishing in his writing by making us sound like a lesser Bonnie and Clyde from the past and probably even a lesser threat than the current Speakeasy Gang who was robbing armored cars all across America. I had read of Bonnie and Clyde at school as them being on the most wanted list of the FBI long before their demise. I once pretended to be Clyde Barrow when Cecil and I were playing cops and robbers. I had only heard of the Speakeasy Gang, and figured they may not be as famous, but were wanted by the FBI just as badly. I barely listened to Frank's limited description of the famous duo of Bonnie and Clyde because what he was saying I already knew, but when he started telling me about the Speakeasy Gang, it took on a whole different feel, as though he knew a whole lot more about them, and I was really impressed with his knowledge, so I listened intently.

The newspaper story included the Sheriff's tale of the two places we robbed in the town of Woodsboro and the cloverleaf necklace, and the story mentioned several robberies that were totally wrong. We had nothing to do with the one in Henley. We had never even touched Henley. Henley was my home town and I so far had convinced Frank to avoid it in our robberies. Even though I had a notion to rob the feed store and get back at Mr. Carson for his unkind words to me as well as the thought of robbing Mrs. Gibson, but if robberies were happening in Henley, it wasn't us. The writer mentioned a gas station job in Pawnee Falls that we did too. It wasn't a gas station; it was a seasonal fruit and vegetable stand. If I remembered correctly, we got a total of $14.00 from that one. The reporter was taking some liberty with his writing and not reporting fact, but rather supposition. I pledged to correct the error if I ever got the opportunity. Boy, I thought, if only the newspaper knew what we were planning for our next caper.

Several days prior to our planned bank job, we were just lounging around the trailer when Frank asked me a question that took me back a bit with astonishment and showed my immaturity.

"Ever shot a gun?" he asked.

I stuttered an answer that I didn't even believe and knew immediately that Frank didn't believe it either.

"Not lately," I meekly replied.

"Yeah right, you liar," Frank said. "You never have, have you?"

"No, have you?" I asked defiantly.

"Of course I have," he confidently replied. "What were you planning to use at the bank, Sport, your finger?" He laughed while emulating a gun with his hand.

I told him about my idea with the note and when he laughed, I asked him to prove himself by showing me his gun. He quickly moved across the trailer and from the drawer beneath the stove, he pulled out a black and silver snub-nosed revolver.

"Wanna shoot it?" he asked while pointing the gun at me.

"Sure," I said. "Can I see it first?" I asked.

Frank twirled the gun around the finger guard and handed it to me butt first. He said it was a Colt .45, which meant nothing to me, but I took it from him gingerly and carefully turned it around and over a few times. I noticed right away that it had no bullets in it and let out a breath. I didn't realize that I was holding my breath at the sight of the gun.

"Relax, Sport, I'm not an idiot, it's not loaded," he said.

"Good thing," I acknowledged. Then as an after thought and to regain some semblance of maturity, I added, "You should never point a gun at people unless you plan to use it, you know!"

"You mean a *loaded* gun, Sport. And, yes I know!" Frank countered.

That was the first time in my young life that I had even seen a gun up close, let alone handled one. Cecil and I made one out of a piece of wood one time. He used one of Mom's knives from her kitchen cutlery without her knowing about it to whittle down the barrel and carve the handle. He did a darn good job, too.

We wanted to paint it black, but didn't have any paint except white, so left it wood colored and played with it that way.

I had not once thought about what to use in the hold up. I guess I was figuring that the note would be all I needed. I envisioned the teller reading the note and out of fear, handing over the contents of the money drawer. There was no need for violence or any kind of threat. But, I hadn't thought what to do if she refused or told me no. I decided that I had some extra planning to do. If the scheduled day for the robbery were to remain, then I had a short time to adjust the plan; and if I was going to learn to shoot a gun, then that had to be done as well. Heck, I had planned and carried out a lot of jobs before now, but with the size of job increasing, so was the risk. I really had just planned to walk in to the bank, hand over the note and expected to walk away with a large sum of money. No mask, no guns, no threats, no worries. Now, things had changed and plans needed to be altered.

In my visits to the bank, I had overlooked their response to a robbery. Did they have bells or whistles? Were they armed or have access to guns under the counter? Was a buzzer or signal wired to the police station in case of a robbery to notify the cops right away? Wow, I had not planned very well. I pictured myself holding the pretty blonde teller at gun point and demanding she put all of her money in my satchel. A bag! Jeez, what was I planning to put the money in? Heck, I hadn't even bothered to think of that. The little satchel we used on the small jobs around the area certainly wouldn't do. Maybe I wasn't ready to go bigger. My planning sure left a lot to be desired. I calmed my nerves and stopped questioning myself and decided to put off the bank heist for another few weeks so that I could properly plan it.

"Can we go somewhere and shoot the gun?" I asked.

"Sure, Sport. I know just the place," he agreed.

We got in the car and headed out of town in a southwest direction. Frank said we would use the old gravel pit where it was away from any neighboring towns. I told him about my failure to canvas the burglar alarm situation and also failed to consider a container to put the money in.

"Maybe I should think things through again before we do the job. What do you think?" I asked.

"It would be better to know all this stuff, Sport. Don't you think? I agree you should re-plan things," he said in almost a condescending manner.

We fired the gun at paper targets that were already shot full of holes. The pit that we were in was an old gravel pit used by a cement company years ago. All of the local hunters and probably some that weren't hunters (like us) used the pit to sight in their guns and rifles. After several lessons of how to hold the gun and how to aim it, I fired several shots at the target and guessed that I had hit it. Who could tell what with all of the holes already punctured through it? The kick-back of the gun was not as bad as Frank had said it would be, so I felt confident that I could handle it, but wanted to *know* that I had hit something.

"Have you got a tin-can or bottle in the car, Frank? I can't tell if I have hit something or not," I suggested.

Frank opened the trunk and found a half filled oil can and an empty pop bottle. He poured out the oil behind the car and walked several yards down range and placed both objects on a large limb from a downed tree about 30 yards away.

"Try your skill at those," he challenged as he returned.

I aimed at the oil can and fired. A puff of dust rose up quite a ways beyond my target. I adjusted my stance and remembering how Frank told me to hold the gun, re-aimed at the oil can and squeezed the trigger again. A loud thud was heard and both the bottle and the can fell to the ground. I had hit the limb, jarring both objects.

"Nuts!" I stammered. "I thought I was aiming right at the can."

"Try again and this time aim just a little higher and stay steady. Don't jerk sideways," Frank advised after returning from up-righting the objects.

I took another stance and took careful aim. I squeezed the trigger slowly while keeping the barrel straight and true. The pop bottle burst into a hundred pieces.

"Bull's-eye!" I shouted.

"Pretty good, Sport. Not bad!" Frank said. "Is that what you were aiming at?"

"You better believe it," I lied.

I wasn't going to be denied the fact that I hit something. The objects were less than a foot apart anyway, so Frank wouldn't know the difference. I aimed again at the oil can and keeping a steadier hand, squeezed the trigger and the oil can went flying off the limb.

"Bull's eye again!" I shouted.

I retrieved the oil can and set it back on the limb. I fired the gun at it three more times and hit it all three times.

"Try your skill at a target further away, A.D. Move the can down range another twenty to twenty-five feet and see how you do with that," Frank challenged.

I moved the can to a spot on the ground about ten or twelve paces further away and six or seven steps to the right of the fallen tree. I reloaded the gun and took aim. Out of six shots, I hit pay dirt five times. The miss was the very first one and it went wide right. By the sixth shot, the can was leaning up against a wall of dirt that stood some four feet high. I was satisfied and so was Frank. He took the gun and emptied the spent cartridges and put them in his pocket. I walked back to the car beaming from ear to ear with pride of how well I did.

"The reason you missed the oil can and hit the bottle is because you let the gun pull to your right. You did the same thing after repositioning the can at the farther distance. Nice job of correcting the problem, though, Sport," Frank praised. "Don't try to fool me again and lie about things like that, it could mean problems for us later on."

I was surprised that he detected my guise, yet humbled and softly told him that I wouldn't do it again.
We returned to the trailer and I got busy with re-planning the job. I made plans to revisit the bank and look for signs of detection, like sirens, buttons to push, or perhaps plain clothed detectives inside acting like customers.

CHAPTER 4

The day for the heist arrived. In re-planning the job, I had visited the bank and inquired about security. I was told by the older teller that all she had to do was push a button under her counter that would buzz the police station in town and cops would be on their way.

"It's called a silent alarm that notifies the police station," she stated.

I strung her along with my story of moving into town soon and opening an account. As friendly as ever, she invited me behind the counter to see the button and also show me the vault.

"That's Brenda over there, and our guard's name is Stan," she said as she pointed at each person. "Our manager, Mr. Massey, is on vacation this week, but if you have questions or anything, I might be able to answer them," she volunteered.

"You have already done more than expected and I thank you," I said.

"My pleasure, Mr.?" she hesitantly asked

"Carpenter. Tom Carpenter," I lied as I tipped my hat.

She caught me by surprise and I really hadn't thought about a name if asked, so I said the first one that came to my mind; one of my teacher's name at Mountain View school.

"Well, Mr. Carpenter, we would really like to have your business, so when you get settled, you be sure and stop in and get that account started," she requested.

"I sure will. Thanks again for your kindness," I said.

Thank goodness she didn't know the real Mr. Carpenter or more lies would need to be told.

I had purchased a suit at the Hardee Mercantile Store and bought a used briefcase at the shoe repair shop. The purchased items would come in handy for the heist. The suit was a disguise so that I would look like a young business man and the briefcase was a prop as well, but figured it should hold all of the money from the cash drawers. A fairly new hat completed the new look and if I say so myself, I look pretty good all dressed up. Hopefully, in my disguise, any roaming eyes outside the bank would not be suspicious of me. A pulled down brim on the hat would assist in hiding my face from a good look. I thought about using a mask, but decided against it.

The morning of the heist the weather was overcast and grey with thundershowers looming. We reviewed our plans over and over again so that we could pull things off without a hitch. Frank would park on a side street close to the intersection and I would walk into the bank, get the money and walk out to the car as though doing a usual routine. We would turn right onto the main street and drive away like any normal person.

The trailer felt damp, so I closed the front door to allow the place to warm up just a bit before we left. I carefully deposited a clover chain into the briefcase and checked my coat pocket to make sure the note was there. I was dressed and ready to go.

"Are you ready, Frank?" I asked.

"Yes. Yes, I am," Frank spoke from his bedroom.

We left the house and headed for Clarkston. It was raining lightly as we left and the skies were really dark in that direction. I figured we would run into a heavy downpour by the time we arrived. Several flashes of lightning occurred in that direction and we were driving right toward it.

"That one looked like it hit right close to town, Frank. I hope we aren't bothered by it," I observed.

"It's probably close, but the distance can be deceiving this far away," he countered.

On the way, I briefed Frank on where to park and which way to turn once I was back in the car. I was counting on my ability to move the tellers to the main lobby and then moving in behind the counter and loading the money into my briefcase. I figured that once the tellers were able to get to the buzzer the cops would be arriving from the right and by us turning right we would meet them rather than the off chance of them following us. The gun was rather cool to my flesh in my belt, so I moved it to the inside pocket of my suit coat. Appropriately, the tie that I picked from Frank's tie rack was beige with three large green 's' shapes that resembled dollar signs on it.

It was 10:25 on the dashboard clock when we parked the car. We met up with the rain storm just a little way out of town and it was giving us everything it had. The dark clouds were emptying their load and the rain was pelting down. In these parts, when a cloud burst happens, water will spill out of the sky like someone pouring it out of a bucket. Things and people get wet real fast.

Normally, the rains will only last about ten to fifteen minutes, but man, can it get wet in that length of time. The windshield wipers on the car had been running at full speed for several minutes. Once we rounded the block and came to our planned parking place, I immediately noticed something that we hadn't counted on; the parking strip had parking meters.

"Do you have a nickel?" I asked Frank, pointing at the meters.

"Heck no!" Came the reply. "Will it take a penny?" Frank asked.

"I don't know," I countered.

Frank began digging into the ash tray where he came up with several washers and lo and behold a nickel. I grabbed it from him and got out of the car, put the nickel in the meter and turned the knob. The front parking spaces are only good for 15 minutes but I figured that would be enough time. My new suit was getting soaked, but if we were fortunate, even if the meter expired, the policeman that checked the meters would not be around in this downpour before we were gone. Frank rolled down his window slightly and yelled out.

"Good luck, Sport. Don't get killed," he said.

I headed to the bank on a dead run while pulling down my hat as tight as possible to ward off the water. I pulled up momentarily and had a sudden chill hit me...a cop car was parked in front of the bank. A slight feel of anxiety washed over me, but continuing, I took the steps to the front door two at a time and stood still for a brief moment and tried to collect my thoughts. As I reached for the door I noticed the policeman coming out and I opened the door for him and put my head down to hide my face. He was in a hurry to get out of the rain, so he never even looked at me, but shouted a thank you over his shoulder as he ran to his car.

Relieved, I entered the bank and got another surprise that boosted my confidence...no one was in the bank...not another customer or anyone. Stan was not at his post and there were no customers, tellers or other bank personnel any where in sight. I walked to the counter and looked in through the grate.

"Hello, is anyone here?" I called.

Brenda, the young blonde teller came from a doorway to the right and answered me.

"Sorry, yes we're here. How can I help you?" she added.

As she approached the counter, I noticed that her dress was wet, her hair was limp and stringy, and she was wiping at her face with a towel. She began telling me as she walked to the counter that Stan, the guard, had called in sick and she was the only one here at the time. She expected Doris to be in shortly, but due to the storm, she was running late too. The storm made her late in opening and someone had called the cops because the blinds were still drawn at 10:20. Apparently, lightening had struck somewhere in the area earlier this morning and briefly knocked out power to homes and businesses. I thought of the flash that we witnessed on the way in. Her getting ready to come to work was delayed due to the power outage and then on her way, she had to drive through a puddle and her car drowned out. The minutes it took for her to be able to start the car again seemed like an eternity, but she eventually was able to get here. She was wet from the rain dousing her on her run from her car to the bank door. She didn't recognize me from before so I proceeded with the robbery. I fumbled around for the note, found it and produced it. She looked at it, and then handed it back to me.

"I'm sorry, but I left my glasses on the sink in the bathroom after wiping the rain off and can't read your note," she apologized. "Would you mind reading it for me?" She asked.

I was put off guard by her response, but recovered quickly and I read the note to her hesitantly and with a disguised voice to hide my real one, just in case. I could tell that I got the message across because the look on her face would have stopped a clock. Using my disguised voice, I asked her to move around to the lobby. As yet, I still had not revealed my gun. She obliged with quick, wobbly steps in her high heels. I couldn't tell if her wobbling was from not seeing where she was going, unfamiliar with the shoes, or just nervous. I quickly changed places with her. We were both as nervous as long tailed cats in a room of rocking chairs, but for different reasons. I got another surprise when I opened the money drawer…there wasn't any money in it. Brenda was so late; she hadn't been able to open up properly, so the money was still in the vault.

"Is the safe open?" I asked, rather confused.

"Ye, ye, yes it is," she stammered. "I just haven't had a chance to move the money yet."

I carefully backed away toward the vault while watching her and slowly opened the big door.

"Where's the money kept?" I asked.

"On the shelf to the right," she said while motioning with her hand.

Stacks of bills were on the shelf she indicated, so I put the money in the briefcase as fast as I could. I kept looking back at her to see a frightened girl staring at the floor. I closed the vault door like it was, walked to the front of the counter where Brenda stood, and carefully put the clover chain in plain sight. She was nervously fidgeting from one foot to the other and showing some obvious fear. She was not looking at me, but was staring a hole through the floor. I didn't talk, but led her to a chair on the other side of the room. She sat down with a plop and began crying. She never looked up to see my face. I headed for the door and turned back to see her holding her head in her hands and her shoulders heaving from the sobbing. I felt confident that without her glasses she hadn't got a good look at me. By me not talking in my regular voice, I figured she couldn't identify me by my voice, either. I felt like apologizing to her for what I was doing, but didn't. She was noticeably upset.

I went out the door and ran toward the car. The rain had practically stopped with just a slight sprinkle falling. The sun was trying to break through a dark cloud bank overhead. I splashed through a puddle at the curb, went around the front of the car, opened the passenger door and got in. Frank started the car and we pulled out into the street and turned right, slowly driving out of town. No one said a word for a long few minutes. I kept looking back to see if we were being chased, but couldn't see anything through the fogged up windows. I suspected that Frank had sat in the car without cracking a window and condensation had formed on the inside. I guess I was holding the briefcase to my chest a little tightly because Frank asked me to put it on the floor. I did so and let out a big sigh of relief.

"You won't believe it, Frank, that was as easy as falling off a log. I have to tell you, I was real nervous, but we got real lucky," I rambled.

I explained about no one being in the bank but the one teller and how it happened that she was the only one there. I mentioned the policeman coming out the door at the start and the reason for it.

"Did you know the bank uses the window blinds as a signal to the cops as to the status of things?" I asked. "If the blinds aren't opened by a set time, the cops investigate as to the reason."

Frank didn't answer me due to my continued blabbing. I kept talking. I told him about the note and the teller not being able to read it and me having to read it to her.

"That made me nervous, I'll tell you," I stated.

Frank just listened to me ramble on and on as he drove us back toward Hardee. I told him how simple it was. Our first bank job went off like a hot knife through butter; smooth and easy. I was proud of myself and couldn't wait for the next one.

After we got home and got inside, Frank went into his bedroom with the briefcase and counted the money. When he came out, he dropped the empty briefcase on the couch and he said we made more on that heist than all the others combined.

"Here's your pay, Sport. Nice job! Don't spend it all in one place," he teased.

He paid me $350 cash. I was thrilled. Frank suggested we lay low for a while and let the heat die down.

I walked up to the mercantile three days in a row to buy a paper and not one word was printed about the *'Cloverleaf*

Bandits'. I was disappointed. Frank told me that he had hidden his money and thought that I should do the same, but I didn't know where or how to get it done. The sock where my other money was hidden wasn't big enough to get my stash into. I thought about it for several days and come up with a plan. The bus station in Middleton had those fancy lockers that you put a dime in and take the key. I had read about it in a leaflet that I picked up at the grocery. Without actually seeing them in person, I imagined them being large enough to hold a suitcase. My little sock would be dwarfed in such a huge space, but it was the best thing I could come up with at the time.

"What about a bank? You know, a savings account," I suggested to Frank.

"What if we rob that bank some time in the future? You want to take your own money?" he asked.

"Of course not. Maybe somewhere else would be better, then," I decided.

I didn't realize that the two things were separate, but didn't stop to think about it either. I took Frank at his word and decided to use the lockers. I didn't like the fact that the money would be so far away and I wouldn't be able to check on it regularly, but it would have to do until I could come up with a better or different idea.

Middleton was a big city in Mavis County that was home to over 20,000 people, 45 miles north on SR313, known as the Middleton Highway. I took comfort in the fact that no one would be disturbing the locker and even if they did, no one could trace the money back to me. The locker would become my own little bank vault. For now, I carefully placed the money into a brown paper lunch sack and folded it over to form the shape of a small brick. I put it in the back of the closet under a tee shirt. I would make up some kind of excuse to Frank to drive to Middleton and deposit the money in one of those lockers.

CHAPTER 5

The first wave of home-sickness hit me one afternoon. The niece was visiting from Albany and Frank had walked over to Mrs. Jenkins to visit. I was taking a break from washing the car after changing the oil and lay back in the hammock with my eyes closed when I wondered if I should share my money with my mom. Lord knows she could sure use it. It had been close to a year since leaving and only a few thoughts of her had entered my mind. I thought better of the idea and decided against it. Besides, keeping her out of the picture would keep her from having to lie about me should she ever be confronted with my life of crime. For her to not know where I was or what I was doing was better for everyone. I wondered if she was still going through a depressed state. I let my mind wander back to some of the more pleasant days of my childhood, but for some reason, my brother Mark's face appeared as mean, old-man Carson, the feed store owner. I shut off the images quickly and returned to washing the car. Frank was returning from the house when I resumed the washing and he stopped momentarily and looked at the job I was doing.

"Not bad, Sport. Don't forget to clean out the trunk," he reminded me.

"Okay," I acknowledged and watched him as he went inside the trailer.

―――

Later that year, Frank caught a real nasty cold that turned into a flu virus and I ended up taking him to the hospital in Clarkston. I drove the back roads so as not to draw suspicion and practically carried him into the building because he was so weak he could barely walk.

I had listened to his hacking cough and complaining long enough and when he couldn't even get out of bed to go to the bathroom; I decided it was time to seek some professional assistance.

It reminded me of the winter when Mom got a really bad cold. She refused to go to the doctor saying she was too weak to drive. Dad was on the road, so no one was around to drive her. She coughed, wheezed, hacked, and barked like a dog for days on end. She was cold one minute and burning up the next. During her hot spells, she would open the front door and freeze everyone else out before getting relief and returning to her bedroom. Once, when Mark complained about the cold air coming in, he suggested that she sit on the front porch...so she did. A neighbor (Mrs. Gibson) happened to notice her while walking by and stopped to find out what she was doing. She made a scene like no one's business, opening the door, putting Mom inside and giving all of us a tongue lashing for trying to kill her by forcing her to sit in the cold air. When we tried to tell her it was Mom's idea, she wouldn't listen. Finally, after two weeks with it, Mom got to feeling better and recovered. It was not a pleasant time.

I couldn't answer a lot of the questions being asked at the hospital, but when I told the lady attendant that I could pay with cash; everything came together like we were celebrities. Frank was diagnosed with pneumonia and was given a shot of penicillin. I handed the lady at the desk four twenty's and we left. I was instructed to keep him warm and keep feeding him a lot of liquids. On the way home I stopped in at the grocery and got some chicken soup and crackers. We both ate chicken soup for more meals than I want to count. I chipped in a hot dog for myself once or twice just to mix things up. It was nearly three weeks before Frank started feeling like himself again. The few nights of moaning and feverish sweats were over, thank goodness.

During the day while Frank was recuperating I would listen to the radio and read Frank's car magazines. I paced the floor so much in those three weeks; I practically wore a hole in the linoleum and carpet. I penciled out several jobs that we might do, too. One was especially interesting and that was the bank in Clarkston. Not the Clarkston County Bank, but Morgan National. Although Clarkston County Bank was easy the first time, I didn't believe for a minute that it would be a push over a second time. Morgan National held a mystique about it for some reason. The other job I was working on was the bank in Middleton. That one would take a lot of planning and the execution would have to be near perfect. I hadn't decided if we were ready for such a large job.

I not only walked the floors of the trailer, but walked the streets of Hardee quite a bit during Frank's illness. I bought a chain from the variety part of the mercantile. I put the key to the locker on it and hung it around my neck. I bought a suicide knob for Frank as a get well present. I just about bought a real pretty vase for my mom thinking that I could drive it over to her one day, but decided not to. I was missing home again. I did buy a small table that I could use for my clock. I stopped in at the hardware store and looked around a bit, but never bought anything. The store also housed the bus stop for Whitney Bus Lines that crisscrossed this portion of the United States. There were four people milling around the store waiting for the bus.

Spring rolled around and I was getting anxious to tackle a big job. The winter months had been pretty slow for us what with Frank's illness and neither of us feeling real chipper. We did pull off two small jobs, though, and I kept my nest-egg in tact in the bus station locker. We drove to Middleton four times over two months to check on things. One of the jobs we did was a small grocery on the outskirts of Middleton. We did that one in broad daylight. It was just something that was there, sort of. We had stopped at the store to get a snack for our return trip to Hardee and one thing led to another and before you know it Frank had the gun in his hand and was asking the man for all of the cash in the drawer. He obliged without hesitation and we drove away with near a hundred dollars and two chocolate candy bars. We laughed about that one several times because, first of all it was unplanned, and secondly, there were no bullets in the gun. I didn't leave our trademark clover chain at that one due to it being unplanned. The other job we did was the filling station in Pawnee Falls. I figured if the newspaper guy was going to accuse us of doing it, then we might as well get credit for it. I also picked up two oil filters for the car on that caper. I left the usual trademark at that one.

"We sure made an honest man out of that reporter," Frank teased.

I turned 18 a few weeks later and for some reason felt like celebrating. I told Frank it was my birthday, just didn't tell him which one. He assumed it was my 21st and agreed that we should celebrate. We had always kept a low profile around Hardee and been really careful where we were seen. Mostly the mercantile store, the filling station, and the barber shop were our usual haunts, but for some reason, we decided to visit one of the taverns in town and have a cold one. I certainly wasn't of drinking age, but didn't say anything. Mudd River Tavern was where we stole the cash box. It was right next to the hardware store and across the street from the US Land Office where that KOC business meeting was held. We walked the few minutes it took to get there and found the tavern to be serving only five patrons when we entered. Two men were seated together at the bar, and an old man was staring down at his glass at the far end of the bar. Two men were playing pool and being pretty loud with their accomplishments of sinking a ball. Four beer bottles were sitting on a table near the pool table. I recognized one of the men as being the same person that worked as a handy man at the mercantile store. He always acted like a jackass and held an air that he was better than anyone else. I certainly didn't like him and avoided him every time I was there.

The juke box in the tavern was blasting out one song after another and Frank selected a table near the door and ordered our drinks. I had never had anything stronger than a sip of wine in my life and definitely hadn't drunk a beer, but Frank had had his share he said and ordered for me. I sipped at it, but never really liked it, so nursed it through several more of Frank's. The bartender brought Frank's third drink over and decided to talk for a while.

"You boys live around here?" he asked.

"Just moved in a few weeks ago. We're from Albany. Got on at the salsa plant and since it's his birthday, we thought we would party a while," Frank volunteered while pointing at me. "Nice place," he added as he gestured out into the room.

"Thanks. I own it now, thank goodness," the man replied. "Happy birthday; your first drink is on the house," he added, gesturing to me.

Frank thanked him for the drinks and after he paid, turned his back on the man. That was his cue and he took it, walking back to the bar with an angry look on his face.

"That was rude, Frank," I said. "He was just being friendly."

"He was prying is what he was doing. And we are none of his business," Frank stated matter-of-factly.

We talked and laughed about some of the jobs we pulled in hushed tones for a few hours. Several men came and went from the tavern, each having a quick drink and leaving. An older man and his wife came in the back door and sat at the bar and talked with the bartender. I found the couple a little funny, because the man had a tiny, squeaky voice while his wife had a big booming voice. We watched the two pool players try trick shots with *"Mr. Perfect"* naturally being better than his opponent. They had put away several drinks in the time we were there and the bragging they were dishing out reminded me of my know-it-all brother, Mark. I had come to hate him in the few years before I left home.

"Ready for another one yet, Sport? I've had six already and you're still sipping on your first one. First timer?" Frank asked.

"Yeah, for beer anyway! I'm fine for now, thanks," I replied.

I could tell that Frank may have had a beer or two before, but he sure couldn't handle the stuff. He was slurring his words and his voice was getting louder with each sip. The bartender told him he better slow down a little and that just added fuel to the fire already raging inside him, it seemed. I had heard stories about people who couldn't hold their liquor, and figured Frank was one of them because of how he was acting.

He got up and staggered over to the pool table and began telling the guys playing how to shoot. They ignored him at first and asked him to go sit down. That was the wrong thing to say, because Frank took a swing at one of them and the fight was on. "Mr. Perfect", who was on the opposite side of the table, threw his pool cue down and grabbed a couple of pool balls off the table and threw them at Frank. The second one nailed him up beside the head. Frank went down as though he didn't have any legs. I jumped up and got into the fray by going after the guy that hit Frank. I connected with a loud crunch to Mr. Prefect's jaw and he reeled to one side momentarily, then straightened up and got me a good one on the side of the head. That blow knocked me off balance and I ran into one of the other two patrons who had joined in. The man pushed me aside and swung at *Mr. Perfect* himself, missing by a good margin. Fists flew, chairs got broken, tables got knocked over, and before things got quiet, a window was broken out. The guy that hit Frank with the pool ball recognized me from the store and told me my loafers were sissy shoes and why didn't I act like a man. I noticed he had logging boots on. I threatened to knock him to the floor so that he could get a closer look at mine.

"Screw you," I said.

I was just about to lay another good one on his chin when a really loud and frightening boom filled the air. We all froze in our tracks and looked to the bar. The bartender was holding a shotgun and pointing it right at us. The man and woman patrons were standing beside him as if to back up what he said if no one wanted to listen.

"That was a blank, gentlemen, but I can't remember if the next is or not," he warned.

The fight stopped immediately and everyone began to straighten things up. The two guys that were at the bar had gotten in a few licks but made a hasty retreat out the back door upon hearing the warning and the bartender waved the gun and told the rest of us to stand still. I picked Frank up from the floor and tried to revive him, but he was still out like a light. I sat him down in one of the chairs that was still on its legs and leaned him against the pool table and turned toward the bartender.

"You owe me money," he said.

"How much?" I asked.

"A hunnered should cover it," he replied.

"What about them?" I asked while pointing to the two pool players.

"They didn't start it, your buddy did," he seethed. "I don't ever want to see you in here again!"

"Mr. Perfect" started to say something, but the bartender held up his hand to stop him.

"Not now, Carl, you need to go on home," he said.

Carl flipped me the bird and called me a queer and walked out of the tavern.

"Same to you fella," I called after him.

I didn't have the entire amount of money on me so dipped into Frank's pocket and got the rest of the money from his money clip and paid the man. I got a nod of approval from the woman at the bar. I got Frank to his feet and slowly left the tavern and started for home. Frank was a cumbersome load and my grip was slipping, so I stopped at the far side of the tavern's parking lot and leaned him up against the wall of the hardware store to readjust things.

"Hey, Blockhead," someone said.

I turned around and Carl was standing there with a stupid grin on his face. Before I could say anything he hit me so hard I saw stars.

"You messed with the wrong person, queer, don't ever get in my way again," he yelled.

I fell to my knees and Frank fell on top of me forcing me to lay prone on the sidewalk with one arm pinned to my side. I looked up from my position just in time to catch a wad of spittle from Carl in my face and he took off running. In anger, I ignored the pain from being slugged, pushed Frank off of me and got to my feet. I dashed around the corner of the building to the front of the tavern just in time to see Carl driving away in a sleek looking black pickup. I vowed to get even as I wiped the spit from my face with the back of my hand and gingerly touched my aching jaw.

We walked to the house with me supporting Frank the entire way. I found it odd that the Cadillac was in the driveway. The lady had just left a few days ago. I wondered if I should enter Frank's bedroom and get him in his own bed or let him sleep on the couch and me sleep on the floor, but I decided to break his house rule and put him in his own bed. I got him laid down and covered up and while turning to leave, I bumped into a stack of suitcases next to the door. A pair of pants was on top of them and the legs draped down the front but I noticed that there were three ivory colored cases, one on top of the other. I closed the door and went to the fridge and put some ice on my jaw to keep the swelling down. I knew I would have a sore mouth when I got up tomorrow. I wasn't sure how Frank would feel because this was the first time in our relationship that anything like this had happened. I figured he would have a good headache though, because that pool ball hit him as squarely as any homerun hitter smacking a baseball. I didn't fall asleep right away for thinking about what Carl had done to me and how I was going to get him back. I imagined me meeting up with him and us going at it and me knocking his teeth out. In my vision, I put my foot in the middle of his chest and spit in his face while raising my hands over my head in victory. I was mad as hell and promised to get revenge. I would hold this little skirmish over Frank's head as collateral for when I needed it. He was the cause of my being angry and he could repay all of the money to me. He owed me that much.

Several days later, Frank was sleeping in so I took the car down to the filling station for gas. A black pickup was in the service bay with its hood up and I saw Carl talking to Victor, the station owner. Victor's employee, Happy, was under the hood doing some work. Happy was one of those people that waited on everyone almost at once. He was very energetic and could talk about as fast as he worked. He came by way of his nickname honestly, due to his constant joyful demeanor and smiling face. Someone told me that his real name was Kenneth, but I never heard anyone ever call him that. The bell rang as I crossed it and Victor came walking out of the bay to attend to my car.

"Where's Happy?" I asked.

"With Carl," Victor said as he pointed over to the garage bay.

I figured Carl would follow Victor out to the island, but he didn't. Victor filled the tank, wiped the windows with a rag and asked for the money. I handed him the money through the window, started the car and pulled away. Carl never saw me. I went back to the trailer and retrieved the gun and bullets. I was not intending to kill the bastard, but scaring him with the gun and making him think about his comments to me was the main thrust. I cracked open Frank's bedroom door and saw that he was still sleeping. I marveled at how neat his bedroom was. Most guys are slobs, but Frank was a very neat and clean person. I quickly wrote Frank a note telling him that I was running a few errands and would be back later. I returned to town and stopped on the side of the street in front of the hardware store and waited for Carl to leave. In just a few minutes, he backed out of the bay and headed north in the direction of Middleton. I let him get quite a ways ahead of me then pulled out and followed him. I did not have a plan, but figured I could think on my feet and was hoping that I had the chance to get revenge.

About two miles out of town, SR 410 crosses the highway and leads past Pawnee Falls and to St. Lawrence. St. Lawrence is 105 miles due west almost to the state line. I followed him out 410 a ways until he turned north on County Line Road, a dirt road that divides Blaine County and Ferry County. I saw dust billowing up from a vehicle that was traveling pretty fast, going away from the main highway so I turned down the road and slowly followed the dust, thinking it was Carl. I soon noticed that the dust was no longer being kicked up and slowed way down to see what was happening. I noticed Carl's pickup was parked along side the road next to a pepper field but no one was in it. As I approached the pickup I saw Carl walking toward it from a clump of sumac bushes nearby and get in. Carl had stopped to take a whiz. I grabbed the gun off the seat, checked the chamber, undid the safety, pulled up beside the pickup, stopped, put the car in neutral and pointed the gun at Carl through the opened passenger window. The look on his face was priceless, but his sudden action caught me off guard.

   He took off like he was shot out of a cannon so I quickly put the car in gear to take off after him. I killed the engine when I popped the clutch and had to take a few extra seconds to start the car again. He was well out in front of me as we raced up County Line Road at speeds approaching 100 mph. Up ahead was Abby's Bridge. It was named after a young girl named Abigail that jumped off the bridge and ended her life. It's one of eight bridges in Blaine County that cross the winding Mudd River and the highest from the river's surface.

   Just then I heard what sounded like a gun firing and suddenly part of a tire came flying off of Carl's pickup and came bouncing right at me. I had to swerve to miss getting hit right in the center of the windshield. The rubber careened off the side of the roof and into the field. I skidded to a stop and watched with wide eyes the awaiting accident unfold in front of me. The pickup began to go sideways and was kicking up dirt and gravel then toppled over and rolled several times before crashing into the bridge abutment on a glancing blow and tumbled into the river. I got out and ran quickly to the spot on the river bank where the pickup went in. It was probably over a hundred feet to the water below and the pickup was lying on the driver's side almost totally submerged about ten feet out into the water. Steam was billowing off the surface of the water and from the front of the vehicle. The rear portion of the bed of the truck was sticking up out of the water like a twisted metal pretzel. I waited for a few minutes to see if Carl was going to surface, but he didn't. I figured if he wasn't killed in the roll over, than the sudden stop certainly ended his life. He could have drowned too, right there in Mudd River. After several minutes of scanning the scene below, I slowly walked back to the car, thinking of what just happened. I turned the car around and drove back to the trailer. I thought to myself that Carl wouldn't be giving the finger to anyone again or making fun of anyone's shoes, nor would he be calling anyone a queer anymore. Calling the cops never crossed my mind.

After I got home, Frank was still in bed, so I tore up the note and as I walked to the couch, it hit me what had just happened. I witnessed the death of another and at my hands, actually, so in a way, I was responsible for his death. Had I not been so mad as to want to kill him, or raced after him in order to do so, he may still be alive. Does that make me an accessory to murder? What was the penalty for that, I wondered. I had to sit down at the table to keep from shaking. After a minute or two, I stood and grabbed a soda from the refrigerator and quickly gulped down two or three swallows of it to settle me down. I thought if I ever get caught, I could be electrocuted or spend the rest of my life in prison. I decided that I would rather be shot and killed than face either of the other alternatives. Here I was only 18 years of age and already had matched Frank in causing someone's death. I didn't light a fire or pull a trigger, but a man was dead just the same. I decided that I wouldn't tell Frank what I did. He was too drunk and knocked out to remember anything about the fight with Carl anyway, so it wouldn't do him any good to learn about it from me.

———

An entire week had passed and there was not a word in <u>The Blaine Gazette</u> about the accident. I stopped off at the filling station and in passing, asked Victor if either him or Happy had seen or heard from Carl. He said neither of them had. I didn't dare step foot in the tavern after being told not to, so inquiring there was out of the question. I thought about asking at the store where he worked, but didn't. I figured if I asked too many people that they would soon get suspicious so I decided to just leave it alone and get on with things. As I was walking back to the trailer, I saw the deep voiced woman from the tavern looking at me from across the street, so put my head down and walked a little faster toward home.

A few days later I was in town and over-heard two women gossiping at the mercantile and one asked the other if she had heard about Carl's death. I stood closer and listened more intently. The funeral for him had been held at the cemetery over near Pawnee Falls. The first lady bragged that her Sonny sold that nice sleek black pickup to Carl. I quit listening when one looked right at me with a glare in her eye that told me I better get on with my own business, which I did.

Over the next few weeks I asked Frank a lot of questions about what he thought would happen to someone that was responsible for the death of another?

Did our state have the death penalty?
Had he ever shoot anyone?
Did he know anyone that had killed another?
Did he know anyone in prison?

I asked the questions at random and at various times over a few days, being careful to add other questions about different subjects so as not to get him suspicious. He answered every one of them and I assume truthfully.

No, he had never shot another person.
No, he wasn't religious but had been raised a Pentecostal.
Yes, he was certain that most states had the death penalty.
No, he didn't like kids and hoped he never had to be a parent.
His favorite color was white, especially white sand beaches.
Yes, he had been in love once at the age of 18 but the girl he had hoped to marry went to Hollywood to become an actress.

Yes, he thought anyone that took another's life should be penalized unless it was justified; like self-defense.

No, he had never married.

His favorite place was the lighthouse at Haven City.

No, he did not know anyone personally that was in prison.

I tried to give an informed comment to some of his answers, stating that I wasn't religious either; I had never seen the beach; I had never been in love or married; my favorite place was fishing at the pot holes; and I had always dreamed of having another A.D. sitting on my knee. If Frank was suspicious of my dealings, he never showed it during the question and answer time. I decided that if Frank was right on a few of those answers, then I was sure that I would spend the rest of my life in jail if I got caught, which reaffirmed my desire to be killed rather than me sitting in a jail cell forever.

CHAPTER 6

The bank job for Morgan National was planned. It had been a while since we had done the Clarkston County Bank job and the other crimes committed had had a chance to fade from memory. The story of the Cloverleaf Bandits had faded with them. Nothing had been written about the robberies or our gang for quite a while. Frank said that was a good thing. He figured we didn't need to call attention to ourselves. If we were in the news, then people would be more alert and more in tune to what was taking place. He said as long as we could quietly move in and take our cut without stirring up a hornets nest, the better off we would be. I had to agree. No one wants that kind of publicity. He admitted that it was nice to be recognized there for a while, though.

Being much bigger, the Morgan National job would need two people, so Frank was in on all of the planning. It was planned much like the Clarkston County job where the tellers and banking personnel would be asked to step from around the counter and one of us (me) would walk back and empty the cash drawers. The other person (Frank) would hold the gun on the tellers, bank personnel and the customers. We had obtained another attaché bag for this job and if we were lucky enough and had the time, the vault was just behind the teller line and would be accessible as well. We wouldn't have enough room in the cases to empty the vault and if we dumped the coin trays in, it would be too heavy to lift, so bills were the only things we would take. Not counting the vault, I figured the cash drawers alone would more than triple Clarkston County's take.

When we were casing the place, I noticed that all but two people left the bank at lunch time, leaving one teller and one office person to serve the customers. The employees ate in a lunch room in the back. Some of them left the building through the back door to go eat at a restaurant, do shopping or maybe just get a breath of fresh air. The employee parking was in the back and the entrance to the boiler room was there too. The bathroom was through a door and down the hall behind the teller line. On one visit I asked to use it so that I could get a look at the rear. A sign above the door to the back indicated that the restroom was for bank employees only, but I faked an emergency and was allowed to go. It was eerily quiet in the back. I could not hear anything that was going on out front. That was the reason I decided to retreat out the back after the robbery. The bank guard also took a lunch break but was only gone for about twenty minutes at the beginning of the hour. I thought that might be just enough time to pull off the job before he returned. It was a fore-gone conclusion that this one wouldn't be as simple as the Clarkston County one.

The plan called for us to park behind the bank, enter from the front just minutes after 12:00 noon, scope out the inside to make sure the tellers and especially the guard had gone to lunch, then announce that it was a hold up and proceed with the robbery. We were counting on the bank guard eating in the lunch room that was closed off from the hall. No one would be able to see us leave by way of the back door and with any luck we would be past the lunch room before the guard returned to the lobby. I figured if anyone screamed or hollered, they would be unheard by any in the back. Frank had done his bit of planning too by getting familiar with the lobby and knowing where to corral the people, plus he had studied the streets and knew how to get out on to the main street the easiest and which way to go from there.

His plan called for us to get into Blaine County as quickly as possible, so we would cross the county line and join Lynnfield road all the way to SR 1212. We would head west until we got to SR 313 (Middleton Highway) and turn north on it and drive straight into Hardee. I was confident in his decision and approved his plan. We neither one had witnessed the counter button to alert the police, but assumed that they had one. There were six teller windows and for all we knew there was a button behind each one. Again, by having everyone in the lobby, access to the button would be delayed somewhat and allow for more time to escape.

I put on my suit and tie, made sure I had a clover chain in my case, checked the gun, handed it to Frank, and the two of us left for Clarkston. It was a clear day and Frank looked good in his sweater and tie.

"Got a hat, Frank?" I asked him.

"Never wear one, Sport. You look good in yours though," he answered.

His wispy, sandy-colored hair moved around like a feather in the wind most times. I could just imagine what he looked like driving a convertible. He greased his hair down with a hair cream on occasion, especially when it was longer, but today's look was fresh and neat.

"Straighten your tie, Cooper," Frank suggested. "We have to have you looking dapper, you know."

The car had been making some unusual noise of late and intermittingly pausing as if it was going to die. It would cough, sputter, and jerk a few times then go on like nothing happened. I had it checked out by Victor at the filling station and the only thing he found was the butterfly choke was sticking occasionally. He suggested that when it happens, just jiggle the throttle arm quickly a few times and it should be okay. He sprayed some type of liquid on the area and called it good. I crossed my fingers that it wouldn't pick today to act up on us.

We parked behind the bank just before noon and walked around to the front and walked up the 16 broad steps and entered the front doors. We were a few minutes early because the guard was still at his post and no one had gone to lunch yet. I busied myself at the service counter that stood in the center of the lobby while Frank sat in a padded armchair at the side of the bank. Once the guard and the staff went to lunch we would make our move. It was only a few moments before the guard left his post and announced to the closest teller that he was going to go get a sandwich.

"See you later, Sam," the lady teller acknowledged.

As though it was a signal, she closed her window. At about the same time, another teller down the line did the same and two people in the office area rose and left their desks. That left two tellers on duty and one person in the office area, so our plan would be altered somewhat due to an additional person being present during the lunch hour. It seemed almost magical; one minute the place is buzzing with activity and the next minute it's so quiet you can hear the slightest noise. I checked the lobby and noticed only six people. An elderly lady with a cane was standing at one teller window and a younger lady was at the other window. Another woman was sitting at a desk in the office area talking to the young man. There was a man and women couple with a child, maybe 3 or 4, sitting on the lobby chairs probably trying to figure out their money woes. Nine people needed corralled and held while I emptied the drawers. It suddenly crossed my mind that neither of us had mentioned the front door or other customers entering. I had a sudden panic and I glanced toward the door and hoped that no one tried to enter while our little caper was happening. I tried to get Frank's eye to alert him, but he was not looking at me. I pulled up my mask and stood spread-legged at the end of the counter.

"Ladies and gentlemen, this is a hold up. Please stay calm and no one will get hurt," I called out.

I made the announcement in a very loud and clear voice so that everyone would hear and understand what was happening. It got so quiet that you could have heard a pin drop. Everyone at first looked at me with confusion, but when I motioned all of them to gather in the lobby, everyone obeyed. The two tellers quickly moved to the lobby area. One of them was slower than the other about moving out around the cage area, but a little encouragement from Frank with a wave of the gun prompted her to quick step her little butt out front. Time was of the essence, so I moved in behind the counter and began at the nearest cage to withdraw the cash from the drawer and deposit into the first bag. I moved quickly down the line and emptied each drawer. I looked up to see that Frank had everyone corralled in the settee area of the lobby with his back to the counter and observing the front door. Fortunately, no one had tried to enter the bank thus far. The small child was making a fuss, asking Frank to see the gun up close. Frank ignored his requests and a stern look at the boy's mommy got her to assist in keeping him quiet. I heard the older lady talking softly to the other lady customer who was calming her with a comforting hand. The slower of the tellers was a little wide-eyed and had a look of concern on her face, but didn't interfere. She was sitting next to the young man from the office area and his lady customer was sitting in a lobby chair next to the couple.

All of the cash went into one bag, and I laid the clover chain on the counter and turned my attention to the vault. The iron gate was partially open and I pulled it the rest of the way and it groaned like a door in a haunted house. I hesitated momentarily to listen for any movement from the back, thinking that the noise from the door may get someone's attention, but hearing nothing except for the whip-whip-whip of the overhead fans; I quickly proceeded into the vault and began filling the other bag with banded stacks of bills. It only took a few minutes in the vault and the new bag was full of money. I closed it and carried it out to the other one. Both bags were pretty heavy.

"Let's go," I called to Frank.

He cautioned all of his corralled customers and staff on any of them trying to be heroes and suggested they just sit still for several minutes. We rushed out the back and down the hall to the back door. We both had pulled down our masks and just as we were opening the rear door to leave, the bank guard was entering the hallway, coming out of the lunch room. He turned toward the lobby and glanced back to see us leaving the back door. I just nodded to him and quickly pushed Frank ahead of me and out the door, closing it gently behind me. A large rock was lying on the landing and I slid it over in front of the door to block it from opening. There was no window in the door and I half expected it to open and the guard to peer out to see who it was that nodded to him, but nothing happened.

We left the parking area like we were just regular bank customers and moved out to the main street. At the stop sign, I recognized one of the tellers returning to the bank, but although she looked right at me as she crossed in front of the car, I don't think she recognized me. Just as we turned on to the main street, the car started coughing and jerking as though it was having a seizure.

"What's happening?" Frank said.

"It's the choke," I said. "We need to pull over and open the hood."

"We can't stop now!" Frank practically screamed.

"It will only take me a second. Pull over," I sternly said.

Frank pulled over to the side of the street and I jumped out and opened the hood. Just then a beat policeman walked up to the car and asked if he could be of help. I had to swallow hard before choking on my own tongue but told him that everything was okay; I just needed to adjust the choke.

"Here, let me do that, you'll get your suit dirty," he volunteered.

And with that, he sort of pushed me aside and reached over and jiggled the throttle arm. The engine began purring like a kitten.

"Thanks," I said haltingly.

"Nothin' to it," he acknowledged. "Ya'll have nice day."

He slammed the hood and sort of saluted me and walked on down the street, whistling a tune. I jumped back in the car and we made a hasty exit from the area to the road leading out of Clarkston to Hardee.

"Can you believe that?" I asked. "Golly, Frank, I just about wet my pants."

Frank was speechless. I could see his hands shaking as he gripped the steering wheel.

"You don't suppose he got a good look at you, do you?" Frank finally asked.

"No, I don't think so. He was too interested in helping and showing how much of a good person he is," I stated.

We talked about the robbery on the way home and wondered how much we took. Frank laughed several times about how the policeman that helped with the car was going to feel when he discovered who he helped.

"He'll be so shocked he'll probably mess his pants," he said.

I mentioned how impressed I was at the cooperation of everyone.

"No one gave a whimper except that kid," I said.

"Did you leave our signature?" Frank asked.

"I sure did," I responded. "Right in plain sight."

The trip home was uneventful. We both sat with satisfied looks on our faces thinking that it couldn't have gone much smoother. The planned route was followed and within an hour, we were pulling into our own driveway.

We knew that we would have to lay low for a spell, so we planned to hunker down in the trailer for several days without going out. I suggested that we each take a bag of money and count it, but Frank nixed that idea and took both bags into his bedroom. I was a little miffed, but didn't say anything. In just a few minutes, he came out and handed me $500.00. That was more money than I had ever seen.

"Know what we're going to do first?" Frank asked.

"No, what?" I asked.

"We are going to buy a new car," he answered.

"That's probably a good idea. Let's go do it now. We can drive up to Middleton and shop around at all the car places. They have Ford and Chevy there and I think there's an Oldsmobile dealer there too. I read an ad in the paper for the new Dodge being on sale. Maybe there's a Dodge or Desoto dealer there too," I said with enthusiasm.

"I was thinking a Cadillac," he said while scratching his chin in deliberation.

"A Cadillac? Are you nuts?" I challenged.

"Why not a Cadillac? We can afford one, and I have always wanted a Cadillac," he argued.

"Frank, we don't need a big car, we need something that we can get in and out of fast, something that is halfway obscure, not too flashy, and reliable," I challenged.

The discussion went on for several minutes and I remember thinking that this was the first real disagreement that we had had since becoming partners. I ended the discussion by telling Frank that he could get anything he wanted; just don't get a red one.

"Where's the nearest driver's license office, Frank. I'm ready to get mine," I informed him.

"About time, Sport. You just might have to drive one of these days and it would go a lot easier on you when the cops ask for it if you have one then if you don't," he teased.

"I'm not planning on getting stopped by the cops, though," I replied.

"You never know, Sport, you never know," he commented. "I can drive you into Clarkston today if you wish."

"Let's go," I agreed.

"Don't you want to study the manual first?" Frank asked, teasingly.

"What for? I know it all, I think. Watching you has done a lot of teaching already. I will be sure and drive better than you do, though," I teased him back.

"Yeah, right! I can drive circles around you, Sport," he argued.

We drove to Clarkston and located the Licensing Bureau. I took the written test and then the driver's test, passing both with near perfect scores. Frank was impressed with my knowledge.

"I would have bet money that you would fail the written test. Did you study a guide somewhere back before we met?" he asked.

"Nope. I'm just smart," I stated.

"Well, I got to hand it to you there, Sport. Nice going!" he said.

"Thanks, Frank. Can I drive home?" I asked.

"Be my guest," he said, throwing me the car keys.

I was lying in the hammock one afternoon when a black Ford pulled into the driveway and stopped at the gate to Mrs. Jenkins's house. A man in a black suit and the tell-tell fedora of a federal agent got out of the car and went through the gate and up to the house. I lowered myself in the hammock and peered over the side. I couldn't see the front door, but heard him knock several times and no one answered, so he turned and looked back at the rear of the property and saw the trailer. He headed back toward it. I stayed still and when he was even with the hammock I spoke up.

"Can I help you?" I asked.

I startled him and he jumped noticeably sideways and hesitantly asked if I could answer some questions.

"Who are you and questions about what?" I asked while standing up.

He flashed a badge and I.D. and said his name was Walt Ballard, a Senior Agent for the FBI and he wanted to know who lived in the house and if I knew whether or not the person living there had a son named Robert. I answered that Mrs. Jenkins lived in the house and no, I didn't know any of her children. He looked around a bit, then looked back at me and asked if I had ever been to Clarkston.

"Yes, Sir, I have been there a number of times," I said.

"Where do you work?" he asked.

"I work over at the salsa plant," I lied.

"Night shift?" he asked.

"No, they don't have a night shift now. Quit running the night shift a few months ago," I said as though I was the one who stopped it. "I'm just off today."

He thanked me and gave me his card and asked if I thought of anything or heard anything that might help him, to give him a call.

"Sure thing," I said.

He walked back through the hanging tree limbs toward his car and after a few steps, stopped, turned back toward me, parted a few limbs and pointed at the new convertible.

"Nice car, is it yours?" he asked, pointing to the brand new '56 Chevy convertible.

"Yep," I said.

"I bet it serves you well," he said.

"No complaints," I said.

"You will call me if you hear anything, right?" he asked.

"Sure thing," I repeated.

He walked to his car, got in, backed out of the driveway and left. Frank came running out of the trailer wanting to know what a federal agent was doing in our driveway.

"Just looking for someone named Robert," I told him.

"I bet he's on a fishing expedition." Frank said nervously. "The name he used is probably a made up name to see if we reveal anything he might want to hear."

"That could be, Frank, but I'm sure it's not about us. No one knows who we are. We have a different car, we've been quiet for several weeks and no one knows where we live. I wouldn't worry about it if I were you," I told him matter-of-factly.

"Still, I don't trust no federal agent as far as I can throw them," he sneered.

"You're probably right, Frank, he's snooping," I said. "But don't get your mind all twisted over it. We'll just take things slow and easy for a while longer and see what happens."

After we went into the trailer, I thought to myself that the agent was probably just inquiring about a case that he was investigating. I knew that banks were insured by the Federal Government and agents like Walt would be investigating our bank jobs, but nothing had pointed to who we were or where we lived. I probably shouldn't have lied about where I work because if he had a mind to he could check that out pretty easy. He may not have thought about us not having a phone, but knows that pay phones are available in Blaine County if I needed to call. I didn't intend to of course, but he didn't know that. He had a good eye for cars, though; I'd give him credit there. I dropped his card on the coffee table as I sat on the couch.

Frank could have been correct in saying that the agent was on a fishing expedition. I figured if he had done his homework, he would have known the name of the person in the house. Asking about a guy named Robert could well have been a guise while seeking information and casing the area. Both of us had been seen fairly clear by several at our bank jobs, despite our attempt at concealment. I really didn't think the beat cop even looked at me, so that was no fear there. If any of the tellers or others gave the Feds a description of us, then maybe he was investigating that, but how did he know to check here? No one had seen us leave a heist I didn't think. The teller that I recognized from Morgan surely didn't recognize me. Shoot, she hadn't seen me clearly in the lobby before she went to lunch. Suddenly, thoughts were bombarding my conscience and I began to get a little spooked. I calmed myself slowly and let it pass. I thought perhaps it was time for us to seek other accommodations, but hadn't discussed the prospect with Frank. I didn't even know how long he had lived in the trailer or how he came by way of getting it in the first place.

I began to feel that maybe I should withdraw my stash at the bus station and put all of it in a bank. It was a good sum of money and I had no plans of how to spend it or what to spend it on. When I discussed it with Frank, he didn't think that was such a great idea.

"I told you before that it wasn't a good idea. What happens when we rob the bank you're using?" He asked.

"I know what you said. I was just thinking that maybe I should move it closer to me. Clarkston is the closest. And we've already hit that one, so we wouldn't be robbing it again. Where's your money stashed, Frank, under your mattress?" I teased.

I recalled the suitcases in his bedroom and wondered if perhaps that was where he was stashing his share.

"You'll never know, Sport," he said.

"I bet I could find it if I looked hard enough," I continued to tease.

"I wouldn't try it if you know what's good for you," he threatened.

"Cool it, man. I don't care where you keep it. I was just funning," I said.

CHAPTER 7

    I bought a brand new, fancy television console with a radio and turntable. I had to move a few items in the living room to make room for it, but it went nicely and looked good up against the partition separating the kitchen from the living room. It took me almost all day to put the two-tiered antennae up on the roof, but I got it done. After making about umpteen adjustments, I had a fairly clear picture. I had the television set delivered from an appliance store in Middleton. The young fellas that delivered it made it clear that they were not going to install the two-tiered antennae that I bought with it. It was a high one so that we could bring in a good signal over the trees. I pointed one section in the direction of Middleton where one television station was located, and pointed the other section toward St. Lawrence where two stations were located. I had difficulty getting the base of it attached to the roof of the trailer, but managed to secure it. The screws that came with it were too short, so I used nails and wire. One of the guide wires holding it straight was attached to the roof and another one was secured to the tree at the end of the trailer. It looked like a botched up job from the start, but by golly, it was up and the reception was good, so I left it where it was. Frank laughed at me several times while in the process of installing it, and motioned over to Mrs. Jenkins roof where for the first time I noticed through the tree a very tall and thick boom-type antenna reaching into the sky.

    "She beat you in height, Coop," he bragged.

"What in blazes?" I questioned as I looked at the monstrosity antenna.

"Beats me, I don't even think she has a television," he said.

My adjustments were successful and the picture was as good as could be. I became mesmerized by this new picture box I purchased. I found it fascinating to watch the pictures flicker across the screen. I could only get one channel in the early hours and then by mid-morning could get the other two. All three of them went off the air at midnight each weekday and one of them went off earlier on Sunday evening. I found myself watching television day and night and other things were getting put aside.

"Are you gonna wash these dishes you dirtied?" Frank asked while standing over the sink one morning after breakfast.

"Yeah, just give me a minute," I said.

"A minute? Gee, Sport, you've been glued to that thing all morning," Frank complained. "Don't forget the house rules," he reminded me.

"Okay, okay. I'll do them," I said.

I had awoken earlier than usual for some reason and was hungry, so I made myself some scrambled eggs and bacon with toast. When I finished, I just stacked the dirty pans and utensils in the sink. I still had my plate in my lap. The counter was messy too, but I turned on the television while I was eating and got engrossed in some kind of news story about the new highways being constructed across America. Seeing as how I had a vested interest, I watched it. I heard Frank get up and use the bathroom, but I could not honestly remember him coming into the kitchen.

One of the house rules was that each of us is responsible for our own messes. If you dirty it, you clean it. Chores like carrying out the trash and dusting the place was shared equally. We each did our own laundry at the coin operated place in town. I folded my bed clothes every morning after I got up and rearranged the couch pillows so that they looked presentable. My area looked pretty good to me, but not as neat as Frank's bedroom. His bed was made every day and his stuff was always picked up. He certainly wasn't like any male that I had ever been around. He took a shower almost daily and had a cologne that almost made your eyes water when he doused it on each day. The smell was lingering in the trailer air most of the time.

"I'm going over to Mrs. Jenkins and pay her the rent money," Frank announced.

All this time with Frank and I still didn't know how he got connected with Mrs. Jenkins. He never visited much. Sometimes he would go over to visit when her niece was visiting. Most times, he would go over at the first of the month to pay the rent. I didn't even know how much that was. I never contributed to the rent. I paid for my room and accommodations by buying some of the groceries and putting gas in the car. Frank had never asked me for more and had never asked me to pay for any rent. I had never met Mrs. Jenkins face-to-face nor been invited into her big house. I only saw her in the yard on occasion and waved at her. I had never met her niece either. I did look forward to her visits though, so I could see her pretty legs. I noticed that she had been coming around a bit more often of late and staying longer. I thought it nice that Mrs. Jenkins had someone that cared about her and was concerned with her well-being.

I was always pretty good about foreseeing things or sensing when things were going to happen, but was totally surprised at the events that took place one early evening right after sundown. I was on the roof adjusting the television antenna (again) when I heard a loud commotion and looking down saw three black sedans in the driveway and about a dozen men surrounding Mrs. Jenkins' place. Two were in the back of the house and four were skirting the driveway. I could hear voices from the front and noticed one man next to a car in the street. One man was right at the rear of our car and making his way down the driver's side. All of them had their guns out and one was holding a shotgun or rifle. I hunkered down and listened for a bit, then saw Frank moving stealthily in behind one of the willows. Frank had his gun, too! I couldn't get his attention by yelling at him, so I found a small rock on the roof and tossed it at him. I hit the limbs of the tree and the rock fell harmlessly to the ground without the slightest attention-getting signal I intended. Knowing I had to get his attention before he did something really stupid, I acted out of pure necessity. I jumped off the roof, hit and rolled, coming up right next to the agent skirting the car.

"Who are you and what do you want?" I yelled.

He was totally surprised and could have shot me, but I was counting on him not wanting to blow his cover. He stuttered a response and quickly showed me his badge and I.D. I glanced over at Frank and secretly motioned for him to stay put.

"You're interfering in a federal investigation," the agent said after regaining his composure.

"Who are you investigating, the mob?" I quipped.

"None of your business," he said. "Just go back to what you were doing and stay out of the way."

"What did the old lady do, rob a bank?" I teased while motioning to the house.

Frank had made his way back into the trailer without being seen and came out the bedroom door as though he were catapulted.

"What's going on?" he asked.

"The feds are arresting Mrs. Jenkins," I told him.

"They're what?" Frank exclaimed loudly.

"Both of you get out of the way before you're arrested for obstruction," the agent said.

Just then loud voices came from the front of the big house and four agents made their way to the gate. They were arguing.

"I told you it wasn't her," one said. "That old lady is way older than the one described."

"Yeah, like you knew from the start, smart aleck," another stated.

"Jim tried to tell you earlier that you were making a mistake," the first one said.

The banter continued until the agent in the rear had heard enough.

"That's enough you two!" he screamed. "Knock it off."

They went through the gate and two agents got into one car and two got into another. Our sentry walked away to join them.

"Sorry to have bothered you," he said over his shoulder.

Within just a few minutes, all of the agents were gone and the area was as quiet as it was an hour before.

"Where did they come from, Frank?" I asked. "What was that all about?"

"Probably the goons from the office in Middleton on another wild goose chase I would guess," he mocked. "I think it's time that we had a talk," he added while motioning me inside the trailer.

For the next half hour or so I basically listened to one heck of a story.

Frank began to explain in detail what had been going on with his life prior to meeting me. I learned that Frank knew a whole lot more than I had been led to believe about his relationship with Mrs. Jenkins. It seems they met six years ago at a small grocery when Frank was attempting to do a job in broad daylight and on his exit with an arm load of cash; he bumped into Mrs. Jenkins' niece entering the store. Money went flying everywhere and Frank went sprawling to the planked walkway. The niece, Molly Joiner, helped him up and figuring what was going on, aided him down the steps and into the floor of her cars' backseat. She quickly went around to the driver's side, jumped in and sped away from the scene. After a few minutes and several miles away from the scene, she stopped her vehicle and told Frank to get up. He did and Molly introduced herself and her aunt, Mrs. Jenkins, who was sitting in the passenger seat. They stopped a ways out of town and talked for quite a spell about what Frank was doing and how he could assist them in their adventure. He was offered the trailer for a mere $20 a month in exchange for his services.

I sat in total awe and spellbound as he related to me their adventures. Mrs. Jenkins was the leader of the Speakeasy Gang, the notorious gang that was wanted all over the Mid-Western United States for armored car theft. Literally hundreds of thousands of dollars had been taken from many armored cars in towns and cities all across Mid-America. The FBI hadn't been able to catch them.

"What about today?" I questioned.

"Like I said, just a wild goose chase. They have no idea, Sport. They're stupid," he answered.

"But don't you think they're on to them?" I asked.

"Nope," Frank replied.

"How can you be so sure?" I questioned him.

"You heard them today, Cooper; they think they have been given bad information," Frank responded.

"Yeah, but how long before they realize that the information they got was for real?" I asked.

"They're too stupid. By the time the feds figure it out, Molly and her aunt will be long gone," he countered.

"Where they going?" I asked.

"Its better you don't know," Frank concluded.

"How do you fit in?" I asked.

"Part of those *'services'* I mentioned was assisting in finding a person who could join the gang. You're it." He said confidently. "With you and me, the five member gang is back in business," he continued.

"Me?" I asked. "How do you figure? We rob banks, not armored cars. I don't get it!" I rambled.

Over the next hour Frank filled me in on what the past year had been all about. Like he said at the beginning, he would train me to rob people and places of their money. Not one of the jobs we did had been done without his involvement. He confessed to purposely being a bumbling idiot in Classic and letting me take over the jobs. He confessed to being on the outside of the bank doors looking in when I robbed the Clarkston County Bank. He was surprised that I didn't notice how wet he was from being rained on while standing outside the door of the bank. His wet clothing was the cause of the windows being steamed up when I got back in the car. The KOC cash box job showed him that I was capable of planning a big job. He had told Mrs. Jenkins about the run in with Carl. His getting drunk was an act to see how I would react. He wasn't planning to get nailed by a cue ball, though. That really hurt. Him being knocked out was not an act. I was followed that day I chased Carl and the wreck that killed him was witnessed by the person who followed me. Victor had followed me on a number of other jaunts, even to Middleton on several occasions. Everything was done in a training mode and reported to Mrs. Jenkins.

The antenna on Mrs. Jenkins house is for a Ham radio in an upstairs bedroom where she gets her information on the armored cars. The basement of her house holds bag after bag of money robbed from them. Molly transports some of it every month to several banks in large cities in Canada. She flies in and out of the United States, leaving and arriving at various airports so that a pattern isn't set for the feds to follow. She always checks two or more suitcases. Each of them is loaded with money and clothes. It's been almost two years since the last robbery and there are still a few money bags in the basement. They are hidden in the coal bin.

Frank explained that the two of us would be replacing two men of the gang that were run over and killed by a train. Just over two years ago, Billy and Daniel were hit by a train while trying to make their getaway from a robbery. The story goes that they were being chased by the local cops and their rented car went through the barrier and was crushed by the train, killing them instantly. The robberies stopped. Not one armored car has been robbed since the accident. Not by the Speakeasy Gang anyway. The FBI has backed off considerably except for some leads of where the money is. That's all they have, some cold leads. They want their money back, of course, but as far as they are concerned, the robberies have ended.

"What about the raid that just happened. Are the feds closing in or just curious?" I asked.

"Curious is a good word, Sport. Yeah, curious is what they are. It's been a long time since the gang has been active, so that's all it could be," Frank stated.

"Where do you fit in to all of this? Were you an active member of the gang prior to the boys getting killed?" I asked.

"Sure. I assisted with the mapping of the banks and the routes of the armored cars. Now that the gang is back to full strength, we can continue like before, except we do the actual robberies," Frank explained.

"So, we are taking up the gauntlet to shake in the face of the FBI," I boldly stated.

"I guess you could put it that way. I think that's more than enough information for you tonight, Sport, let's go to bed," Frank announced as he got up and headed for his bedroom.

I nodded in agreement and just sat there, bewildered. Wow! My brain couldn't hold any more. I walked over to the opened door and looked through the screen at the evening's starry sky. Molly's Cadillac was in the driveway. Probably here planning the first return heist, I thought. So, little Mrs. Jenkins is the master mind behind the Speakeasy Gang, huh? Who would have ever thought that? But, wait a minute…Frank said we would be putting the team of *five* back together; Mrs. Jenkins, Molly, Frank and me only makes four…who was the fifth? I walked back to his room and knocked on the door. I heard shuffling inside the room and thought for sure I heard a woman snicker. I knew that Frank listened to the radio a lot before going to sleep and figured that was where the noise was coming from.

"Hey, Frank. Who is the fifth person of the gang?" I asked through the door.

After a short pause and nothing except some additional giggling and rustling of clothes or bed covers, I got impatient.

"Frank, did you hear me? Who's the fifth person?" I repeated a little louder and up close to the door.

"Mr. Jefferson," Frank said, flatly.

His voice was like, right there. He was standing just on the other side of the door when he spoke.

"No way!" I gasped in a whisper.

"Yep. In the flesh," Frank mused.

Mr. Jefferson is the old black man that lives next door to Mrs. Jenkins. I was flabbergasted.

"One more question and then I'll shut up," I said softly. "How does the money get to the basement?"

"Mr. Jefferson picks it up from Molly most times and puts it down there. He sometimes brings it over when he mows the lawn or delivers merchandise for Mrs. Jenkins," he stated. "Now, go to bed," he demanded.

I went to bed totally alert. I was so anxious I would never get to sleep. The information I had received over the past few hours was mind boggling. I had been used, abused, and confused. I first got angry for being lied to, but then the thought of me being the chosen one made me feel great! Imagine, me, Adam Dwayne Cooper, a notorious gang member. I did go to sleep, but long into the wee hours of morning and fitfully at best.

Over the next two weeks, I met all of the operatives in the gang, began to learn Morse code and to read <u>US </u>armored car schedules. The radio room is upstairs in the big house and along with the radio equipment is a huge wall map of the Central United States with certain areas marked over with lines and circles. Those markings are the banks where an armored car has been robbed. On the adjacent wall hung a form with lines, markings, and jumbled up letters and numbers on it. Molly and

Mrs. Jenkins took me under their wing and explained to me what the markings and numbers meant.

The armored car schedules are written in a coded number/letter sequence. The code is four numbers; a letter; two numbers; a letter, followed by four numbers, like: **1073-N27B-3099**. The first set of numbers is the armored car division; the number of cars making the drops; and the day that the drops are made. The second set tell the area being delivered to and the last four numbers tell how many drops the car will make and when. In this example, 1073 would indicate company number 10 making 7 drops on Wednesday (the third day of the week).

The government divided the entire U.S. into 48 regions and assigned a specific number of armored car companies to each region. The gang focuses on regions 27, 28, 29, 30, and 31 in the central part of the United States. There are a total of 20 armored car companies in those regions with each having an identifying number; 1-7. Each region is divided into four sections and each section is divided into eight zones. So, N27B would convert to Section N, Region 27, and zone 2 (the letter B is the second one in the alphabet).

The last four numbers represent the number of banks the car will be serving, the hour that the car will arrive, and the last digit of the car's number. 3099 would indicate that 3 banks in the assigned area would be getting drops around the 9 o'clock hour by car number 9. The schedule will vary depending on the size of the area being served. The number 1 will always precede the entire code when a really large amount of money is being delivered; like 1-1073-N27B-3099. Through experience, it was learned that the 1 is only present on deliveries to very large banks in large cities. The gang had learned to stay clear of such deliveries and concentrate on small towns and smaller banks where security was less and the amount was adequate.

"You mean that robbing a car in New York City would never be attempted?" I ask.

"That's right, A.D. Detroit, Washington D.C., Philly, Chicago, none of those large cities will ever see our faces or experience our specialty," Mrs. Jenkins stated.

The two of them had detected a pattern in the sequences where the fourth month began the sequence over again, except in reverse order. All you had to do was check it for possible errors and proceed. The brains behind the outfit could easily schedule a heist in any part of the country they wanted. I commented that it looked to me like a pretty easy thing to decipher.

"You have to remember, we are talking about the feds," Molly stated.

"How do you know which banks are being served?" I asked.

"That one takes a little more effort. Each bank is served on the same day of the week every week, unless there are certain circumstances to alter that, so knowing the section, region, and zone helps in determining which banks are getting drops. See, this one is for Wednesday, so we have learned over time that these seven banks will be served on that day between 8 a.m. and 3 p.m.," she said as she showed me the schedule.

"But, if you hit the first drop of the day, isn't there money bags left in the cars for the other drops?" I asked.

"Very good, A.D. Yes, there are bags left in the armored car, but it's very dangerous to try and rob them," she pointed out. "First of all, the driver is still inside and the back door is locked. Besides that, the driver has access to a scatter gun, and you don't want any part of that, believe me. Secondly, the areas are usually rid of traffic in the mornings, whereas, more cars, people, and cops are present in the later times. We have been quite successful in hitting the very first drop of the day in these regions and feel strongly that it's the best way."

"Have you ever hit the cars at a later time?" I asked.

"Yes, and that is when Daniel and Billy got killed. Danny is the one that suggested the later hit and he paid dearly for it," she explained. "We should never have agreed to it."

There was a long pause in the dissertation for reflection on what was said. After a few minutes, I continued.

"Do you suppose the schedule is the same after so many months being idle?" I asked.

"Again, A.D. we are talking the U.S. Government. They haven't changed the way they do things for centuries. They literally live by the expression "if it ain't broke, don't fix it," she said. "Trust me, the schedule is the same. I have been checking it regularly the past few months just to make sure."

She proceeded to explain in detail, the various aspects of the job, the events that take place and the order they are to be handled.

The United States Government has twelve major currency warehouses and twenty-four smaller ones across America. The currency warehouses are protected like Fort Knox. Tall fences (with barbed wire strung at the top) encircle every complex. Armed guards protect the gates that provide entrance to the compound as well as walk the perimeter 24 hours a day. Three U.S. coin mints are strategically placed across the States and they stamp out the coins used in commerce. Four paper currency mints in America provide all of the folding money circulated by the U.S. government. The U.S. Army guard and protect the

U.S. currency every minute of the day at every location. The currency is distributed by the U.S. Government agencies to the twelve major warehouses and smaller units of the government supply the smaller warehouses.

I had heard while in school how Fort Knox was heavily protected. One of my teachers mentioned that it was better protected than the President of the United States was. I envisioned the currency warehouses being guarded by a huge army.

All of the armored car companies in America are licensed and certified by the U.S. Government. They too are guarded by armed sentries. The only time that the country's currency is not under heavy armed guard (other than when it sits in the local bank) is when the money is transferred from the armored car to the bank being served. After a lot of research and observation, it was decided that the cars were easier to rob than the buildings where the money was located, so the Speakeasy Gang concentrated their efforts on them.

Usually, three guards occupy each car; two in the cab and one in the back with the money. All three have side arms and the driver has access to a shotgun. Depending on the area, more than one bank is served each day by most armored car companies. In the smaller towns and burgs, Mondays, Wednesdays and Fridays are most commonly the only days served. The larger cities, like state capitals and large metropolitans get pick-up and delivery every day, and sometimes twice a day. The first delivery is always best because it occurs in the morning before the bank opens. The Speakeasy Gang tries to target the smaller areas to avoid traffic, people congestion, and detection.

"As you have rightly discovered, we would never attempt to pull off one of our jobs in, say New York City or Chicago," Molly said.

"What happens if the schedule is changed at the last minute?" I asked.

"If it is due to weather or manpower, then we would be notified by our contacts, but if it's due to human element, Mother Nature, or mechanical failure, we are helpless," Molly explained. "We fall back and regroup."

She went on to further explain the procedure.

The gang members arrive at the targeted city by way of a rental car picked up at an airport that is about an hour away. That buffer of distance is used for the purpose of protection and to prevent detection. The rental is driven to the targeted bank and arrives ahead of the scheduled armored car delivery. After the heist, the gang members return to the airport city to rendezvous with their contact, make the payload drop, and return home the way they came, most times at separate intervals. Usually, one will return by plane and the other by bus. Many times, Molly will be on the same flight as one of the members. Mr. Jefferson will substitute for her on occasion.

Home is at one of three airports in the area and the bus station at Hardee. They alternate the airports according to the schedule and the members doing the heist are not told which one until they are sent out. Nor do they know which one of them will be flying and which one will be riding until they receive their job orders. Molly will usually meet the money bags and load them into suitcases for their flight home. She may take the bus on occasion just to keep the feds confused if they happen to get wind of things. Mr. Jefferson meets Molly at the airport or bus terminal and becomes a porter of sorts, taking her bags and delivering them to the basement of Mrs. Jenkins' house.

"I've never flown before, and I'm anxious to do it," I interjected.

"You'll love it, I'm sure. Now don't interrupt and let me continue," she said with an annoyed look.

"Sorry," I apologized.

Molly just held up her hand and continued to explain the procedures. I felt like a kid in a classroom.

Clarkston Municipal Airport is the closest one to us, but the airlines serving Clarkston make small hops to larger cities and do not have major airline capabilities without transfers. Plaster Air Field is about forty-five minutes away in Middleton and has two major airlines that serve large and small cities alike. Albany International is over an hour south of here, and also has two major airlines that make two more flights a day than Middleton. The jobs are done at random. Sometimes a job will be on the first Monday of the month, the second Wednesday, or the last Friday of the month. We may do two jobs in the same week then again; do nothing for a whole month. It all depends on how Mrs. Jenkins perceives the situation and what the schedule reveals.

At a bank drop, two guards of the armored car accompany the transfer from car to the building, leaving one guard in the car to protect what is still to be delivered and what has been picked up. That guard will have the shotgun. The robbery takes place while the money is being delivered outside between car and bank just before the guard rings the bell at the rear door. The masked gang members approach the guards with guns in hand and demand the money. The money is usually hand carried but, sometimes it is carted. When a cart is used, the cart leaves with the money bags. The cart is left next to the parking space where the rental was parked. The gang members move the guards out of sight of the general public and tie them up using clothes line rope. If a pole or post is handy, tie them back to back with the post in between them. If a post or pole is not available, they are tied back to back sitting on the ground. Stuffing a rag in their mouths helps to quiet their resistance.

There was a pause in her presentation and I started to ask if anyone had ever been bitten, but saw the look on Molly's face and decided not to. I wanted to know what kind of rag was used, too, but didn't dare interrupt. She continued.

Taking the money before it arrives at the bank means more to be gotten. If you wait and rob the money being picked up, chances are you won't get a whole lot. In all of the robberies, not one time has a guard delivered the money to the back door with his gun drawn. For that reason, only one time has a shot been fired in a heist and that was a few years ago when Billy had to fire at a guard who resisted taking orders from him and tried to draw his gun during the robbery. The guard was not wounded, only scared. However, his actions prevented the heist from going down.

It's a pretty slick operation from the sound of it, I thought. Being there and actually performing the robbery will be a different set of circumstances, I was certain.

"Now, Mr. Cooper…did you have a question?" Molly asked when she finished.

"Yes ma'am. Who provides the gags and what are they made of?" I asked.

"We provide all of the equipment needed for the heists, including the gags and they are simply white washcloths, A.D. Anything else?" she asked.

"Where do we get the guns and what do we use for masks?" I asked.

"Boy, you are full of questions," she commented. "We give you the guns, A.D., they are Colt .45's. I think you are familiar with them," she said while looking right at Frank. "And the masks are my specialty, made from my nylon hosiery. Frank will show you how they work. Now, anything else you're wondering about?" she asked.

"No ma'am, I think I understand most of it," I stated.

"Good. Our first job back will be coming up soon," she said.

CHAPTER 8

Mrs. Nora Jenkins has the deftness of a much younger person. I questioned whether or not she was actually in her 80's as was told. She could decipher an armored car schedule with ease and picked the most opportune jobs available. She wasn't partial to any particular bank branch, but did like the ones that had a wide area between where the car unloaded and the door. In the larger cities where an alley or street may be adjacent to the back door of a bank, she would avoid them, preferring smaller towns and banks with a lot of ground surrounding them. When someone cased the various banks she had marked, (usually Mr. Jefferson) they would always be asked the distance between where the armored car parked and the rear door of the bank. If the report came back with a number she was not comfortable with, the job would be changed to the alternate location or perhaps scrubbed all together. She was crafty in her work. She would normally have two locations and sometimes a third from which to choose.

Her radio sessions varied in length as well as time of day. She listed over 20 Ham operators in America and several in Canada that she made contact with on a regular basis. She had her own routine and reasons for when she talked to each. She never broke silence between 9 p.m. and midnight, but was often up before dawn and keying messages or talking on her set. Her various contacts kept her informed as to routes and schedules of 16 of the 24 different armored car companies across the central states. I listened in on several conversations (that sometimes were also in code) and practiced my Morse code by watching her use the key. I would listen and identify the letter she was keying and try to decipher the message she was sending. I wondered how she formed the network of helpers that she communicated with, so I asked.

"How did you establish your network of operators, Mrs. Jenkins?" I asked.

"Well, Molly introduced me to the Ham radio a number of years ago and taught me the codes and procedure. It was just a matter of time before we narrowed the operators to location and the information they could provide," she informed me.

"Do any of the radio operators on that list share in the money we get, or are they just in it for the joy of participating?" I asked.

"Depending on whose information we use, that operator is sent a small retainer fee that we decided on. It isn't a lot, but keeps them from blowing the whistle on us. They don't even know whose information was used until they get an envelope in their mail box," she explained.

She stated that we are just as likely to hit a small hick town with one bank as we are to hit a larger city with multiple banks if all of the coordinating aspects warrant. The feds were always guessing as to where the gang would hit next. For nearly two years now, they have thought that the robberies had ended. If they only knew.

Mrs. Jenkins may be the leader of the gang, but Molly Joiner does the leg work and Mr. Jefferson assists her a lot of the time. Molly flies to the major airports, rents a car, and drives to banks both big and small to appraise each one as to their potential. She observes both inside and outside of the bank for traffic patterns, getaway routes, police coverage, and personnel. When she feels that she is being watched or is following a certain pattern, she switches with Mr. Jefferson and he cases the places two or three times just to break up any pattern that may be detectible.

A lot of the smaller banks do not have a guard inside, and the ones that do are not at work when the heists are being done. A lot of the smaller banks in small towns are wedged in between other buildings and do not have access in the back except for maybe a back door that leads to a trash can or something. At those banks, the armored cars deliver from the front, making any attempt at robbing them almost impossible, so those types of places are avoided and banks that allow for a rear approach are selected instead. Banks that are on street corners are also avoided, due to exposure. They normally have both front and rear doors exposed to the casual observer.

The distance that the gang members have to drive from airport to bank may be an hour or more, but allowing that type of distance gives them a better chance to make a clean get-a-way. Several times, members have left the rental in a different airport or abandoned it and stole another vehicle to ward off the cops and FBI. On top of all of her other duties, Molly also travels to Canada to deposit the money from the heists into several different banks in different provinces. That's one portion of the job that only she accomplishes.

"There has to be a lot of money in those banks," I thought. "She goes to Canada once every month to deposit the loot and they have been doing this for a long time, so there has to be a lot of money there," I surmised.

I began to wonder how we were to get paid for the jobs. Working for someone else was going to put a little kink in my step. I was getting a good wage with Frank and I wondered if I would better it or have to take a cut. I remembered them saying we would get paid every Friday, but how much? The curiosity overwhelmed me, so I asked.

"Excuse me, Molly, if I may...how much is that pay on Fridays you said we would get?" I sheepishly asked.

"To answer you question, A.D...you and Frank will get $100 every Friday. Okay? I trust that will sustain you for a while." Molly answered in a condescending manner. "And you'll get that <u>every</u> Friday whether we do a job or not," she added with a wink and reached over and patted my shoulder.

My mouth must have dropped open because she gently pushed my chin up to close the gaping hole. I could certainly live with that amount. She explained that the airline tickets, the rentals and all incidentals were paid for by the boss. If for some reason either of us had to pay for something out of our pocket, we would be reimbursed when we returned to the house. However, one thing must be understood: if we get caught and arrested, no one will protect us. If we get shot and killed, no one related to the gang will see to our body. We are all on our own.

I liked Mr. Jefferson; he was one cool cat. He always appeared to be an old man, but in reality he was only 54 years old and quite active. He was living on disability from an accident at the salsa plant. (Plus what he garnered from the heists) His grandson, Willy, was nine and all boy. Willy's parents were separated and getting a divorce, so Willy was living with his grandpa. Apparently, there was no grandma for Willy to be with. I didn't know how that affected anything, because I never had a relationship with either one of my grandparents. Mr. Jefferson never explained the reason for not having a woman around and I never asked.

Mr. Jefferson preferred to be called Dr. J. He was a medic in the war and the name got hung on him then and just stuck. So, Dr. J it was. Dr. J's job with the gang was caretaker. Not only did he take care of the yard and odd jobs around the house, but he took care of the money once it was back in town. Either he or Molly would pick up the money at baggage claim and drive it to the house. When Dr. J was on a job, a young mother just a few doors away took care of Willy. Molly used her Cadillac and Dr. J used his old pickup for the hauling. Dr. J was also responsible for packing the money into suitcases for Molly to take to the Canadian banks. I wondered how Molly got to make such large deposits so often without drawing suspicion. It would be worth a big steak dinner to find out.

Our first assignment was told to us at Willy's birthday party in Mrs. Jenkins' back yard. The presents were all opened and Willy and Dr. J were playing with his brand new Daisy Air Rifle. Of course, being an experienced grandfather, Dr. J. laid down the law regarding the loading and shooting and care of the gun. Mrs. Jenkins served the cake and ice cream on paper plates and while we were eating, Molly told us where, when, and what of the upcoming job.

Frank and I would be leaving in two days out of Middleton, flying to Harrington, renting a car and driving to Calvert to rob the armored car serving the National Bank of Commerce. Our tickets were at the First Class/Will-call window in separate envelopes. Frank would be leaving on the 10:30 flight and I would follow on the 1:20 flight. Harrington was just shy of an hour and a half flying time. Once there, we were to hook up and drive over an hour to our destination. The N.B. of C. has an armored car delivery each Monday and Wednesday before 9 in the morning and a pick up on Friday around 4 pm. Dr. J had cased the place and figured the Monday delivery would contain the most cash seeing as how it was following a Friday pay day and a weekend. Molly handed each of us $50. Mine was in tens and Frank's was a fifty dollar bill.

"Try not to spend it all in one place," she quipped.

She smelled real sweet and I admired her nylon legs beneath the hem of her skirt as she walked away. I wondered if our masks would carry her scent as well, seeing as how they were made from her nylons.

"Keep your mind on your work, young fella," Frank teased thinking that I was admiring Molly's rear end.

Two days passed at a snails pace, it seemed. I was full of nervous energy and chomping at the bit to get going. My leaving several hours after Frank just added to the anxiety. Frank tried to calm me several times when I was rambling on about nothing in particular, just a nervous babble.

"It'll be here before you know it, Sport. Just relax," he said.

The harder I tried, the worse it got, so I turned on the TV and just stared into the picture not really seeing or hearing anything. Frank must have walked from the trailer to the house and back a dozen times in preparation, so it was obvious that he was anxious too.

"How much rope do we need, Frank?" I asked him after the third time he brought in a roll of it with washcloths for stuffing the mouths of guards.

"Just loading up on supplies for other jobs, Sport. It's not a big deal," he replied. "Do you want me to show you how the masks work?" he asked.

"Yeah, could you?" I eagerly asked.

The demonstration was quick and easy. I marveled at the concept. You simply pull the cut nylon hose over your face and the material hides your features while letting you breathe and see. How clever is that, I thought.

I didn't eat much nor sleep well for all of the tossing and turning I did, but finally, D-Day arrived and even though I had to wait a while longer than Frank to get on the plane, at least we were moving and doing something. I rode with Frank to Middleton. He dropped me off in town and the plan was for me to catch a taxi or ride the bus to the airport for my flight. He mockingly waved to me as though he was dropping off a little boy for his first day at school. When he drove away I gave him the finger.

My first ever air plane ride was amazing. The takeoff was the best part just to feel the power being expended to lift the beast into the air. Looking down on the top of clouds was kind of weird, and the roar from the engines was almost soothing, but I was too excited to sleep. The landing was a different body experience all together. My ears plugged up, released, and plugged up again several times before finally popping the final time as we set down. I figured out that I could yawn and my ears would unplug. A stewardess evidently saw me doing it and gave me a tip; chew gum during the flight and the ears won't plug up as often. I thanked her for the advice. After landing, Frank met me in baggage claim and we walked to where he had the rental parked. We jumped in and rode toward Calvert on one of those new Super Highways. Wow. It was exhilarating. We talked sparingly on the way, mostly just sat with our own thoughts as we gazed out on the new roadway and thought about what we would be facing at our destination.

We arrived in Calvert in the late afternoon and not having anything to eat for most of the day; we stopped at a drive-in restaurant for a bite.

"They have waitresses that come out to your car to take your order; do you want to eat in the car or go inside?" Frank asked.

"I'd rather eat indoors at a table, I think. I've never been very good at eating off of my lap," I stated.

We left the car and walked into the restaurant. A man behind the counter told us to sit wherever we wanted. A young girl came by to take our order and Frank ordered both of us a Coney Island and a root beer. It was my first ever hot dog with chili, but boy was it good. We talked in whispers and Frank was constantly watching over his shoulder at the front door.

"What are you looking for?" I asked him.

"Just a bad habit, Sport. Don't worry about it," he said.

"Well, stop it. You are making me nervous and you are drawing attention," I said.

"Then switch places if it bothers you so much," Frank requested.

We swapped places and then I found myself looking over my shoulder at the door.

"See, it's not as easy as you think, is it?" he teased.

"Maybe we should have eaten in the car," I commented.

We left the drive-in and drove around for a little while before finding the bank. It was getting darker outside and seeing street signs and the like was getting a little harder in the twilight hours. We drove around the block and observed the area to determine the best place to attack and the best way to get out. The bank building was part of a larger brick building that housed offices for an accounting firm and assorted businesses. The two story building housed an attorney's office next to the bank and an insurance office was right next door to it. There may have been other businesses inside, but those three were the main ones. The bank occupied that portion of the building that was next to a driveway that led to the back of the property with a large parking lot. From the parking lot of a furniture store across the driveway in the back, we could observe the back of the bank and the parking lot without being detected. There was an enclosure behind the bank along side the walkway that led to the back of the building. The driveway had several parallel parking spots along it and a sidewalk leading to the front of the building. A fence bordered the walkway the entire length of the driveway and stopped about three feet before getting to the enclosure. The brick structure had a stately look to it and the pillars in the front added to the façade. The bank's wooden sign board out front looked to be brand new. The spot lights shining on it made the paint glisten with a glaring reflection. Across the driveway from the bank was a large two story building with a music store on the ground floor and what looked like apartments on the second floor. There were no doorways on the driveway side of the building, but there were several windows on the ground floor of which most of them had posters and advertisements in them. The smaller windows on the second level were all dark.

Frank pointed further back into the furniture store parking lot.

"We can park right over there and wait next to the enclosure for the guards to walk by. The fence will hide us from the armored car when it arrives and the enclosure will provide a good cover for us when we return to the car. We can easily get back out to the street without any fuss," Frank observed. "If we wait just a bit, the guards will pass behind the enclosure and be out of sight of the armored car when we make our move."

"What if the armored car parks out front, Frank. What will we do then?" I asked.

"Then we won't be able to utilize the enclosure for cover. I doubt the car will park out front though because it's customary to deliver from the back to avoid exposure," Frank said, matter-of-factly.

"What time do you propose we get here and set up?" I asked.

"The schedule says 8 to 9 doesn't it? We should be here and ready before 8 then," Frank stated.

We returned to town and found a motel with a vacancy. Frank paid for a room while I stayed in the car. We parked right in front of our unit's door and went inside. Frank asked if I had ever been to a drive-in movie. I told him I hadn't even been to a movie theater. He insisted we treat ourselves to a drive-in movie, so we drove to it and paid a dollar to watch a *'shoot 'em up'* western. I enjoyed it and compared it to the television; longer and on a bigger screen. We returned to the motel and Frank slept in the bed and I slept on the floor with a blanket and a pillow.

I was awakened in the wee hours by a freight train rumbling through town that passed real close to the motel we were staying in. Frank slept right through it without even turning over. I went back to sleep only to be awakened again a few hours later by the same noise. I swear the train was coming right through the motel room. Again, Frank was undisturbed. Unable to go back to sleep, I got up and washed my face, combed my hair and brushed my teeth and readied myself for the job ahead. It was still dark outside, so I decided to go for a walk and perhaps look for an all night diner so I could get a cup of coffee.

I found one just about a half a block away. The clock on the wall behind the counter showed the time to be 5:20. I grabbed a newspaper that had been crumpled up and thrown on a chair and was reading it when the older waitress came to my table.

"What you going to have, sweetie?" she slurred.

I looked up to meet her eyes and discovered the reason for her slur; she had a half burned cigarette clinched between her lips and was trying to talk without dropping it.

"Just a cup of coffee, please," I requested.

"Want any water?" she asked.

"Sure," I said.

She left and a circle of smoke stayed back and hovered over the spot where she stood. I watched it dissipate and returned to reading the paper.

The paper was *The Chronicle* and the article I was reading had to do with the government's push to pave America with as many Super Highways as they could in 10 years. I thought to myself that Mark could be working for a long time if he got on with those companies that the government was contracting with.

After I finished drinking way too much coffee and reading the paper from front to back, I decided to mosey back to the room and arouse Frank. I went to the toilet and when I returned to the table, I folded the paper, left it on the chair next to mine and walked to the counter to pay.

"Just a quarter will do you, young man," the waitress said. "The water is free," she laughed and then smiled, showing yellow teeth.

I paid her and gave her a dime as a tip. She had a fresh cigarette lit and clinched between her lips and was trying to see through the smoke to take the money from my hand.

I walked back to the room, woke Frank up and sat around while he got cleaned up and dressed.

"Can you wipe off the windshield on the car, A.D.? You might want to check our bags too to make sure everything we need is there," Frank requested.

I went out and wiped off the windshield; I checked the gun, checked to make sure we had our needed equipment, and rearranged the things in the bag.

"Everything present and accounted for there, Sport?" Frank quipped as he emerged from the bathroom.

"It appears to be," I responded.

"Good," he said.

We hauled our things out to the car and loaded up. Frank drove over to the bank and we parked in the furniture store lot where he suggested and waited for the armored car to arrive. There were two cars parked out in front of the bank and a station wagon in one of the driveway parking spaces with the driver still inside. A few people were walking by on the street as if heading to work.

"I hope that person either leaves the car or drives away before the armored car arrives or we are in trouble," Frank offered regarding the station wagon driver.

He hadn't more than got the words out when a car pulled in to the driveway, parked in back and the driver walked to the station wagon, got in, and the car pulled away and entered the street traffic and drove out of sight.

"Thank goodness. That could have been bad," he stated.

With only the newly parked car in the parking lot of the bank, I wondered if we were too early and said so to Frank.

"It's better to be early than late, Sport, don't you think?" he said.

"Yes, Frank. You're right. I'm just a little nervous," I replied.

"Don't let it mess you up with the job," Frank said.

"I'll be okay," I said. "Do you suppose anyone's here to let the armored car guys in?"

"I sure hope so," he quipped.

Frank looked at his watch and said it was time. We walked cautiously over to the end of the fence and hunkered down next to the enclosure. I looked through the fencing and noticed the enclosure was used for trash cans and a lawn mower. Just then, the armored car pulled into the driveway and drove right past us and around back, parking next to the curb. We watched the guard in the passenger seat get out and walk around to the back of the car. He knocked on the door and the guard opened up and passed three money bags to him. The driver then got out and stood guard at the back of the car while the guard inside stepped down and joined the other one in a walk to the back door of the bank. Once they passed behind the enclosure and out of sight of their driver, we pulled on our masks and with guns in hand, moved in.

"Good morning gentlemen, let us lighten your heavy load," Frank demanded softly as we surprised the guards. "Be ever so quiet, if you will," he added while waving the gun.

The heist went smooth and within just a few minutes both men were tied back to back and seated on the ground behind the fence of the enclosure. The rags in their mouths kept them from hollering and drawing attention to the robbery. Frank and I removed our masks and walked quickly to the rental keeping hidden from the third guard the whole way with all three bags in our arms. We tossed them in the back seat, covered them with a blanket, and drove away toward our rendezvous with either Molly of Dr. J. I looked over at Frank with a grin on my face and found a smiling Frank grinning back at me.

"Not bad, Sport," he said.

"It went smoother than I figured it would," I replied. "I was shaking like a bowl of jelly."

"Who ever taught you how to tie a knot, Sport?" he asked, teasingly. "That rope you tied probably won't stay tied too long once those two start moving around," he laughed. "You're going to have to work on that."

I just sat and said nothing. I knew I wasn't the world's best at tying ropes, but thought I had done a decent job. At least we got away before the ropes came undone. We rode in silence for quite a while and just let the events go through our minds.

"Any guess as to how much is in the bags?" I asked.

"I really don't know, but I would estimate a few thousand," Frank replied.

"Have you ever wondered if you'll ever see more than the $100 a week?" I hesitantly asked.

"You haven't even got that yet, Sport. Why the worry? Don't you think that's enough?" Frank countered.

"Plenty," I said. "I was just wondering, that's all!"

"Maybe if we do a really great job and don't get caught anytime soon, we will see some of what we have taken," Frank said.

"That would be nice," I said.

We drove the speed limit back to Harrington where Molly met us at the prearranged rendezvous sight. We loaded the bags into suitcases and because they were pretty heavy, Frank lifted them into the trunk of the rental and slammed the lid.

She asked how it went and we both said in unison that it was successful. She told me that I was to return to Hardee by bus and her and Frank would fly.

"Maybe next time it'll be your turn to fly," Molly said to me.

We discussed the procedures to be followed and we drove into Harrington. Frank dropped me off at the bus station, saying that he would see me at home, and I purchased a ticket to Hardee on Whitney Bus Lines and waited in the terminal for the bus to depart. I had no idea how long of a ride it was or how many stops or exchanges I would have to make before arriving at my destination. Molly had already purchased tickets for her and Frank for a flight to Middleton on the popular Guinness Air. He figured they had only one stop-over before arriving, and an hour's drive home. They would obviously be home hours ahead of me.

My ride was not too bad, although I had little to compare it to. The only other buses I had ever been on were the school bus and the work bus to the pepper fields. This one was much nicer and the seats were a lot softer. The bus stopped over a dozen times on the way home and just before 6 p.m. I stepped off in front of the hardware store and walked home. Molly's Cadillac was in the driveway and the convertible was parked in front of the trailer. Frank must have heard my footsteps on the gravel, because he came out of the trailer and greeted me as though we were long lost buddies and walked with me inside. The first return job of the new Speakeasy Gang had been pulled off without a hitch.

The gang met that night in Mrs. Jenkins' house to review the heist and go over any ideas or suggestions that needed to be presented. Molly asked me directly if I could think of anything that could have been done differently or should have been done that wasn't. Not having any previous experience, I told her I didn't have anything to add or take away. She asked the same of Frank and he too told her that he couldn't think of anything that he would change. Mrs. Jenkins took over the meeting and stressed the importance of keeping our jobs and travels under wraps and secretive.

"My Uncle was once a captain of a merchant marine ship and he always told me that *'loose lips sink ships'*. I'm a firm believer in that saying and want you to be advised that silence on what we do is paramount," she stressed.

She indicated that in all likelihood we would be doing another job within a few days, so be ready. She said the proceeds from this last job had not been totaled, but looked as though it could be close to fifty thousand dollars. I must have audibly released a gasp because she looked directly at me before she continued. She said the next heist could possibly be even more. She added that the details are still being figured for the job and the results and final plans will be revealed in plenty of time for the team to make the hit.

I was already overwhelmed with visiting cities that I hadn't even heard of but to be traveling by air to places miles away from home was exhilarating. In the last 48 hours I had done a number of things for the very first time in my life. I flew in an airplane; I stayed in a motel; I ate a hotdog with chili; I saw a movie; I robbed an armored car with a mask on my face; and I rode a commercial bus. I thought of myself as a pretty important person, seeing as how there would be thousands of people right here in Blaine County that not only hadn't done any of that, but was most likely to never do any of it in their lives. That in itself was amazing. I felt good!

Just about the time I was mentally popping my buttons, Mrs. Jenkins brought me back to earth with her statement;

"Always remember that this is a dangerous job and you could get shot and die just like that," she said, as she snapped her fingers for emphasis.

The reality was that there is no guarantee in life. The task of robbing armored cars just compounds the likelihood of the job ending in death. Care and caution should always be thought of and taken on any job. I figured her statement would mentally be played over and over in my head in the coming months and years. How long before I would take a bullet ending my life or maiming me for life? Her words reminded me of Frank's former speech on getting too familiar with your work. He was probably repeating then what Mrs. Jenkins was voicing right now.

"You can probably think of people in your past that became complacent with their job or with the way they were doing something, only to be caught by surprise," she stated.

My dad came to mind. His wreck was probably due to being too familiar with either his truck or the road he was traveling. He probably took an unnecessary risk and it cost him his life. I made a mental note that I would forever be extremely careful doing my job. Obviously, retirement seemed like an eternity ahead, but wouldn't it be nice to live long enough to experience it?

We were reminded that we would be contacted soon with the details of the next job. The meeting ended with chocolate ice cream sundaes being passed around and enjoyed.

The mood changed from serious to a more relaxed gathering. Dr. J excused himself and went home after the dessert. Molly and Frank were teasing one another with a spoon from the ice cream treat and I asked Mrs. Jenkins how the gang was formed and where the name came from. The next hour had even Molly's attention on what was being said.

Mrs. Jenkins' husband Arnold actually operated a Speakeasy bar in Lonsdale during the prohibition. Mrs. Jenkins often assisted as a barmaid and even entertained the bar with a tune once in a while. I learned what a Speakeasy was and how the illegal sale of alcohol transformed into banks being robbed and then armored cars. Arnold Jenkins was shot and killed by revenuers while resisting arrest during a raid at the Speakeasy bar. Mrs. Jenkins was injured in the raid and has walked with the aid of a cane ever since. She vowed revenge while serving her imprisonment and once released, joined up with a group in Tennessee that were robbing banks across several states. The bank jobs became too difficult due to her crippled state, so she quit the gang. Still angered at the FBI, she studied the flow of money in the United States and decided that armored cars were the way to strike back at the Federal Government. She formed a gang down south in a town called Putman and began robbing armored cars in Georgia and Alabama. She operated the gang for two years and had good success, but it soon became too localized and dangerous. She moved back to Hardee to the home she was born and raised in and became close to her niece.

Molly is the daughter of Mrs. Jenkins' younger sister, Bernadine. They are twelve years apart. She lives in Albany. Bernadine married an Army soldier from a base nearby (Sgt. Noah Joiner), late in her life and it was feared that she wouldn't be able to have children due to her age, but she conceived and had a beautiful baby girl. They named her Molly. Sgt. Joiner was killed in a jeep roll-over accident while being transferred to a base in Kentucky when Molly was just a toddler. When Molly was twelve years old, Bernadine contracted polio. Her care fell on the young shoulders of her daughter. Molly still lives with her mom and continues to take care of her. Bernadine lives her life in an iron lung. Once Mrs. Jenkins returned home from her ordeal, she got reacquainted and began spending a lot of time with her niece. During that time, Molly learned of her uncle's demise and her aunt's passion for getting even.

The Ham radio started as a hobby for Molly. She became a licensed Ham operator with the call letters; W7-CFC. Her slogan was '*W*ill *S*even *C*ops *F*ind *C*harlotte'. Molly's former fiancée' got her hooked on the idea and taught her the ropes of being an operator. She learned with precision and soon became very skilled in the art of keying. Due to a few misconceptions by her future husband, the engagement was broken off and the man disappeared, never to be heard from again. To console herself and heal the wounds that the breakup caused, Molly buried herself in solitary with her Ham radio and the many contacts she had made.

Molly moved her radio components into her aunt's house and taught her how to operate it. Mrs. Jenkins learned Morse code and became proficient in the art of keying the dots and dashes. She soon became a favorite of many of Molly's contacts and used Molly's call letters as her own. After just a few months of getting acquainted with the operation, Mrs. Jenkins started up the business again with Molly's help and used the contacts for planning the heists. Molly named the business from what she knew about her aunt's past. Mrs. Jenkins approved and told her to begin hiring the help and planning the jobs. They have been in operation for eight years.

CHAPTER 9

Another job was in the making and Mrs. Jenkins was at the helm with the details. She gathered the gang together in her parlor and with the help of Molly, set the stage and directed the show.

Frank and I were scheduled to drive to Middleton the next day and fly to Charlton. Our flights aboard Guinness Airlines were scheduled four hours apart with Frank leaving at 9 a.m. Molly handed us our tickets in the meeting and smiled big at Frank as she did so.

"I will rendezvous with you in Charlton and we will make our way back home," she said right to him and winked.

I'm not the jealous type, but her constant cooing and flirting with Frank was getting a bit much. I felt like an outsider a lot of the time when those two were making eyes at one another. Mrs. Jenkins saw it too and stepped forward to continue with the job instruction. Molly resumed her position at the side of the presentation and didn't interfere further.

The plan was for us to drive to Cayman and rob the armored car at City Bank & Trust. According to Dr. J's research, the area behind the bank has several possibilities for hiding and attacking the guards. A street construction project on the road that the bank is located should assist us in our get away if we work it right. It was suggested that we scope out the area before the heist and make a plan of departure. He was kind enough to sketch the area on a piece of paper and point out where the construction was in relationship to the bank. The direction we took afterward was left up to us because several ways would put us back on the road out of town.

At the close of the meeting, Mrs. Jenkins handed us each an envelope and wished us luck in our assignment. The envelopes contained $50 in small bills. We talked in generalities for a few moments and then made our way to the trailer to get ready.

"I'm going over to the Road House Tavern for a beer," Frank stated as we entered the trailer.

"Do you need some company?" I asked.

"You don't drink beer, Sport, and besides, you might get in the way. Molly is meeting me there. You might want to get some extra rest because you may have to drive to Middleton in the morning," he suggested.

I was stunned momentarily. This was a first since we have been working together. Frank's attraction to Molly seemed to be getting more and more serious.

"Well, don't overdo it!" I warned. "You want a level head tomorrow, you know!"

"Don't worry about me, Sport. I can handle things just fine. See you in the morning," he said as he walked out the door.

Since our little ordeal at the Mudd River Tavern a while back, Frank had not been to either tavern as far as I knew. I was worried that this may be the start of something that could work against us. But, on second thought, I decided that I was still just a boy in their eyes and probably was to a degree, and when my time with the ladies arrived, I too may be stricken to the point of not making wise decisions. Still, I didn't think Molly was right for Frank...there were just too many red flags to feel good about it.

The alarm sounded like a bell was stuck in my ear. Sometime during the night, my alarm clock had fallen from the arm of the couch and landed next to my pillow. I was roused from sleep very rudely. I jumped out of bed and began to make ready to depart. I remembered putting the alarm clock on the arm of the chair after I set it instead of on the table, thinking that I would hear it better up close. I was right about that.

"Frank! You awake? It's time to roll," I hollered.

There was no response from his bedroom, so I walked to the door and knocked rather harshly.

"Frank, my little buddy, it's time to get up," I whispered.

After not hearing any response at all, I opened the door slightly and peered at a neatly made bed, expecting to see a sprawled, half-clad body. There wasn't anyone in the bed or on it. I opened the door further and checked out the floor next to the bed, but Frank was not there either.

I walked back to the living room and finished making my bed while thinking of what to do and where to look. While I was folding my blanket, I looked out the door and saw Frank sitting in the front seat of the car. I ran out to the car and opened the door and caught a sleeping Frank before he hit the ground. He woke up as I caught him and begin to fight to keep upright. He stood up next to me and patted me on the shoulder and walked into the trailer.

"You better hit the shower, Frank. You'll feel better, I bet," I suggested to his back.

He just held up his hand to acknowledge that he heard me and kept walking. I walked in after checking out the car and while closing the door I heard the water running in the shower.

The ride to Middleton was quiet. I drove as Frank suggested. Not that he could have, but he was a little hung over was all. He slept some of the way and we talked briefly a time or two, mostly to review our job and discuss a few aspects of it. I tried a few times to get some details of his night at the tavern, but he was not in the mood. We drove into the parking lot of the airport and made our way to the terminal. I didn't lecture him or try to be his momma, but he knew how I felt about his actions.

"See you in Charlton. Try to get some sleep on the plane and have a rental ready when I get there," I instructed.

"I will, don't worry. See you there," he said as he headed for his boarding area.

I watched him walk away and then turned and headed for the airport restaurant for a late breakfast.

My flight went smoothly. I read a little and nodded off a few times, but for the most part just gazed out the window at the milky white sky. Frank was waiting with a rental right outside the Charlton terminal and we took off for Cayman.

"How about you and me getting a big steak dinner tonight?" Frank asked.

"That sounds good to me. Any special reason?" I asked.

"No, but it beats a hamburger and besides, I'm so hungry I could eat half a cow all by myself," he answered.

"Hang-over wearing off, is it?" I teased.

"Yeah, my head is feeling normal again. Be glad you didn't join us. Wow, that Molly can put it away. She drank me right under the table last night," Frank confessed.

"Was she tipsy, too?" I asked.

"I don't know. I started feeling poorly, so left to come home. I got as far as the car and felt like I was going to pass out, so I stopped there to get my head straight. Obviously, I didn't make it any further till you showed up," he continued.

"Where did you leave Molly?" I asked.

"She was still downing the beer and singing with the juke box when I left. I have no idea what time it was," Frank stated.

"I sure hope she makes the rendezvous spot on time, then," I said with some concern.

"Oh, I'm sure she will. She's never let us down yet," Frank assured.

"But, what if she doesn't make it? What will we do then? We don't have anything to put the money bags in and we certainly can't check them by themselves. We probably better think about that and be prepared just in case," I advised.

"You worry too much, Sport. Trust me, she'll be there waiting, I just know she will," Frank tried to bolster my feelings.

We traveled for just over an hour and topped a hill that looked down into the town of Cayman. There was a lake in the distance beyond the town that looked as though it could be a great spot to fish or boat.

"I don't see any ranches around these parts. We might end up eating a bass or trout from the looks of things," Frank muttered.

"I'm sure they have a steak house of some kind in town. We'll check it out once we get settled in and find out," I suggested.

The streets of Cayman ran in wide arcs. There weren't any traffic lights for control, just stop signs. We went through one intersection of the downtown area and after about a few hundred feet, the street turned in a slow arc to the left and then another stop sign. The street would run straight for a few more hundred feet and circle around to the left again. We entered the town going east and in two arcing left turns was heading north without noticeably turning that direction.

"I think the road planners must have had a night like mine before they built these streets," Frank kidded.

"I have never seen the like," I commented.

We soon came to a little road side motor lodge and decided to stay there. The main area of town was back behind us a few blocks and Frank said that if we stayed on this road we would probably come right past the motor lodge again in a few minutes. I had to agree, seeing as how the roads seemed to make a big circle.

"Strange way to lay out your streets, here," Frank mentioned to the clerk when we checked in.

"You like that? The city founders think they are a bunch of big wheels, so the streets are appropriate," the male clerk laughed.

"I have never seen such," Frank stated.

"It is unorthodox, but the uniqueness of it has its rewards. Makes for great conversation with strangers like yourselves," he laughed again. "Just one room, one night, mister?"

"Yes, please. Is there a steak house nearby where we can get a bite?" Frank asked.

"Best little steak house for miles around, mister. Called The Oxcart. It's over one street, called Kramer, and back that way about a block," he said as he pointed out the window. "Look for a giant Paul Bunyan statue out front."

Frank paid for the room and waited for his change.

"Have a good evening, fellas. Tell your hostess over there that Jerry said hello, will you?" he said as he handed Frank a room key with his change and motioned for us to turn left when we left the office.

We parked in front of our unit and put our stuff inside.

"Want to walk there or take the car?" Frank asked.

"It's still early, Frank. Do you think the place will be open for dinner this early?" I asked.

"If they aren't we can look around a while," he answered.

"We better take the car then. We need to find the bank anyway, so we can do that before we stop and eat," I suggested.

"Yeah, you're right. Let's take the car," Frank agreed.

As suspected, the restaurant didn't open for dinner until 4 p.m., so we had a little over an hour to check things out. We rode the arcing streets for a few minutes before we ran into some road construction.

"It has to be right around here somewhere. Dr. J said there was some street project going on near it," Frank observed.

"There it is, right up there," I said as I pointed through the windshield to the building in the next block.

"The road is closed. How do you get there?" Frank blurted.

"There has to be a way. Let's go around and come in from the other direction," I suggested.

We went down a few side streets that connected to the main one and soon came out on the other side of the bank building. The road was torn up in that area, but passable. Flaggers were all over the place and road machinery was running in every direction it seemed. The area around the bank was one busy place.

"This is gonna be a challenge, Frank. With all of this activity, robbing an armored car will be next to impossible. What are we going to do?" I asked.

"I'm not sure just yet. Let's park over there in that parking lot and think this through," he suggested while pointing to the area he saw.

We swung back around a large hole in the road and drove into the parking lot he saw across from the bank and turned off the engine.

"I can't imagine the bank working as usual with all this activity going on outside. Heck, you can't even get into their parking lot from here. How's the armored car going to deliver anything?" Frank was agitated.

"Maybe we should call it off and regroup. I thought Mrs. Jenkins always had a back up plan in case something of this nature happened. Did you get a back up plan on this one, Frank?" I asked.

"Not that I'm aware of. At least she never gave me one," Frank answered. "I have an idea; the bank is closed for the day, A.D., but I want you to walk over there and see if you can roust anyone and ask them if they are doing business elsewhere or in a different manner than usual," Frank directed.

"You mean just knock on the door or window and ask that?" I hesitantly quizzed.

"Yeah. Can you do that?" he urged.

"Okay, sure," I agreed.

"Don't get hit. There's still some concrete up there to walk on, so you might want to go that direction and cross over to the bank side," he suggested while pointing to the existing road surface.

I got out and slowly walked to the area where no construction was taking place and crossed the street. I walked up to the front door of the bank and knocked on the glass. A pretty young girl came to the door and shouted that the bank was closed.

"I know, but can you help me?" I hollered back.

She fumbled with a key ring and inserted it in the door and cracked it open being careful to block the bottom with her foot.

"How can I help you, Sir?" she asked.

"Are you keeping different hours during the construction?" I asked.

"No, we're keeping the same hours as usual," she stated.

"Then, where can I park to use the bank tomorrow? Your driveway is all torn up," I asked.

"In back. The construction company has made another entrance from the street behind us," she pointed.

"How can you think with all this noise," I laughed.

"It's difficult, but we manage. It'll be worth it in the end, I think," she said with a smile.

"Thanks," I said and left to return to the car.

"See you tomorrow," she said as she shut the door and locked it.

I told Frank the news when I returned to the car and suggested we drive around and take a look. We drove over to the adjacent street and parked across from the new entrance to the bank parking lot. From the street behind the bank a narrow graveled driveway had been laid down in an open lot between two businesses. The sides were real muddy as though rains had flooded the area recently. Both businesses on the street had large front parking lots and one had a fence running down the entire side to the entrance to the bank's lot. Just about that time, a water truck pulled into the driveway and doused the whole thing all the way to the lot and then turned around in the lot and ran back out to the neighboring street with the water drowning the area again. The mystery as to how the mud got there was answered.

"We can park right back there against that fence, I think," Frank noted as he pointed to the fence that bordered the bank's right side.

"There's no place to hide from the driver of the car, though, Frank. We can't take them out in the wide open spaces, can we?" I was getting a little nervous.

"Let's drive back there and take a look, Sport," he suggested.

Once the water truck was out of sight, we drove down the graveled driveway into the bank's lot. The rear of the bank was untouched by the construction. A sidewalk led to the back door and was bordered by green grass on both sides. An out building of some kind was on the concrete apron about ten feet to the left of the door.

"There's our cover, Sport," Frank stated while pointing. "We wait right there and make our move when the guards walk to the door."

"What about the construction, Frank. What if someone sees us?" I wondered.

"Hopefully, they are too busy to look back here and the noise of the machinery will drown out any noise we make. I think we'll be okay," Frank guessed.

"Where do we park the car? Against that fence isn't going to work, because we have to go out that driveway. The armored car will be right in our path. Dr. J said there were a number of ways to escape, but I don't see it," I questioned.

"Wait a minute. Look there," Frank said while pointing to the building next door. "That lot has a driveway going toward that side street," he emphasized as he pointed.

Sure enough; the business to our left had two driveways; one toward the street under construction and a perpendicular one that ran toward the area not under construction. We could park next door and make the heist under cover and get away without, hopefully, the construction being a problem. There was a short railed fence between the properties, mostly used for decoration. It could simply be stepped over for clearance.

We left the bank parking lot with our plan in place and headed for the restaurant. I felt better and the nervousness I previously felt had subsided. Dr. J was right. With a little luck, everything should go off without a hitch.

We ate a delicious meal of T-bone steak with a baked potato and creamed corn. Frank had a bowl of split-pea soup before dinner; I had a roll with butter. Our plates had been removed and coffee was served and we sat back and chatted for a while and let our dinner digest. I had wondered a number of times about our jobs and what would happen if we got caught or something prevented Molly or Dr. J from rendezvousing with us. I asked Frank for his explanation.

"We've been told a number of times, Sport, that should we get caught, no one is going to bail us out. We are on our own. The same goes for the time that no one is there to pick us up. We make it back on our own, no questions asked," he explained.

"Ever been tempted to take any of the money from the bags before meeting up with our ride, Frank?" I asked.

Frank looked around our area for eavesdroppers and leaned across the table and quietly answered.

"That is the most asinine question I've ever heard. Of course not; we would be foolish to try such a stunt. I would advise you to never attempt it if you had the chance and banish such an idea from your head," he stated with a very stern voice.

"Okay, cool it. I was just asking, that's all. I wouldn't try it, ever," I stammered.

"Make sure you don't!" he cautioned, and then sat back in his seat.
"You never bite the hand that feeds you, man."

I had never lit a fuse like that in our relationship and got to see a side of Frank that I had never seen before. He was actually protecting our bosses and warning me against crossing them. How interesting. And this coming from a guy that I didn't think had any morals at all. I vowed right then and there to watch my words a little more carefully and be more selective on my topics of conversation.

On our ride back to the motor lodge, I recalled that we didn't say hello to the hostess on behalf of Jerry, the clerk at the motel. Oh, well.

We arrived at the bank just before 8 and parked in the lot adjacent. There was a car already in the lot and we figured it belonged to someone that worked at the business. Frank parked right next to it with the front of our car facing the bank. We didn't talk and kept an eye out on the back door of the business where we were parked. A curious employee or manager could cause some anxiety with an inquiry as to our presence.

"Let's go," Frank said and opened his door. "It's noisy enough out here that we may have to yell to be heard," he commented.

We were half sneaking, half trotting across the lot to our hiding spot when suddenly, the noise of a truck was heard above everything else and our attention went to the graveled driveway where the water truck was busy watering down the road. We froze momentarily and then literally had to jump to avoid getting wet. The driver roared into the lot, flashed a big smile and turned around and quickly went back out the way he came and never once turned off the water. Water cascaded toward the curbs of the parking lot and splashed up over the sides, then slowly flowed into a drain in the center of the lot. Fortunately, neither of us got wet.

"Stupid idiot," Frank mumbled.

We proceeded to the small outbuilding and within a matter of seconds looked up to see the armored car slowly entering the lot. With the other construction noises, we couldn't hear the car and were just lucky enough to spot it. It circled around and parked with the back door facing us. We watched as the guard in the passenger seat jumped out and walked around to the back door of the car and knocked twice. The back door opened and the guard inside handed the other one two money bags and then jumped down to join his partner. That guard was a small man with a wiry build. They didn't speak as they neared the bank door (not that you could have heard them anyway) and Frank quickly stood and motioned with the wave of his gun for both of them to step behind the small shed.

"You won't get away with this," the stouter of the two yelled.

We quickly got them on the ground back to back and tied their hands together and stuffed rags in their mouths. I was careful to make good strong knots. They were both mumbling and thrashing to get loose. Frank smacked the smaller one across the forehead with his gun and he slumped over. The bigger one hushed immediately.

We made a mad dash across the grass and parking lot toward our car. We hoped that the driver of the armored car was not looking out his sideview mirrors to see us. I threw the bags in the back seat and climbed in an already running car. Frank backed out of our spot and roared out of the parking lot. At the street where we planned to turn left and head back out of town; Frank had to turn right because a big grader was sitting in the road to the left of the intersection.

"We need to go the other way, Frank," I yelled.

"I couldn't because of that stupid grader. I'll try to turn left up here and circle back around," he shot back.

I glanced back in the rear seat and noticed that I had forgotten to cover the money bags. I turned around and put them in the floor and quickly spread my jacket over them, hiding them totally.

"What are you doing?" an excited Frank asked.

"Hiding the money bags, just drive," I practically yelled at him.

Frank passed a worker with a stop sign out and then turned left at the intersection. The guy holding the sign yelled for him to stop, but he continued on without even slowing down. He speeded up as we crossed over the torn up road and both of us bounced around like we were sitting on rubber balls. He hit the end of the dirt road and rammed straight into the broken concrete of the street causing the car to jump up and scrape the undercarriage as we drove on to the main street surface. Frank turned left at the next intersection without signaling and right in front of a cop car.

"Oh cripes, Frank. That's a cop right there," I blurted as we turned.

"Keep an eye on him and see if he follows us. I may have to try and lose him if he does," Frank commented as he slowed a little.

I watched over my shoulder with held breath as we distanced ourselves from the police car.

"He just turned left at the intersection, Frank. I think we're okay," I witnessed.

Frank suddenly turned right and I went scooting across the seat and up against him. I held up my hand and pushed myself back up against the passenger door.

"What are you doing?" I asked. "Take it easy!"

"There's another cop car right up there," he stated and pointed back to his left.

He slowed down and turned into a grocery store parking lot and parked next to a station wagon with a big dog in the back. It began to bark on seeing us.

"What's the plan, Frank?" I asked.

"You go in the store and purchase something, quickly," he instructed.

"What do you need?" I asked.

"Not anything, just buy something. The delay may help take the attention off," he was talking fast and had a furrowed brow.

I walked fast to the store and glanced back at the car a few times as I went. Once I got into the store, I walked up and down a few aisles and grabbed a bottle of vinegar off of a shelf and stood in line at the check out counter.

"Nice day today, isn't it?" the male clerk stated to me.

"Yeah, nice," I agreed.

"That'll be 61 cents with tax. Do you need a sack?" the clerk asked.

"That'll be fine, thanks," I replied as I handed him a dollar bill.

He bagged my purchase, handed me my change and a receipt and wished me a good day. I left the store and headed to the car. I stopped suddenly. A cop car was parked behind our car. A policeman was at the driver's window talking to Frank. I turned down the next aisle of cars and walked with my head down avoiding eye contact. I slowly walked to a pickup truck at the far end of the parking lot and placed my package in the bed right behind the driver's seat. I looked back toward our car and noticed that the cop was leaving and in a hurry. I quickly ran to our car and got in.

"What was that all about, Frank," I asked breathlessly.

"We don't have a license plate on the rear of our car, Sport. Did you know that?" Frank laughed.

"What did you tell him?" I asked.

"That it was a rental and I hadn't noticed it. I showed him the rental papers and he was looking at them when his radio announced the bank robbery, so he threw the papers back in my lap and tore out," Frank explained.

"Wow, we were lucky there. Let's get out of here fast and avoid any road blocks they may put up," I said with a degree of urgency.

We traveled the distance to Charlton with a little taste of victory inside. Things could have fallen totally apart in the beginning, but with some quick thinking and a little bit of luck, we were successful in our job. We discussed the various aspects of the job and how things could have worked differently the entire trip. Frank laughed at my grocery purchase.

Our rendezvous site was at a roadside park just a few miles from the airport. Molly's rental was already there and she had a concerned look on her face as we drove up beside her.

"Where have you been? I have waited for nearly and hour for you. Did you have a problem?" She was talking as she got out of her car and opened my door.

"We had a little run in with a city cop. We're fine, though," Frank said with a big grin.

He went on to explain our close encounter and told her that he would tell her all about it on the plane.

"Well, A.D. will have to tell me the story then, because you're taking the bus," Molly stated.

"Me? Why can't I take the plane with you?" Frank's earlier grin was replaced with a scornful look.

"Because you are taking the bus, that's why?" Molly said emphatically.

Frank actually looked hurt by her comment. I was smiling inside, but didn't let on like it affected me one bit.

We transferred the money bags to her suitcases and closed the trunk. I drove Frank to the bus station in total silence. When he got out of the car, he slammed the door in anger. I felt like telling him that I would see him back at the house, but decided not to further his anger any.

I actually enjoyed my flight back to Middleton. Molly and I sat together and I softly told her about our ordeal at Cayman. She was all ears and asked a lot of questions, mostly about what Frank did and his reaction to each obstacle we ran into. I tried to bolster his stand as a worthy employee by bragging on him a little and expressed how much I have learned from working with him. She seemed to understand where I was coming from and told me how happy she and her aunt were that I was a part of their operation.

CHAPTER 10

Molly revealed the details of our next job one night over dinner. Just the three of us were present. Mrs. Jenkins was not feeling good and Dr. J was at a Town Hall meeting in the Community Center. Frank had worked on preparing the dinner most of the afternoon. I got the feeling that he was trying to impress Molly with his cooking abilities. Perhaps trying to win her favor again after having to ride the bus after the last heist was a part of it, too. I knew he was attracted to her physically, but didn't think anything romantically could become of it due to their age difference. I figured Molly to be in her mid-thirties, remembering the stories told, and Frank was only 26 or so. In my way of thinking, 10 years difference in age was a big gap. The spaghetti and meatballs with a tossed green salad was delicious. Frank was upset though, because Molly asked for some garlic bread and Frank had not prepared any. He offered to go to the store and purchase some garlic powder and make her bread for her, but she told him not to worry about it.

"You did an outstanding job, Frank. It was scrumptious and I loved it. Don't worry about the bread; it's not a big deal," Molly told him.

Her compliment helped a little, but you could still tell that Frank was agitated by the miscue.

We cleared the table and Molly spread out a couple of maps and several pieces of paper and we got down to business regarding the next job. In just two days, we would be on our way to another part of the country and pulling another heist. Frank would be leaving from Clarkston on the early morning flight westward to New Brahms. The flight stops in Albany where Frank would change planes before continuing on and I would get on the same plane. After landing, we would get a rental car and drive to Lake Cameron. We would be staying in a motel in Lake Cameron for the night and hitting the bank at 8:30 the next morning. Our target is the Lakeview Savings and Loan Bank on the lake front. Dr. J had canvassed the area six months ago, but the feeling was that nothing had changed a great deal to alter the plans. The bank was two years old and the only bank in town. The bank in Crofton (across the lake) was where a lot of the citizens had previously done their banking and although some of them had stayed with the old bank, many had transferred their accounts to Lakeview and were doing their banking with it.

The lumber mill that was located in Lake Cameron had a large employment and a campaign early in the opening of the bank convinced a lot of them to bank with Lakeview. Dr. J's analysis was that Lakeview would reap a large reward. Drawings indicated that we could safely approach the rear of the bank without being seen. Dr. J's report indicated that a sidewalk led to the parking lot and it was covered by a large trellis covered in ivy and honey-suckle vines. The cover provided a good shield from being detected by the driver of the armored car or other patrons due to it being on the opposite side of the trellis from where we would approach. If we could time everything perfectly, the whole job should be a cinch. The post supporting the trellis would be ideal for tying up the guards. Frank elbowed me as a reminder of my knot tying prowess. Molly noticed it.

"What's that all about?" she asked.

"Nothing really. I'll tell you about it some other time," he replied.

I slept fitfully the night before we left. The alarm clock was set for 6 a.m. but I was awake at 3:20, at 4:30, and again at 5:20, so just got up and got ready. Frank was going to drive to Clarkston while I got to ride the Whitney Line to Albany. Our return home was in reverse order, so I would be riding the bus home as well. I really didn't mind, seeing as how I trumped his return on the last gig. The transfer rendezvous was to take place just outside New Brahms in the parking lot of the big Union Grocery Warehouse. It was just about a mile to the airport from there. I was nervous early and tried to calm myself as I rode south. I had never been this direction before and didn't know where the airport was, but was relying on Molly's directions. The airport was exactly where she said I would find it. Just as you enter the outskirts of Albany, the airport is in clear view to your left…easy as pie. I was dropped off at the intersection and as I walked to the terminal, a man in a pickup stopped and offered me a lift. The wait for the plane coming from Clarkston was not all that long. Once it arrived, Frank and I boarded the Southern Metro Airlines plane for our flight to New Brahms. After being seated, I glanced down the aisle for Frank, but couldn't see him. I sat next to the window and watched the ground fade from view. The flight was announced as an hour and twenty minutes and coffee was served to everyone that wanted it. I took a cup and sipped it hoping that it would calm me.

We landed in New Brahms on time and Frank was ahead of me at baggage claim. He ignored me the whole time and headed for the rental booth after getting his bag. I walked to the area where the rental cars were parked and waited for him. In just a few minutes he drove up in a small foreign sports car convertible, smiling like a Cheshire cat. I put my bag in the back and jumped in. We drove the next two hours talking like we had never talked before with the wind blowing our hair all over our heads. We climbed out of a valley and entered a forest of trees and drove on narrow roads lined with evergreens. The curves were plentiful, but the traffic was minimal with logging trucks passing by every once in a while and just a few cars, making the time go by quickly.

In our conversation, Frank told me his feelings toward Molly and was wondering what I thought. Heck, I didn't know anything about girls or romantic stuff. I just listened to him for the most part and he revealed some things that I really didn't care about or need to know. He confessed that the squeaks and the snickers that I may have heard coming from his room that night was indeed Molly sharing his bed. I was totally shocked. I didn't even know what to say. I stammered something undetectable above the wind noise and he just grinned. God, I thought, how am I going to get out of this? Frank was hooked on Molly.

"Were you in love with that gal that went to Hollywood?" I asked out of the clear blue.

"I don't know. I may have been. We weren't together very long, though," Frank commented as though he was expecting the question.

"How long have you known Molly?" I asked.

"Quite a while. A lot longer than I knew Dorothy," he announced.

"Isn't Molly a bit older than you, Frank?" I asked.

"What difference does that make if you're in love with the person, Sport?" he questioned to my shocked face.

I regained my composure from the shocking news and tried to talk like an experienced adult. I reminded him that he couldn't jeopardize our mission and he couldn't afford to get involved with someone you work with. I rambled on for several minutes without making any sense, but hoped I got through to him with my wisdom-sounding advice.

We soon topped a summit that opened up below into a beautiful valley surrounded by trees and a huge lake sitting between two towns, Lake Cameron was just below us and Crofton on the other side of the lake. The smoke and steam from the saw mill was spread wide with a layer of it seemingly transfixed over the lake. We descended the hill on a winding road that seemed like it took forever to reach the base of. We pulled up in front of a small motel just as we passed the city limit sign of Lake Cameron.

The night went quickly, it seemed, and before I knew it, Frank was jostling me awake. We got dressed, checked our gear, and headed out to get a bite of breakfast before driving to the bank. A small diner just a block or so away was flashing an *Eats* sign so we stopped and had breakfast. The only waitress was a cute little thing and the place was fairly busy. She was scampering between tables trying to keep up with the demand. I overheard the table talk next to us and discovered that the Lakeview Savings and Loan Bank had been robbed last night. I looked at Frank to see if he had overheard the same thing and his face said it all. He got up from the table and went to the cash register and asked our waitress if what we heard was true. She acknowledged that yes it was apparently true. She had heard that the bank would be closed for awhile due to the break-in and the FBI would be arriving later. Frank made some excuse for us having to leave and asked for our bill. Even though we hadn't been served anything but coffee, he paid for our two breakfast orders and we left the building.

"What are we going to do, Frank?" I asked when we got outside.

"I don't know," he replied.

"Do you think the armored car will still make its run?" I asked.

"Heck, I don't know, Coop," he blurted. "We're going to go ahead with our plan, though, just in case."

"Don't you think the FBI will forewarn the armored car company about the robbery and stop the delivery?" I asked.

"Like I said, I don't know, but I'd sure hate to go home empty handed," he stated.

Frank was thinking clearer than me because all I had was questions. At least he was making sense in thinking that we might still be able to carry out our mission. Who knows, maybe the armored car will still try to make its delivery. But I figured with the robbery, the bank will be swarming with cops and later FBI agents. Our being there may draw suspicion that we don't want.

We slowly drove over to the bank and noticed immediately that cops were all over the place. State troopers, sheriff's cars, and the local cops were in force. Flashing red lights were penetrating the air like a 4th of July show. There was no way we were going to be able to carry out our plan. Frank continued to drive on past the bank and we parked in the lot across from the grocery store. We could see some of the activity and we watched with furrowed brows. Someone or some people had ruined our plans. There was another gang of robbers at play in this area. I guess in some way, that was good news for us. At least the FBI would not be looking for us on this job. I wondered what Molly and Mrs. Jenkins would think. Surely, they would understand. They had put out a good bit of money to put us here and we were not going to be able to perform. More money would be spent to get us home and there will be no return on that expenditure either.

"We'll drive back to New Brahms and meet up with Molly like we planned and tell her the news," Frank said factually.

"How do you suppose she will take it?" I asked.

"You're just loaded with questions, aren't you Sport?" Frank replied. "She'll understand. Heck, what else is she going to do, fire us?" he continued.

The ride back to New Brahms was quiet. Each of us was harboring our own thoughts for the entire 88 miles. The weather had changed along with the mood. Cloud cover blocked the sun and the wind had a chill to it. Frank stopped the car and put the top up. I helped lock the latches in place. We rolled up the windows and we continued on our way. We drove into a rain storm within just a few miles and I mentally kept time with the windshield wipers for a long time. We arrived at the rendezvous site almost an hour before we were scheduled to so we just sat in the car and waited. Frank tried to find some music on the car's radio but for some reason all he could get was static. I figured the electrical storm was hampering the radio signals. We sat in silence.

Molly drove up along side the car on my side. Her window was already down as I rolled mine down to talk to her.

"Hey!" I said in greeting. "We have a problem."

Molly had already heard about the robbery. She heard from Mrs. Jenkins who heard by way of Ham radio about it. Molly had stopped at a pay phone upon hearing about the robbery on the car radio and checked it out with Mrs. Jenkins. She confirmed that it was fact. She had told Molly of her alternate plan...the bank in Crofton had ordered an additional sum of money to be delivered to cover the payroll of the mill and other transactions that would take place due to the robbery in Lake Cameron. The armored car was to be arriving at the Bank of Crofton tomorrow morning at 8 a.m. Our orders were to return to the lake and take the money from the Crofton bank's armored car delivery.

Molly explained the circumstances as best she could with what information she had. It seems that when an act such as a robbery occurs, other banks step in and assist the one that was robbed with services needed. In this case, with the bank in Lake Cameron closed due to the robbery and the start of the FBI investigation, the bank in Crofton picks up the slack. With the mill getting paid tomorrow, the workers would need a place to cash their payroll checks and Crofton would be the natural place to do it. The report that Mrs. Jenkins got regarding the special delivery meant that a lot more money than usual would be arriving at Crofton. That was our new assignment. There was no preliminary report on the conditions or surroundings, so we would basically be striking in the dark.

Frank suggested that we return to Lake Cameron immediately and check out the bank in Crofton tonight and get a feel for how it could go down tomorrow morning. Molly agreed and told us that she would meet us here at this site tomorrow morning between 11:30 and noon. We both nodded our approval and got under way.

"I want us to trade cars, Frank. You have been seen in that fancy little sports car already and you never know who might take an interest. You don't need to draw unwanted attention. You take mine and I'll take the convertible," she said.

"Okay. It's probably better that way, anyway," he replied.

I was actually surprised that Frank didn't put up a fight about that, but instead readily agreed. We transferred our gear into the sedan that Molly was driving and swapped vehicles and drove away.

"Good luck!" she called out and threw us a kiss.

"I think she likes you too, Frank," I said. "She just blew you a kiss," I teased.

"Knock it off, Sport," he replied. "That gesture was meant for both of us and you know it," he blurted.

"Yeah, so you say," I continued to tease.

We got back to the lake in a few hours and went straight to Crofton to locate the bank. The road leading to Crofton is called Lakeside Boulevard. It circles the lake and once you enter the city limits of Crofton, businesses are built all along the waterfront. The Bank of Crofton was one of those businesses. Frank slowly cruised past and we looked over the situation. A three story office building was adjacent to the bank parking lot and we pulled into its dirt lot and drove to the back to hopefully get a better look at the rear of the bank. Mud puddles dotted the lot. A delivery truck was parked in the rear and provided protection for us to park and observe the back area next door. We parked next to it in a huge mud puddle.

The parking lot of the bank had a marked off area next to the sidewalk and an enclosure next to the steps leading to the water's edge. An outbuilding of some sort was about ten paces away from the back door of the bank and Frank thought it might well shield our attack due to its size. The distance from where we thought the armored car would park to the back door was more than a hundred feet and the guards would have to go around the outbuilding in order to get to the back door. That is where Frank suggested we make our move.

"We should probably park right here and make our move from here. It's out of sight and would provide cover for our approach," I suggested.

"Provided the truck is here tomorrow morning; that would be a good idea," Frank confirmed.

I was proud of myself for the idea. With the one guard left in the armored car unable to see us crossing the parking lot, we could catch the others by surprise as they emerged from the back side of the outbuilding.

We returned to the main part of town and thinking possibly that several people in Lake Cameron might have seen us, it would be better for us to find a motel in Crofton to spend the night. We found a nice little motor lodge just a few blocks away from the bank that offered kitchenettes and a view of the lake from your room. It was late afternoon when we settled in so we drove to a grocery on the street and bought a few things to munch on and drinks for our nights stay.

"It'll be safer if we are not seen by anyone. I hope you don't mind eating in the room, Sport," Frank commented.

"Not at all," I agreed.

Frank was up early and was outside wiping the windshield of the car when I got up. I got dressed and we ate toast and jam with coffee that Frank had purchased at a small diner down the street. Not being seen by a lot of people (like in a restaurant) was being adhered to proficiently. We ate in silence with our own thoughts. Once finished, we loaded up and headed for the bank. We passed by the Cottage Café where Frank got the grub and noticed a lot of cars, trucks and logging trucks. Passing by the front of the bank, we noticed that there were not any cars in the lot on either side. We parked on the back side of the delivery truck out of sight from the street with the entire bank parking lot in front of us. Frank purposely parked to the side of the big mud puddle so that we could move in and out without wading in the water to do so. We were a half hour earlier than planned but it was a good thing we were, because we had only sat for a few minutes when the armored car pulled up.

"The car is early, Frank. Do you suppose there is anyone in the bank yet?" I asked.

"I hope so. Someone has to let them in. It's probably already been arranged," Frank surmised.

"And if no one is inside, what do we do?" I asked.

"Maybe that one belongs to someone inside," he said as he pointed to a car that was parked out in front of the bank.

"You could be right," I said.

"Sometimes the armored cars are early and have to wait for someone to get inside to open the door for them. Maybe this is one of those times, considering the situation," Frank explained.

His explanation made sense but it didn't make me any less nervous. We could see the guards begin to prepare for their delivery by moving in and around the car. Suddenly, the back door of the bank opened and a man propped it open. He whistled and motioned for the guards to come in. He went back inside, leaving the door open. The guards got out of the car and began their walk, each carrying a large bank bag. Frank and I got out of the car and quickly rushed to the scene to do our job. I didn't have time to put on my mask, so pulled my hat down over my eyes as much as possible and still be able to see where I was going. We surprised the guards without saying anything by stepping onto the sidewalk as they came from around the outbuilding. Frank waved the gun at them and they stopped and hesitated prior to handing over the bags. I walked slowly backwards to the open door and closed it quietly. As I did, one of the guards made a break for the armored car and pulled his revolver. He turned as he ran and he and Frank both fired their guns at the same time. The guard went down. I was stunned, but recovered quickly and noticed that Frank had the gun aimed at the other guard.

"Don't shoot mister," he begged.

"Don't you move a muscle, friend," Frank told him.

Frank grabbed me by the arm and we made a run for the car. I had both money bags in my grasp. They were quite heavy, but manageable.

"Get us out of here, Sport," Frank said as he threw me the keys.

I trapped the keys on the top of the money bags and lowered them into the car's back seat. I jumped behind the wheel, started the car and backed out of the space. I glanced over at the bank and the man that had opened the back door was running toward the downed guard. The other guard was running toward the street to intercept us. I didn't even stop at the street to see who might be coming. Some car screeched to a halt on seeing me dart out of the driveway and into the street. As I zoomed past the bank, the guard was shaking his fist at me and yelling obscenities. I drove fast down the boulevard to the road that circled the lake back to Lake Cameron. I slowed down through Lake Cameron so as not to attract attention and made my way to the main road that would lead us to New Brahms. I glanced over at Frank and he had his head against the window and his hand on his shoulder. It was red with blood. Frank had been shot.

"Oh my god, Frank. Are you going to be okay?" I asked.

"I'll be okay, Sport, just get us out of here and don't get pulled over by a cop, please," he grunted.

The main highway leading out of Lake Cameron was being repaired in a few spots that morning and two men were out with the road crews directing traffic. We had to stop for just a few minutes in traffic for a loader to back into place, then we were allowed to resume. The man with the flag was on Frank's side of the car and he got a real good look at Frank as we slowly went by. Hopefully, he didn't see the blood or become suspicious of the situation. Once clear of the traffic, I picked up the pace and drove faster than the speed limit toward New Brahms. Frank had found a rag in his bag and had it soaking up the blood oozing from his shoulder wound.

"I told you not to get stopped, A.D. You best slow down and don't attract attention," he said.

"Okay!" I replied, and slowed down to under the speed limit.

The rest of the way to our rendezvous site was mostly done in silence. Frank either passed out or went to sleep about half way there and didn't awake until we were just about to the warehouse parking lot. I tried twice to get him to talk but he was out. I knew he was still alive, because he snored a few times and moaned a few times as well. I couldn't find anything on the radio but static so just drove and tried not to think about what lay ahead.

The sports car was already at the site so I pulled up beside it. Molly immediately knew that something was wrong because I was driving and Frank's head was leaning against the window. She jumped out and opened Frank's door almost before I got the car stopped.

"What happened?" she blurted.

"He took a bullet from one of the guards," I answered.

"Good God," she flushed. "Are you hurt?" she asked me.

"No ma'am," I said.

She started administering aid to Frank by getting him eased down into the seat and taking off his shirt. He was awake and could assist by moving his own body. It was obvious to me that Molly had experience in this sort of thing with the way she was handling herself and being gentle, yet stern with her nursing duties. She opened one of the suitcases and withdrew a limited first aid kit, but adequate for what she needed. Within a few minutes she had a bandage on the wound and secured it with a bandage around his upper arm and shoulder. A makeshift sling supported the arm. She eased his shirt back on, leaving the left sleeve vacant.

"We need to get him to a doctor, A.D," she said. "Put those money bags in the trunk and follow me."

She tidied up by throwing the spent bandages and bloody rags in a nearby trash can while I transferred her suitcase into the sedan's trunk with the money bags. We drove out of the lot and toward town. We slowed after just a few minutes and Molly stopped in the middle of the street and asked an old man walking his dog where the nearest hospital was.

"What is she doing?" I asked.

"She's getting directions, I bet," Frank guessed.

"Excuse me mister, can you direct me to the hospital?" we heard her call out.

He was very cordial and with a look of concern, pointed to our right.

"Take the next right and go about six blocks. It will be on your right hand side," he called back. "Can't miss it."

"Thanks!" I heard Molly say and we immediately turned right at the next street.

"Told you so!" Frank said.

Within just a few minutes we entered the emergency area of a local hospital. I assisted in getting Frank inside and Molly talked to a man in a white coat. We were asked to get Frank into an examining room and after we did, Molly quietly told me to go ditch the little car somewhere and meet her back here.

"Do it quickly, A.D., but don't get caught," she whispered as she handed me the keys.

I had never ditched a car in my life, so was going on instinct alone. I had never driven a sports car before, but discovered it drives pretty much like our own. I drove around for quite awhile looking for a place to ditch a car. Finally, I noticed a new and used car lot on a street corner and figured that would be a good place to leave it. It would blend right in, I thought. I went around the corner and turned around and drove up on the sidewalk and into the lot, pulling right up beside another convertible. I checked over the interior to make sure I got everything that belonged to us. I checked the trunk for anything Molly may have left, then put the keys on top of the dashboard, shut the door and started walking back to the hospital.

I met Molly and Frank coming out of the emergency room door as I walked up the sidewalk. Frank was leaning on her for support.

"It was just a flesh wound, the bullet went clean through," Molly said as she looked around for eavesdroppers. "Did you get rid of the car?" she asked.

"Yes, I did," I replied.

"Good," she said.

"Is he going to be okay?" I asked her of Frank.

"Yes, he's going to be fine. He'll be a little sore for a week or so, but he will recover nicely," she assured.

Frank mumbled that he'll be just fine and tried to say Sport, but it came out like Shirt.

"They gave him a pain pill and I think it's already working," Molly explained.

"Didn't they ask how he got shot?" I asked

"Sure they did. I told them it was an accident that the gun went off accidentally while I was loading it. I took the blame for not handling the gun properly. I gave them a false name and address. They were fine with it. The emergency doctor even said that he had another one just yesterday," she explained. "Money talks, you know. I gave the lady at the desk two hundred dollars and she was in total shock, but released us."

Molly handed me the paperwork and I looked it over while she drove us to the airport. I noticed that she had presented the hospital as them being Mr. and Mrs. Frank Smith. I looked over at her at the wheel and she knew why I looked at her, and she just grinned.

"Did you know that Frank was crazy about you?" I asked her while I looked in the back seat to make sure that Frank was out.

"Did he tell you that?" she replied.

"Yes ma'am he did," I said.

"He is cute and I do like him a lot, but I think he's too immature for me," she said. "Someday, he'll find his love and get on with his life. That is if he doesn't get himself killed first," she said as she looked back at him lying in the back seat.

"Yes ma'am," I said and turned my eyes back to the road.

We pulled up to the curb at the section marked *'Departures'* and started unloading the car. Molly asked me to help her get Frank into the airport and to the boarding area.

"What about the car?" I asked.

"We'll just leave it there. They'll find it and return it to the rental place," she said.

I wasn't comfortable leaving the car in the drop off area, but didn't argue and followed her while pushing the suitcases and bags on a luggage cart to the ticket counter. Frank was awake and walking on his own, although a little wobbly, but with Molly's help, he made it fine. Molly bought three, one-way tickets to Middleton and checked all of the bags. I thought that was really risky but figured she knew what she was doing and didn't say a thing. She must have seen the concern on my face.

"Relax, A.D. Everything will be just fine," she assured me as we turned from the counter.

"Excuse me, sir, could I speak with you for a moment," a man in a black suit was speaking to a man right next to us. "My name is Agent Quinn of the FBI. Could you answer some questions for me?" he asked.

We all froze in our tracks, momentarily.

"Sure, I guess; what about?" the man agreed.

"Just some questions to clear up a few things is all. Step right over here if you would, please," the agent gestured at some chairs next to the counter.

"Is everything all right, mister?" Molly asked the agent.

"Everything's fine, ma'am. You can go on about your business and let us handle this situation," the agent returned.

"Okay!" Molly said and hurriedly turned and walked toward our gate with Frank and me in tow.

"Is he on to us, you think?" I whispered on our way.

"I thought so at first, A.D., but he gave us the go ahead, so we're taking it. That guy might be suspected of robbing the bank in Lake Cameron. I'm glad we weren't the ones," she stated as we walked.

CHAPTER 11

Frank recovered nicely and his wound healed. He would be sporting a scar the rest of his life, but something he would have pride in telling his friends about, no doubt. The Speakeasy Gang cooled their heels for the better part of two months. That time was spent mostly just hanging around the trailer, walking to town occasionally, and washing the car every now and then. Molly only came around a few times in that span and Frank noticeably missed seeing her and talking to her. I asked why she wasn't around and was told that she was probably searching out some new jobs for us to do. I taught Willy how to play cribbage and we spent a lot of time playing and keeping track of who won how many games. He got really good at the game and was soon quite a bit ahead of me. I visited with Mrs. Jenkins a number of times while helping her weed or cut flowers. She was really a sweet old lady, but you could tell there was an under lying anger about her

"So when do you think we will do another job, if it's any of my business?" I asked her one time.

"You are part of the business now; Mr. Cooper," she responded. "To answer your question; pretty soon. We're working on something."

We were cleaning up some weeds and dead flowers out of the flowerbed when I asked the question and she walked to the front porch and propped her cane against the house and motioned for me to sit in the straight back chair beside her rocker.

She asked about my past and about my family. I filled her in on as much as I dared reveal and she seemed satisfied. I told her that my mom was sick and lied to her that she was in an old folks home in Woodsboro. I told her about Cecil drowning when he was young and confessed that my older brother was a know-it-all and had no time for me. Mrs. Jenkins shared her condolences for me having to be raised in such a messed up environment.

As we talked, she revealed to me that Molly had deposited well over a million dollars in the Canadian banks over the years. I was flabbergasted. Where ever Ottawa, Ontario, and London were, they had a lot of money there. I had heard of London when I was in school and thought it was the capital of England, but didn't argue. I had learned that there were a lot of towns and cities that shared the same name and figured this was just one of those. She asked me if I was pleased with the arrangements of my pay and asked if I thought it was sufficient. I assured her it was more money than I had ever received and was very satisfied. I didn't dare ask if Frank and I would ever reap any of the million she mentioned.

Her questions started me thinking of what I was going to do with all the money I had. The savings account that I opened a few months ago was getting regular deposits and I knew to the penny what I had in the account. The money and change I carried on my person was more than a lot of people make in a month, but I was used to having it and felt comfortable having it available if ever I needed it. The money envelopes came every Friday whether we were working jobs or not. Even in this idle state we are in now, the envelopes kept coming. I made a trip to the bank in Clarkston every Monday to deposit my pay. Where to spend it and what to spend it on were big questions for me.

Not having any experience at travel to see sights, I didn't know about retirement areas or vacationing spots, other than what I had read in books or seen on television. The Riviera sounded good, but I had no idea where it was other than somewhere in Europe and close to the water. I had never seen the ocean or sandy beaches in my life, so settling in such an area was as foreign as a different language. Canada sounded nice too, but could only relate it to what I had read. My dad spoke passionately about an area in Arizona that he would like to settle in. I knew that was out west somewhere, but had no idea as to why it was so coveted. Nor did I know how much I would need to settle in any of the areas I thought about. How many more Fridays would I have before having enough to live on for the rest of my life without having to work.

"Do you have a girl somewhere, A.D.?" she asked.

I was startled at the sudden break in silence we were enjoying, so the answer to her question came out in a squeaky voice.

"No ma'am I don't. Not yet anyway," I confessed.

"Well, don't rush it, young man. You have lots of time," she counseled. "One thing I will advise you on though, always be honest with whoever it is you settle down with," she stated.

"Oh, I will. Trust me!" I told her.

"Well, you haven't been totally honest with us, have you?" she questioned.

"What do you mean?" I asked, confused and with the sound of concern.

"How old are you really, A.D.?" she asked.

"Oh, I see what you mean. I'm only 18, ma'am," I confessed.

"I thought so. But rest assured, young man, your secret is safe with me. What Frank Epperson doesn't know won't hurt him. But, you be sure and mark my words when the time comes to take a mate. You be honest with that someone. Understand?" she instructed.

"Yes ma'am, you bet I will, and thank you!" I said. "I assume your experience in these matters helps with your decisions," I added.

"That's a good assumption. Molly knows a thing or two about being honest during a relationship, too," she revealed.

"How's that, Mrs. Jenkins?" I asked.

"Her mother, my daughter, has polio and lives in an iron lung. Molly lied to her fiancée about her mother. It ended their relationship when he discovered the truth," she revealed.

"Couldn't he have forgiven her? I would have if I loved her and intended to marry her," I confessed.

"If only you were a few years older, A.D. However, her beau was a little higher strung and demanded the ring back. Molly was devastated, of course, but she recovered. Who knows if she will ever lend her heart to a man again? It pays to be honest with your mate, A.D., believe me," Mrs. Jenkins stated.

I liked her. She was smart enough to see through my disguise. I thought about telling her the truth about my mom, but decided not to. However, I decided that I would be a little more cautious in the future when hanging out with Frank. I wondered if he knew the story about Molly that was just revealed. I began to think about what Mrs. Jenkins said about being honest with my future wife. Heck, I didn't even know a person of the opposite sex, except Molly, and she was out of my reach both in age and experience. I figured that someday, I would meet that special someone and one day have a family.

Of course, all of the thinking I was doing was assuming that I didn't get killed or spend the rest of my life in prison. And what happens to all of my money if I do get killed or have to spend my life in prison? Would it just sit in the bank and draw interest for eternity? I could tell someone where my money is and ask them to take care of it for me. I don't know who that would be, other than my brother, but being separated from him for so long, I didn't even know what he was up to or if I could trust him to take care of things for me. I didn't have a wife or kids to share my wealth with and didn't even have a girlfriend to spend any of it on. The thoughts just kept coming and with no answers or decisions. I thought that when the time came, I would know where, what, and how much. Meanwhile, I would continue to sock it away and plan accordingly.

"Frank, do you smell smoke?" I yelled as I pounded on his bedroom door.

There was no answer, so I opened it slowly and discovered no one in the room, but the door to the outside was ajar. I went out that way into the dark and noticed the sky being very bright from the fire that was raging nearby. I ran back inside and put on my pants and hurriedly headed for the fire.

I came up behind Frank who was standing near the road out front, watching the house across the street go up in flames. I had noticed the house a number of times, and Mrs. Jenkins told me that an older couple lived there off and on. They rode the bus to Middleton quite often and stayed with an ailing relative there. The house was partially hidden from view by overgrown, unkempt bushes and shrubs out front and I often thought that it was an eyesore to the surrounding homes, but didn't say anything.

Just then the sound of a wailing siren penetrated the night air and a fire truck approached from town. No sooner had the firemen started dousing the fire with water, another team of firefighters arrived and then another. I noticed the insignia on one truck as being from MacAfee. I looked down the street toward town and a wall of people in all matters of dress was watching the blaze as well. Their blank faces were partly revealed in the light of the fire. From my vantage point, it appeared that the fire was contained to the close side of the house in the rear because I could see smoke pouring out of the screened-in porch at the far side.

"Thank goodness they were not at home," a lady nearby commented.

"Do you know that for sure? They will be devastated to learn of this, though," another female voice stated.

"Yeah, they left yesterday afternoon. I wonder if she left her iron on or the stove. It looks like the fire is coming from the kitchen," the first one observed.

The firemen had the blaze knocked down and under control in a matter of minutes, it seemed, and began mop-up procedures. The excitement was over and people dispersed to their homes. I didn't say anything to Frank as we moseyed back to the trailer and went back to bed. I looked at the clock and noticed that it was 2:45 a.m.

Other than the excitement of the fire, our time off was mostly boring for me. Frank longed for Molly more and more. She was gone for better than a week at one stretch during the lull and on her return, she revealed that her mother had passed away and she went back to Albany to take care of things. I was not aware that Mrs. Jenkins went with her. On her visits afterward, she spent a lot of time with Frank and he faked that his injury was not healing as fast as it should and asked her to stay longer. She could see through his ruse like it was clear glass and just laughed him off. I wondered if she had told him that his interest in her was one-sided. It would devastate him, I was sure, and maybe she realized that and hadn't told him for that reason. She really hadn't helped him because she wasn't interested in him as a boyfriend, but strictly as a partner in the business of robbing armored cars. Molly soon moved in to the big house and lived with her aunt.

I had a lot of time to think about any future relationships I might have. I had never had a girlfriend, let alone a love life. I thought about what I would do and how I would act with one though. I didn't think I wanted to use Frank as an example that was for sure. His constant whining when he was around Molly was almost sickening. I vowed to never be like that with my girl, if and when it happened. I envisioned myself with a younger Molly, holding hands and looking at a full moon from the hood of my own car. I had a lot of dreams and thought a lot about what I would do when this part of my life was over. That is if I don't get killed or wind up in jail somewhere before it all ends. The time off was boring, to say the least, and I was getting antsy to do something. One thing I did get from the time off was some good advice from a smart old lady.

CHAPTER 12

Mrs. Jenkins called a meeting of the gang one week night and after hearing about the job upcoming and the details of it, I realized that Molly's visits were not just to agonize over Frank and get him all agitated. A lot of time had been dedicated to this one. Her previous comment that she was working on something was becoming evident.

Mrs. Jenkins prefaced the meeting like all the others except with a bit more emphasis on the danger involved. She recalled the last job and how the daring of an obviously rookie guard brought havoc to an otherwise successful heist. Her contacts had relayed to her that the guard that Frank shot was just wounded and had left his employment due to the danger involved. Both banks had been recouped by the Federal Government and the top officers of both banks had stationed armed guards inside the banks for protection. Apparently, sixteen banks had been robbed in the past three months and the government was doing something about it. The FBI had hired more agents and several were being trained to work solely on bank jobs and had formulated a *'task force'* to deal with it. The banking industry had been mandated to provide guards inside of the banks to ward off would-be robbers. Large banks had as many as three guards and the smaller banks had at least one. The industry figured that a few outlying banks in isolated places may not get the problem resolved for a few months, so their hours of operation had been reduced to four hours a day. I wondered how that was going to prevent the bank from being robbed at night. Mrs. Jenkins must have read my mind because she said the exact same thing just moments later, except Mrs. Jenkins answered the question of wonderment with an actual fact.

The U.S. Treasury Department had mandated that all banks were to keep a minimum amount of cash on hand overnight and on weekends. The amount varied due to the size of the bank and the areas they served. The armored car companies were going to be making a lot more trips weekly to keep that law in check. That meant that some of the late afternoon and evening hauls could possibly contain more cash than the early morning delivery. It also presented the possibility that some competition may develop as well. One plus on our side was that each car would only have two guards accompanying the money.

"How interesting," I thought.

I had never considered that others were doing the same thing we were doing. I wondered what would happen if two gangs hit the same armored car delivery or same bank at the same time. Now that would be *really* interesting.

The new plans called for a twist in our regular routine. Due to the new government regulations, we were going to start hitting two armored cars at once, at night and with three people; me, Frank, and Dr. J. When that announcement was made, mine and Frank's mouths dropped open like the door of an oven. This had taken a lot of preparation. Molly confessed that her trips to and from Hardee over the last few months were for the gathering of facts and figures from the state capital to better plan the robberies. The new regulations pertaining to banks' operations were especially pertinent. The new directives were implemented immediately. To expedite matters, several armored car companies were combining their efforts by establishing rendezvous points and consolidating their loads so that only one car had to make the trip to the depository. That way, they would save time and money. The rendezvous point was where we were going to hit. If successful, we would double (or perhaps) triple our usual take.

The first of the night time heists was set and the plans were being carried out. Our usual preparation had been altered a bit and although travel was still a part of the job, we were not robbing during the day time but during the dark of night. Molly's research, with the help of her Ham operator bunch, had uncovered the place and the time of several of the transfers. She even observed a few in operation. All of them that she had observed had been done around 10:00 at night and one was after 11:00. That meant that our travel was being done late in the day with an over-night stay and return travel in the early morning hours. I had little experience in driving at night and hoped that Frank could handle all of it. Rendezvous spots for our own transfers would have to be altered as well if we were keeping the same routine. Molly had not indicated that that portion of the heist would be different.

We set out for Hillsboro (our first destination) at four in the afternoon. I rode the bus to Middleton's Plaster Air Field and caught the 7 p.m. flight and Frank and Dr. J drove to Albany for their flight. Once in Hillsboro, we were to rent a car and drive to the rendezvous spot where two armored cars were consolidating their load. Mrs. Jenkins had described the scene like an overview. Each armored car would travel from their respective spots, bank A and bank B; meet at point C, with only one of the cars continuing to point D, the depository. The other car would return to its depot or continue on in another direction as a decoy. If we were successful, both cars would be empty no matter which way they traveled.

My flight was delayed in Middleton for about thirty minutes and I began to fidget thinking that I would be late for the party. But, upon arrival in Hillsboro and entering the terminal, I saw Frank and Dr. J waiting in the busy lobby.

"Well, it's about time," Frank complained. "Plane problems?"

"Something about an aviation light blinking, I heard. I did see a man on a ladder inspecting a light at the wing tip. Are we still okay for time?" I asked.

"We're fine, A.D. Don't let him spook you," Dr. J assured.

Frank walked off toward the rental booths and secured us a late model station wagon. I had never before rode in a station wagon and thought it might be interesting. We loaded up and made our way out of town with Frank driving and Dr. J in the front seat. I sat in the back and looked out on a very dark night.

The rendezvous site was the intersection of highways US 202 and the Inland Empire Road running north and south through Ramsey County. One corner of the intersection was once a filling station, now closed and abandoned. The closest town to the meeting spot was Pottery, about 8 miles further south. We didn't know which towns the armored cars were coming from, but Molly had guessed which depository the money was headed for. This transfer was to take place at 11 p.m. Frank had studied the maps of the area and drove right to the designated spot. We parked on the side of the road about 50 yards from the designated intersection, right at an entrance to a field of alfalfa. We parked a good half hour before the transfer was scheduled to happen and waited.

Not having done a job this particular way before, we discussed how we would approach it and who would do what.

Frank took the lead in the discussion and instructed us on how it should happen...with masks in place, we would attack the cars just as the transfer was taking place. Frank was to hold the gun on the guards and Dr. J and I would relieve them of their money bags. We would tie all of them up in one car, close the doors and make our get away. We were to meet up with Molly at a motel in Kingston (a town nearby) and make the transfer of money bags to her rental. We would stay the night and depart for home tomorrow.

The night sky was really black with few stars visible. Only one vehicle had passed through the intersection during our wait, and then lights of another vehicle appeared to our left. We watched as it slowed down for the intersection and then it pulled over to the side of the road at the old gas station building. It was an armored car. We watched closely for lights from any direction to appear indicating the other armored car. Moments later, lights were spotted in the distance headed straight for us.

"You suppose that's the armored car, Frank?" Dr. J. asked.

"How would I know, Doc?" Frank answered.

In anticipation, Frank started the car and moved forward toward the intersection very slowly with no lights. The crunch of the gravel was deafening inside the car, so figuring the occupants of the armored cars may be able to hear it too, we stopped and moved in on foot. I didn't close my door all the way for fear of being heard. We huddled together in front of our car and watched the latest car back up to within a few feet of the car that was already there. The drivers of the cars got out and spoke to one another and then opened the rear doors. The open doors provided a wall between the cars and all we could see was the legs of the guards in the opening below the door.

Both cars had their interior lights on and the transfer was under way without any chatter.

It wasn't explained why the cars would need to back up to one another, but thinking it was for security purposes, we figured it was to our benefit because they couldn't see our approach. The statement that Molly made about the feds never changing their ways came to mind. It seemed that just transferring a few money bags from one car to the other was a simple task and backing up to each other was unnecessary.

We hadn't counted on the doors providing a barrier of sorts, and how to overcome the obstacle presented a challenge. Frank stopped our pursuit with an outstretched hand and with his hands and arms, indicated that we were going to go around the front of the cars and approach from the other side. He put his finger to his pursed lips in a gesture of keeping quiet.

Frank hit the door with such force that it not only caught the men by surprise, but knocked one of them to the ground. The look on his face was pure astonishment. The timing was perfect because we caught the others with their backs turned while transferring the bags of money.

"Don't move gentlemen. This won't take long if you cooperate," Frank's announcement left no doubt in the minds of the guards as to what was taking place.

His gun waving in their faces was convincing, so they froze with faces startled, but with no resistance. Dr. J put his foot in the middle of the man that was down and he didn't move. The man in one car handed me four of the six bags being transferred to his rig without a word. I looked at the other one and he obliged by handing me the rest of the bags. Dr. J had asked the other man that was outside the vehicles to get on his knees. Frank instructed all of them to get on the floor of one car and sit back to back. They obeyed with speed and accuracy. I was about to tie them up when Frank put the rope in Dr. J's hands and motioned for me to stuff the rags in their mouths. I knew without asking that Frank was thinking of the rope tying job I did on a job and trusted Dr. J to do a better job. I stuffed rags in their mouths and grabbed several bags, and headed for the car. Dr. J was right behind me carrying just as many. Frank grabbed the remaining bags and ran to catch up with us. He left the rear door of one armored car open with the light shining into the night.

"I thought we agreed that we were going to shut both doors of the armored cars, Frank," I stated.

"I figured they could use some fresh air, Sport. Besides, passers by may not be as suspicious," he said.

"Good thinking," I said.

"I thought it was," he bragged.

"Let's get out of here," Dr. J. said.

Frank turned west at the intersection and drove away from the scene.

"Did you see the look on that guard's face after you hit him with the door, Frank?" I asked.

"Yeah, he was scared out of his mind," Frank replied.

"He was shaking beneath my shoe," Dr. J. said with a laugh.

"How many bags did we get, Sport?" Frank asked me.

I turned around in my seat and counted the bags lying in the back behind me.

"I count ten," I reported.

"That should amount to the largest haul we have ever done, gentlemen," Frank boasted. "Wouldn't you say, Dr. J.?"

"As far as I know, it is," Dr. J attested.

We were used to motor lodges where we could park right in front of our unit. Molly had us staying in a hotel with three floors. She met us inside the lobby and gave us our room keys. I had heard of buildings with elevators, but was like Dr. J and didn't care to ride one, and opted for a room on the ground floor. Once checked in and settled, we met in the parking lot and walked to a restaurant less than a block away for a late supper. We talked in low voices and tried hard to look normal.

"I have a question, Molly," I said softly.

"Let's hear it, A.D.," she stated.

"How come we have never hit any banks around home?" I asked.

"Because it's too close to home, dummy. Did you think about that?" Frank blurted almost loud enough for others to hear.

"Shhh, not so loud, Frank. But, he's right, A.D. I was taught a long time ago that you don't mess in your own nest. Aunt Nora taught me that," Molly added.

I felt a little humiliated, but understood what she was saying. I had to agree that Mrs. Jenkins was one smart lady.

We each paid for our own meals and walked back to the hotel. Frank and Molly went to the cars to transfer the money to suitcases and Dr. J and I went to our rooms. I wondered if Molly and Frank were sharing a room tonight. Once I got into my room I went to the window and looked out. A bush was blocking my view of the parking lot where our cars were parked so I couldn't see them. I went to bed wishing that Molly would not string Frank along with ideas that he was making headway in their relationship. I knew it was none of my business, but felt for Frank.

CHAPTER 13

Our departure from Hillsboro went smoothly and we were all back in Hardee by mid-day. Molly told us that she would be away for a few days and for us to take care of ourselves and things around home. She would be contacting us by next week and work on the next job. Frank asked her where she was going and she told him.

"I will be making a trip to Canada tomorrow," she said. "I'd ask you along, but I'm afraid you would just get in the way," she laughed.

"I could help with your luggage," he volunteered.

"No need, my darling, the porter at the airport will take care of it," she responded.

"What about at the bank?" he asked.

"The bank guard is too happy to oblige me," she snickered.

"Does he have your best interest in mind?" Frank asked, almost begging.

"Are you jealous, Frank?" she retorted.

"Heck no. I was just curious," he replied.

"Yeah, and you lie a lot too," she said laughing.

After Molly left, the conversation between Frank and me became not just heated, but defensive. I was curious as to why we couldn't share the huge amount of cash in the Canadian banks being as how we stole an awful lot of it. Frank was defending Molly and Mrs. Jenkins in them being the brains of the outfit.

"Had they not canvassed the various jobs we have pulled off, there wouldn't be any fortune to share," he stated. "Besides, a lot of what is there wasn't any of our doing. You should be happy with what you're getting. It's more than deserved."

He raised his voice as he spoke and reminded me that they had been doing this for years before we were involved and we should respect their position. I told him he didn't have to raise his voice at me and I was really quite satisfied with what I was getting. I emphasized that it just didn't seem fair that we were being denied a portion of the huge amount of money that we were instrumental in taking. We argued for quite a while and I became fully aware that Frank was not siding with me, so quit arguing and stormed outside to get some air and stop the tirade.

It seemed that a wedge was forced in between us from that moment on. Frank became distant after that conversation and hardly ever conversed with me on anything. We worked together, but we weren't close like before. With the attitude he was portraying, I started doubting his allegiance to me as a friend or partner. I chose to be a lot more observant, more careful with my words and actions, and to be more vigilant when performing my work.

I sat and thought about our conversation for hours on end, battling the various scenarios that were flashing in and out. What if Molly had promised Frank a portion of the stash? What if she is putting on an act when she says she thinks Frank is too immature for her? She sure loves to tease him, and them sharing a bed on occasion conflicts with her *'immature'* comment. Then the thoughts would bombard my mind with what was I going to do with hundreds of dollars anyway. Heck, I have already wondered what I was going to do with what I have, let alone ten times more. I was having terrible thoughts one minute and warm thoughts about everyone the next. I had to remind myself of my vow...to be real careful, cautious and vigilant in everything I do from now on.

The following weeks were spent with somewhat of a strained relationship between Frank and me. I would sit and watch the television without really looking at it and he would sit at the kitchen table and bury his face in a mechanic's magazine without really reading anything. I knew that, because he hardly every turned a page. I could feel the gap in our strained relationship widen by the minute. We ate sparingly on what we individually fixed and cleaned up after ourselves. During the two weeks, I only went out a few times. I walked up town twice just to clear my head, and mostly just walked back and forth to the street and back to the trailer. I saw a taxi cab in the driveway one day and just figured Mrs. Jenkins needed to go to town for some reason. That wasn't unusual, other than she normally waited for Molly to take her. Dr. J did a lot of her shopping for her, but obviously, he couldn't shop for personal things.

One day during the lull, I walked to town just to have something to do and ran into my own brother, Mark, coming out of the barber shop.

"Long time, no see," I said to him.

"Can you take time to buy me a soda?" he asked.

"Sure. I think I can afford that," I accepted. "How did you find me?"

"The sheriff told me that he thought he saw you here back a few months ago, so I thought I would take a look. The barber in there said he thought you were living over in the old school house," Mark revealed.

I was curious as to how the sheriff or barber would know, but let it go.

We walked over to the mercantile and sat down in the chairs outside on the creaky boardwalk. I went inside and purchased two bottles of pop and handed one of them to Mark on my return. There were few cars and less people milling around town, so we were alone to talk to one another.

"So what have you been doing with yourself, Punk?" Mark scowled.

Same ole Mark, I thought; got a chip on his shoulder the size of a boulder.

"Not a whole lot of late. How about you?" I asked.

"Same thing. Just work, eat and sleep it seems," he answered. "Are you working?" he asked.

"Yeah, I'm on at the salsa plant," I lied.

"I hear that's a good place to work," he commented.

"I got to drive on one of those new fang-dangled super highways a while back. They are really nice. Are you still working for that road building company?" I asked, changing the subject.

"Still there. I don't have anything to do with the new roads though," he confessed. "I work mostly on culverts and preparing bar ditches."

"Have you been back to see Mom?" I asked, changing the subject.

"Yeah, Birdbrain. That's why I'm here. Apparently after you left, Mom had another episode like that time she was yelling at the make-believe guy re-roofing the garage, remember. Well, this time she yelled so loud she woke up the neighbors and they called the cops. Our mom was arrested and committed to that insane asylum in Middleton. They said she suffered from schizophrenia; some type of mental illness. Anyway, Mom passed away at the institution. I asked if her mental illness could cause her death, and they told me she had a brain aneurysm. It's a blockage in the blood vessel that supplies the brain with blood," he explained. "The authorities found me and I had to take off work to deal with it. Where were you?" he asked in a very accusing tone after explaining things.

The news was like a kick to the stomach and I paused for a bit to catch my breath.

"I'm so sorry, Mark. I didn't know," I solemnly said from the shock of hearing such news. "Actually, I've been right here all along. Of course Mom didn't know that because I never told her where I was going. She wouldn't have understood, anyway," I explained. "When did it happen?"

"I'm not sure. I was contacted last week about it and took care of everything at the funeral home," Mark replied. "Why would you care, anyway? It's no skin off your nose," he said like a challenge. "Did you even try to tell her where you were headed?"

"I tried, but she didn't want to talk to me, so I just left. I wish now that I had said something." I was feeling sad. "Did she suffer?"

"Couldn't tell you. She apparently died in her sleep. She had that insurance man, Dale, listed as one of her emergency contacts and he told the authorities where to find me. He's the one that told me what happened to her. Everyone's better off now, anyway," he said.

We both just sat motionless for a few minutes and sipped our sodas, letting what had been revealed flood our minds with thoughts of bygone days. I broke the silence.

"Are you still driving the old Plymouth?" I asked.

"Nope. I traded it for that car right there; it's mine," he bragged and pointed to a nice looking car in front of the barber shop.

With that, he got up and walked down the steps to the street. I got up and walked to the steps and stopped, watching him walk to his car. When he opened the door he stopped and turned back to me.

"Mom's buried next to Dad over at Pawnee Falls, in case you're interested," he said smugly. "As far as I'm concerned, little brother, I don't care if we ever see one another again, so take care of yourself and have as good of life as you can," he added as he got in and drove away.

I was stunned. I knew my brother was a loner, but I didn't figure he would totally disregard his own blood just like that. I couldn't form any clear words to reply, so just nodded my head like I agreed and understood and watched him drive off. I was saddened by the news he brought plus the declaration he made, but took solace in the fact that Mom was in a better place now and I was better off not having to worry about my brother for the rest of my life. Still, both announcements were hard to shake.

On the way back to the house, I thought of some of the better times that we had together. I recalled a few of the talks I had with my mom. I had to agree with Mark that Mom was definitely better off now than she was, but wished that I had gone back to see her before she died. I appreciated Mark telling me where she was buried, and now had two very sad realizations...one, I would never see Mark again, and two, I knew I would never visit Mom's grave.

Dr. J tapped on the door one evening and announced that a planning meeting for our next heist was being held at the house. Man, that was like a needed break in the rising discomfort. Frank and I left the trailer and walked with Dr. J to the house and into the drawing room where Molly was seated. She excused Mrs. Jenkins from the meeting because she wasn't feeling well and welcomed us like long lost family with hugs and handshakes. I wondered if the gestures were sincere or done for show. After all, it had only been two weeks since we last spoke or seen one another. Frank acted relieved that the gang was back in business. Molly caught us up on her trip and mentioned that the weather was getting cold up north. She indicated that the upcoming job was similar to the last one, just in a different part of the country. We were to fly to Camelot; drive about an hour to

Mosley and perform a robbery of two armored cars in the rear parking lot of Francine's Department Store.

"I checked this one out while I was gone, so it's fairly fresh. The cars didn't park back to back the first time, but did the second, so be aware and act accordingly," she instructed. "Frank, you took the lead on the last one, so do the same this time."

Frank acknowledged with a nod and straightened himself in his seat. Molly proceeded with instructions noting that I would ride the bus again; to Clarkston this time and get a flight to Albany where I would change planes and fly to Camelot. Dr. J and Frank were to drive together to Middleton and catch a different flight to Camelot.

The bus ride was slow for some reason and the bus driver had to visit with each passenger getting on board, it seemed, slowing our progress. I really didn't care that the large lady carrying two shoulder bags was headed to see her grandkids; nor did I give a hoot whether the little guy with the older lady was old enough to have his own ticket. I had another short delay at the airport and just knew that I would show up last again at our destination, giving Frank another reason to jab insults or in some way show that he was the leader.

I arrived first, surprisingly, and only had to wait about fifteen minutes for them. I felt like teasing Frank and saying *'It's about time'*; but decided not to. Our relationship was still widening lately and he might not appreciate the humor. He could dish it out, but was not very good at taking it. We left the baggage claim area and got a rental. The dark blue sedan was brand new and smelled new too.

Driving the 48 miles to Mosley was done mostly in silence. I remarked to Dr. J as to how dark the night was and got a grunt in response. Dr. J had the overhead light on so he could read the map and instruction sheet and it was somehow disturbing Frank and he reached up and turned it off.

"I can't read the map without a light, Frank," Dr. J announced.

"Well, you should have it memorized by now. You've been studying it ever since we left the airport," he replied with a smirk.

"Don't get all huffy with me, Jack. I don't need that kind of talk," Dr. J returned.

"Sorry man, it's just that the light bothers me," Frank apologized.

"Just say so, then," Dr. J stated. "I think I can get us there, but you back off of your high horse, okay? I been doing this a lot longer than you have."

The talk subsided and the remainder of the trip was done in silence. I was proud of Dr. J for speaking up and putting Frank in his place.

Once we arrived into town, Dr. J instructed Frank on how to get to the store where we needed to be. Francine's was a huge store and Frank drove around back and parked at the end of the building near an exit to a back street. As we waited for the armored cars to arrive, we reviewed our plan of attack and discussed what to do if the cars parked side by side like Molly witnessed.

The armored cars arrived on time and we watched them get into position. They maneuvered so that they were back to back. Once they were in position, we walked from our vehicle to where they were parked, donning our masks and readying our equipment on the way. The whole operation went smoothly and much like the last one. I got to tie the guard's hands together while Dr. J stuffed their mouths with rags. Frank insisted that we leave a back door open like the last time, so we did. We took eight bags in the heist and threw them in the trunk. On the way out of the parking lot and onto the back street, a police car showed up behind us, so Frank signaled and turned left onto a side street. The police car followed.

"Don't look back at him. I'll try to lose him first, but if he stops us, let me do the talking," Frank announced.

I was getting noticeably nervous and put my hand on the back of the front seat, only to have Dr. J. put his big hand on top of mine and squeeze as though to tell me not to worry. We met eye contact and I could see the assurance he had in the situation and the *"not to worry"* advice was heeded.

Frank turned at one intersection and then the very next one and the cop car followed both times. We traveled down a wide, well lit street for several blocks when Frank suddenly rolled down his window and put his arm out to signal a left turn. He slowed almost to a stop and then turned and slowly drove down a residential street, pulling easily into a driveway about half way down. The cop car followed us, but drove on by and turned left at the end of the block. We sat in silence for a few minutes watching the corner for the cop car to return, but it never did, so we returned to the main road and headed for the motel.

"That was smart thinking, Frank. I will have to remember that," Dr. J. said, bragging him up.

"It worked for us a few years ago, so I thought I would try it again," he replied, smugly.

He was reminding me more and more of my braggart brother. I was beginning to get very uneasy being around and associating with Frank Epperson.

Molly met us at the motel where she had made reservations and we made plans to go to dinner like before. Frank told her about our encounter with the cops and Molly seemed overly concerned about our near miss, but complimented Frank on his savvy.

"Just to be on the safe side, Frank, park your car up against that fence over there and we'll take care of things after we get back," Molly instructed.

"Why? Do you think the cops will be looking for it?" Frank asked.

"That would be my guess. I would if I were them. Parking it over there will deter their search. We can transfer the bags to my car when we finish dinner," Molly confirmed.

We talked in hushed tones and very little was said at all during the entire meal. It was obvious to me that a rift had been widened in our relationship and I felt that Molly could feel it as well. Even Dr. J seemed withdrawn from me and my presence for some reason. Frank seemed cozier than usual toward Molly and was doing little things for her that he didn't normally do, like offer her the salt and pepper, or ask the waitress to fill her water glass and then like an after thought include the rest of the table. She dropped her fork and he left the table to retrieve a clean one for her. He took his own napkin and dabbed at her mouth to remove a small morsel of food. Things like that. I was wondering if she had been leading him on lately or was he just trying hard to please her.

We each paid for our own meal, leaving the restaurant and walked back to the motel.

"You and Dr. J. go on ahead, A.D. Frank and I will transfer the bags to my car and we'll be all set for tomorrow," Molly instructed.

To satisfy my own curiosity, I took note of where Frank's room was and discovered that indeed he and Molly were sharing a room. My trust in both of them was becoming less and less. I couldn't let them know that I knew, so I avoided any conversation that would give suspicion. I began to wonder if Dr. J was a partner in the sharing of the stash or was he too being used and paid the weekly salary. Suddenly, I didn't feel I could trust anyone in our gang.

The next morning after arriving at the airport, Molly instructed all of us on how we would return to Hardee. We were all booked on the same flight to Middleton where the cars were located. The six suitcases were heavy with money bags and Molly's clothes in them, so we got a cart to haul them to the counter. Molly and Frank checked four bags and Dr. J and I checked a bag each. Dr. J and I sat together on the plane and we were instructed to drive the convertible back to Hardee. Molly and Frank would sit together on the plane, like a couple, and drive to Hardee in her car. We were told to deposit our bags inside the front door of the house and go about our business as usual. Her and Frank would take care of everything else once they got there.

"Going shopping?" I asked out of curiosity.

"We might, so what if we do?" Molly answered.

"Nothing. Just asking, that's all," I replied.

"We have a few errands to run, so we will be later in arriving home," she stated.

The curiosity about the money was bugging the heck out of me, so when she was finished with the instructions, I asked her straight out how much she thought we had gotten from last night's heist.

"Oh, it was a lot A.D. Why do you ask?" she said with a wave of her hand.

"Just curious, I guess, ma'am. Do you think it was more than last time?" I asked.

"I have no idea, A.D. probably, but I haven't counted it so I don't know," she replied.

"Will you be making another trip to Canada after we get home?" I asked.

"You're sure full of questions this morning, A.D. Why is that?" she asked me.

"Like I said, ma'am, just curious," I returned.

"Well, don't you worry your little head about it. You let me handle that end of things and we'll do just fine," she instructed.

"Yes ma'am," I said.

She answered my question without answering my question, other than the amount. What she told me with her wisecracks was I was not going to know how much the bags contained and for me to pursue the question would not be a wise decision. You could almost feel the cloak of doubt spread over our relationship. I felt like I was getting used and when they decided that enough was enough, either I would be eliminated or turned over to the FBI. It was not a good feeling.

The rest of the ride to the airport was in silence and I boarded the plane with the rest of them. Molly and Frank sat together four rows in front of Dr. J and me. Frank flirted with the stewardess every time she went by and Molly's giggling voice was heard each time telling him to stop it. Molly stood up in her seat and looked back at me twice during the flight and I pretended to not see her by burying my face in a magazine from the pocket in front of me.

"Don't let her get to you, son. The two of them deserve one another as far as I'm concerned," Dr. J surprisingly stated.

"Where do you fit into the scheme of things, Doc?" I asked softly.

"Miss Nora and I go way back. I've worked for her ever since she returned to Hardee. Nice lady. Too bad she let her niece run things, though," he continued.

I thought about what he said and changed my mind about him. He was being treated much the same as me and he didn't like it either, I gathered.

"Do you think you'll get any of their stash some day?" I asked.

"Nope. You won't either, I doubt. It won't be long now that I 'speck we'll stop what we do and you'll have to live on what you have saved," he said. "Me too, for that matter."

"Do you think Frank will get any of it?" I asked.

"Not if the lady has any brains. Course, I could be wrong," he stressed. "If it was up to Mrs. Jenkins, I know he wouldn't, though."

Our conversation ended and we both just sort of stared into space for the longest time. I looked out the window for a long while and my dad came to mind...the ground really did look like a hand drawn checkerboard. When the plane landed in Middleton, Dr. J and I got off before Frank and Molly and made our way to baggage claim.

"Did you notice they were holding hands when we went past?" I commented to Dr. J.

"No concern of mine. Yours neither I would say, so let it go," Dr. J stated.

We got our bags and headed for the car. It took a few minutes to locate it, but once in it and headed toward Hardee, I felt a little more relaxed. We didn't talk much on the way, and once in the driveway, Dr. J took both bags to the house and sat them inside as instructed and walked to his house. He looked back to where I was standing in the driveway and waved at me before going inside.

I sat in the trailer watching the driveway for Molly and Frank to arrive. I thought about what had been done over the last few days, months, even and wondered where all of this unrest would wind up. I wasn't comfortable with things and I was sure no one else was. Something had to give. I turned on the television and plopped down on the couch. The reception was snowy, but the sound was good, so I decided to climb up on the roof and adjust the antenna for a better picture. I had nailed pieces of timber to the side of the tree at the back of the trailer for easier access to the roof when I first got the television so used them for my climb. The first adjustment was better, but still not real good, so I did it one more time with better success. I had learned that just moving the antenna a little bit in either direction was plenty to adjust the picture. The first time, I moved it a touch to the right…the second time I moved it back to the left. I climbed back down and entered the trailer to scope out my adjustments. I hadn't been seated for more than a couple of minutes when Dr. J knocked on the screen door.

"What's up Doc.?" I asked.

"Molly wants to talk to us over at the big house," he replied.

Somehow during all of the messing around with the antenna, I had failed to see Molly and Frank drive in.

"Okay. I will be right with you," I said, thinking that he would wait for me.

But, he didn't. I guessed that he never heard me. I wondered what the meeting was all about. I got up and turned off the television then went to the bathroom before walking over to the house. I walked up the steps and entered the house and followed the noise to the drawing room. The gang was all assembled except for Mrs. Jenkins. Molly left the room and left everyone sitting quietly and patiently for her return. The room was deathly silent for what seemed like a long time.

"What's going on?" I finally said to Dr. J.

"I don't know, we were just asked to meet here," he answered.

We both looked at Frank and he just shrugged his shoulders. He too looked as though he was as much in the dark as we were.

"I'll answer that question," Molly interjected as she returned to the room with a large bowl of popcorn and offered some to everyone.

She sat down next to Frank and explained what was happening.

"We have it on good authority that the FBI is closing in on things; perhaps by tracing the money or perhaps it's due to a total unrest in the financial world, we aren't sure," she started. "We have decided that the gang is going to pull one last job and then we are going to disband and everyone will go their separate ways."

Dr. J and I looked at one another and he nodded, knowingly.

"Who decided that?" he asked.

If looks could kill, Dr. J would be dead on the spot. Molly was not pleased to have her authority challenged.

"Okay, Dr. J if you must know, I decided it," she said emphatically. "Aunt Nora and I have been discussing it on and off for a few months now and before she left for Canada, the decision was made to end it," she added.

"Your aunt's gone?" I asked.

"Yes, A.D. She has gone to Canada ahead of me and after this last job, I plan to join her there," Molly explained.

She paused momentarily and then with a sigh, decided to explain the situation to all of us.

"Seeing as how I am the only one left to continue the work, it is my decision. Aunt Nora and I anticipated that this would happen some time, just not as soon as it did, but the changes in the system are making us change the way we do things," she said. "We decided a while back that we would continue until the feds altered the way they operate the system and talk about it again. We did and the decision is to close it down," she added. "The gang will do one last job and discontinue the operation before it becomes too dangerous and costs a life or two," she concluded.

There was some discomfort shown by our collective sighs and shuffling in our seats.

"I realize this may be a surprise to all of you, but believe me you will not be disappointed," she stated.

She went on to explain that the last job was going to be a big one and the haul would be more than any one single heist we had ever done. It will take about two weeks to put together, but it will be worth it. Each of us was to receive $500 as a bonus for doing the last job. She further explained that Mrs. Jenkins' early departure to Canada was to better facilitate things and that she was looking forward to retiring.

"Once the job is complete and I'm there with her, you will be on your own. It's been a very profitable couple of years and all of you should be proud of yourselves for the job you've done. To say thank you seems so small, but Aunt Nora asked that I convey her thanks as well and congratulate all of you on a job well done," she stated.

Frank appeared to be as surprised by the news as Dr. J and I were. I could envision his little balloon bursting and his dream floating away.

There it was, I thought. Molly had played her trump card. The work we had performed for the good of all was being rewarded with a measly $500. So much for sharing in the treasures in Canada, I thought.

"Frank, I want you to assist me in planning this last job. You will head it up and lead the others through it, okay?" she stated.

Frank nodded and tried to smile, but it was a weak attempt.

"What do you expect us to do in the meantime?" Dr. J asked.

"Just keep your mouths shut," she snapped. "Once this job is complete, you can do whatever you like. With the money we have paid you and the bonus you will receive, all of you should be set up pretty good and have enough to do what ever you desire," she explained.

The meeting ended with all of us having quizzical looks on our faces. Molly saw our concern and in an attempt to ease the tension, she assured us that everything would be just fine and for us not to worry.

"Everything will be okay. I promise," she said. "All of you will do fine. Aunt Nora and I put together a great team and all of us have done very well. We feel it's time to close the operation down, that's all," she concluded.

You could tell she was trying to recoup the feeling of a team. She told all of us that she would have the details of the last job of the Speakeasy Gang finalized and ready to implement in less than two weeks. We left the house with our heads down and a mood to match.

CHAPTER 14

Over the next two weeks, Molly came and went from the house a number of times. Sometimes she was gone for two or three days, and just as often was at the house for two or three days. She was driving a different car. The little two-door sedan didn't look as good on her as her Cadillac, although her legs were as pretty as ever. I wanted to ask about it, but thought better of it. Frank spent a lot of time at the house when Molly was home and when he was in the trailer, he was quiet and appeared to be busy doing something with pencil and paper. I was reluctant to ask what he was doing due to the widening gap in our relationship, but his actions were getting the best of me.

"What's with the different car, Frank? Any idea?" I asked.

"It's a rental she said. None of our business, apparently," Frank mumbled.

"What's with all the paper shuffling you're doing?" I asked.

"Just helping with the last job like I was instructed," he stated with a note of anger.

After he answered, he stood up, grabbed the papers and headed for the house. In his absence, I undid several papers he had wadded up and threw away, but there was nothing but a few lines drawn and some doodling on them. I couldn't help but think even more that Frank was being fooled into thinking he was going to get some of the big treasure and have his romantic wishes fulfilled.

My thoughts as to what I was going to do and where I was going after it was all over occupied my mind constantly. I didn't dare ask Frank what I should do. It was obvious that he didn't care about my future outside the gang. He had recruited me and trained me to be a thief and now he was abandoning me. I felt confident that I could continue in my life of crime all by myself, but wondered if I should. I could look for a partner and train him to rob banks like Frank and I used to do. Once trained, we could take the gang's place and rob armored cars. It was a good job and if done right, no one gets hurt; unless of course someone on the other end decides to stop the heist by interfering. I wondered how much money it would take for me to get started again. The Clarkston County bank job came to mind and I wished simpler times could return. Frank and I pulled those early jobs with basically the clothes on our back. We did have a gun, though, but never fired it on any of those jobs. My thoughts were interrupted by the man himself.

"Hey, Cooper! We need to see you…come 'eer!" Frank yelled from the porch of the house.

"Be right there," I called back through the open door.

While I was thinking all of these mixed up thoughts, I unconsciously picked up the FBI agents card and was playing with it. I glanced at it and recalled the incident the day I got it. I put the card back on the table and walked out the door and headed to the house expecting to hear instructions on this final job as a member of the Speakeasy Gang.

After hearing the details of the last job, I had to admit, it was not only daring, but well designed. It appeared that Molly had certainly done her homework. Of course the proof would be in the actual performance.

Fort Cummings Army Base in Ashton is commonly used for processing troops that are getting out of the service. Those troops are awarded separation checks in various amounts according to how long they've been in as well as how many days of leave they have accumulated. Hundreds of those checks are cashed at the Base Exchange, which means huge amounts of cash needs to be on hand to accommodate them. Molly's contacts revealed that three entire companies of soldiers (over 500 of them) were <u>ALL</u> being discharged after a special ceremony at the base on the 30th. That coincides with the regular payday for the entire base. She said that her contacts noted that there are well over 1,500 soldiers on the base, meaning that more cash than normal was necessary. Our job was to intercept the armored car that was making that drop and take all of the cash that was intended for the base.

The guards of the armored car servicing the base have a habit of stopping at a local wayside, all-night diner for coffee and donuts each time they deliver to the Base Exchange. The diner, Lola's Café, is just off highway <u>US </u>314, only a mile from the main gate of the base and just over three miles from Ashton. It sits on a popular truck route and a lot of truckers patronize Lola's Café every day. The café's specialty is chicken fried steak, served each weekday from 6 a.m. to 6 p.m. The donuts and coffee are pretty popular as well.

The armored car usually delivers to the exchange every Monday and Friday, but will be making a special delivery on Thursday before the 30th. The extra day is thought to be for the base personnel to get additional help lined up and for readying the cash they will be handing out. The guards normally arrive at

Lola's early, around 5 a.m., park at the side of the diner where there is little congestion, and once parked, one guard stays in the rear of the car while the other two get the coffee and donuts to go. When they return, one guard delivers the goodies to the back while the driver gets in the rig and starts it up. The back door is knocked on with two quick raps as a signal and the guard inside opens the door to receive his food and drink. This routine was supposedly witnessed a number of times, so it was established. Our attack would occur when the two were inside the diner getting the coffee and donuts. One of us would be inside and jump in line before the guards to delay their routine. At that hour of the morning, only a few men, mostly truck drivers, were in the diner anyway. After a short pause, the others in our gang would knock on the rear door as if delivering the goods and rob the armored car. It was believed that if the person inside the diner could delay the guards long enough, the entire heist could be done and over with in a matter of a few minutes. The driver of our car would pick up the inside man on the other side of the diner and the three of us would make our get-a-way without confrontation.

"Pretty smart!" I said.

"Who's the inside man?" Dr. J asked.

Frank immediately pointed to me. I felt honored to be the decoy in the heist and began to plan how I would go about my job. The first part of the plan called for all of us to fly to Ralston, rent a car and get a motel room there. The next morning we would drive the hour long trip across the state line into Ashton to do the job. Once the job was accomplished, we would rendezvous with Molly in the parking lot of a large trucking firm; make the transfer of money bags to suitcases and return to Ralston Airport. Molly promised to have our pay envelopes with her and give them to us at the transfer. She was booked to fly on to Canada while the rest of us would return to Hardee. It dawned on me why she was driving a rental instead of the Cadillac…she was not coming back.

"I will say my farewells to all of you at the airport. I know I will cry, but hope you understand how much all of you mean to me," she said.

As was already stated, Frank was appointed the leader and Dr. J and I were instructed to follow his orders. Neither of us liked the idea because we had already been in that situation and knew how domineering Frank was in his role as leader. Molly was acting as gang leader now, and taking charge in her aunt's absence was very enjoyable for her it seemed. It was obvious from past dealings that she had a thing for Frank anyway, and she was making him more important than the rest of us by making him the leader. Frank loved every minute of it and we all knew that he would flaunt his superiority every chance he got.

The day of departure started like normal. Both Frank and I were up at daybreak and moving around in preparation for the trip. I grabbed my paper bag full of money and was about to put it in my bag, when I had second thoughts and returned it to its hiding spot in the closet. I left my usual black bag next to the door.

"I may need the money later." I thought.

I normally had about a hundred on me, but would be making this trip with a measly $30. If things worked as planned, I would receive the bonus money at our rendezvous point, then I would be solvent again. As I was closing the closet, Frank entered the living room from his bedroom.

"You go over and get Dr. J, and I'll go gas up the car," he stated like an order.

"Okay! And meet back here?" I asked.

"Sure, that would work. We can load our bags when I get back," Frank replied. "Oh, by the way, neither of you have to ride the bus on this one; we are all going in the car to the airport," he disclosed.

"Why is that?" I questioned.

"Because I said so," he stated very smugly.

Great, I thought. We aren't even on the job yet and he's already acting like he owns the place.

Frank left to gas up and I walked over to Dr. J's to get him. Molly's car was gone and I wondered what she was up to so early. No one answered the door at Dr. J's and I wondered if he had slept in. I knocked again louder and waited. No one answered. Just then, Molly drove by in her rental and turned into the driveway. She got out and came running over to Dr. J's. She looked harried and confused. Her hair was not combed.

"Dr. J's in the hospital over in Clarkston. I just got back from taking him," She panted.

"What?" I blurted.

"I think he has food poisoning. He's pretty sick so we are going to have to do this job without him. Where's Frank?" She ran her words together as she said and asked everything.

"He's gassing up the car," I answered. "Is Dr. J going to be okay? Where's Willy?" I asked.

"Sure he will, A.D, he just won't be with you on the job. Willy is at the hospital waiting for his mother to arrive. The hospital called her," she said as though irritated at me for asking.

We walked together back to the big house and were standing on the porch pondering our situation. Frank returned from gassing up and Molly ran to meet him at the car door as he got out. She hugged him and began quietly telling him about her trip to the hospital. Frank was all ears and as I approached the car, both of them turned and walked toward the trailer.

"Be a dear, A.D. and get my bags for me. They are in the parlor. Just put them in the back seat," she called back over her shoulder.

I nodded in agreement and turned back to the house. The suitcases weren't in the parlor, so I looked in the dining room and noticed that the table and chairs were gone but no bags. I turned back to the foyer and was planning to go ask Molly where the cases were when I spotted them sitting next to the front door. Her wrap was on top of them and I had walked right past them. I picked them up, noticing that they were quite heavy, and carried them outside and put them in the back seat. I walked on to the trailer to let her know that the job had been done. As I approached the front door, I overheard Molly explaining in detail what occurred with Dr. J, how it happened and how the job was going to continue in spite of it.

Apparently, Dr. J's grandson awoke Molly early this morning and told her that his grandfather was sick. Molly went over to see if she could assist and immediately decided to get him to the hospital. He was pale, throwing up violently, and as weak as a newborn kitten. She and Willy got him in Molly's car and she drove him to Clarkston. He was admitted and they started IV's and everything.

Molly was sitting on the sofa facing Frank as she spoke and wiped the tears from her eyes. She got up from the couch and walked out the door. When she saw me, she looked surprised, suddenly stopped and just about lost her balance. She hesitated and took a moment to regain her composure.

"Did you get my bags in the car?" she blurted.

"Yes ma'am," I replied.

"You will go with Frank to the airport and the two of you will have to take down the armored car by yourselves," she said. "I know you can do it and I'm sorry you won't get help, but you'll be fine, I just know you will," she stated as if trying to assure herself in the process.

Frank had followed her outside and she grabbed him around the waist and hugged him with a long caress.

"You guys have to pull this off," she said to Frank with a begging look as she stepped away.

Frank put his arm around her and drew her close to him and assured her that things would be fine and almost guaranteed her that the job would be successful.

"You just leave it to me. I will see you at the drop sight like before. You'll see," he assured her.

I wondered if he left me out of the picture on purpose or was he just trying to be comforting to Molly. I took a dim view of his statement none-the-less. I left them alone as they embraced and comforted one another and I walked into the trailer to grab my bag. It wasn't there.

"Frank, did you take my bag?" I called out the door.

"Oh yeah; it's in my bedroom. I thought it was mine by mistake. Sorry," he returned.

I walked back to his bedroom and found my bag on his neatly made bed. I grabbed it and carried it out to the car.

The ride to the airport was mostly quiet. Frank acted the boss once or twice with comments reminding me of certain aspects of the heist.

"I hope you're thinking about your role inside the diner," he said. "Let me check us in at the ticket counter. You can wait in the lobby for me or meet me in the waiting area," he advised. "You got your bag, right?"

"Yeah; it's on the seat." I said as I pointed over my shoulder to the rear seat. "Where's yours?"

"In the trunk," he stated, almost absent mindedly.

I <u>was</u> thinking about my role once inside the diner, but wouldn't let him know that he was right. I just continued to stare out the window. His know-it-all attitude was beginning to get my goat and I again thought of my older brother. After parking the car, we walked to the terminal with our bags in hand. Frank headed for the ticket counter while I walked on into the waiting area. I looked back and saw that there was a line of maybe 10 or 12 in front of Frank.

"He may have wished that I would stand in line instead of him," I thought.

Our flight was announced and the ropes were removed so loading could take place. I stood in line, but hung back knowing that I didn't have a boarding pass yet. Suddenly, Frank was standing next to me and handed me my ticket.

"How did you get this so fast? There was quite a line out there," I commented.

"I paid a man at the front of the line to let me cut in. It's amazing what a little ten-spot will do," he said.

"You take the cake, Frank," I said.

The weather was a little gusty outside and several comments I overheard while boarding mentioned that the weather sure had been weird of late. We boarded our plane and actually sat together. I didn't really mind, but decided that I would read the entire time, or pretend to sleep so that I wouldn't have to bear Frank's know-it-all jabber. I thought of Dr. J and wondered how he was doing. The two-hour flight seemed short to me and we landed in Ralston without any problems. On the way out of the plane the pilot was standing at the door thanking the passengers for flying Guinness Air and commented to one of them that a tailwind had aided his getting to our destination ahead of schedule. That explained why it seemed short, I decided.

Frank rented a dark brown, late model four-door sedan. He said he had no choice in the matter. It was one of only three left. No matter, it was a car. It just wasn't a very pretty one.

"What an ugly color," I stated.

"It's inconspicuous. Next time you can get it," he said.

I noticed that lately, Frank was not referring to me as *Sport* like he normally did. I wondered why and if it was because of his stepped up leadership role. I sort of missed it. Molly probably told him to drop it and he would do anything she asked of him. You could be sure of that, I thought.

We drove into Ashton and located a motor lodge on the same road as the base. The main gate of the base was one mile east of the city limits.

"I paid for the rental, so you can pick up the room and dinner," Frank stated matter-of-factly.

"What do you want to eat?" I asked, thinking that I only had a few bucks from what I usually have.

"How about pizza. Or a nice open-faced, hot roast beef sandwich. It doesn't matter," he replied.

We could see a restaurant sign just down the way a few hundred feet called Ziggy's Pizza Parlor. We checked in and walked to the restaurant. I was not accustomed to eating pizza and really didn't know what to order so while at the *"Order Here"* counter, I overheard the person in front of me order a pepperoni pizza with extra cheese, so I ordered the same.

"How big you want it, son?" the man at the counter asked.

"Large should do it," I said as I looked on the wall and noticed the sizes being displayed.

"You want drinks?" he asked.

"Do you have beer?" I asked.

"Yeah; what kind?" he asked.

I ordered a lager for Frank and a cola for me and paid the man. He gave me a large metal piece shaped like a key with the number 33 on it and told me to place it on our table.

"My gal will deliver your pizza to your table. Thank you for your business," he said. "Don't forget your drinks," he reminded me and pointed to the counter where they were sitting.

"You're welcome," I returned and picked up the drinks and walked to our table.

"This might be our last meal together, you know," Frank stated. "Have you thought about what you're going to do when it's all over?"

"Not really," I answered sadly. "But I will be just fine if you're concerned," I added.

"I figure you'll land on your feet," Frank said. "You've proven to be strong and capable," he continued.

"Thanks for the vote of confidence," I sincerely said.

"I'm not kidding. I think you'll do fine. After all, I trained you, remember?" he bragged.

We stopped talking for a while when the pizza arrived and just ate our supper. I felt that Frank was throwing out all the compliments as a way of saying goodbye and maybe a touch of an apology. There was certainly no hint of remorse on his part. He could brag with the best of them, though. I just knew he was hoping to cash in on the pot of gold at the end of the Canadian rainbow.

"What are _you_ going to do, Frank," I asked between bites.

"Don't go worrying your little head about me. I too will be fine. I plan to see Molly off on her flight, and then join you for our flight home," he volunteered. "What about you?"

"I think I will drive into Clarkston first and visit Dr. J. I wonder how he's doing. Do you suppose Molly will pay him the bonus too?" I asked.

"I don't know; haven't thought about it to tell you the truth. She might," Frank pondered the question.

"Do you want to join me at the hospital?" I asked.

"No. Instead, I think I will pack up and head for my favorite spot on earth and enjoy life for a while. I have always longed to retire on a beach somewhere warm and sunny. If I get bored, I will open up a garage and fix exotic automobiles like Jags, Mercedes, and Bentleys," he said as though he had given a lot of thought to his future.

I hadn't heard of any of those cars before, but didn't give him the satisfaction of knowing that. He was probably making it up as he talked anyway, I figured. He sure dismissed the invitation quickly. I wondered how he and Dr. J got along anyway. To my recollection, he had never mentioned the beach to me in any conversation we had ever had. And why the hurry? I wondered about his earlier years as a child growing up and thought that maybe he was raised near a beach and that was the reason for his dream. Maybe his home that he set on fire was near the beach. The whole conversation over dinner was one that was odd for both of us. It was like two people putting on airs to one another in hopes of covering up the real truth about matters. I was getting uncomfortable and decided to end it by leaving.

"Through eating already?" Frank asked as I got up from the table.

"Yeah, I've had enough." I stated. "You go ahead and finish up. I'll walk back to the motel and get ready for tomorrow," I added.

"I'm done, I guess. Let me finish my beer and I'll join you," he said.

We returned to the motor lodge and lounged around the room. Frank asked me to walk to the office for drinks from the pop machine, so I did. He was inside his bag getting playing cards out when I returned. We played some rummy but my mind was not on the game and whether Frank cheated or not, it probably wouldn't have made any difference. We finally went to bed after I lost four dollars. I slept okay, just not soundly. I woke up before the sunrise and dressed and played solitaire with the deck that was left on the table until Frank got up. He cleaned up and got dressed while I cleaned the windshield of the rental from the light of an overhead light and tinkered around with the loose door handle on the driver's side. I couldn't see well enough to do any good, so left it. We drove to the diner without saying a word to one another. The sun was still sleeping.

Only two semis were in the parking lot when we drove in to the diner. Both of them had their clearance lights on and one of the trucks was still running. Two cars were parked right in front, so we parked down the way as planned. The lights from inside the diner reflected a harsh glare through the windshield. I could see streaks made from my earlier attempt at cleaning it. I got out and Frank told me not to forget my bag.

"You may need it," he said.

I again waited for him to say my nickname, *Sport*, but it never came. I reached into the backseat to get my bag and noticed that Frank's wasn't there. I figured he put in the trunk and was saving the backseat space for the money bags. Why I was in need of mine was a mystery, but I didn't ask.

"Good luck," I said to Frank as I closed the door.

He nodded and began looking over his shoulder to get his bearings. I walked into the café and sat down close to the front counter, facing the door. I placed my bag in the chair next to me and looked around. A few of the patrons looked up to see me, but no one made eye contact. The waitress came over and greeted me and put a glass of water and a menu on the table and asked if I wanted coffee. I nodded and picked up the menu and began reading without really seeing any of it. I looked out the window at the car and saw Frank sitting behind the wheel. His car door was open and his left foot was touching the asphalt. The sun was coming up to greet the day.

The café was filled with the aroma of fresh donuts. I started looking at the large display of them in the glass case and deciding which ones I would order when the time came. I didn't see any cinnamon twists and decided that I would request one. Perhaps I could delay the guards a little more if the waitress had to try and find one or at least take some time in explaining why they didn't have any.

Just as the waitress returned with the coffee, cream pitcher, water, and silverware, I saw the armored car turn into the parking lot from the main road. They parked just two spaces away from Frank; closer to the door of the café. I glanced over to our car and Frank was not in sight. I sipped some coffee and while looking over the rim of the cup, I noticed Frank sit up in the seat. He had laid over when the armored car drove in to keep from being seen. Just as the guards entered, I got up and went to the counter.

"I changed my mind about breakfast and those donuts smell so good, I decided that I would have a couple," I began as I stepped in front of the guards as they were walking to the counter.

"They do smell good, don't they?" the waitress returned.

"Could I get two cinnamon twists to go and make my coffee to go as well?" I asked.

"Oh, I'm sorry sir, but we don't have any cinnamon twists this morning," she apologized. "I have plenty of sugar donuts, though. Would you like two of those?" She asked.

"No thanks. I had my mind set on those twists," I moaned. "Let me think?"

I looked down on the massive display and started slowly oohing and aahing and asking about first this one then that one. A rack with trays of donuts was standing close to the counter and I strained my neck to see what I might want from its collection.

"Is that one lemon-filled?" I asked as I pointed at one on the rack.

"Yes sir, and so are these," she volunteered and pointed to a row in the case. "And these here are custard filled," she added, indicating another row.

The guards were being patient and I was wishing I could look out and see what was happening, but I couldn't. Frank was on his own and I just hoped I was giving him enough time. I continued to think of things to ask and prolong the delay without drawing suspicion. One of the guards was talking behind me about some family thing he was involved in when he suddenly blurted out.

"Come on buddy. We have work to do and need to get going. How much longer are you going to be?" he asked.

I looked back and pretended to see their uniforms for the first time and apologized for the delay.

"Oh, sorry officer, I didn't realize I was holding you up," I said.

"I'm not an officer, but an armored car guard…and you are holding us up. We have a schedule to keep. Do you mind if we go ahead of you so that we can get on with our work?" he politely asked.

I noticed that he was about to turn and gesture toward his armored car, so I quickly grabbed his arm and eased him to the counter. The other guard had already stepped to the counter and was gazing upon the display of donuts.

"Not at all, mister, you guys go ahead and order. I have decided to just get coffee anyway," I stated. "Can you just get me a coffee to go instead?" I asked the waitress.

"A large or small one?" she asked.

"Oh large, please," I requested.

The waitress sort of apologized as she poured a coffee into a to-go cup so that I could go. As she did, I glanced out the window and noticed that our car was gone. I took my time paying for the coffee by fumbling with change and trying to get the exact amount and after paying, again apologized to the guards for the delay.

"That's okay, mister. You have a nice day," the talkative one said.

I grabbed my bag from the chair and walked out the door with my coffee in my hand. I longed to see our car at the end of the sidewalk at the side of the café with Frank at the wheel waiting for me. I turned the corner and he wasn't there. I walked down the side of the café thinking he might still be pulling around, but there was no sign of him. I walked across the back of the café and around the other side and still no Frank. I slammed my coffee cup to the ground in anger and walked toward the armored car. I noticed that the back door was ajar and a light was on inside. I had a notion to open the door and see the knot-tying job that Frank did on the guard, but decided not to. I walked back into the café and passed the guards on their way out. They looked at me funny, but continued on. I told the waitress that I had dropped my coffee and needed another one. I wasn't lying when I told her that I missed my ride.

As I sat down again at the table, one of the guards came rushing in and asked to use the phone. He was agitated and I assumed that our heist was successful. I looked longingly out the window hoping that Frank would come driving by, but knew that it wasn't going to happen. I had assisted in the gang's last heist and was set-up in the whole thing. I figured that Frank and Molly thought this up when we found out that just the two of us were going to have to do the job. Had Dr. J not gotten sick, I bet all three of us would be headed home now. Damn you Frank. You bastard, I thought. I will get you for this. I will cover every inch of the earth in search of you and when I find you I will make you pay for this little deceiving ploy.

All I could overhear from the guard's conversation was his heightened voice when he asked what he should do. He hung up the phone and left the café in a huff. I watched as he chatted with the other two guards outside the truck and then they all got in the vehicle and left. The one tied up in back was rubbing his wrists, so I assumed that Frank had tied them pretty tight. The driver looked really angry.

"Join the club," I said under my breath.

I sat for close to an hour and drank way too much coffee. The waitress was apologetic and even asked if I wanted to use the phone to call someone. The truck drivers left for their runs and four or five other patrons had come and gone in that time. My mind was filled with thoughts of what was ahead of me and several times I had to fight off the tears welling up in my eyes.

I had money in the closet and the bank even if it were several hundred miles away. If I had to work for a while in order to afford a ride back to Hardee, I would do so. Meanwhile, I was stuck in the middle of nowhere with little money and no way to get anywhere. I kicked myself for being so frugal and putting my sack of money back in the closet.

About that time, three military vehicles full of uniformed soldiers entered the parking lot and I decided it was time to go. I got up, threw two quarters on the table and as I was walking out into the early morning air, a dozen or so soldiers were walking into the café. I overheard a few of them talking about a class they attended or were going to attend, maybe, but decided that I was better off not sitting around waiting for any of them to start a conversation with me.

As I began my walk across the parking lot to the road back into town, three semis's pulled into the café. As I turned toward town, another one pulled in. Lola's was filling up with the morning rush. I noticed that the morning traffic was getting heavier, too. I guessed that the extra traffic was the morning rush-hour traffic you hear about. I walked like I was taught as a youngster, facing the traffic. A thought of my mom crossed my mind that she would be proud of me for doing that. I walked toward town with my head down and my mind was just full of jumbled thoughts. I wondered how the boys in the armored car were going to explain their dilemma. I figured I too was in one and began to wonder what I was going to do. Where was I going to go? How was I going to get home? Why didn't I see this? I have always been able to foresee such things. Why hadn't I seen this coming? I was the idiot in this case. Frank's probably laughing his butt off right now. I hope Molly dumps him good and proper and he doesn't get a thing. That would certainly serve him right. He would be smart to just keep the money he just grabbed and make a run for it... *Wait a minute*! That is what he's doing. I would bet my life on it. I bet he was planning this all along. Dr. J. getting sick and not making the trip just helped his plan work better. I wonder what he was planning for Dr. J. if he had been with us. I bet Frank finally figured out that he had already been shafted by Molly and decided to rebel. Good for you Frank. That may be the smartest thing you've ever done. However, shafting me in the process was not a smart thing to do. You have messed with the wrong person, my friend, and I will find you if it's the last thing I do. You taught me well, Frank Epperson, and I will get you back, I guarantee. What beach did he say he was headed for? I can't remember. Warm and sunny, he said. It had to be in the south, southwest, or Mexico I figured. No matter, I will find him if it takes the rest of my life. My mind was made up; I would look for and find the money that belonged to me.

CHAPTER 15

It was just before nine o'clock when I finally arrived in town. My feet hurt! Penny loafers are not made for walking long distances. I had a notion to walk barefoot or at least in my stocking feet, for a ways, but the terrain was a little rocky and not good for walking without some padding. I stopped a number of times to give my one toe a rub because it was rubbing up against a fold in my sock and causing problems. I even considered walking to the other side of the road and hitch hiking into town just to relieve the stress, but figured I could make it, even if it took me a while.

I decided to find the bus station and get a ticket to Hardee or at least to a town as close to Hardee as I could afford. I asked a lady sitting at a city bus stop where the Whitney Bus depot was and she pointed me the way. I found it after several blocks and went inside and promptly sat down on a bench for a spell to rest my feet. After a few minutes, I walked to the counter and inquired about the cost of a bus ride to Hardee. The attendant looked it up and told me it would cost $32.00 with a change over in Layton and another one in Neels. The fare to Neels was $24.00, but it was another 91 miles to Hardee. The bus to Layton was scheduled to leave at 11 a.m.

"You could catch the Express in Layton and double back to Albany for another $5 bucks if you've a mind to," the man told me.

"Let me think about it for a bit," I told the man behind the ticket counter.

I sat down on the lobby bench to gather my thoughts. I counted my cash and lacked a few bucks to have enough for the entire fare. Doubling back to Albany still left me a number of miles to home and the way my feet hurt, I couldn't imagine walking from Neels or Albany. I could hitch hike I suppose, but I had never hitch hiked in my life, so was reluctant to start now. Maybe I could sell my new watch and gain enough to buy the ticket I needed. I could find a job for a day or two and make enough, maybe. The thoughts were coming faster than solutions and my mouth was dry, so I looked for the drinking fountain and noticed a sign on it that said "Out of Order". I opened my bag to get a piece of gum instead and was taken by surprise; in my bag was an envelope with $500 in it. I let out a gasp and looked up to see if anyone had seen or heard me. I was by myself on the bench and quickly put the envelope back in my bag and closed it. How did that get in there and when, I thought. This whole thing was a set up from the start. It had to be. That's the reason Frank reminded me to get my bag at the diner. He knew that the envelope was in my bag and he was kind enough to not leave me with nothing. When did he put it in there? My bag was out of my sight before we left for Ashton, so maybe Frank put the envelope in there then. He and Molly spent a lot of time together the night before we left, so they probably plotted the whole thing then. Wait a minute…they were together for a few minutes after the news of Dr. J. They walked to the trailer just before deciding that Frank and I together could do the job without a problem. Frank said he mistakenly took my bag for his. Was that the truth? That had to be when the money got put in my bag. But, then again, I was out of the motel room for a while last night. He could have planted the envelope then. He could have put the envelope in my bag at several different times, I decided. I wondered if Dr. J would find an envelope in his bag. I couldn't figure why Frank would leave $500 on the table, though, especially if he knew that he was going to bolt.

Perhaps he didn't know, but then why would he remind me to take my bag? Nothing made any sense.

Finding the money altered my plans immediately. I walked outside and began to think of things I needed to do. I could get a taxi to the airport and buy a ticket to Albany or Clarkston. I could rent a car at both places and drive back to Hardee. Once I got home, I could decide what I was going to do and where I was going to go. I vowed again to get even. Frank had a few hours head start on me and probably had a plan being implemented already, so I was slow on the upstart. I walked back inside the terminal and told the clerk that I changed my mind and needed a phone to call a cab. He pointed to the wall of pay phones on the opposite wall. I called a cab and walked back outside to wait. I got a pop from the machine and waited for about twenty minutes before one showed up. I asked the driver to take me to the airport.

"Which one, buddy?" the cab driver asked.

"You have more than one?" I asked.

"Nope. We don't have any, but there's a big one in Ralston and there's a small one over in Kingly," he stated. "The air base has a big one, but we aren't permitted to use it, I'm sorry to say," he added with a laugh.

"Ralston, then," I stated. "How long of a time and how much will that cost me?"

"I'll drive you there for twenty-five bucks. It shouldn't take more than an hour," he guessed.

"Okay, it's a deal," I said.

The driver smiled like he just made the deal of the century and got out of the cab and assisted me with my bag and opened the door for me.

"I'm not much of a talker and would prefer to sleep the whole way. Okay?" I said.

"You just lay back and leave the driving to me," he said, smiling.

I did go to sleep for a bit. The cab driver woke me up when he pulled up at the air terminal. He was anxious to get back to Ashton, so I paid him his fare and carried my bag into the terminal. The one Guinness Air flight daily to Albany with connections to Clarkston had already departed. I talked with the lady at the counter for a while trying to figure out another route, but really didn't want to fly all the way to Eastwick and wait for a flight to Albany from there.

"Elway Air flies out of Middleton to Albany and then to Clarkston, but unfortunately the connection from here has already left for the day as well," she volunteered with a sigh.

We both figured that a decision to wait for the Guinness flight tomorrow morning would be the best and fastest way. So, that's what I decided to do. I purchased a ticket to Clarkston by way of Albany and wondered what I was going to do till then.

"Any good movies showing in town that you know of?" I asked her.

She smiled and shrugged her shoulders and asked the next person in line if she could help them.

I wondered around inside the airport for hours and looked at the many pictures depicting the early flying days of several airlines. I had a bite to eat in the airport restaurant and stopped a number of times at the drinking fountain. I sat for a while, walked for a while, stood for a while, and even slept for a brief while, but nothing I did could break the boredom of waiting. All I could think of was how I got swindled and the growing time span that Frank had prior to me getting on his trail. Heck, he would have better than a day's head start on me. More than that, probably, because I still had to figure out where he was headed.

―――――

My plane loaded and took off on time the next morning. I had a bite of breakfast on the flight...a donut and a cup of coffee; it was just enough. I didn't think I would, but I fell asleep on the flight and was awakened by the stewardess prior to landing in Albany. I walked to the other concourse and waited for my flight to Clarkston. My mind began its battle once again on how to find Frank. I boarded my plane for Clarkston with my mind racing about the things needing done. The time went by so fast I didn't even realize that we were in Clarkston until I felt the wheels touch down. I hadn't really concluded anything as to where I was going to go or what I was going to do. I couldn't get rid of the thought of Frank off somewhere laughing his guts out over the ruse he pulled. I did make a few decisions, though. I needed to rent a car and before heading home, go to the bank and get my money out. I planned to go to the hospital and visit Dr. J while I was in town and tell him what happened. I was real curious to see if he got his money. Once back home, I wanted to make plans to find the weasel that shafted me.

The Mercy Hospital in Clarkston sits on a hill overlooking the eastern portion of Blaine County. I had been there a few times, but from my new perspective, it looked different. I parked the rental in the lot and walked in through the front door. I inquired at the information desk about Mr. Jefferson. I just realized that I did not know Dr. J's first name. The lady looked at her record book and asked me if I were family. I found that kind of funny, but then realized that she didn't know that Dr. J was a Negro.

"I'm just a good friend is all; I came by to check on him," I told her.

She took my name and asked me to take a seat in the waiting room and someone would be with me in a minute. I walked to the area she motioned to and found a seat and sat down. There were a few others in the room, mostly couples sitting together, a family of four, and one other lone person besides me. Soon, a man in a dark suit appeared in the room and in a fairly loud voice asked to speak to Mr. Cooper. I acknowledged his request with a raised hand and got up and walked to him. He asked me to accompany him to a room just off the waiting area and we entered and sat down.

"I'm Chaplain Perry. Were you close to Mr. Jefferson, son?" he asked as he shook my hand.

"Yes sir, we worked together," I hesitantly revealed.

"Well, Samuel died the other morning just after arriving at the hospital," he said.

"What happened?" I stammered quietly, thinking what a nice name Dr. J had.

"His appendix ruptured and there was nothing the staff could do to save him," he solemnly said.

Poor Dr. J, I thought; he won't get his fair share of the money.

"Does his family know?" I asked.

"Oh, yes, son, they know. Mr. Jefferson's body was taken by the funeral home yesterday afternoon," he said.

"Which one?" I asked.

"Pawnee Falls, I believe," he paused. "Yes, Pawnee Falls," he said after looking at a piece of paper.

I immediately thought of Willy and wondered where he had gone and who was taking care of him.

"What happened to Mr. Jefferson's grandson? Wasn't he here?" I asked.

"His mother came and picked him up. He's fine," the man stated.

I thanked the chaplain and left the hospital. I drove to Morgan National Bank and walked in just prior to them closing their doors for the day. I hadn't realized the time until then. I closed my account and took the money. I got my entire life's saving; $12,000 in a cashier's check and the rest, $337.47 in cash. I walked out of the bank a rich man.

I entered Hardee with a purpose and pulled the rental into the driveway half expecting the convertible to be there, but it wasn't. I noticed that a station wagon was sitting in Dr. J's driveway behind his pickup. I walked over and met Willy's mom. I gave her a hug and told her I was sorry.

"Anything I can do, ma'am?" I asked.

"I don't think so. You have been very kind. Miss Molly left us some money. We will be fine," she said.

"Where's Willy?" I asked. "Is he okay?"

"He's fine. He's packing up his things," she explained.

She also explained that Willy got the entire Ham radio set-up. Apparently, Molly was a busy girl before she left for our rendezvous. I wonder how she reacted when Frank never showed; maybe thinking that she was the one that got shafted. I decided that I couldn't worry about that now; I had a job to do and needed to get going. I put $50 in her hand and told her how much I was going to miss her dad. She thanked me and I left the house.

I walked back to the trailer wondering if Molly knew that Dr. J was dead. She was all teary eyed before we left for Ashton so she could have known then. Did she leave the money as a gift like she did mine, hoping that he would find it when he got home, or did she already know that he was dead and left the money for Willy's mom to find? I had a feeling that I would probably never find out the answer. At least I could take solace in the fact that Willy had someone he could lean on. I hoped that she would take good care of him. I wished that I had told him bye.

My future, however, was in doubt. I didn't have anyone right now. I began to feel sorry for myself but decided that that attitude wouldn't get me anywhere. I grabbed my stash from the closet and sat down on the couch to count it. I started seriously thinking about revenge and how to get it accomplished. I had enough money to do a whole lot of things right now and if I was careful, I could last for several years. I saw the calling card on the table from the FBI agent and I began to think that maybe the FBI would be interested in finding the leaders of the Speakeasy Gang.

I had read once (at the barber shop, I think) that the FBI was contemplating the use of a new program where they protect people that turn evidence over to them that they can use to arrest and convict a felon. The person telling on the law breakers would be pardoned of their wrong doing and the FBI would protect the witness forever. Maybe I could get Agent Ballard to enlist me into that new program if it ever got off the ground. Getting revenge for what Frank put me through was going to happen one way or another anyway. If the FBI believed me, then they could go after the gang and get them convicted. I wondered if there was a reward on our heads.

I decided that I needed to pack up my things and get out of here. I needed a suitcase and remembering the ones in Frank's bedroom, headed that direction. I looked in Frank's bedroom and noticed that all three of the suitcases were gone. Where was I gonna get one, I wondered. My mind recalled that Frank didn't have his usual black bag at the café. I opened his closet and it was bare except for several clothes hangers. I assumed the suitcases were probably in the trunk of the convertible with all of his belongings and a lot of money. I noticed something on the floor next to the bed and reached down and picked it up. It was a leather luggage tag with a small silver chain hanging loosely from it. I looked at the tag and saw the name, *Grace Miller*. Under the name was an address that was ink smeared, like it got wet at some time, but looked like; *1289 Atlantic St. HO Fl*. The other side of the tag had a lighthouse burned in to it. Frank's story about the luggage tag came to mind. This was it.

I dropped the luggage tag on the made bed and quickly ran to the big house. I was actually surprised to find the front door unlocked. I began looking around inside. The house was almost empty. I had only been in a few of the furnished rooms before so it was strange to see the others totally empty. I walked into the kitchen and there were pots and pans hanging from the high ceiling on some round contraption over the counter. The stove looked twice as big as Frank's and a partially filled canister of popcorn was sitting on the side table.

I went upstairs and looked in the bedrooms to find all of the beds made and the rooms filled with covered furniture. White linen covers were draped over the dressers, wardrobes, and night stands. I looked in the wardrobe closet for a suitcase, but didn't find one. I checked out the radio room and discovered that the radio transceiver, amplifier, and power supplies were all definitely in Willy's hands. I didn't think I would find a suitcase in here, either.

"I hope Willy can learn to operate that thing and have some great times with it." I said out loud.

Speaking of Willy, I thought; maybe his mom can find me a suitcase. If not, then I will have to go to town and buy one.

I walked over to Dr. J's house and knocked on the door. I asked Willy's mom if I could borrow a suitcase. They were just fixing to leave and thinking that her dad had one in the bedroom; she went to fetch it and carried it back out to me.

"Let me buy it from you, ma'am. That's the least I could do," I stated.

"Nonsense. After all you've done, forget it. You keep it and do with it what ever you wish," she said. "Willy and I will be eternally grateful for your kindness.

"Goodbye, A.D.," Willy softly muttered.

"See ya, Willy. You take care of your mom, understand?" I solemnly said.

"I will," he uttered and then walked behind his mom as though embarrassed.

"Come back here and give me a hug, Willy!" I demanded.

He gingerly sidled over to me and put his arms around me and quickly hugged me and returned to his hiding place.

"You take care, ma'am. Again, I'm sorry for your loss," I stated.

It was a nice piece of luggage that should work fine. I thanked her and reached out and lightly knuckled Willy's head as a gesture of friendship and returned to the trailer. I packed up my things and set my stuff by the door. I sat on the couch and thought of several things that I might do, one of which was just getting as far away from this place as humanly possible. I decided that I would drive to Middleton and try and locate Agent Ballard. I didn't have a lot to tell him, other than the names of those that were in the gang. I had no idea where any of them were, but could point them in the right direction. I wondered if the FBI had jurisdiction in Canada.

I got up early after a fitful night's sleep and loaded the car with my stuff. I didn't bother folding up my bedding and left a few dirty dishes in the sink for spite. I looked around the trailer for anything that I may have missed and longed to take my television, but knew that was impossible. I got in the rental and took one last look at the house and trailer before backing out of the driveway for the last time. I doubted I would ever see this place again. I stopped to gas up at Victor's without revealing anything about what was going on.

"Where's the convertible, A.D.?" Happy smilingly asked as he filled my tank.

"Frank's got it. He's out of town doing some things for the old lady and I need a car, so rented one," I explained.

"Those things expensive?" he asked, meaning rental cars.

"Not bad. I've only got it for a few days," I lied.

"You still working at the plant?" he asked, still believing that I worked there.

"Yep. Nothing better anywhere around, you know," I commented.

"Got that right," Happy laughed in agreement.

He went on with his chores while talking the whole time, but none of it was audible. I paid for the gas and drove away. I looked in the rear view mirror and saw a smiling Happy waving as I left.

Middleton was the closest FBI office around as far as I knew. Frank had mentioned it after the agents were around Mrs. Jenkins home that one time. I had no idea where it was and there was no address on the card, just a phone number. I drove the distance to Middleton in just over an hour, arriving around 9:30 and stopped at the bus station and called the number on the card. There was no answer. I hung up and called again. Still no answer. Just then it dawned on me as to the reason. It was Saturday. No government offices were open on Saturday, what the heck was the matter with me. Now I had to wait until Monday to get in touch with the FBI. What the heck was I gonna do until then, I wondered. All of this excitement had clouded my senses and made me forget things. My recent vow of being cautious had already been broken with the heist at the diner and I didn't want to get sideswiped again. I needed to think more clearly. I stopped at a restaurant and got breakfast. I sat for over an hour after eating and just let things run through my mind. I thought of my mom, Cecil, Mark, and my dad. I thought about Dr. J and I thought of Frank and the dastardly deed he did to me. I wondered how I was going to find him.

"Anything else I can get for you, dear?" the waitress broke my train of thought.

"No thanks; just my bill, if you would, please," I stated.

I left the restaurant and just drove around for a while and couldn't help but notice the new and used car lots in Middleton. There were a lot of them. I got to thinking that I probably should buy a new car. I certainly could afford one, and when I figured out where Frank was, I would need one to get me there. I drove around for a bit and looked over the town and drove by several car dealerships. I stopped at three different lots and looked at the new models. The sales pitches were enticing. I drove four different styles of car before settling on a brand new two door hardtop for $2,300 cash.

"Can you take care of that thing there? It's a rental and I can't drive two cars," I mentioned to the salesman about my car.

"Sure thing, mister; leave it with us," he volunteered.

After transferring everything from one car to the other, I drove to a nearby barbershop and got a crewcut. The barber was not as friendly as the one in Hardee, so I basically just sat and listened to the sound of the clippers. I paid him and drove to a department store where I bought some new clothes. I picked up a new pair of penny loafers and a new fedora as well. On the way back to the car, I saw a store with sunglasses in the window display, so walked in and bought a pair for myself.

I walked around the town for a while just looking and thinking. I decided to see about getting a room for the weekend and call the FBI office first thing Monday morning. I had to figure out where Frank was so that I could get moving in that direction. Shucks, he already had several days head start and I wasn't close to getting started in my hunt for him. It was getting on toward mid-afternoon, so I drove back out to the edge of town and located a Motor Inn where I could bed down and wait out the weekend.

Over the next few hours, I sat in my motel room and recalled some of the things that I had done over the past few years; the jobs I pulled; the acquaintances I met; the good times and the bad. Frank had made a fool of me and for that I would never forgive him even if I was asked to. I didn't figure the FBI could hold me accountable for much; after all, I only got paid a wage for working the jobs. Not much different than working in the salsa factory or the pepper fields, really. I knew the city in Canada where Mrs. Jenkins and Molly were, but would have to guess as to what warm and sunny beach Frank was on. He could be talking the west coast as well as the east coast for all I knew. The FBI could look until the cows came home with that kind of information and never find him. I thought back to conversations we had in hopes of him mentioning any particular beach. I couldn't come up with one.

I hadn't had anything to eat since breakfast and I was getting hungry, so decided to visit the restaurant I passed just a little ways back toward town. The restaurant, named The Copper Kettle, featured a family atmosphere and a daily special. I had their evening special of meat loaf and mashed potatoes with green beans and a roll. My mom would have been disappointed in me not cleaning my plate, but it turned out to be more than I could eat. When I left after paying the bill, I walked away from the motel for several blocks before turning around and coming back, just to walk off the over indulgence that I did.

As I walked back through the parking lot of the motel toward my room, I saw a black pickup parked in a space near the office and had a flashback of Carl's truck in the Mudd River. Then as if a light bulb suddenly went on, I remembered the conversation with Frank that told me where he might be. When I was asking him all of the questions about prison and the death penalty, I remembered him saying that his favorite place was Haven City.

Night time was falling as I drove back into Middleton to locate the town's library. I hoped that it stayed open for a while during the evening hours. I needed to find an atlas or map to locate Haven City. If I could find it, I might be able to find Frank on my own, or at least have some detailed information to share with the FBI.

I spotted a policeman walking his beat and stopped and asked where the library was and if it was still open. He was happy to respond to my questions and even told me where to park.

Not ever being in a local library I wasn't sure what to look for, but remembered the school library and figured all libraries were pretty much the same. I located the research section and found the 'H' encyclopedia and looked up Haven City. It described the area briefly and the town's motto was mentioned as having the whitest sand on the Florida coast. I found a book titled *Florida, the Sunshine State* and read several pages describing the Gulf Coast, of which a whole half page was dedicated to Haven City. Amazingly, a picture and a detailed map of the area were present on the page. The picture was of a pure white sand beach and the bluest water I had ever seen. The story mentioned a new concept in town layout...making the entire town center a pedestrian area called a *'mall'*. It was being practiced apparently at a number of resort towns and cities on the coast. A lighthouse was in the background of the picture and I recalled Frank saying how much he liked the place. The map showed the Gulf Coast and the towns and cities on both sides of Haven City.

"There you are," I thought. "It may take me some time to get there, but I will see your *'warm and sunny'* beach, Frank, ole buddy," I said to myself.

I decided that I needed to pick up a road map or two and plot my way to the place. If the atlas I looked at was correct, I guessed it would take me about three or four days or more to get there. I asked at the check out counter for a pencil and paper. I wrote down some of the information accompanying the article in the book. I closed it and returned it to the shelf, put the borrowed pencil on the counter, folded the paper and stuck it in my pocket, and left the building. I drove back to the motel with a new determination and a better feel for what I was going to do. I stopped at the office to see if they could direct me to a place that sold road maps.

"Do you know if the filling station down the street has road maps?" I asked the lady clerk.

"I can't say for sure, but I would guess that they do. If they don't, then the truck stop on the edge of town near the main road I know has them and the Visitor's Bureau downtown has them too," she volunteered. "They are closed on the weekend, though."

"Thank you. I appreciate that," I told her.

"You're welcome," she said with a smile and turned to continue her work.

I walked to the filling station and discovered that indeed they had road maps. I looked at them for a few minutes and noticed the clerk eyeing me.

"I gotta close up, mister. You gonna buy something?" he asked.

I apologized for the delay and decided on a map that depicted roads in the southeast portion of the United States and bought it. I walked back to the motel and went into my room. I studied the map for a bit and kind of plotted a way of getting to the area. I jotted down a few things I was planning to ask the FBI and made a note to be sure and ask Agent Ballard about protecting me.

I slept like a log and awoke Sunday morning with the sun shining through a break in the window curtain and into my eyes. I washed my face, brushed my teeth, dressed in my new clothes and walked to the office to get a cup of coffee. What I was going to do for the whole day was a mystery, but I had an inkling to put a few miles on my new car by taking a trip further north and seeing some country that I had never seen before; not that I was aware of, anyway. I could have seen some of it from the air during one of my travels, but was not sure.

"I want to do some sightseeing today. Is there any place you would recommend me seeing around here?" I asked the same lady from last night.

"If you're interested and have the time, the Amish country would be a good visit. Their compound is just about a half hour's drive out Highway 206," she suggested. "They actually set aside a few hours every Sunday for tour visits from outsiders. You might get lucky and be able to join in on one of those."

I had no idea of what or who she was speaking, and decided not to ask. I thanked her anyway and just decided to take out on my own and see where the road took me. I drove on some of those new types of roads that you read about. It reminded me of my brother, though, and that was thoughts that I would just as soon stay away from. I took a turn down an old country road and pulled off to the side near a river crossing and got out and walked around for a while. The river was a long way down there and reminded me of the Mudd River and that reminded me of Carl's death. Those thoughts just began to conjure up bad memories, so I returned to my car and drove back to town. I passed a drive-in movie place on my way back in to town and decided to see a movie tonight. I really didn't care what was showing; just passing time was the main thing to accomplish. I was anxious for Monday to come so that I could get on with my plan.

CHAPTER 16

"Could I speak with agent Walt Ballard, please?" I asked the receptionist who answered the phone at the office of the FBI.

"One moment please," she said.

"This is agent Ballard. To whom do I have the pleasure?" he courteously answered.

"My name is A.D. Cooper. I have some information for you regarding the Speakeasy Gang," I announced.

"Like what?" he asked.

"Like their names and their location," I replied.

"Where's that?" he asked.

"It's not going to be that easy, Agent Ballard," I warned.

"What do you mean? You're the one with the information you said," he commented.

"I will exchange the information I have on their location for your promised protection of me," I told him.

"Protection from what?" he asked.

"The gang members," I said.

"What makes you think you need protection from them? Are you one of them?" he asked.

"I used to be," I volunteered.

"And you expect me to believe that you are just going to rat on your former gang members and give me the information of their location just like that, huh?" he asked.

"If you promise me protection, yeah," I replied.

"Okay, I promise you protection, now where are they?" he stated.

"Not so fast. I told you it wasn't going to be that easy," I repeated.

"What else is there? I told you I would protect you. What more do you want?" he asked.

"Come on man, I'm giving you the Speakeasy Gang," I said.

"What you're giving me could be a bunch of malarkey for all I know. You could have been left holding the bag and just want revenge, Mr. Cooper, or whatever your name is. If you want to come in and surrender yourself and do this properly, then I will listen, but otherwise, let the FBI do their job," he stated loudly and then Agent Ballard *hung up on me.*

I hung up the phone and took a deep breathe. This wasn't what I envisioned at all. The FBI isn't buying the fact that I know where the gang is? I felt that Agent Ballard was trying his best to be uncooperative. I guess that's the way they perform their jobs; act tough and reluctant and see what comes out of it.

Frank said once that they are stupid and I'll have to agree with him on that.

    I started thinking ahead for a few minutes and decided to put all of the information I had on Frank and the gang on paper and mail it to Agent Ballard. If I gave myself up and surrendered, they would have to keep me in jail until they could locate and arrest the other members. Who knows how long that would take? I didn't want to be in jail at all, let a lone until the rest of them could be found. My first inkling to cooperate and be a witness had been replaced with the idea of finding Frank on my own and wishing the FBI good luck on tracking down the others. I mentally apologized to Agent Ballard for attempting to assist him in his case and decided that he could just work on it with the small bit of information I could provide. I asked the lady at the desk for a piece of paper and a pen. I quickly jotted down the information I was going to reveal and signed it. The lady at the desk provided me with an envelope and I bought a stamp from her and mailed the information to Agent Ballard at the FBI.

    I was finally headed for the white sand beaches of Haven City. It would probably take me four to five days drive to get there, but I was in no real hurry. The anger and revengeful thoughts were enough to drive me for quite some time. Besides, I needed the time to think of how I was going to find Frank and hopefully, the money. I tuned the radio to a western music station out of Chicago, turned the volume up about midway and headed for US 34 while tapping my fingers to the beat of the music.

    I enjoyed my first ever road trip away from home. Up to now, I had only driven on the open road for an hour or so between heists and rendezvous spots. Being on the road for hours on end would certainly be different. The traffic headed east was pretty light and the cars and trucks I met were few and far between. I pretty much had the road to myself.

I recalled a few of the towns I would pass through on my way and had to laugh at a few of them. Who would name their town Ulcer, for example? Another one that touched my funny bone was a small town in Georgia called Ty Ty. The founders thought so much of that place they had to name it twice, I guessed. I would pass through an Oasis; come face to face with a Moosehead (in Tennessee); could see water at Lakeside; and even breathe in the sweet smell of Cologne on my journey. They were all towns that dotted my route to Haven City.

Just before 1:00, I stopped in a small town just a few miles from the state border called Prather and pulled into a road side diner for a bite to eat. The waitress that served me reminded me of Molly; really nice legs, but older. She showed me to a table and placed a menu in front of me. I opened the menu and noticed that the Coney Island was on special for a dollar. Deciding on the special, I closed the menu and opened up my map.

"Where you headed, son?" a voice from behind me asked.

I turned to see who was speaking and an older man with real bushy eyebrows was looking me right in the eye. His cap was pushed back on his head revealing a bald head. My first thought was he could transplant some of his eyebrows to his head and have enough for both places.

"Haven City. Ever hear of it?" I stated.

"Yep. Just a few miles from Blister Cove. Been there a few times in my travels," he said. "It's got the whitest sand in the whole world, you know."

"So I hear," I replied.

"I'm headed that way," he said as he walked back to his table. "I could wait for you and show you the way," he volunteered.

"Thanks, but that won't be necessary, mister. I'm in no hurry anyway; just moseying," I commented.

"That's a good thing 'cause the Patrol are out in force I hear," he stated as he walked to the counter. He turned back to me and warned me about a particular stretch of road.

"There's a lot of road construction near Crow's Junction. That's 'bout another 60 miles east where US 151 takes off south, so be careful." he warned and then turned back to the front counter.

I acknowledged his message with a nod and returned to my map. US 151 was my planned route south connecting to US 24 that turned east again.

The waitress waited on him with his bill and once finished, said goodbye to him and walked to my table.

"I'll have the special, please," I told her.

"You can get a bottle of soda for another twenty cents if you wish," she suggested.

"Okay. I'll have a root beer to go with it," I said.

"Coming right up," she said and picked up the menu and returned to the kitchen. I admired her legs as she walked away.

As I turned back to studying the map some more while I waited, I saw the bushy-browed man climb up into a large truck and trailer rig. He was a truck driver. No wonder he knew where Haven City was...and undoubtedly had been there a number of times. I watched him pull out onto the main road and could almost hear the gears meshing into place as he took off. I thought of my dad. I never did have the opportunity to ride with him. I day-dreamed for a few moments and thought of my mom and brothers. The thought of Mark brought me back to the present, swiftly.

I was studying my map when the waitress brought me my meal and sat it down in front of me. I folded up the map and enjoyed my meal. I thought of my trip and what all I would encounter. I envisioned myself walking on a white sand beach looking out on a deep blue ocean; neither of which I had ever seen in my life. As I paid for the meal, which was as good as or better than the first Coney that I had, I asked the waitress taking my money if there was a filling station close by.

"About a half mile down the road, young man. You can't miss it," she stated.

I thanked her and expressed my satisfaction on the meal. She said she would pass it on to the cook.

I drove less than a half mile and I pulled into the station to gas up. The gas gauge was almost resting on the **E** mark and I wondered what kind of mileage I got on the new car's first tank full.

"Fill it up, please; regular," I told the attendant when he came out of the station.

"Can I check your oil, mister?" he asked.

"Sure," I agreed.

"Nice car. Had it long?" he asked as he raised the hood.

"Nope. Just got it a few days ago. I sure like it," I commented.

After about an hour or so of driving, road signs warned of construction ahead. I got stopped behind two other cars for a few minutes and then a pickup with a sign on the back saying "Follow Me" pulled up and led the cars through the construction area. After a few minutes of driving slowly on a new surface, another area of road construction stopped the same cars for about ten minutes. We all got to move through the construction area by again following a truck with a sign on it. After resuming the regular roadbed, the two cars in front of me soon out distanced me and were out of sight. I rode along for the better part of an hour with just the music keeping me company, when I noticed a pillar of smoke or dust up ahead a ways. I first thought it was farmers stirring up dust while plowing or harvesting, but the closer I got I could tell it was smoke rising and drifting south over the landscape. I slowed and decided that it was a wreck up ahead. Red flashing lights from a police car were emitting a harsh beam of light intermittingly over the scene. A truck cab was on its side in the bar-ditch and the engine was on fire. The trailer had apparently come unhitched and went through a fence and was nose down in the adjacent field. The black smoke was like a curtain as I drove through it and then as I passed the cab, I saw the bushy-browed trucker from the diner sitting on the edge of the bar-ditch holding his head in his hands.

"Is he going to be all right?" I asked the trooper as I was slowly passing by the scene.

"I think so. He suffered a blowout and lost control of his rig. He'll be okay," the trooper stated.

"Can I help?" I asked.

"No, but thanks for the offer," the trooper said.

I slowly drove on by and mentally wished the trucker good luck. He had warned me about the road construction and told me to drive carefully and then something like a blowout ruins his day. Several miles further down the road, I met an ambulance simply flying toward the scene of the accident. I figured the trooper called it in, thinking that it was better to be safe than sorry concerning the truck driver. Then within just a few seconds, a fire truck went zooming past with its lights and siren on. The man was getting help, after all.

The afternoon drive was warm, but pleasant. There wasn't a lot of traffic on the road as I went through small town after small town. They reminded me a lot of the area around Hardee. Most of them were just like small spots in the road, with an occasional larger one that had a few stores and businesses in it. The occasional four-lane highway I encountered was really something. The surface was smooth and hypnotizing. After the second time of almost dozing off, I decided I better find a place to bed down for the night.

I entered the town of Rochester around 4 p.m. and looked for a place to spend the night. It appeared to be a nice town. Green grass covered almost every lawn and the trees and flowers were really pretty. I found a gas station and had the tank filled up and inquired about a place to stay.

"There's a new motel just down the street. It's real nice," the older man attending the pumps told me. "They opened up just last month. Real nice folks own it."

After getting the car filled up, I turned down the street he said and just a block further was the motel. On the same side of the street was a restaurant that I could walk to once I had checked in. The newness of the place was still evident in the smell of fresh paint and carpet. The man at the desk was very cordial and kind.

"Just driving through, young man?" he asked.

"Yes sir, just driving through," I confirmed.

"Nice weather for traveling, I suppose. Not too hot and not too cold. Suppose to rain tomorrow, though. Where's home?" he talked in a streak.

"A small town named Hardee, near Albany," I told him. "I'm headed for Haven City. Know of it?"

"Can't say that I do. You have a nice stay," he stated and handed me my room key. "Just leave the key on the desk when you leave in the morning."

"Thanks. I will," I said.

After I put my stuff in my room, I walked to the restaurant and had some supper. I sat for quite a while after eating and tried to think through where I was, where I was headed, and what it was that I proposed to do once there. I could still envision very clearly the scene at the donut shop. Every time I thought about it I got angry at Frank and renewed my vow for revenge. I would be in Haven City in a couple of days and begin my search for him. I thought about the trucker and wondered how he was doing.

———

Some grey skies and a slight mist greeted my departure from Rochester just like the man said. My new car was getting rained on for the first time. The rain got a little heavier as I joined the main highway at the light and drove to the beat of the windshield wipers. I drove for three hours during the morning, going through one town after another with intermittent rain showers the whole time, and then suffered from the mugginess of the late morning humidity for more than an hour. I came upon a road junction where SR98 crosses the state from east to west and noticed a road sign stating that New Brahms was 254 miles back west of the intersection. That brought back some memories. I had no idea that I was anywhere close to one of our jobs. New Brahms was where Molly took Frank to the hospital when he was shot at Lakeside. I envisioned it like it happened just a minute ago. That was a scary time, I recalled, but Molly handled it like it was just another ordinary day. She was pretty special, but she showed her true colors with the Air Base job. I hoped she would get what was coming to her someday.

I stopped for lunch and gas at a little wide spot in the road called Bliss. The rains had stopped by the time I pulled back on the highway and about mid-afternoon I saw a road sign that said the Tennessee state line was 62 miles ahead. I pulled over to the side of the road and checked my map. Three larger towns were in route, so I decided to stop in Prophet (the first large town) for the night and continue my trip to Haven City tomorrow.

As I approached the town of Prophet, I kept seeing small sign boards along the road's fence line announcing what I thought to be biblical quotes. I was never a biblical scholar, nor a religious person, but recalling a few of my Sunday school days, the words looked like they came from the Bible.

It appeared to be a laid back town. A few cars were in the parking strip in the downtown area and an old Model T met me as it chugged down the street. Two old Negro men were sitting on the steps of a mercantile store; one of them doffed his hat at me as I passed. I thought of Dr. J. A large white church with a steeple that reached way up into the sky sat on my right as I left the major business area. There were two cars in the lot next to it.

I located a small motor lodge at the outskirts of the city and stopped for the night. There was only one other car in the parking lot right in front of unit number 4. I walked into the office and thought I had walked into a church. There were pictures of biblical times on the walls and candles burning everywhere you looked.

"Need a room for the night, sir?" an older lady with white hair came from behind a wall and asked me.

"Please, if it's no bother," I said.

"No bother at all. Are you traveling?" she asked.

"Yes. Headed to Florida," I answered.

"Sure hot there, I bet," she guessed as she filled out a card.

"Probably so," I agreed.

"That will be $8 even," she stated with a smile.

I paid her the money and she marked the card with the amount and stuck it under the counter. She pulled out a key from a metal box and handed it to me.

"There you go. Unit 7 across the way. Have a good stay. Just drop the key in the door when you leave tomorrow," she instructed and pointed to the front door.

"Okay, thanks," I said, observing the open slot in the door.

It was an older place and the walls were scuffed and a rusty stain was in the bathroom sink and toilet, but it was clean and the price was right. Two pictures of biblical scenes were hanging on the walls of the room. The face of Jesus was depicted in a painting on the wall behind the door and a painting of praying hands was above the bed. I dropped my stuff on the floor and went back to the office. A buzzer sounded when I entered and a young teenaged girl came to the counter.

"Is there a café or restaurant in town where I can get a good meal?" I asked her.

"Freda's Cottage Inn is just a block over and a little way down Second Street," she offered. "She has really great fried chicken and collard greens, if you like that sort of thing. You can leave your car here and walk. It'll be safe."

"Thanks," I replied.

"God bless you!" she called to me as I left the office.

Her salutation left a weird feeling in my body.

I walked to Freda's as the sun was setting for the day. Instead of the fried chicken, I ordered a hamburger and homemade potato salad. I wasn't the only one in the place, but I was the only one eating. A boy I guessed to be about 10 was at the counter talking softly to the waitress, whom I assumed was his mom. He was dressed like he just came from church. A young couple was seated at a table across the café and next to the counter. They had pamphlets of some kind in front of them and were reading from them. They read aloud at first, but I guess I spooked them of doing that by looking right at them a few times.

A large wooden cross was hanging right in the middle of the wall behind the counter. Plates and bowls were stacked on shelves to the right of the cross and glasses were placed in neat rows on shelves to the left. An open window ledge was on that side as well and that is where the waitress retrieved my order. I assumed the kitchen was behind that wall. I noticed the boy had a small Bible under his hand on the counter. He looked over at me a number of times during my meal, but never said a word. I kind of felt like I was being talked about for not saying grace, but couldn't even remember the last time such a prayer was uttered. The food was very good, though and plentiful.

I was done with my food and asked for my check. Just as the waitress put it on the table, a man in a suit walked in accompanied by a pretty young woman that was dressed to the nines. I thought it strange that she would be dressed as such in a small mom and pop diner, but there she was in all of her glory.

"Hello, Pastor Graham. Hey Miss Flo," the waitress said to them as she walked back behind the counter. "Sit down anywhere ya'll would like," she said. "The others should be here pretty soon."

I noticed a huge diamond ring on the finger of the lady. She was younger than the man by several years, I thought, but could very well be his wife. If he purchased the ring for her, than preaching is a pretty good paying job, I figured. I paid for my meal and couldn't avoid the smile of the young man. It seemed as though it was plastered on his face. He hadn't moved from the same spot since I arrived.

"Thanks for coming in. You're welcome to stay if you'd like," the mother said to me.

"No thanks," I said and opened the door.

As I was walking out, three couples dressed as though they were attending a wedding, were walking in. The door shut as the waitress was welcoming them to the café. I had a notion to change my mind on her invite if for nothing else but to find out what all the pageantry was about, but decided to let it be. As the door shut behind me, the little boy turned the open sign to closed and pulled down the window blind. I looked at my watch and saw that it was almost 9:00.

I walked back to my room and dressed down to get comfortable. I sat at the desk in my skivvies and studied my map for a while, trying to pick out the easiest path to my destination. A knock came to my door. A little startled, I jumped up, put my pants back on and walked to the window curtain. I peeked around the side to see who might be knocking on my room door at this hour. I saw the young girl from the motel office standing at the door.

"Can I help you?" I called through the door.

"I'm here to invite you to the prayer meeting in room 10. Everyone is invited. Are you interested?" she called back.

"No thank you. I'm in bed. I have a long day of travel tomorrow," I lied.

"Sorry to disturb you. Godspeed," she said and walked away.

I thought it pretty odd that a business place would do such a thing as go around to the guests and invite them to a meeting. A prayer meeting at that. And late at night on top of it. Weird, I thought.

———

Day three on the road started well. The sun was shining brightly and there was not a cloud in the sky. I planned to turn east in a while, near noon I figured if everything went smoothly. A full day of travel today, another night's stay in a motel somewhere on Highway 24 and about four hours more would get me to my destination. I hoped like crazy that I wouldn't be disturbed tonight and asked to attend a meeting like last night.

I was enjoying driving my new car. I was enjoying driving, period. My road trip was pretty cool. I thought I just might do this for a while after I get my business done. Who knows, I may drive up north to Canada and then west to the Pacific Ocean. I could afford it. If I could find the money that Frank took from me, I could afford to do even more than that if I wanted to. My thoughts centered in on Frank for a moment and I wondered where he was hiding the money and what he was up to. I sure hoped that Haven City was his planned stop. He had a good couple of days' head start on me, but hopefully he hadn't got his fill of white sand just yet.

I pulled into a roadside truck stop outside the town of Carney for a bite to eat. It was not all that busy, but then it was mid-afternoon, too. I had turned east onto US 24 just before noon and bypassed lunch time due to having a large breakfast, but hunger was now attacking my stomach, so I thought it best to feed it. I parked and walked in. The café reminded me of Lola's a little…it had a donut rack behind the counter and the tables were set up similarly. That brought back the memory of me being shanghaied.

I just sort of automatically brought my map in with me. I didn't really need it, but it gave me something to look at while I ate or waited for my meal. I seated myself and laid out the map in front of me. The waitress came over with a water glass and menu.

"Coffee?" she asked.

"No thanks, but a soda would be nice," I told her. "How about a root beer?"

"Sure thing, darling," she replied and walked away.

I had heard other women talk like that—words of endearment to someone that they don't even know—and guessed that those people were either not married, or had other pet names to call their loved one. I knew I didn't care for it, but what are you gonna do?

"Where you headed, young fella?" an old man asked as he sat down at my table.

"Florida," I said as I looked at him carefully.

"From where?" he asked.

"Albany. Know of it?" I asked.

"Sure I do. I've been in every state in America, sonny," he bragged. "Why are you driving? A lot quicker if you fly."

"I suppose you're right, mister. I enjoy driving though," I told him.

"Yes, I've been in New York many times in my day and Albany quite a few times," he bragged as he rubbed his head.

"Not Albany, New York, I'm afraid, but the one in Pot Hole Country," I told him.

"What's a pot hole?" he asked almost before I finished my sentence.

"A bunch of small holes in the ground where water collects. That's all I know," I explained.

He didn't say anything more, just got up and wandered on out of the restaurant. The waitress appeared with my pop and to take my order.

"Did Jake bother you, hon? He has to talk to everyone that comes in, I think," the waitress asked and volunteered.

"No ma'am. Is he a regular?" I asked.

"Regular as clockwork; the old coot. As long as he doesn't run off the customers, I guess he's harmless," she replied.

"Said he's seen all of America. Told me I should be flying, not driving," I said.

"He's so full of it, he stinks. As far as I know, he ain't ever gone anywhere. He has lived his whole life right here in Carney. What can I get for you, hon?" she asked.

I ordered a BLT and potato chips. After the waitress left, I got to thinking as I scanned my map, that I bet Frank flew to Haven City. He could certainly get there sooner and if he did fly, he would have had time to figure out what he was going to do with the thousands of dollars he took. Heck, he may have already started spending it. I began to think that it may take me a while to find the rest of it, should that prove true. I wondered what he did with our car if he flew.

"He probably sold it to someone trying to rid himself of the memories it holds," I thought. "That old man may have something there about flying instead of driving. I guess I have all the time I need, though," I figured.

I finished up my meal, paid at the counter and drove on into town to gas up before resuming my trip. I found a popular station right away and filled up the tank. Right across the street was a bank. That brought back a flood of memories. I wondered if it had ever been robbed.

Just then an armored car drove in to the bank parking lot and made its way to the rear. Sure a weird time to be arriving, I thought. It's after 3:00. Whatever company is providing armored car service around here are doing it after the bank closes not before it opens, I decided. That's different. Maybe that's one of the changes that Molly referred to.

I drove across the Alabama state line just minutes after leaving Carney and started thinking about a place to bed down for the night. I tried to recall a town on the map that I might stop at, but everything I saw in my head had the name Lola on it. I decided I needed a rest badly. The town of New Holland was only 74 miles ahead, so I decided I would stop there for the night and venture on into Haven City tomorrow. A good night's rest and a hot breakfast tomorrow morning would put me in a good mood and the several hours of driving could be done with a new attitude.

I came upon some road construction signs in just a few minutes and slowed down to the new posted limit. Apparently, the new highways were being laid down in this area too. They were nice to drive on, I had to admit. I could just see the next generation of drivers fully enjoying the super roads the entire distance from coast to coast.

The road detoured to the right up ahead and circled around some farmer's crop, from the looks of it. I followed a flatbed Army truck in front of me loaded three high with large wooden boxes of something. The boxes were partly covered with a tarp and tied down with a rope and one rope was tied to the bumper. I could see the driver in his sideview mirror and he looked to be about fourteen. He kept bobbing his head up and down as though keeping time with some sort of music. He never did look out to see me. The crop in the fields was either peanuts or possibly potatoes, I couldn't tell, but the field was massive. It reminded me a little of the pepper fields, except much bigger.

The gravel road got bumpier and I had to slow even more to keep from being bounced out of the seat. The Army truck didn't slow down, though. I thought to myself that he could easily lose his load if he hit one of the holes really hard. The detour circled around the field and went through an open field before returning to the main highway. The flatbed truck had distanced me by quite a ways, but I could see it entering the main road.

"He's going too fast—he's gonna lose his load," I thought.

Just about that time, the flatbed hit the new road bed and bounced in the air. Before the front tires could touch down, the rear duals hit the road's edge and the truck almost turned over, but stayed upright. That last bump, combined with the others on the detour, caused his load to shift and the ropes snapped from the weight of the cargo. Practically every box on the truck came off and was dumped on the road and the shoulder. Several boxes broke open and the contents scattered like seed in the wind. When the carnage was over, hundreds of military flashlights were scattered from here to kingdom come.

I had to stop and the car behind me stopped, but a pickup and a car behind that one took off across a dirt field and rejoined the road after crossing the shallow bar ditch.

The kid driving the flatbed was a young soldier. He stepped down from the cab of his truck and pushed his cap back on his head.

"My CO is going to have my hide for this," he said while blowing out his breath in a big sigh.

"Let me help get you picked up and get you back on the road," I stated.

"Much obliged. Those two boxes are shot so let's see if we can get a few flashlights in the ones that are still together," he suggested while pointing at two of the boxes smashed to pieces.

He went to the cab of the truck and came back with a crowbar and a hammer. He swiftly opened several of the crates that were in one piece by lifting the tops off.

"The packing can be removed and those loose ones can go in these," he instructed.

I got the feeling that this young man had done something like this before.

The name tag on his fatigues read Macalister. He had no stripes on his sleeves, so I assumed that he was a Private.

"What do most people call you, Private?" I asked.

"Mac will do just fine. My first name is Bernard, but I prefer Mac," the young man stated.

"My name is A.D. Nice to meet you," I said as I shook his hand.

He was probably about my age, but I figured I had him in maturity by a bunch.

Two other people from the car behind me walked up and offered their assistance. They introduced themselves as brothers; Joe and Phil from Miami. The four of us worked steady for the better part of an hour and finally had all of the flashlights picked up. Amazingly, only a hand full were damaged so bad that they couldn't be used. The young soldier threw them in the cab of the truck. He closed up the boxes he opened and hammered them shut. We stacked the good boxes on the flatbed, covered them with the tarp and tied them down.

"Where you taking these?" one of the brothers, Joe, asked.

"To Fort Kingston, just another thirty miles away," the soldier stated.

"Is it near New Holland?" I asked.

"Yes, Sir. Right outside of town about three miles," he replied.

"Well, you almost made it unscathed," Joe said.

"That's a lot of flashlights for one Army base. Planning a night time invasion?" Joe's brother, Phil, smirked with a big grin.

"Fort Kingston is an Army Supply Depot. These units are bound for places all over eventually," Mac stated. "I picked them up at the train station in Mobile," he explained further.

"Did you damage the truck any?" I asked.

"I don't think so. I will be going a little slower the rest of the way, though," he guessed. "Thanks for your help. I wish there was something I could do to repay you."

"No need. You serving your country is payment enough for us," Phil acknowledged.

"Thanks again. You guys have a nice trip," Mac said as he got in the truck and headed for home.

We watched him head out and returned to our own vehicles. Surprisingly, only two others had stopped in that time.

"Where are you two headed," I asked Joe.

"Miami. We operate a deep sea charter out of there. We have been over in the Bayou for a week checking out spots for maybe expanding our operation,' he informed me.

He handed me his business card and I read it.

J & P Deep Sea Charter, Miami was typed in bold letters. A telephone number was below the writing in one corner and their names were in the other—Joe and Phil Stafford.

"Nice to meet you. Thanks for your help back there. Have a nice trip," I told them as I got in my car.

They both acknowledged my departure with a wave of their hand and I joined the road and resumed my journey to New Holland.

I passed the Army truck about a mile down the road and honked and waved as I passed. Mac flashed his lights at me as I pulled ahead of him.

CHAPTER 17

The next morning, I had breakfast at a nice restaurant and filled up at a station that offered a car wash for an extra quarter with the fill up, so I gave the car its first official bath. After the detour yesterday, it could use it. After getting the car dried off, I headed for the main road and the white sand beaches of Haven City. I figured I could be there in about four to five hours. The blue skies of the south are sure pretty, I thought. I could get used to the warm climate, but the humidity may take a little longer to get accustomed to. I had never seen the ocean nor been on a beach of any kind, so I was looking forward to it. Not being familiar with the area, I figured it may take a week or two to locate the whereabouts of Frank if he was even anywhere around. A local motel or motor lodge would suffice for a place to rest and gather the needed information in my search. Hopefully, I wouldn't have to stay around long enough to get familiar with the humidity.

I had smooth travel the entire way. The new car was performing excellently. The radio stations were too far apart though, I decided. Miles on end with nothing but static on the radio is not a good background noise to drive with, so I drove with just my thoughts and the noise of the car the rest of the way. As I crested a hill in the road, the view of a lifetime appeared in front of me. I pulled over to the side of the road and got out of the car and just stood and stared at the most beautiful blue water I had ever seen. I was looking at the ocean for the very first time in my life. The white sand beaches were so pretty. The smell of the ocean was really strong and I couldn't wait to put my feet in the water.

I entered the city limits of Haven City with the sun almost directly overhead. I noticed the slogan at the bottom of the welcome sign; 'Home of the whitest sand on the Gulf Coast'. The temperature was pretty warm and I had noticed the high humidity in the air for the past several miles. I passed a spot where I could see the water and beach again and had to admit… the sign was the gosh-honest truth. The whitest sand on the coast was right in front of me.

Haven City was a tourist town. Little shops and boutiques were everywhere. The center of town had been closed off and made into one of those "pedestrian mall" places that I read about. No vehicles were allowed in the center of town and parking lots had been formed on three sides of the square. Stairways and steps led down to the beach in dozens of places. People walked anywhere they pleased; crisscrossing the area at any point they wanted and actually walking, standing and sitting in the middle of the former street. There was no danger of getting run over, obviously, so it was a safe practice. The long plaza had several little pockets where benches and tables were available for the guests of the city as well as the townsfolk. Large beach umbrellas provided shade for those places. I enjoyed the atmosphere and the uniqueness of the place.

There weren't a lot of young people around, I noticed, mostly older citizens shopping and chatting to one another. It was summer time, so school was out. I did notice a few kids with their parents further down the walkway. I ambled in and around various groups and gatherings and looked in the windows of the shops and glanced over things being displayed on the sidewalks outside the shops. I bought a bag of taffy for later in my room and stopped in at the drug store soda fountain for a cold drink. While standing in line to place my order, I noticed a young lad of maybe 10 lifting a wallet from an elderly gentleman. The man had purchased something and had laid his wallet on the counter after getting his money out and the boy grabbed it. The man had seen the act and reached out and grabbed the kid by the arm and snatched his wallet from the kid's fingers.

"Oh no you don't, you little urchin," the man said.

He loosened his grip just enough for the boy to jerk his arm away and hightail it out of the store on a dead run. Thoughts of my younger days came to mind. I could still hear and envision Mr. Carson yelling at me when I worked at the feed store. I figured this young man would be on the road to a life of crime if someone didn't straighten him out in a few years. I noticed something that caught my eye…the kid had a clover chain necklace around his neck.

That fact may not be significant to anything, but it got me thinking. I had showed Frank a long time ago how to make a clover chain. He was impressed with the procedure and had insisted that we make more than we needed for future jobs. I didn't check the freezer before I left, but I bet there was still clover chains inside. It was a wild guess, knowing that anyone could make a clover chain, but I wondered if Frank had taught this kid how to make them. I may be closer to finding him than I thought an hour earlier.

I took the long walk down to the beach in the early afternoon after a nice sandwich at a deli restaurant on the plaza. It truly was beautiful white sand. There were a number of people walking the surf's edge and a few walking very slowly and looking down at the sand as though they had lost something. It took a few minutes, but I soon realized that they were looking for seashells.

As I walked, I looked out on a really blue ocean. Breakers were calmly rolling in and birds were soaring overhead. A family with two kids and a dog were flying a kite down the beach aways and the dog appeared to be barking at the kite. The two little girls were enjoying the adventure and Mom was encouraging Dad in his efforts of keeping the kite in the air. By looking out over the area, I could understand the draw such places had on the human mind. It was serene and really peaceful. I wouldn't mind living here, I thought. I looked down the beach in the other direction and saw the boardwalk and in sight up behind it was a lighthouse. I walked that way.

I took off my shoes and socks and walked barefoot for a little ways and let the sand and saltwater wash between my toes. Looking back up the bank, it was a long hike up to the top, especially near the boardwalk where the lighthouse stood. The long winding pathway to the top near the lighthouse was dotted with people both going up and coming down. I met a young couple walking toward me carrying their shoes. The man had rolled up his pant legs and the woman had on peddle-pushers. I nodded to the man and he waved a hand in return. I noticed that the lady had a clover chain around her neck.

"Excuse me," I called back. "I noticed your necklace…would you mind telling me where you got it?" I asked.

The man was a little defensive at first, but stated that he had picked it up for his wife at a shop in the square. It only cost a nickel and she thought they were pretty, so she got one.

"Can you remember which shop it was?" I asked.

"It was at Thimbles Gifts, I think," he said.

"Yes, it was," his wife agreed.

She reached up and touched her necklace as if to make sure it was still there.

"Thank you," I replied, and walked on.

I decided to check out the shop and see what I could find out. I walked to the water, washed off my feet and put my shoes and socks back on. Unfamiliar with the procedure, I lost my balance and fell to one knee, getting my pants wet. I was laughing at myself on my way back up to my car. I drove back to my room with ideas of getting down to business as soon as possible. I changed into a fresh pair of pants and returned to the square to find Thimbles Gifts and inquire about the necklaces.

The lady behind the counter of the shop was a young blonde girl with glasses. She reminded me of Brenda from the Clarkston County Bank in Clarkston. But, that's impossible, I thought; Clarkston is miles away. It can't be her, just someone that looks like her. I saw the small display of clover chains and asked her about them. She told me that she made them. She had seen one where she used to work and thought they were really neat, so she tried making one and it was easy. When she moved here, she got the job in the shop and being a trinket, knick knack and gift store, she thought the necklaces would fit right in.

"Don't you think they look a lot like shell necklaces?" she asked.

"I suppose you could see them that way," I replied.

"Customers seem to like them, and for only five cents, it's a good buy. I just wish they lasted longer," she rambled on. "I make up about a dozen or two a week."

"They're flowers, aren't they?" I asked quizzically as if I knew nothing about them.

"Yes, they are," she answered. "I pick them in a field not too far from where I live."

"You make these other flower arrangements too?" I asked as I motioned to the array of arranged flowers and weeds.

"Yes. I love to arrange flowers and play with that sort of thing. My aunt tells me I come by it naturally because that is what my mom always did. She was a florist at a store here once, but it got destroyed by a hurricane," she talked leisurely.

"Mind telling me where you moved here from?" I asked. "I once saw a girl that looks like you in a town I used to live in," I told her.

"Really?" she blushed. "I kind of doubt it, because I worked in a bank in a town named Clarkston; many miles from here, I'm afraid. The bank got robbed and I was let go by the manager saying I wasn't cut out to be a banker," she said. "Oh, by the way, that is where I saw the clover chain. I guess the robber dropped it," she explained. "I got my severance pay, bought a bus ticket here and found a job and a place to stay," she went on.

I was totally flabbergasted. The impossible had happened. This girl was the same one. She obviously didn't recognize me, which was a good thing, so I decided to play like I was seeing her for the first time.

"Sorry to hear that. No, you're right, it couldn't be you. The girl I remember worked in a restaurant," I lied. "Where's your family?" I asked as a second thought.

"I lost my parents in a fire when I was three years old," she answered. "My Aunt Beth and Uncle Melvin took me in and raised me. My aunt said that my brother was put in a foster home the year before the fire because he was a problem child and my parents couldn't do anything with him. I don't remember him and have no idea where he is today or even if he is still alive. When I turned 17 a year ago I moved out of my aunt's place and got a job at the bank. Now I'm here," she explained.

"I'm sorry about your family," I said. "What was your brother's name?"

"Owen. I don't know much about him and can't remember him at all," she confessed as her voice trailed off.

"Nice necklaces," I said, changing the subject.

"Yeah, they are, aren't they?" she agreed, returning to the present.

"Maybe I will see you around," I said as I left the shop.

"I would like that. Come by anytime," she called.

I left the shop with my mind racing like a fan blade on an engine. It's Brenda; the same cute young blonde at the Clarkston County Bank. Wow! This is amazing. I wonder if she is seeing anyone. Could it be that we were meant to be together? I was never one to believe in fate, but I could start. I'll have to ask her out. Oh man, this could be neat-o. If I can find Frank and if he still has the money and I can find it and if Brenda and I can get together and we can marry and move away to a deserted island or a foreign country we could live happily ever after and,...the thoughts just kept coming all the way to my car and to the motel that I was staying at. I lay down on the bed and drifted to sleep with wonderful thoughts of me and Brenda

I woke up and it was dark outside. I looked at my watch and it was after 10 p.m. I got up and walked outside and breathed in the fresh salt air. It was real pleasant, temperature wise, and the slight ocean breeze was playing with the loose papers and small trash close by, causing little whirlwinds. I walked through some of the town on my way toward the beach. All of the stores were closed and the breeze was blowing a few shop signs back and forth. I found a picnic table on the bank above the beach and sat down and looked out over a pale moonlight reflection glancing off the water. The plaza shops were about fifty yards away to my left. A lone beachcomber made his way toward the lighthouse. The light from the lighthouse moved across the breakers and the boardwalk every thirty seconds or so and the whole scene was a peaceful setting. I then saw a few couples walking the beach to my right and a beach fire glowed some distance away. I looked up into the sky and saw the flashing lights of a plane overhead. That brought back the conversation with "Jake" about flying instead of driving. I really did figure that Frank flew here rather than drive. It would fit him to a tee. He never really liked to drive, anyway, so why would he drive the many miles to here if he didn't have to.

I had to formulate a plan in finding Frank and hopefully the money. I couldn't believe that Frank would put the money in a bank. I was convinced that he had never used a bank...at least while I lived with him...and that the money was very possibly in the ivory colored suitcases. I was certain that he would put them in a locker, or a closet, or the trunk of a car, or maybe bury them somewhere. Burying them would be simple I would think, just a bit awkward when you needed to dig them up to get some spending money. Privacy would be a must and most of the beaches were not private, so another area would have to suffice. Sand is easy to dig in, but it being unstable, maybe a more solid area would be better. Regular dirt would work, I thought, and rocks could be used to mark the spot; like the buried treasure in a storybook. There were literally thousands of places where buried treasure could be hidden. I vowed to look at every conceivable spot I could think of and find the money. Money that rightfully was part mine. If I could find it, I would take it all as punishment for what he did to me. In reality, I may have to stick around here for quite some time waiting until Frank either showed his face or I could find his stash. I sure hoped he was still in the area. But, if Brenda and I could get together, the wait may not be so bad. I walked back to my room with some pleasant thoughts about us and what the future may hold.

My room was one in a motor lodge on the south part of town. When I arrived from the north, I slowly drove through town and saw the shops that lined the main street. I didn't know then that those same shops were open to the pedestrian mall on the other side, facing the ocean. The street to the lighthouse and parking lots branched off from the main street and passed the upper end of the mall shops. When I got to the sign that gave the mileage to the next town, I figured I better stop and get a room, so I rented one for a month at White Surf Lodge.

Over the next few days, I made it a point to stop in at Thimble's Gifts and see and talk to Brenda. I learned her full name (Brenda Pearson) and told her mine and we talked in generalities each time I visited. I really liked her and wanted to find out how she got here from Clarkston.

"Do you take a lunch break?" I asked.

"Sure. My boss insists I take an hour each day, except when she's not here, of course," she replied.

"Maybe we can have lunch sometime," I suggested.

"Anytime," she said enthusiastically. "Most any day is okay," she said a little more cautiously.

"How about tomorrow?" I asked.

"Tomorrow will be fine," she blushed a little as she answered.

Brenda and I had lunch on the beach. We sat on a blanket and ate fish and chips that I purchased from Ian's Fish Bar (a walk-up stand near a set of stairs to the beach) and shared a cola drink. She sure was pretty. Her shoulder-length blonde hair was pinned up on the sides with barrettes that had butterflies on them. She wore a pretty lavender dress with small white flowers on it that tied in the back and had a white sweater over her shoulders. She confessed that she loved the ocean and that her lifelong dream was to live near it. Her aunt and her mom were sisters and they lived in Haven City when they were young before better paying jobs for their dad moved the family down the coast to Blister Cove. (That name rang a bell, I thought, and then remembered it being mentioned by the trucker at the diner.) Her mom was older than her aunt by four years and got married and had kids before her sister did, moving back to Haven City with her new husband (Brenda's dad, whom she can't remember at all, and just has glimpses of memory of her mother). She was told that her mom's first husband and father of her brother passed away and was not told any of the details.

"My aunt had pictures of my mom and dad, but that's all the memory I have of either of them," Brenda confessed.

Her aunt and uncle moved west due to her uncle getting a job as a mechanic in a factory. After the fire killed her parents, they took Brenda in and raised her. Her aunt had shared a lot of stories about the area over the years about the seaside and especially Haven City where she and her mom were raised. Most of the memories about her parents are from stories told by her aunt. She only mentioned her brother occasionally if at all. According to her aunt, he wasn't a very nice boy, anyway. Brenda went to school in Clarkston and got the job at the bank right after she graduated from Clarkston High. With no job and a desire to live by the ocean, she made her way back to the place where she was born.

"I have always dreamed of moving back here and living on the coast," she confessed.

She said she had visited the site of the fire. From the description given to her by her aunt, she located the old neighborhood and discovered that it had been torn down after sustaining horrific damage when hurricane force winds swept through the area almost 12 years ago. The whole area had been rebuilt into what is now part of a large medical center. She was told by her aunt that she nearly died in the fire that claimed her parents, but some heroics by a fireman saved her life. The local newspaper gave a very good depiction of what happened. Apparently, someone notified the brave fireman that a little girl (Brenda) was somewhere in the burning house. The fireman entered the blaze and called out for her several times. His keen sense of hearing detected a slight muffled whimper coming from a bedroom closet. Brenda had closed herself inside to escape the heat and flames. After an even lighter whisper (thought to be caused by Brenda losing consciousness) the fireman literally ripped the closet door off the hinges and carried her to safety. She was totally overcome by the smoke and passed out in his arms on the way out of the burning structure. She was resuscitated at the scene and spent the night in the hospital, but otherwise just fine. She never learned the man's name and even after many inquiries, it was never learned and the event is basically a vacant memory now.

"I asked Auntie Beth to inquire about the man through other channels, but she never did," Brenda said.

Afterward, anytime the subject was brought up, her aunt would quickly change the subject or down play the whole thing as one of life's fates. The cause of the fire was never discovered. Arson was ruled out and the incident was finally logged as accidental. A few years later, a letter was forwarded to her aunt and uncle from the State Fire Marshall signifying that the fire was indeed accidental. Today, the letter is the only article of proof anyone has that says the fire actually took place. Brenda took it from her aunt's papers and has it in her possession. The foster home is gone now, too; it was also in the neighborhood that was destroyed by the hurricane.

I told Brenda that I once knew a guy that shared some of the same experiences she revealed. He was raised in a foster home and said he was responsible for burning down a house that his parents lived in. He too hoped to some day live on the beach. I told her that this was my first ever sighting of the ocean and besides a bath, the pot holes near my home were the closest thing to water I had ever been to. She recalled some pot holes near her home, too, but she had never been to them. I mentally kicked myself for almost letting the cat out of the bag about my past. She obviously meant the pot holes in nearby Jasper.

"I was told that there were a few over near the place that Uncle Melvin worked at," she stated.

I vowed to watch things a little closer and not reveal too much. I would have to improvise and embellish my stories carefully so that she wouldn't be able to tie me to any wrongdoing. I learned that she was 19 years of age and lived alone in a furnished house she was renting. Her favorite color was pink and her pet peeve was people who pretended to be someone they're not. When I heard that I just about swallowed my tongue.

"So, what brought you here, Adam?" Brenda asked.

"Please, it's A.D. Call me A.D," I requested.

"Okay, A.D…what brought you here?" she repeated.

I told her I was looking for a new adventure and I wanted to start over. She didn't know that she was older than me, because I let her think that I was older than her. I told her that I had not intended to stay very long here, but meeting her had changed my mind.

"Good. I like that," she said. "You could look for work around here if you've a mind to. There are plenty of jobs to be had."

"I could do that," I agreed. "Would you like to go to the drive-in movie tonight?" I asked, changing the subject.

"I would love to," she smiled.

She didn't know that I did not intend to look for work unless I couldn't find the money. Perhaps a little entertainment in the meantime would satisfy both of us.

She asked her boss if she could take the afternoon off and the request was granted. We spent several hours together on the beach. We walked up to the boardwalk and circled back into town and talked the whole time. She pointed out the lighthouse and several nearby sights as we walked up the boardwalk. I figured she would make a great tour guide. The lighthouse sat high on a cliff above the beach and was surrounded by jagged rocks and big boulders. A long and winding path serpentined up the cliff and ended right next to the lighthouse. The lighthouse sat a ways out from the street with a long sidewalk leading to it. It was rectangular in shape at the bottom and then round from about twenty feet up to the light itself, probably another fifty or so feet up. The light had to be 60-70 feet in the air I guessed. A large gift store sat in front and to the side of the lighthouse and sold souvenirs associated with lighthouses and the beach. A seafood restaurant was on the other side of that and appeared to be the end of town, because houses were on both sides of the road afterwards and the side street joined up with the main road in another block or so. Brenda said the main floor of the lighthouse was used as a tourist attraction and had a display that changed with the seasons. It was arranged by some ladies every so often, one of which was her boss. I learned that the caretaker lived on the second floor and owned the gift shop.

"Mr. Gunther has been sick I think, or has gone away for a spell. I'm not sure. Anyway, there is a stranger in town that is filling in and taking care of the place. I think he might be worth a lot of money because he drives a really pretty and expensive convertible. I've never seen him up close, but of course he's only been here for a few weeks," she explained. "He helped my boss and her friends arrange the latest display. Shall we go take a look?"

"I'd love to, but let's leave it for another time. We better get ready to go to the movie," I said.

I found out where she lived and we set a time to go to the movie. A western, starring Steve Hutchinson as Wild Bill Cody was showing on the big screen. I was to pick her up at her house at 8:00. I walked back to my car in the parking lot thinking about what I would say or do on our date. I was proud that I actually had the courage to ask her out...this would be my very first date ever. I knew I would be nervous and I figured I would probably not see much of the movie; I would be too distracted.

Over the next few weeks, I spent a lot of time looking around the area for Frank. Haven City is a fairly large town and covers a lot of area. I think I covered the majority of it in about a week of searching. I thought I spotted Frank once near the path to the lighthouse, but when I got closer, I called out to him and whoever it was, just turned and walked away back toward town. I figured the person either didn't hear me over the roar of the surf, or ignored me as just another tourist seeking information. I saw the convertible Brenda spoke of...it was a foreign job a lot like the little fancy one we rented the time Frank got shot. It had Florida plates on it, though, so I figured if it was his, it was rented. He could certainly buy one, I figured. With the money he had from the café heist, he could afford it. But, if he flew in to the area, he probably rented a car for the time being. I would if I were him. I decided to keep an eye on the car and discover who owned it.

I thought about walking out to the lighthouse and seeing the display Brenda mentioned and look around, but decided not to, maybe later. It would be more fun with her anyway. I would have to remember to ask her if she had ever seen the substitute caretaker and compare the description to what I know Frank looks like and see if they could be the same person.

I drove out to the main highway and drove down the coastline road for a few miles, just looking and thinking. The houses were sparse that way and very little beach activity going on because the rocks come back down to the water's edge and the beach disappears. A few scuba divers or snorkelers may search the waters for shells or treasure every now and then, I supposed, but for the most part, I figured it stays deserted. The drive was pleasant and the view was breath-taking. I figured I could really get use to life on the beach. I stopped at a roadside monument of some kind and just looked out over the Gulf. Thinking back over the past few weeks and taking assessment of what had transpired, I had to believe that Brenda and I were meant to meet up. I still believe Frank is in Haven City and I believe with all my heart that he has a lot of money with him. I need to be patient and careful, however, because things could escalate the other direction pretty fast. I had to find him before he discovered that I was in the area looking for him.

When I returned to town, I parked the car at the motor lodge and walked down to the beach. The area of beach above the lighthouse stretches out farther than the other direction by several hundred yards. It is a lot wider and the majority of beach activity is in that area. A roped off portion of the water is for swimmers and the rougher area further up from the lighthouse is where some try their hand at surfing. I looked at a lot of people on my walk and tried to see their faces whenever I could, but didn't see Frank. I spotted a person sitting in a low beach chair quite aways up the beach and all alone. I wandered that way thinking it could be Frank. It was definitely a man and he was either asleep or reading because he had his head down with his chin almost touching his chest. When I got within a few yards, he looked up and I knew immediately that it wasn't Frank.

"Hey there! Sorry to wake you. You reminded me of someone I know from a distance and was just checking it out," I apologized to the man as I walked up to him.

"No apology necessary. It's a free country," the man said.

He was a lot older than Frank. He looked to be in his seventies, maybe eighties. His hair was snow white under his hat and his several days' worth of stubble was white as well. A fishing rod and a tackle box were next to his chair.

"Been doing some fishing?" I asked.

"The bite's off today; just relaxing more than anything. Maybe I'll try again tomorrow," he stated.

"I guess being retired you don't worry about not getting any fish today because you can always go fishing tomorrow, huh?" I commented.

"Son, the only thing I worry about is whether the tide hits my chair," he said.

"I understand what you mean there," I replied with a laugh.

I left him alone and walked back down the beach and wondered again about my own retirement. I never did get shot at or wounded in all of the jobs I did. And not having to spend my life in jail meant that I just might see retirement some day. I guess I could hope for that time, anyway. I envisioned me and Brenda together in our eighties with her having white hair and me as bald as a billiard ball. I shook my head to clear that thought. I moseyed back toward the town square and spent a little bit more time looking for Frank and then decided to give it a rest.

I visited with Brenda every day and got to liking her more and more. We had lunch together often, ate out a few times and had supper at her place on several occasions. She was a good cook and enjoyed teaching me my way around the kitchen. I could cook a few things, but she instructed me on a few finer points in the task. She was a real neat house keeper and she loved to lounge around and just chat or snuggle, and we did a lot of both. I shared with her a little of my background, just left the crime spree out of the stories. I learned a lot more about her and discovered she loves to laugh. She has one of the prettiest smiles I have ever seen. Her beautiful white teeth were straight and even and the small dimple in her left cheek appeared even deeper when she smiled. We got along really well together and I started fantasizing about the possibility of us making another *Bonnie and Clyde* duo. She was used to the banking procedure and I had the experience. Heck, just a few jobs would set us up for life. No, I thought, I couldn't do that to her even if she was interested in trying it. If we were to have a life together, I would either have to get a good paying job or find the money that Frank took from me. If I found the money, how I would explain my sudden wealth to Brenda was a mystery. I could never tell her how I came by it I didn't think. I began to think that I was falling in love with her, though, and that could complicate matters.

One afternoon while I was waiting for Brenda to get off work, I moseyed around a few of the shops in the area and saw something that jogged my memory. In the little shop called

The Sand Piper, several souvenir luggage tags were displayed on a board and a picture showed one hanging from an ivory colored suitcase. My mind immediately jumped to the suitcase in Frank's room and the luggage tag I found on the floor. I could picture the name and address, but it was not clear. I recalled what looked like an H and an O and wondered if it could indeed be HC for Haven City. I couldn't recall the numbers, but thought they too could have been mistaken for other ones. I made a mental note to search the city for Atlantic Street and see if I could be in the exact place that a Grace Miller lived?

Brenda and I did some shopping when she got off work and she noticed that I was a bit preoccupied. Several times she asked me about my day and I didn't answer her. She brought me out of my haze with a slap on the arm and asked me where I was.

"A penny for your thoughts," she said.

"Just thinking about us," I lied.

"What about us?" she asked

"I was just thinking how nice it would be for us to spend the rest of our lives together," I lied again, but closer to the truth than the first one.

"Oh?" she quizzed. "Are you thinking of proposing or something?" she teased.

I turned as red as a beet and felt the heat, so I tried to conceal my embarrassment by changing the subject.

"Do you want to go look at that dress in Hafner's?" I asked.

"Don't try to change the subject, A.D. Cooper, you tell me right now what you're thinking," she blurted.

"No, really," I stammered. "I just think it is something that we should talk about sometime," I excused.

"I don't know you very well, A.D. I don't know anything about your background, where you lived, your folks, your family, your wants and wishes. You want to tell me a little more?" she asked.

I launched into a story about me and my family and how we grew up and where. I was mixing the truth with fiction, lies and half truths throughout the entire explanation. I included the deaths of my dad and brother and how my older brother abandoned me. I made up the story part of where I worked and what I did so that she wouldn't catch on to what I really did.

"There; now can we talk about our future and what we plan to do the rest of our lives?" I asked after my dissertation.

"I would love to spend the rest of my life with you. Do you love me?" she asked.

"I think so," I said hesitantly. "I am not sure what it is, but I sure like you a lot," I went on.

"I know that I love you, but let's think about it for a while and then decide," she wisely suggested

"Okay!" I said quickly as if to get a different subject matter started. "Now can we go look at a dress for you?" I asked.

We started walking to Hafner's Clothing Store and I was more occupied than ever with the conversation that we just had. She says she knows that she loves me. Is the feeling I have in my stomach and the tingle that I get every time she touches me, love? I'm feeling it right now just holding her hand. But, what about Frank and my pursuit for him and the money? Can I do both? I guess I will just have to work it out. I certainly don't want to give up this relationship…no way. Maybe I can have both and work it so that they don't conflict, especially when we are together.

I had lived a lie for over three years, but lying to Brenda made me feel really cheap and dirty. I avoided subjects now that would require me telling another lie, but knew that some day, I would have to either come clean and confess as to what kind of life I led prior to meeting her or continue to lie with the possibility of losing her forever. Old lady Nora Jenkins came to mind and the conversation we had when she warned me to always be truthful with the one you love.

"My aunt would kill me if she knew I had a man living with me." Brenda stated. "I was taught to only give the one you marry your love and devotion," she continued. "But, I don't care what she thinks, I love you and I want to marry you. Us living together just makes sense to me. Besides, you can't live in a motel all your life, huh?" she reasoned.

After three weeks of dating and seeing one another every day, Brenda suggested that I stay the night with her after our date and I did. We had made love only once before (our very first ever) but I went back to the motor lodge that time. She suggested that I move in to her house and us live together, so I did.

"No sense in you spending money on a motel when you can live here for free," she announced.

The next day, I checked out of the motor lodge where I was staying and moved in to her house. I knew what she was saying about us living together to be true because my mom preached the same thing to all of us. I wasn't raised as spiritually as Brenda was, obviously, but although we weren't heathens, we sure weren't saints. I didn't have a problem in living with her. It was sure a lot more convenient and cheaper too. This way, I could search around during the day for Frank and use the house as a sort of headquarters.

The dishes were done and Brenda had assembled about a dozen clover chains one evening and joined me on the couch. We were holding hands and listening to music on the radio when Brenda told me her thoughts.

"Did you ever wish you could just snap your fingers and money would suddenly appear?" she asked. "I wish we had a fairy godmother or genie to grant our wishes. Don't you?" she continued.

"Whatever are you talking about?" I asked.

She wasn't making any sense and it bothered me just a bit that she seemed concerned about money.

"I was just wishing that we could start that *'live happily ever after'* story book dream right now and not have to wait for it to happen," she explained.

"I used to have a little bit of money put away for a rainy day," I began. "But, like I said, my ex-partner took it all. Maybe some day I can dig up some for us to live on and then we can begin to *live happily ever after*," I told her.

"Like a sunken treasure?" she teased.

"Aye Matey. A hidden treasure it is," I returned, trying to talk like a pirate.

We both laughed. Little did she know that I was speaking the truth for the most part. I was sure the money was hidden, and if I could find it, her wish of being granted lots of money would come true.

We embraced and kissed before she went to the bedroom to get ready for bed. I walked out onto the back porch and looked out toward the ocean. The light from the lighthouse was moving in its wide arc across the water and the sound of the surf in the distance was soothing to the ear. Suddenly, arms encircled me and I could feel bra-less breasts pressing into my back. Brenda was in her night-gown and moved to my side and joined me in looking out over the view.

"Did you ever get up to the lighthouse and see the display?" she asked.

"Not yet," I answered. "Maybe I will tomorrow."

"No hurry; I just thought you might want to see it before it changes. Grace is pretty proud of it," she said.

"Who?" I asked.

"Grace Miller, my boss. I told you that she and some of her friends arrange the display in the lighthouse every so often," she explained.

"Oh yeah, I remember you saying that," I commented.

My mind almost snapped with the sudden realization that this could be the same person that had her name on the suitcase in Frank's room. Where did she fit into Frank's life?

"How did she get started doing that?" I asked. "Do you help with it?" I continued.

"No, I don't help, silly; it's the old ladies that do it. The town folk call them the *'Old Ladies Society'* because of their age. I think Mrs. Miller is in her late 70's. She says she will retire and sell the store someday," Brenda stated. "I don't know much about her, but before she bought the shop, she used to have a foster home, supposedly, but the state made her stop, due to her age. The foster home is gone now. It also was damaged in the hurricane and had to be totally demolished. Folks here say that the boy that burned our house down was one of her foster kids, the one I told you about. I once asked a few questions of her about her former life, but she can't remember much about it due to a fall she had some time ago. Apparently, she hit her head in the fall and got a concussion. Her memory was already a little suspect, but hearing that, helped explain a few things," she laughed.

My mind again went speeding around all the information being received and trying to make sense of it. I now have heard two stories from two different people that had so many familiar happenings; it's all a little spooky.

First of all, Frank said he was raised in a foster home; he was placed there by his family; his family was killed in a fire that he set; and he had a sister that he says died in the fire too.
Brenda was rescued from a fire that killed her parents.
Her brother was put in a foster home and she lived with her aunt.

She has lost all contact with her brother and has no idea of his whereabouts.

Luggage with the name Grace Miller was in Frank's possession.

Mrs. Miller is Brenda's boss and she was possibly Frank's foster mom that he stole the luggage tag from.

Frank's favorite place was the white sand beaches of Haven City.

The lighthouse has a temporary custodian that could be Frank.

There were way too many facts for it all to be considered coincidences, I think. And if I was thinking straight, I am in the presence of Frank's sister. Oh my God, could it be that Brenda and Frank are brother and sister?!

The look on my face must have shocked her because she slowly and hesitantly touched my face.

"Are you okay? You look like you just seen a ghost," she stated.

"Yes, I'm okay, just a little light headedness, suddenly. I'll be fine," I quickly stammered.

I don't know if she bought it or not, but I walked back inside and went to the bathroom. She followed me into the house and sat at the table waiting for me to return. I sat on the toilet and thought about what I had just learned. Brenda doesn't know her brother is here, if indeed he is. She doesn't know or suspect that Frank was in Mrs. Miller's foster home. Just as she has no idea that it was me that robbed her bank and got her fired, she has no idea that her brother was my partner in robbing it. Her own brother killed her parents and thinks he killed his sister in the fire.

"Good God Almighty," I thought; "What if it's true? And if it is, how am I going to handle it?"

"I thought you were going to bed," I said to her when I entered the kitchen.

"I'm worried about you. Are you sure you're okay?" she asked, truly concerned.

"I'm fine, Brenda, really. I'm sorry if I scared you," I apologized and gave her a hug.

"Well, you did," she said. "Don't do that again," she warned as she slapped my back.

"I promise," I assured her.

"Well, I have to go to bed. Are you coming?" she asked.

"Not right now. I'll be along soon. Goodnight," I replied as I kissed her.

After she had closed the bedroom door, I started thinking of a way I could prove my suspicions. The fact that Frank's last name was Epperson and Brenda's was Pearson was due to her mom remarrying, no doubt, but she said her brother's name was Owen. That's not even close to Frank. Of course Frank could be a middle name, like Franklin. I figured there was close to five, maybe six or seven years between her and Frank's ages, so that portion of the story could very well be true. Perhaps I can find someone in town that can confirm my suspicions and put an end to the mystery. I still was confused about how the two of them wound up in the same area of the country, although that could be total coincidence.

I went to bed with my mind a mess thinking of all the scenarios. Brenda didn't wake up when I got into bed, but she rolled over and caressed my body and stayed close to me. My mind was spinning with all of the information I had garnered in the last few hours and wondered if I would sleep. I had a lot more thinking to do and was now more determined then ever to find Frank and locate the money. I finally fell asleep with Brenda's hand lovingly placed on my chest.

CHAPTER 18

    I made an earnest effort to find Frank over the next few days. If he was here in Haven City, I was determined to find him. I remembered an exercise that one of my teacher's suggested to the classroom…make a *'To Do'* list of the things that need done and rank them as to their importance. When they are accomplished, mark them off. I made the list and then I began to tick them off as I ruled them in or out of the equation. Once I had covered the list, I checked it again for oversights and decided if it was relevant or not. The one that stood out the most was the Atlantic Street address. I also had not visited the lighthouse display, but didn't give that one a lot of credence. The man I yelled at that day near the lighthouse did give me concern, though, because that just may be Frank. I had to check that possibility out right away. The other one that stood out like a beacon was the new dress for Brenda. I intended to buy it for her, just hadn't done so. I vowed to do just that and soon.

    I inquired at the filling station about Atlantic Street and was told that it no longer exists. The area where it was is now part of the medical center. The station attendant was a talkative type and while standing in the bay, I asked a few questions about the hurricane and the area where it hit. I told him that my girlfriend once lived here and after being gone for a number of years, returned to find the place totally changed.

    "When that hurricane hit, the whole town figured we would all be wiped out, but it just sort of swept up that way and destroyed everything in its path," the older gentleman explained while pointing toward the medical center.

"Did you know the Pearson family?" I asked.

"Sure did. Patrick and Sue were friends of mine. How do you know them?" he asked.

"They were the parents of my girlfriend," I said.

"Brenda? How in the heck is she doing? I was her godfather prior to the fire, and then her Aunt Beth took her in. I haven't seen her since," he confessed with excitement in his voice.

"She's fine. She just lives right up there on Blake Street," I said as I pointed in that direction.

"I'll have to go up and see her. Has she told you about the fire that almost took her life?" he asked.

"Yes, I know about it. It's a long gone memory though. She was only three, you know?" I replied.

"Oh I know very well, young man. I was on the fire department at the time and helped douse the blaze. That was one hot fire. I wish we could have saved Pat and Sue, but due to that heat, we couldn't. We barely got Brenda out," he said. "I still believe that no-good brother of hers was responsible."

"You mean Owen?" I asked.

"Yes. He changed his name to Frank when he got put in the foster home. He was born as Owen Franklin Epperson. Sue was married briefly right after high school to a soldier named Franklin Epperson. He was killed in the line of duty and never saw his son. Sue remarried a few years later to my friend Pat and they had that sweet little girl. Owen became a rebellious no-good. He became a real trouble maker and was in hot water all the time. They did everything imaginable to rectify the problem, but in the end, they had to place him in a foster home," the older man related. "Excuse me, I have a customer. Be right back," he commented and left the bay.

I thought to myself that things were as I suspected. Frank and Owen were one in the same and he was definitely Brenda's brother, although he was a step-brother. The story he told matched up pretty close to everything else related.

"Brenda's rescuer that night of the fire; did you know him?" I asked when the older man returned.

"Yes. Why do you ask?" he inquired.

"She says that no one could remember who it was. They tried a number of times to find out, but have never been able to," I told him.

"He sustained burns on his body that he never recovered from. He died about two weeks later in the hospital. His name was Hank O'Hara. He was a single man from down around Fort Myers. His body was returned to his hometown for burial," he revealed.

I thanked the man for his time and information. I had proven the majority of things and now knew truth from fiction. The older man's story was proof that Brenda's information about the hurricane destroying that section of town was correct. I was anxious to tell her that I found out the name of the fireman that rescued her.

I drove over to the area that the man described and found the medical center...a huge area with multiple buildings that housed pharmacies, doctors' offices, medical labs, and several dentists' offices, too. Just a block away was the new hospital...a towering ten-story building that was the most modern facility in the area. The whole complex accounted for nearly a six-block area that used to be where Brenda's home was as well as where the foster home was. I mentally scratched that item off on my list.

"You'll never guess what I found out today, Brenda?" I started as we sat down for supper.

"That you're hopelessly in love with me and you can't wait to marry me and settle down," she teased.

"Well, I didn't have to find that out. I have already discovered that. Really, I found out the name of your rescuer from the fire," I stated as I put a fork full of food in my mouth.

Her face went solemn and her mood went down to match.

"What's the matter? You've never found out, you said. Don't you want to know?" I asked, concerned.

"It just conjures up bad memories, A.D., that's all," she divulged.

"Sorry, I thought you would want to know. Let's drop it, then," I suggested.

"Who told you?" she asked.

"The man at the service station. I didn't get his name. He said he was your godfather prior to the fire. Told me that he was friends with your parents," I revealed.

"Were you checking up on me?" she asked.

"No. He asked me if I was new in town and I told him I was staying with you. He volunteered everything else. Nice guy!" I told her.

"That had to be Wayne Mott. Aunt Beth told me about him. She said he's owned the station ever since it was built," Brenda recalled.

"You don't want to know the name of the fireman, then?" I asked.

"Not really. It's not that important to me anymore. You understand don't you?" she asked.

"Certainly," I stated.

The subject was dropped and we ate in silence with our own thoughts. I cleaned up the table and washed the dishes while Brenda dried them and put them away. We didn't talk a lot the rest of the evening and went to bed early.

During the weekend, I tricked Brenda into thinking that we were going for a stroll on the beach and got her to commit to a dress at Hafner's. It was a pretty teal summer dress with a huge pink and white gardenia encircling the majority of it. The flower covered most of the front and circled all the way around her left side and covered most of the back of the dress.

"What's wrong with the right side? It doesn't have any of the flower on it," I observed.

"Not enough sun hits it I guess," Brenda teased.

We both laughed and she went into the dressing room to try it on. She came out and modeled it for me; I fell in love all over again. Wow, was she a beauty in it.

After the purchase, we were both in a great mood, so we had an ice cream sundae at the ice cream parlor, then I asked if she would mind showing me the display at the lighthouse. She gladly agreed and we walked up to the lighthouse holding hands and almost skipping along like a couple of school kids. The room where the display was located was a forty foot circle, I guessed. There were a few people in the lighthouse when we entered and I noticed immediately how the sound echoes around the room. The lighthouse was really old and smelled musty. The planks used for the flooring were old and worn. Several squeaked when they were walked on. Two portholes were used as windows, but appeared as though they wouldn't open. They did permit light to enter the dark room and assist the three light bulbs hanging from the high ceiling forming a triangle around the room.

Paintings hung on the walls depicting the beach from various artists' perceptions. A display of oranges and grapefruit was on one side of the room. The smell of the fruit mingling with the musty smell of age was not unpleasant, but unusual. A fake palm tree was in the center of the display and a few crates were scattered around. Unlike the tree, the fruit and the crates were the real thing. A harpoon and old spear gun were on display on one wall to the left of the front door and on the other side of the door were ropes, buckles and a large fishing net. The net had replicas of crabs and starfish hanging from it at various places.

Other fishing gear and related items were scattered around the rest of the rooms' walls.

In the center of the room was the display that Brenda referred to. The display was on a raised platform about 6 inches off the main flooring and about 12-feet wide and 8-feet deep. It faced the front door and was positioned so that it was very noticeable. It consisted of four mannequins representing a family on vacation. The boy was standing in front of the man mannequin wearing blue shorts with a blue and white Hawaiian shirt and barefooted. The girl was standing between the man and woman mannequin, dressed in pink shorts with a pink and white striped shirt and sandals. The man was standing very erect dressed in tan Bermuda shorts with a brown Hawaiian shirt and loafers. The lady was seated on a suitcase in white shorts and a red blouse and white sandals. The entire *'family'* had leis around their necks and the man had a box camera hanging from his shoulder.

The boy was holding the pull strings of a yellow and white canvas beach bag that was sitting in the white sand; neatly arranged to compliment the display. A Guinness Airways sign hung on a backdrop behind the family and in big letters it announced **"Fly to Hawaii"**. The whole scene was well done and well thought out. The ladies that built it were to be congratulated. The one thing that drew my attention however was what the lady mannequin was sitting on...an ivory colored suitcase sitting upright on the sandy floor. A similar suitcase was next to the man's leg. Sand had been piled up the side of it about four inches. I immediately thought of the missing suitcases from Frank's bedroom. Could they be one in the same? Would he be as bold as to hide the money in his suitcases and then put them in plain sight? Not a bad idea, really. After all, who would expect money to be in cases out in the open being used in a display? I decided to check it out for myself...after dark and when no one else was around.

I looked around the room for any sign of occupancy and noticed the most likely door to the caretaker quarters. I thought it very possible that Frank could be the temporary custodian of the lighthouse. How I was going to get confirmation of that feeling, though, was another thing. I couldn't just hang around the lighthouse all day waiting for him to show his face. But, a few things added up whereas he could certainly be the man. First of all, the suitcases could be his and secondly, the little fancy foreign car could easily be his as well. If in fact he's here, he is a bold man for returning to the scene of his most dastardly deed. I just bet he has no idea that his sister is also here. He thinks she's dead. I wondered how Brenda was going to handle that bit of news if and when she heard it. What if he has seen me in town and is planning to do something to me? I would if I were him and knew all the stuff about him. My mind was racing again with all the possibilities and I had to stop it before Brenda got worried about me again. We walked on around the room and out the door.

"What a great job on the display," I praised as we walked out of the lighthouse. "It makes a person want to go to the islands."

"They did a great job, didn't they?" she agreed.

I continued the conversation for more facts about my idea as we made our way to the gift store.

"Where do they get all of the items for the display?" I asked.

"I'm not sure. The mannequins could be from Hafner's or Trina's Togs and the clothes could be from either too, I would imagine," Brenda volunteered. "One of Mrs. Miller's friends owns Trina's store and is one of the group, so that makes sense. The travel agency probably provided the signs as well as the leis. I recall that sign, or one like it, hanging in the agency office.

I don't know about the suitcases, though, probably borrowed from one of the ladies," she guessed.

"How long has that *vacation* display been on show?" I asked.

"Oh, it was just done a short time ago. Not long before you came to town," she answered. "Mrs. Miller worked on it with the others for several nights I know."

I was asking to determine if by chance the suitcases were put on display about the same time Frank arrived on the scene. It appeared that that is what happened. I thought back about four weeks and figured that was about the time he would have arrived here. I thought maybe when the ladies came up with the idea for the display, they asked the man in the lighthouse for assistance and the suitcases were added to the scene for effect. He wouldn't have had a lot of time to hide them elsewhere and what a better way to hide them then right in plain sight? I could just imagine him volunteering to place the heavy bags on the sand. He would relish in that bit of chivalry. He may not be the temporary caretaker, but I would lay odds that he knows who is and is getting cooperation in providing a place to stay…if indeed he is staying at the lighthouse.

"What does the temporary caretaker look like, honey?" I asked

"I haven't seen him up close, so I don't really know. I have seen him get out of his little car and walk into the lighthouse though. He's a slight man of around 40 I'd say. He was wearing a hat, so it was hard to see his face," she decided.

That didn't give me a lot for comparison. True, Frank was not a very big man, but he wasn't close to 40, and he didn't wear hats. Or at least he didn't when we worked together. Still, it could be him, I thought.

I bought a small sailboat replica for Brenda to add to her small collection and we left the gift shop and headed for home by way of the beach. We arrived back at the house after dark and I fixed a bite to eat. While sitting on the settee after supper, Brenda curled up in a ball and dozed off. After I cleaned up the kitchen, I put on a stack of records on the hi-fi and listened to music for quite a while, thinking about how I was going to get the suitcases, check them out and get out of the place without being seen. Around 11:00, I awoke Brenda and got her to go to bed.

"Please set the alarm for me, would you?" she asked.

"Sure. Goodnight. I'll see you in the morning," I told her.

I covered her up and tiptoed out of the bedroom and closed the door.

I left the house and walked up to the lighthouse. There was not a lot of light emanating from around the area. An overhead street lamp shone dimly on the path to the front door and the trees nearby caused a shadowy effect. Several cars were parked near the curb on the tree lined street under the lamp. A little foreign car was among them. It certainly looked a lot like the little convertible we rented in New Brahms. I looked around for anyone that might be wandering by and seeing no one, I walked around the side of the lighthouse on the gift shop side and skirted the wall to the rocks. There were no windows or doors to be opened. A porthole window was too high to reach and another larger window was above it, probably in the caretaker's quarters. The electric meter and fuse box was attached to the wall on that side at about eye level. Huge rocks covered the remaining terraced slope to the beach.

    I returned to the front of the building and looked inside through the door window. A man walking his dog appeared up on the sidewalk and I froze and hugged the lighthouse wall trying to blend into the darkness. He didn't notice me, so I looked into the room again. I could see shadows of the display, but little else. I reached down to check the door knob and found it locked, but the door hadn't completely closed, so when I touched it, it came ajar. I froze and listened. Nothing. I looked around the area, glancing back up toward the street, but saw nor heard anything. I stepped around the side of the building to look down on the beach for any movement and there was none. I returned to the door and opened it a little more and stepped through into the room. I partially closed the door leaving it ajar just a hair. I tiptoed to the display, trying to avoid any squeaky boards beneath my feet, and carefully stepped up onto the sand covered area and removed the suitcase that was next to the man. It was heavy so I carried it with two hands to the open floor where a little better lighting from the door window would assist. I laid it down and released the latches as quietly as possible, slowly opening the lid. I caught my breath…two money bags were inside. Frank had not disappointed me. My calculations were correct. The stamp on both bags read; *Property of the U.S. Treasury*. My heart practically stopped.

    I quickly opened one of the bags and not only smelled the bills inside, but could see that it was full of money. I put it aside and quickly went over and took the lady off the other suitcase, gently laying her to the side. When I let go, her arm came loose from the shoulder and I almost dropped it. I laid the arm on the floor and took the suitcase to the open floor next to the other one and went through the same procedure. The second case seemed a little lighter than the first one. Perhaps Frank had used some of the money or put some of it in a different place.

I slowly opened the case and again found two bags of money. One had been opened, so I looked in and saw that nearly half of the bag was empty. Frank had definitely removed some of the money. From what I could see, the bills were in large denominations. I wanted to shout out with glee, but contained myself and got busy working on a plan to get the money out and leave the suitcases. I wanted to take the money and leave the display the way I found it. I looked around for something to put the bags in but couldn't see anything. I remembered the crates and walked around the display to the other side of the room and took one. All four bags fit in the crate like it was made for them.

Now, if I could just carry it out without waking the dead. I would need to get it somewhere so that I could go get the car and haul the bags away. I decided I would chance being seen and lug it up the walk to the street and leave it there while I went to get the car. I went to work replacing the display. The lady didn't want to cooperate in reattaching her arm, but I finally convinced her and got everything where it was suppose to be. I spread the sand around as close to what I could remember as possible, then scattered it to hide my foot prints, (being careful to stomp the sand off of my shoes), and left the building. I lugged the heavy crate for several steps, put it down and rested, then picked it up and hauled it a bit further. I was keeping a close eye on the sidewalk and the path leading up from the beach to avoid being seen. If I was caught, I would have to come up with something convincible quickly to hide my covert task. I made it up the path to the street finally, and was sweating like a pig from the effort. The area was deathly still and no movement from anyone anywhere. I noticed a trash can on the sidewalk next to the streetlamp and a shrub was right next to it. I figured it would be a perfect place to put the bags until I could come back with the car. I set the crate down next to the shrub. I pulled my shirt off and covered the crate with it.

I half walked, half jogged to the house and got the car. The ocean air on my bare chest felt good. The house was dark and to avoid any noise, I let the car roll out of the driveway and onto the street before starting it. I turned on the headlights and drove to the lighthouse. I pulled up to the lamppost and opened the trunk. I put my shirt back on and hefted the crate into the trunk and slammed the lid. I drove back to the house, locked the car and entered the house as if nothing had happened. I sat down on the couch and tried to plan my next move. Now that I had the money, I figured I needed to get out of here as quickly as possible to avoid being discovered or seen by Frank. How I was going to explain my sudden departure to Brenda remained a problem. I had the money that belonged to me. I had been very lucky and successful again in a heist. I felt good but anxious at the same time. I knew sleep would not come easy tonight.

I was still sitting on the couch when Brenda got up. It was 6:30. I had dozed on and off during the night, but nothing substantial. She asked about me and I said that I must have fallen asleep on the couch.

"Are you okay, A.D.? Is whatever happened last night still working on you?" she asked.

"Of course not. I am fine. I just fell asleep on the couch and slept here all night, that's all," I lied again.

"Okay. That was really weird, though," she commented.

"I think I will drive down the coast a ways today and look for work," I stated, changing the subject.

"Anything particular you're looking for?" she asked. "Blister Cove may have an opening in the bookstore," she suggested.

"Where'd you hear that?" I asked.

"Mrs. Miller mentioned it the other day when I told her you were looking for work," she volunteered.

"How far away is that?" I asked and remembered seeing it on the map.

"It's only about twenty minutes or so. It's the next large town down the coast line," she answered.

"Could you marry a man that worked in a bookstore?" I asked, teasingly as I wrapped my arms around her.

"As long as he read me a bedtime story every night, I wouldn't mind at all," she teased back and kissed me on the cheek.

She showered and got dressed, put on her make-up and came into the kitchen to make breakfast. I had put on a pot of coffee while she was in the shower and was looking for the bread when she came into the room.

"What are you looking for, A.D.?" she asked.

"The bread. I know you like toast and jam, so I was going to get it ready for you," I replied.

"How sweet of you. You might make some lady a great husband some day if you keep that up," she teased. "Its right here," she added as she opened a drawer and took out a loaf of bread.

We ate toast and drank our coffee and talked small talk for a few minutes. Brenda put the dirty dishes in the sink, cleaned off the counter and grabbed her bag to head out the door.

"Don't bother with those; I'll wash them up before I leave," I volunteered.

"Thanks. Will you be home when I get here tonight?" she asked.

"Of course," I said. "I don't think it will take me all day to look for work."

"I will try to think of something scrumptious to eat for supper," she stated.

"Whatever it is will be fine with me. I'm not real fussy when it comes to food," I stated.

I walked to the door with her and kissed her goodbye. She wished me luck and went out the door. Brenda didn't own a car. When I inquired about it earlier, she simply stated that she didn't need one. The few times that she did, she borrowed Mrs. Miller's.

"I can't afford one anyway," she had stated.

The shop opened at 9:00 and a sale was going on so she had to be there a little early. As I watched her leave, it suddenly struck me that I could not leave her in a lurch. I would somehow get her to marry me and together we could resolve this whole situation. I had to come up with a good one though, regarding the money. I still can't believe my luck there.

On the way down the coast, I passed a convoy of Army vehicles. Soldiers waved at me each time I passed one. Two trucks were loaded with olive-drab duffle bags and two soldiers were sitting on top of each of them as though claiming *King of the Hill*. One truck was pulling a water tank and another one was pulling a trailer with a jeep on it. The others had troops in them hanging out the back and sides and legs dangling all around. The canvassed covers kept the sun off of them during their trip and there were probably enough lies and tales being told to occupy their time the whole way. The commander jeep was out front with the company flag waving from a tall pole attached to the bumper. I didn't know where they were headed, but I didn't envy them one bit. If only they knew what I had in the trunk, I bet I could get every one of them to go AWOL. I grinned as I speeded up and passed the lead vehicle with a honk of my horn.

I got into Blister Cove and looked for a place to think. I found an off-the-road monument and parked there and sat on the bench provided. The monument depicted a sign with VFW (Veterans of Foreign Wars) on it and the little park setting was dedicated to them. A flag pole stood in the center of the park, however, there was no flag flying from it.

I decided that I needed to transfer the money from the bags to something else and ditch the bags somewhere. The crate could be disposed of fairly easily, I thought. If I was caught or found with the bags, I would have a lot of explaining to do. I could maybe shop for a bag big enough for all of the money. Or I could get a bag big enough for half of the money and stash the rest. Where that might be was a mystery in itself. What kind of bag would be big enough for all of this money? I also needed to come up with a way of telling Brenda how I suddenly became rich. I could say that a genie or fairy godmother was looking out for us. I could invent a story and tell her I located the pot of gold at the end of the rainbow. The story I told would need to be one that left no questions. After this whopper, I promise to never lie to her again. Of course, honesty was the best policy and Mrs.

Jenkins' sermon on the subject came to mind, but I didn't think I could be totally honest with Brenda without losing her for good. I definitely needed to think this problem through.

For some reason the military convoy that I passed on the road came to mind and I decided that I needed to find a duffle bag. Where was I going to find one? I wasn't planning on going into the service and didn't know anyone that had been in. Then I remembered the summer display where the money was...the beach bag. If I could find one, it would be perfect. I jumped in the car and headed for town. I searched the small shops in town looking for just the right thing. There were gift stores and souvenir shops all over and I saw two or three clothing stores, but no beach bags.

It was close to lunch, so I decided to grab a bite to eat and resume my search on a full stomach. A small café was nearby, so I stopped in and ordered a hamburger, fries and a cola. There were several patrons already seated and enjoying their meals. The place had a counter with six stools at it, all vacant, so I sat at the counter and looked at myself in the big mirror that covered the entire back wall. Drinking glasses and coffee cups were neatly displayed on several glass shelves attached to the mirror. A big clock was on the wall to the left of the mirror. The kitchen area was at the opposite end and a pair of saloon type doors separated the kitchen from the counter area. The place reminded me a little bit of the café with all of the religious folk.

"What will you have, young man?" the motherly waitress asked.

I ordered my meal and watched the other patrons in the mirror while I waited. It was a good burger, but I sure didn't need the onions. I made a mental note to remember to order my meals in restaurants without onions from now on.

I paid for my meal and walked out of the place determined to find a beach bag. I stopped in at two gift shops, thinking that I might get lucky, but found nothing that even resembled a beach bag. In the second one, I asked the clerk before I searched the store.

"Do you have beach bags for sale?" I asked the young lady clerk.

"No we don't. Sorry. Have you tried Glen's Surf Shop? They just might have what you're looking for," she volunteered.

"Thanks, I will try them. Can you point me in the right direction?" I asked.

"Oh, sure. I guess I just figured you knew," she stated.

When she walked out from behind the counter and walked to the front door, she reminded me of Molly. The seam up the back of her hose was just as straight as hers always was and she had legs to match. She walked out the front door and stood on the sidewalk and pointed toward the shop further down the street.

"Right there. See their sign?" she asked.

"I see it. Thank you," I said to her.

"You're very welcome. I hope you find what you're looking for," she said as she walked back into her store.

I walked to the shop and went in. I looked around the store and found beach umbrellas, sand buckets and shovels, surf boards, kites, beach blankets, and a whole section of swim suits. Still no beach bags. Then, in the corner of the store I found a shelf with three beach bags covered up with a beach towel that someone had thrown aside. Only two looked large enough to hold all of the money. The third one was definitely too small. Both were an off-white colored canvas bag with draw strings. One had a blue dolphin painted on it and the other one had an orange crab on it. I chose the one with the dolphin on it. Perfect, I thought.

    I returned to the roadside bench and made the transfer of the money to the new beach bag. It all fit nicely with enough room at the top to tie the draw strings tight. Now I just needed to dispose of the money bags and the crate and get back to Haven City. I tossed the empty bags in the trunk and carefully put the beach bag, now stuffed with banded bills, on the floor of the back seat. I drove through town and headed for the main road while thinking of a way to rid myself of the money bags and crate. The county garbage truck was making its rounds through the downtown area and a man was dumping cans of trash into the back of the truck. A light bulb went on in my head and thinking that the truck would be a great way to rid myself of the money bags, I followed the truck a ways. The man dumping the cans never was very far away at any time, so throwing the bags in the back of the truck was out of the question because the act would be witnessed. Too risky, I decided. I joined the main road back up the coast and headed for home thinking hard on a solution.

    I hadn't driven for more than a mile up the coast when I spotted the crew that picks up the trash at the state parks. They were driving their green truck to all of the roadside view spots as well as dropping down to the various beach spots that catered to tourists and visitors. I thought this one would be easier to utilize then the downtown truck. I drove ahead of them about a mile or so and stopped at a view spot that had a large viewing area and waited. I pretended to be reading while waiting for someone and looked at the little book that came with the car papers that were in the glove compartment. Soon, the truck pulled into the area where I was stopped and I looked up to see the men jump down from the cab to do their job. While they were walking away to retrieve the trash cans, I quickly jumped out of my car, grabbed the money bags out of the trunk and threw the bags in the back of the garbage truck and ran back to my car. I resumed my position of reading behind the wheel. The men did not see me. They finished up their chore and returned to the main road. I waited a minute or so and then drove out of the area; joined the main highway; and resumed my trip to Haven City.

———

I pulled into the driveway at the house, got out and locked the car door, and started running to Brenda's shop. I slowed to a walk once I entered the town square and caught my breath. I entered the shop and spotted her in the back stocking some knick knacks. Two ladies were in the shop looking at some costume jewelry and the display of clover necklaces. I walked back to where Brenda was and grabbed her, turned her around and planted a big kiss on her lips.

"What was that for?" she asked.

"We need to celebrate, honey, we have hit the jackpot," I whispered. "I dug up my buried treasure, matey," I hammed.

"What are you talking about? What jackpot? Where?" She kept asking questions quietly. "A.D. you're scaring me. Now quit being goofy and tell me what you're talking about?" she asked again.

"Can you get off right now?" I asked.

"We don't close for another hour, sugar, can it wait?" she answered and asked.

"I guess it will have to," I answered disappointingly.

"I have work to do, now go away and let me. I want to hear all about it, though, so be ready to tell me later," she demanded.

She sort of waved me off and waited on the ladies with answers to their questions. I walked out of the shop and wandered around the square and down to the beach. I looked up at the lighthouse and wondered how long it would be before Frank discovered the missing money. Hopefully, the ladies would leave the summer display up for a long time. I should have loaded the suitcases with something heavy to ward off the immediate suspicion when they were lifted…twenty-twenty hindsight, I figured.

I must have been gone longer than I thought, because just as I was walking up the steps from the beach to the square, Brenda practically knocked me down when she jumped into my arms.

"Whoa, missy," I shouted. "Where are you going?" I asked as I straightened myself up.

"Tell me, tell me, tell me," she insisted.

"Tell you what?" I teased.

"About the jackpot! How much did you get? How did you get it? Where did you get it? Oh, A.D. I'm so excited. Tell me," she ran all of her questions together in a rush.

"Slow down before you have a heart attack. I will tell you the whole story, believe me," I assured her.

We walked to the house and she was all ears. I told her to go in and change her clothes and I would tell her all about the newly found treasure. She went in the house and I retrieved the bag from the car and hauled it inside.

"What's in the bag, A.D.?" she asked as she emerged from the bedroom dressed in a pair of light blue peddle pushers and a pink t-shirt.

"The buried treasure I spoke of," I said. "But first, you have to hear what I have to say."

I was nervous and a little shaky. I had decided to tell her the truth and tell her my findings about her brother. She may not believe any of it and then again she may only believe portions of it, but I hoped she would want revenge just like me. I led her to the couch and with me standing, I started in. I began by reminding her of the person I spoke of earlier that had a similar experience as she did regarding the fire that destroyed her home. She nodded that she remembered, so I told her about Frank; how I met him and how I learned that he was her brother. I related the things that Mr. Mott at the station told me. I shared with her the information that Frank had shared about his childhood. I wondered how it was that the two of them happened to land in the same area, just a few miles apart. I briefly mentioned the gang and Mrs. Jenkins and Molly. I told her about the set-up where I was shanghaied and how Frank took money that I worked for and did not get. I confessed that my trip here was with motivation and meeting her was a blessing in disguise. I tied everything together for her with Mrs. Miller, the fire, the foster home and the luggage tag. I told her about finding the money in the display's suitcases and buying the beach bag. I left out the parts of robbing her bank and the fact that I was the one that got her fired.

"I know this is a lot for you to fathom in one setting, but what do you think?" I asked.

I hadn't been looking at her much during my tale, but instead, had been walking and pacing around the room while talking. I looked at her now after questioning her on what she thinks and tears were running down her cheeks. She had let me talk the entire time without interrupting and me being unaware of her physical state, just kept going on and on without considering that it may be too much for her to grasp all at once. I quickly rushed to her side and sat down next to her and put my arm around her. She almost collapsed into my arms.

Through sobs, tears and gritted teeth, she managed to utter a few words.

"Is that the truth, A.D.? You wouldn't make that kind of thing up, I'm sure," she softly said.

"That's the gosh honest truth, Brenda. I swear!" I stated.

"I knew about my mom remarrying and my brother being a step brother, but I sure didn't know that he was responsible for my parents' death," she stated.

"Sorry, babe!" I tried to console her.

"That bastard!" she barely whispered. "I will kill him for what he did," she vowed.

Her anger was welled up deep inside and her face became redder as it emerged.

"Can I help?" I asked, trying to lighten the mood a bit.

She was not amused, but suddenly got up and went into the bedroom and brought out an envelope. She pulled out a letter and handed it to me. I got up and walked to the window for better light and read it. The letter was the one she took from her aunt from the State Fire Marshal informing her that after extensive research, the fire at her sister's home had been determined as accidental. Investigation turned up proof that the fire started in the back of the house caused from a match or possibly a discarded cigarette. Although it first appeared as though it was arson, there was no founding proof to substantiate it. The letter went on to give condolences to the remaining family and considered the case closed. The letter was signed by a James Mc Bride, State Fire Marshal, Tallahassee, Florida.

I handed the letter back to her and as she took it, she let her hand linger on mine and looked me in the eye.

"You swear what you said is the truth, A.D. Did my brother tell you those things?" she asked.

"Yes, he did, Brenda, I swear. And I believed him. I always wondered how he could live with himself after admitting that he killed his family," I answered, honestly. "After the story about him from that man at the filling station, it all makes a lot of sense."

"Well, I will see that he suffers as much or more than my parents did. Believe that, too," she said through softened sobs.

"But, he's your brother, Brenda," I said with a questionable slowness.

"He's no brother of mine. A real brother would be remorseful and try to make amends. No sir. He's got to be punished," she was almost boiling with anger.

"My brother disowned me, too, so I can sympathize with you, honey. I will help you wherever I can if you are serious," I said.

"I am dead serious. A.D., and the sooner we get to it, the better. I will not rest until he meets his demise, legally or not," she blurted.

"So, we keep the money, then?" I asked of her with hesitation.

"For what he did, what ever is there is not near enough to pay for his sins," she said.

She was mad, and rightly so. But, I still wondered how she would react to being rich. I drug the beach bag over to the couch and dropped to my knees next to it and started opening the draw strings.

"Want to count it?" I asked.

I pulled banded bundle after banded bundle out of the bag and her eyes got bigger with each one.

"Your dream has come true, Brenda. Your genie has granted you your wish. You have all the money you will ever need. Come on, you're not counting," I teased.

"Okay, A.D., I'll help, but the new me is going to take some getting used to," she consented.

"What do you mean the new you? Are you going to become someone else?" I quizzed.

"Of course not, but lots of money has changed a lot of people in the past," she mused.

I pulled her to me and gave her a tight hug. I kissed her soft lips and could sense that she was buying into our newly found fortune. We parted and began to count the money for real. We stacked it on the kitchen table and each counted their stacks and then we totaled our sums. The more we counted the more we were both amazed. The total came to $240,000. Holy Moly, what a haul, I thought. I thought Brenda was going to faint. I figured it would be several thousand more if Frank hadn't taken some. Still, I couldn't be happier.

Brenda quickly rose and grabbed my arm and pulled me to the living room.

"We need to think about what we are going to do now, A.D.," she said sternly. "Do we continue like nothing happened or do I quit my job and we move out of here right away? We have to make some decisions," she stated. "If I quit my job, there will be questions. What do I tell my boss? If we move out right away, a lot of people are going to question why? Will that catch up with us? And if we move out of here, where are we going to go? Is this money being looked for by others?"

She then pointed back to the kitchen where the money was lying on the table.

"And how do we handle that?" she asked.

I knew what she was referring to and agreed that hiding and/or taking care of that much money could be a problem.

We sat at the table and I logically tried to answer her many questions. Brenda played with first one stack of bills and then another as we talked. I told her that the money was probably being looked for, but assured her that it would never be found. We agreed that she would not quit her job immediately, but in a few weeks, perhaps. We could say that I was looking for a job in another town, when in actual fact I would be looking for a nice home on beach front property in a nice location. That would cover me not being around during the day. We could get married by the Justice of the Peace and that would cover our departure from here. I quickly inserted the fact that she may have wished for a big fancy wedding, but under the circumstances, I didn't think it was feasible. She just poopawed that notion and continued to figure out our situation. We could keep the money in the closet momentarily until we figured out where to hide it. And in a month or so, when everything had settled down, we could begin living the life of luxury. It wasn't a foolproof plan, but at least it was a plan. My mind went to the possibility that the money could be traced, somehow. I hoped it couldn't. And then a light bulb came on.

"Does Haven City have a bus station?" I asked.

"Sure. The Southern-Trails bus station is downtown next to Wayne's gas station. It's a new building that just opened this past spring. Why?" she answered.

"Oh yeah, I remember seeing it. I was thinking about those new fandangled lockers that some of the bus stations are getting. That's all," I said.

"I heard someone say the bus station has those. The one in Blister Cove has 'em too, I think. What are you thinking?" she asked.

"A place to hide the money. We could bank some of it, and hide the rest of it until we needed it," I told her.

"I think that's a great idea. We can transfer it as we need it. Good thinking," she said.

"I'm not just a handsome face, you know," I teased.

Brenda threw a bundle of bills at me with a laugh.

We proceeded with putting the money back in the bag and I put it in the closet. Brenda was still sitting at the table pondering our situation.

"What about getting even with that bastard, Owen, or Frank?" she asked. "We have to resolve that situation before he is allowed to go any further."

"I will work on that over the next few days and if we can locate him, we will see to it that he is stopped permanently," I promised.

"Locate him? I thought you said he was the substitute caretaker at the lighthouse?" she questioned.

"No, I said I thought he was. When you described him the other day, I thought perhaps it could be him. Everything points to it, but I have not seen him at the lighthouse or any place else, for that matter. We need to ask around and covertly discover his whereabouts," I told her.

"The sooner the better, A.D.," she said. "That bastard has to pay." she solemnly said.

"I will get right on it," I promised her.

We both sat down and just sort of let the last hour or so of discovery wash over us. I felt exhausted and remembered that I hadn't had a lot of sleep in the past 24 hours. I still needed to get rid of the crate too. I looked over at Brenda and she forcefully smiled at me and took my hand and squeezed it.

"I know you love me A.D., otherwise, you could have taken off with all that money and left me to wonder what I had said or done to make you leave me," she stated. "That means a lot to me, and I thank you for wanting to share your life with me," she continued and leaned over and kissed me on the cheek.

I had been combing the city in search of Frank and was not having any luck. I checked the little car a few times by glancing in the window on my way by but couldn't see anything that rang a bell. One time I stopped and peered in through the window close to the curb and noticed a yellow invoice of some kind on the seat, but I couldn't read it. I tried the door on the sidewalk side, but it was locked. I walked around the car to the driver's side and looking for wandering eyes, tried the door. It opened. I quickly got in the car and looked at the paper. It was a rental form. Frank's name was at the top and the car was rented at the Gulf Stream Airport in Blister Cove.

"Now we're getting somewhere," I said aloud.

The car did belong to Frank, but it was not his. He was renting it. I looked in the back seat and noticed a black bag like the ones we carried on our heists. I quickly opened it and found a pair of pants and a tee shirt inside. I zipped it back up and got out of the car.

"Nice car. I had one similar one time." A man on the sidewalk was speaking to me as I got out of Frank's car.

"Yeah. They're okay. Not a lot of room in them though," I said nervously, trying to cover up my invasion. "Have a nice day," I said as a sign that I didn't want to talk.

The man must have got my drift, because he turned and walked away toward the town square. I hoped I didn't show signs of being a thief or robber.

I wandered into the lighthouse and looked over the display out of curiosity more than anything to see if it had been disturbed. It appeared to be like I left it. I tried the door to the living quarters as I passed by and it was locked. I am not sure what I would have done had it been open, but it wasn't, so I didn't have to worry about it. I did need to know if indeed Frank was staying here, though. I figured I could plan better if I knew where he was. I decided to grab Brenda for a bite at lunch and catch her up on what I discovered, then resume my search in the afternoon.

Brenda was in tears when I walked in. Mrs. Miller was trying to comfort her.

"My uncle died, A.D. He had a heart attack. I have to go to Clarkston and be with Auntie Beth. Can you take me to the airport?" she sort of mumbled and slurred her words while holding a Western Union telegraph letter.

"Sure thing. Is there an airport here in Haven City?" I asked.

"No, you'll have to go to Blister Cove. The major airlines go out of there," Mrs. Miller answered the question.

"When do you want to go, Brenda?" I asked.

"Right away if I can," she replied as she looked at Mrs. Miller.

"You go and take all the time you need, sweetheart. This job will still be here when you get back," Mrs. Miller commented.

"Thank you!" Brenda said.

We headed for the house and she quickly threw together a bag with a change or two of clothes and some personal items. I put her suitcase in the car and went back inside to assist her if she needed it.

"I don't have enough money to buy a plane ticket, A.D. Can I take some of the treasure?" she asked.

"I have enough, I'm sure. Don't worry about it," I assured her.

I made sure the door of the house was locked. I really didn't want anyone finding our treasure. I thought about taking it with us for protection, but decided not to.
The ride to Blister Cove was pretty quiet and subdued. Under the circumstances, I could understand why. I tried to make light conversation to take the gloom away, but wasn't successful. Obviously, Brenda's uncle meant a great deal to her. I suppose it makes sense though, after all, he was more of a father to her than an uncle. All I could do was assure her that everything would be okay. She flew here from Clarkston, so she was familiar with flying. I thought back to my first flight and how my ears popped a thousand times, it seems.

"Do you have any chewing gum?" I asked. "They say it helps to keep your ears from plugging up."

"Yes, I have some in my purse. Thanks," she solemnly stated.

Brenda told me where to turn and within a few minutes we were parking the car in front of the terminal. I escorted her in, carrying her bag and walked to the ticket counter. She booked a flight to Clarkston by way of Miami, then to Chicago, and then to Albany before the short hop to Clarkston. The ticket wasn't all that much, I didn't think. Brenda offered to pay me back, but I paid her no mind. Her flight was familiar, because she had to change planes in Miami, Chicago and Albany. I knew about changing planes because I had done it a time or two. I gave her $50 to use wherever and sat with her in the waiting room and hugged and kissed her before she went out the door to load up.

"I'll be back as soon as I can, A.D. Will you still be here?" she asked when we parted.

"Of course I will. You can't get rid of me that easily," I assured her. "Let me know when you are coming home and I will pick you up right here."

"Promise?" she asked.

"Promise." I stated.

I waited around and watched the plane lift off and get airborne before heading back to Haven City. I thought of the flights that I had enjoyed the past few years.

The next day was met with a little degree of anxiety. With Brenda gone, I felt alone, suddenly. I recalled other times that I felt this way and decided to just buckle down and get on with things. She would be back in a week or so and things could get under way toward our future. Meanwhile, I needed to find Frank and try to think of a way that he can be punished. I would get busy trying to locate him first by asking around as to whether others may have seen him.

After a busy morning cleaning and sprucing up the house, I drove over to Mott's Service Station to ask the town's "historian" if he knew anything about my adversary.

"I heard about a man taking Bert's place while he's recuperating, but I haven't seen him. A friend of yours, too?" Wayne inquired.

"Not really, just curious about that little foreign car out front. I'm told it belongs to this guy," I hedged.

"Nope, can't help you there, I'm afraid. I did hear that the man is seeing a gal that works at the restaurant next door, though. You might ask someone there," Wayne volunteered.

"Thanks, I'll do that," I replied.

I drove to the restaurant on the other side of the lighthouse gift shop for a visit. Wayne's tip made sense, seeing as how the restaurant was so close to the lighthouse. The restaurant was called **'The Crab Pot'** and naturally featured seafood on the menu. I walked up to the front door and saw the sign… CLOSED. The place was closed and the small sign in the corner of the window indicated that they opened at 11:00. I had turned and was walking back to the car when a lady dressed as a waitress opened the door and called out from behind me if she could help me.

"Yes you can. I am looking for a friend that recently moved here and was wondering…have you seen the man that is tending the lighthouse? I was told to check here, but you're closed," I stated while pointing over to the lighthouse.

"You must mean Frankie?" she knowingly said. Then after seeing my face, asked, "What's wrong?"

I must have looked at her with a strange face or something, but hearing him referred to as Frankie, the strange look was not surprising.

"Nothing, I was just surprised to hear you call him Frankie. He hated that term when we were working together," I confided.

"That's what we call him and he doesn't seem to mind. He's Vickie's friend, anyway. At least he was. He went down the coast a few days ago to do some business. She's not real happy about it, but he should be back either today or tomorrow. That's his car right there," she pointed toward the line of cars in front of the lighthouse. "That little sports car. He used Vickie's car for the trip. That's the reason she's not real happy…that and the fact that he took Linda with him. Can I tell her you're looking for him?" she volunteered.

"That's a little confusing, but no thanks." I said. "Just out of curiosity, how do you know all of this?" I quizzed.

"He's taking care of the lighthouse while Mr. Gunther recuperates from his hip surgery. Mr. Gunther is staying at his sister's place down in Gulfport. Frankie has dinner here at the restaurant almost every night while he's staying at the lighthouse and he and Vickie hit it off right away and have been dating," she said.

"Who's Linda, then?" I asked.

"She works here too and she's the one that is trying to make Vicki jealous…doing a pretty good job of it right now," she replied while smacking her chewing gum. "Who are you, I might ask?" Now it was her turn to be suspicious.

"Like I said, just a friend. Today or tomorrow, huh? I can wait that long," I said as I tipped my hat, pulling it further down over my eyes and then walked back to the car.

As I got in the car, the friendly and helpful waitress was still standing in the door of the restaurant watching my departure with a furrowed brow.

"So," I thought, "*Frankie* was the temporary caretaker of the lighthouse. He's only been here for a few weeks and already seeing the ladies. I recalled his big attraction to women… apparently it was still being exercised."

I again started thinking of a way for Frank to meet his demise in a way that would be swift, accurate, and final. If I knew what kind of car Vickie's was, I could run Frank off the road and into a deep canyon on his way back into town. Knowing him, he may just drop Linda off somewhere and continue on his way and never look back the way he did me. No, on second thought, he wouldn't leave the money. He will be back if for nothing else but that. I began to think of ways for Frank to meet his end rather than the canyon drop…hmmm, I wonder if I can get him to fall from the ledge at the lighthouse to the rocks below? I wonder if I could poison his food at The Crab Pot and he could suffer and die from that. Are there sharks in the water around here? I could get a gun and just shoot the bastard and be done with it. I decided to visit the restaurant and perhaps meet and talk with Vickie.

"Just one?" The hostess asked me as I entered the restaurant.

"Just me," I acknowledged. "Is Vickie working today?" I asked.

"Yes, would you like to sit in her section?" she asked.

"Yes, Please. That would be great," I said.

I was seated and a menu was placed in my hand. I was glancing through it without really seeing it when a female voice asked if I was ready to order. I put down the menu and looked up into the most beautiful blue eyes I had ever seen.

"I'll just have a cup of clam chowder and a glass of iced tea, please," I said.

As she was writing it down on her pad, I noticed her name tag said **Victoria** in large black letters.

"I understand you may know a friend of mine. Frank Epperson?" I stated.

"How do you know that weasel?" she asked.

"He and I worked together a while back. I'm trying to find him to return a few things to him that he left behind," I lied. "He said that he was headed to Haven City, so I came to find him."

"Well, he's not here today. I don't know how well you know him, mister, but I'd watch my P's and Q's around him if I were you," she said through clinched teeth. "I have only known him for a short time and already he's jilting me," she added.

"Sorry to upset you, ma'am," I said.

"I'm not upset, just warning you about your friend, that's all," she said. "Some day he will get his. People like that always pay for their crimes against society in the end."

"Your co-worker told me he drove down the coast in your car...is that right?" I asked.

"Yes, and took that little she-devil, Linda with him," she sneered. "Is that all you wanted?" she asked as she picked up the menu.

"Yes, thank you," I replied.

She took the menu and walked off toward the kitchen. She had a great figure too. I could see the attraction that made Frank want to date her. This Linda girl must be prettier yet, or Frank was playing one against the other, I thought.

Vickie didn't return with my soup; another waitress that was older and larger named Pearl, did. I didn't ask about Vickie, just figured she didn't want to renew the conversation about the man she was despising. It was obvious that she was not real pleased with the situation.

The soup was delicious. As I ate, I tried to think of a fitting end for my former friend and co-worker. I thought of Brenda and what a surprise I had laid on her. Poor thing. She certainly deserved better. I wondered how she was coping with the death of her uncle and couldn't wait for her to return. I missed her already.

I tried to recall any details about Frank that I may be missing in order to better prepare a way for him to meet his maker. I couldn't think of a thing. I came here thinking that I could find the money and get the heck out of here, leaving Frank holding the bag, so to speak. Then I run into Brenda and that changed everything. Well, almost everything. I found the money, but now I need to fulfill a promise I made. Frank has to die and I truly want to have a part in his death, but couldn't think of a way to do it.

CHAPTER 19

Brenda made it back and it was so good to see her. We embraced like never before and for a long time when we met in the airport boarding area. Our trip back to Haven City was filled with talk of her trip, our future, the money, how Clarkston had changed in the time she was away, and how much she missed me. I didn't get to say a lot because she pretty much dominated the conversation the whole way. But I didn't mind. It was really good to have her back. I fully realized in her absence that I was in love with her and wanted to spend the rest of my life with her.

"Thanks for keeping the house up," she said as we entered.

"Not a problem. I did what I could," I hammed it up, wiping the pretend sweat off my brow. "I ate out every night so as not to dirty any dishes and I slept on the couch so I wouldn't have to make the bed," I continued.

"You liar. You did not," she laughed; then paused for a moment. "Thank you for being here. I love you, A.D.," she added as she came to me and hugged me close.

"I love you too, Brenda," I whispered in her ear.

The evening was spent mostly reminiscing and talking about our future. I caught her up on my hunt for Frank and what I found out. We made a few plans to enact over the next few days; I would look for us a place to live and she would work out an exit from the store without giving away everything. We both would think really hard for a way to get even with the man that brought us together. We agreed on our plan and went to bed. Brenda was exhausted and was asleep almost before her head hit the pillow.

My trip down the Gulf Coast was done with several things in mind other than look for a place for us to live. A way to dispose of the man that at least three people now hated (me, Brenda and his former girlfriend, Vickie) was a huge priority and how to dispose of our massive amount of cash was high on the list. I drove through the small town of Seaside without even realizing it because my mind was filled with jumbled thoughts. On the other side of Blister Cove, the highway Y's with Route 16 headed inland to Mandrill and because of my inattention, I took the Y to the left and was almost to the little town before I put a stop to the waywardness. I turned around and noticed a billboard near by. The billboard read *'12 miles to Highland Beach'* and under it read; **'the home of the world famous Gretchen Lighthouse'** and below that, it read; *in Jinks Harbor*. The sign advertised the opening hours for tours was at 10 a.m. and the gift shop was open daily from 10-4. I had never heard of the Gretchen Lighthouse and didn't remember seeing Jinks Harbor on the map, but out of curiosity, and to get back on the main road, I drove the 12 miles to Highland Beach.

The small town was not much more than a wide spot in the road. The remains of a lighthouse could be seen in the distance as the small town came into view. I stopped in front of the monument sign and joined two other people in reading an inscription of the famous place. It told of the lighthouse being fired upon during an invasion by war ships in the early 1800's. Supposedly, a cannon was fired at the lighthouse to extinguish it from sending out a beacon. The cannon ball did its trick, but in the process, the lamp oil was splattered all over and set the rest of the building on fire. The lighthouse was destroyed and burned to the ground. All that remains today is what was left after the fire went out. It's a skeleton of a partial wall that's a tall, jagged, charred sliver of wood reaching into the sky. The story continues to explain that the pirates invaded the small village and pillaged and burned everything in sight, leaving it wasted and destroyed. The pirate was Brie Augustine and he was trying to escape from the rascal Roberto Gallatin. They later teamed up and ran rampant for over a year before they were both caught and hung outside Jinks Harbor. The town folk carried them both out to sea and dropped their dead bodies into the ocean. A gift shop had been built next door to the former structure and had a lot of lighthouse replica's and of course hundreds of plagues and signs depicting the famous Gretchen Lighthouse and the pirates and ships that did the damage. The usual assortment of seashells and other items depicting the beach and ocean were also available.

An interesting story, I thought, but a greater ending would have been for the two pirates to have walked the plank. A new lighthouse was built not too far away and has been serving the area for many years since that horrible day. The idea of firing a cannon into the lighthouse that Frank was living in came to mind, but where was I going to get a cannon. The idea of burning the place down crossed my mind, but a person could be put away for a long time for the crime of arson and I had no desire whatsoever of spending any time in jail. Then, I thought back to the old place and remembering the dry conditions, I figured it would go up pretty good if a method could be figured out on how to do it.

I drove on down the coast a ways further and entered Pleasant Beach, a nice little town that sits about fifty feet up off the shores of the Gulf Coast. I parked the car at a roadside monument and looked down and out over the Gulf. The sand wasn't as white, but it sure was pretty. The beach meanders around a jutting hillside further down the way and the beach extends as far as the eye can see. There were four people riding horses on the beach below and they were looking up toward the town. I waved with little thought of them seeing me and was surprised that one of them actually waved back. Friendly place, I thought. Of course they are probably tourists visiting the area and just being overly friendly. This could very well be a place for us to live, I thought.

I returned to Haven City with an air of excitement. I thought living out the rest of our lives in a place like Pleasant Beach wouldn't be all that bad. I drove the whole way with ideas of settling in the area while thoughts of ridding ourselves of Frank kept interrupting me. I kept coming back to the idea of burning the lighthouse down with him in it. I was anxious to tell Brenda about the town of Pleasant Beach and my idea of living there. I was also anxious to tell her of my idea on burning the lighthouse down. I didn't resolve the situation with the money. That was going to have to be dealt with soon, though.

Brenda had never been to Pleasant Beach, but said it sounded nice.

"Aunt Beth spoke of it a few times, I remember; why, is that where you want to live?" she asked.

"I don't know, honey. We agreed that we can't live here, though. You want to live on the beach, you said. That's all I was trying to find, was a place near a beach," I commented.

When I told her my idea about the fire, her face lit up like the lighthouse itself. She thought it was not only a great idea, but fittingly proper. The man that killed her parents and thought he killed his sister in a fire that he set should meet his own destiny in a fire. She couldn't think of a better ending for him or a better beginning for us.

"How do we do it?" she asked with sincerity.

"I have no idea, right now, sweetie, but if that's what we are going to do, we need to come up with a way," I told her.

Over the next few days both of us racked our brains trying to come up with a solid plan that would rid us of the evil man. I had never messed with fire of any kind, other than making one in the family wood stove. I had heard of people being referred to as pyromaniacs, and learned in school that it meant the person lighting the fire was fascinated and addicted to the flame and blaze it created. I couldn't imagine anyone being so drawn to that type of destruction. I guess it takes all kinds to make a world.

Brenda said she used to make camp fires when she was growing up during outings to the woodlands with her aunt and uncle, but nothing on the scale of what it would take to light up the lighthouse. The lamp of the lighthouse was electric now as opposed to candles and oil lamps of the past. I thought if it was the olden days, causing a fire would be easier. While on the porch, I noticed the sacks of dried flowers and weeds that Brenda used for her designs and remembered Frank telling me about the fire that he set by accident that killed his family. The little bit of dried grass or weeds in the sacks wouldn't be near enough to put the lighthouse ablaze, I didn't think.

"You're sure he lives in the lighthouse?" Brenda asked through the screen door.

"I don't for sure because I haven't seen him, but from the information I got from the restaurant, he's the temporary man in the lighthouse, so at least we know where he should be," I answered from the porch.

The next day, Brenda came home after work and I was fixing a screen on the bedroom window. I never heard her come in and when she entered the room she instinctively turned on the light. Something popped inside the fixture and the light bulb exploded. Brenda screamed, I jumped, and a whiff of smoke came out of the light fixture as we both looked on with astonishment.

"What the heck?" I blurted.

"I told the landlord the wiring in this place was rotten," she exclaimed. "He said he planned to rewire it next spring."

"Do we need to call him?" I asked.

"Well, I'm sure we blew a fuse. We can either call him now, or temporarily fix it and call him later," she volunteered.

"Fix it; how?" I asked

"You're a man and you don't know that?" she teased as she walked over and turned off the switch.

"Heck no, do you?" I asked

"Yes, I do," she bragged.

"Then why don't you fix it, smarty britches," I challenged.

She asked if I could remove the base of the light bulb while she got another bulb.

"I think so. I am scared of electricity though, I'm telling you right now," I said.

"Okay, let me do it and you watch. It's not a big deal. The light switch is off, remember?" she patronized. "Do you have a penny?" she asked.

I questionably reached in my pocket and handed her a penny.

"You'll see…just wait a minute," she answered my question without it being asked.

She left the room and came back with a chair and a clothes pin in her hands. She placed the chair under the light and stood on it. She put the working end of the clothes pin into the light socket and squeezed the prongs together causing pressure to the inside and rotated them as though removing a screw. The broken bulb base unscrewed and was removed. She handed it to me and stepped down and stooped to pick up the broken bulb. I started to question her about the penny, but she held up her hand as if to say 'wait' and left the bedroom. I followed. We went to the kitchen and she dumped the broken stuff into the trash. Brenda got a fresh bulb from the cupboard and handed it to me.

"Hold this for a second," she instructed.

She opened the fuse box next to the refrigerator. She unscrewed a fuse from the box, looked at it and then put the penny behind it and screwed it back in. We walked to the bedroom and she asked me to screw the light bulb into the fixture. I hesitantly and nervously did so and she flipped the switch and the new light bulb shone brightly just as though nothing had ever happened.

"Wow. You're a magician," I exclaimed. "How does that work?" I asked.

She explained the theory and also the dangers of bypassing a fuse. Copper is a natural conductor of electricity and the penny bridges the contacts of the burned out fuse fooling the system into thinking that a new fuse has been installed. It is not a good idea to leave the penny behind the fuse for long, though, because fuses are designed to counter overloads by breaking and stopping the power from being transferred. If a power surge occurs and the fuse doesn't stop it, then a fire could erupt in the box and spread rapidly throughout the structure it serves.

As soon as she said it, we both looked at one another and knew how we could burn down the lighthouse. All we needed was a sure proof method of making it work…and a penny or two.

We worked on the plan for several hours over the next few days. The plan was to cautiously place a piece of copper under a couple of fuses in the box at the lighthouse and wait for an overload to cause the electrical fire that hopefully would destroy the place with Frank inside. It was a long shot at best, but the only way we could think of to cause the fire other than to torch it. The overload could occur when the big light came on or even something in the lighthouse being turned on, like the oven, or a light switch. It may not happen for a day or two, and then again, it may not happen at all. The real challenge was if it did happen; would Frank be caught inside the burning structure?

The likelihood of the fire starting at night was as remote as it happening in broad daylight...one just never knows. We decided to try it anyway and see what happens. We agreed that it wasn't foolproof, but at least it's an idea and we figured we had to start somewhere.

I cased the lighthouse on two different nights to get an idea as to the timing of when Frank was inside. I also noted the time the big light came on and tried to get a sense of when other lights in the dwelling portion were being turned on and off. My vantage point was with binoculars (borrowed from Mrs. Miller) from the back of the restaurant. The watching and planning reminded me of some of the bank jobs Frank and I did. This was different in several ways, but the concept was the same.

The first night I settled down on a grassy knoll behind the restaurant and focused the binoculars on the windows of the second floor of the lighthouse. The lighthouse was quite aways further out toward the beach than the restaurant or the gift shop, so seeing it clearly was not a problem. After about an hour of watching, I heard arguing from the front of the lighthouse, but couldn't see anything from my position. It was definitely a man and a woman in a heated argument and I thought it might be Frank and Vickie, but couldn't decipher either one.
I watched for nearly two hours and Frank never appeared. It was possible that he was inside, just never crossed in front of the window that I had a bead on. I never did see anyone cross in front of the window, but a light burned all night long through it. The big light went out at sunup, 5:10 a.m. I figured if this type of routine continues for several nights, I may have to pitch a tent on the lawn behind the restaurant in order to stay the course. I wasn't really sleepy after the all-night ritual, but knew I needed sleep, so bedded down on the couch until Brenda went to work and then transferred to the bedroom and slept soundly until after lunch. I tidied up around the house during the afternoon

and had supper ready when she entered the door after working until 6 p.m.

"You didn't need to fix dinner, A.D. I could have had a peanut butter and jelly sandwich, but thank you," she praised. "Did you get any rest?"

"I did. And fixing dinner is not a big deal. Toasted cheese sandwiches are one of my favorites anyway," I told her.

"Mine too," she said.

"I fixed the shower for you, too," I admitted.

"What was wrong with it?" she asked.

"It was just a mere drip rather than a stream, silly. You had to turn around a hundred times just to get wet," I joked.

"Does it work better, now then?" she asked.

"Of course. I fixed it, I told you," I bragged.

"Thanks. It's nice to have a man around the house for that sort of thing," she commented.

"You could have done it probably, but obviously it didn't bother you the way it was," I said. "You might want to back into the stream slowly in the morning so as not to get knocked over," I teased.

We visited with idle chit-chat and listened to records until after dark and then I got ready to do another night of watching.

"Do you want to take something to nibble on, A.D.? You didn't eat a lot at supper," Brenda said with concern.

"I'm fine. Hopefully, I won't have to spend the entire night this time," I replied.

Not more than an hour after settling down behind the restaurant for another night of watching, I spotted someone through the upstairs window. I couldn't swear that it was Frank due to the shadowy figure, but figured it had to be. It was male at least, although a woman could have short hair too, I suppose. The figure passed by the window several times before whoever it was went to bed for the night. I was still sleepy from the previous all night vigil, so decided to leave it to chance. If the big light coming on for the evening could cause the surge of electricity we needed, then setting the copper piece behind the fuse would need to be done after the light went out. Which fuse was a mystery. I took a risk and eased my way down the side of the lighthouse and opened the fuse box. It was larger than Brenda's and there were big fuses about three inches long and small ones like in Brenda's box. I figured if we put a penny behind all of them, we couldn't miss. It would be risky, but I made the decision to do the deed at 5:15 a.m. and hope no one saw me. We would have the entire day to pack and get out of town to some far away place, letting the dastardly deed take place when we weren't anywhere close. All we could hope for was that the deed <u>would</u> take place.

I returned to the house a little after midnight and explained everything to a wide awake Brenda. She explained that the larger amp fuses would be the secondary fuses for the big light and that they were most likely the long ones I saw. She wasn't sure how to rig one of the large fuses, but figured there had to be a way.

"Maybe some copper wire would work. I have some in the drawer in the kitchen. We can take it just in case," she suggested.

"Why aren't you in bed? It's really late and you have to go to work tomorrow. It's your last day, you know and you have to tell Mrs. Miller that you're leaving," I half scolded.

"I couldn't sleep with you out there, so I waited up," she stated

She was sold on the idea of us leaving and decided to tell Mrs. Miller about our plans to get married. She hoped that Mrs. Miller would agree that today would be her last day at the shop.

She had listed the things needing done prior to our departure and thought that I could do most of them. We went to bed with an air of excitement for what could occur in a little over twenty-four hours.

The next morning, I drove to the post office and filled out a change of address card, stopped in at City Hall and notified them to return the water and electricity to the landlord's name, sending the final billing to General Delivery in care of Brenda at Blister Cove's post office, and then stopped in at the telephone office and had her phone turned off.

"Where do we send the final billing, sir?" the lady at the counter asked.

I gave her the forwarding address we agreed on for all of the final stuff. I drove to the filling station and gassed up the car before meeting Brenda for lunch.

"Where you headed, young man?" Wayne asked while filling up the car.

"I'm going down the coast a ways to see about a job with a charter outfit; J and P Charters, heard of them?" I lied.

"Can't say that I have. Good luck!" he wished as I paid him for the gas.

"Thanks," I said, and drove away.

———

I met Brenda for lunch at an outside café on the boardwalk. I told her about my day and the success I had in getting everything done in order for us to depart the area.

"Mrs. Miller is not happy with me, you know," Brenda started. "She was hoping that I could buy her out or at least talk about it. I don't know where she thought I was going to get the money to do that, but it was nice of her to consider me anyway," she added.

"Isn't she happy that you found a man to marry you?" I asked.

"Oh, of course she is. It just caught her by surprise, that's all," Brenda explained. "She wished us all the luck in the world. She said she had hopes that I would someday want to buy her out and take over the shop. I told her thanks, but no thanks."

"Do you think you would have, had I not happened by?" I asked.

"I don't know. I never thought about it, really," Brenda commented.

We held hands on the walk back to the shop, kissed goodbye and parted. During the afternoon, I used the crate to pack a few things and got out Brenda's suitcases along with mine for her to pack when she got home. I emptied the refrigerator, packed the food from the cupboard and packed up a lot of the knick knacks, pictures, and things sitting out. I packed the car with everything that I had packed up and made sure that I left room for the suitcases and the bed covers and pillows. None of the furniture was hers due to her renting a furnished house, so nothing big had to be moved.

When Brenda got home, she changed clothes and packed all of her belongings. We didn't talk a lot during the evening, but every time we passed one another we would either kiss lightly, touch one another lovingly somewhere, or touch hands...all of it being a sign that both of us were nervous and excited at the same time. After completing the packing and doing a walk-through to make sure everything was packed, we drove down to the drive-in for a hamburger. We ate inside and mostly sat in silence. We sat across from one another and looked at one another like two lovesick cows. Neither of us ate much of our order.

"Did you get the bag safely in the car?" she asked.

"Yes! All that is left is our bedding," I answered.

We went to bed in our street clothes and slept fitfully until 4:30 a.m. After washing our faces and brushing our teeth, Brenda packed up the bedding and the toiletry items and I hauled them to the car. We left the house, drove to a side street near the lighthouse and walked to it. The big light was out and it was light enough outside to see how to work. I walked with her to the building and waited in front while she scaled the side wall to the box. She insisted on doing the deed and her being more experienced, I let her. She closed the fuse box quietly and returned to the front of the building where I was watching.

"I wired the big fuses with copper wire and joined them to the buss bar in back. I put pennies under the small ones just like at the house. Keep your fingers crossed that one of them will do the trick," she informed me when she returned.

I had no idea what she meant regarding the 'buss bar' and didn't ask. The trap was set and we needed to hope like crazy that our plan worked. We walked rapidly back to the car and left town headed south. The sun was starting to peek over the horizon in the east and bless the day. I looked over at Brenda and smiled. She grabbed my hand and smiled wryly at me. I read it as being very nervous, but excited about our new adventure.

CHAPTER 20

3 Years Later

Brenda is expecting our second child. We have spent the last few months going through names for boys and girls. Brenda wants a girl this time and has two names picked out. She says she will know which one to choose when she sees her *daughter*. The names are Beverly and Susan. Sue was her mom's name. She just likes the name Beverly, for some reason. Either one would be okay with me…and I'm okay with a girl; I just want a healthy baby.

Our plan to rig the fuse box and set fire to the lighthouse was done. And believe it or not, the fire happened twenty four hours after we left; but not by the rigged fuse box…or at least it was not listed as the cause. We can't take credit for the fire that killed the occupants, either. But, justice prevailed. The paper's account of the fire stated that the girl Vickie, the waitress that Frank borrowed the car from that day, was arrested and jailed for setting fire to the lighthouse and killing both Frank and his other girlfriend, Linda. Vickie will undoubtedly spend the rest of her life in prison for arson and a double homicide. What's the saying…something about a woman being scorned…Anyway, the lighthouse was destroyed and the bodies were found in the rubble. Like I figured, the place went up like it had been soaked in gasoline.

Our plan was successful, although it wasn't carried out by our hands. The story never indicated an electrical short or electrical fire; it said that Vickie threw a Molotov cocktail through a second story window. She was spotted by a passerby that tried to stop her as she ran away. The male witness yelled for her to stop and when she ran toward him, he stepped in front of her to stop her. Vickie pushed the witness to the side of the sidewalk, knocking him down, and ran into the street and got behind the wheel of a car that was already running. The man quickly got up and ran after her, but was unable to see any license plate number due to the darkening night. The time was just minutes after the big light came on at 8:54. I guess Vickie figured the big light wasn't bright enough and decided to boost the output a little. We would never know if the copper wire or the little pennies we placed under the fuses were instrumental in the place going up in smoke.

The police were notified and the fire department was called. The old place was so dry there was no way the fire department could save it. The writer of the story embellished a little saying that it was unlikely that the nearby waves crashing on the beach would have been enough to save the place. Another article accompanying the original story quoted the Fire Chief as saying almost the same thing; that the ocean tide would have had a problem dousing that fire. The police located Vickie in the plaza two days later disguised as a man; trousers, trench coat and a fedora pulled down over her face. She was in a woman's boutique looking at sweaters and the clerk of the store recognized her from being at the restaurant. The clerk watched her for a bit and then thinking something wasn't right, asked her assistant to seek the police. The clerk should have been a detective or a police woman, because she actually engaged Vickie in conversation about what she was looking for; enabling enough time for the police to arrive. They arrested her when she was leaving the store and took her into custody. It was not revealed as to why she was sticking around the town after torching the lighthouse.

We live in a really nice area more than fifty miles down the Gulf Coast from Haven City and 35 miles south of Blister Cove. We decided to live in Pleasant Beach after all. The house we bought (for cash) is just a little bit out of the city and sits on a low cliff overlooking Cape June and the Gulf. It's just north of the Shank Peninsula that juts out into the ocean. The house is not anything elaborate, but a really comfortable, three-bedroom job that was only vacant for two weeks before we found it. Brenda loves the kitchen and I have a small shop to putter around in. There are two trees on the property, one in front of the house and one in the back. We had a cement patio poured right after we bought the place and we can sit in our lounge chairs and look out over the ocean in the evenings from it. The thing we use for a table on the patio to sit our drinks on is the crate I took from the lighthouse to carry the money bags in. I decorated it up a bit with some trim pieces and a little bit of paint. It serves as a reminder of how I got back at the one man that tried to ruin my life. Brenda has her own little memory joggers, but keeps them locked up in her mind. We are both pleased that justice was carried out.

Our closest neighbor is about seventy yards away, back toward town, and ironically, a clover patch grows about half way to their house from ours and both Brenda and I have made necklaces from it a few times. She modified the necklaces a bit with Butter Cups; they grow wildly in the same field. The splash of yellow in the necklace changes the looks of it considerably. A well-built staircase leads down to a fairly private beach, but the sand is not as white as we would like. The whitest sand on the coast is still in Haven City. Neither of us works. We don't have to because our money will last us a while.

After we got married by the Justice of the Peace in Blister Cove, we did a little vacationing as a honeymoon. Neither of us had ever been deep sea fishing and wanted to try it, so we drove to Miami and spent a few days there. During that time, I called the charter guys I met on the road, J & P Deep Sea Charters, and they took us out. We were two of seven people on the boat and we both got a chance to work the poles when we latched on to a barracuda. We weren't good enough to haul it in, (the big fish broke the line) but everyone had a great time and the best part for us was we neither one got seasick. It was good to see the gentlemen again, too. As a honeymoon gift, they didn't charge us for the fishing trip.

Brenda does some home craft things and still messes with flower arrangements when she has time. She just sold a few arrangements at a bazaar she attended in Haven City. She ran into Mrs. Miller at it. Brenda said she was doing good but missed assembling the displays at the lighthouse. Apparently, a new lighthouse is being constructed on the same sight. I haven't returned to Haven City since that night and the bazaar was Brenda's only time. I help her with the arrangements she takes to the bazaars once in a while, but haven't ever gone with her to them. Brenda takes the car on her weekend trips and I mostly sit with the baby. I have taken up the hobby of drawing and spend a lot of time sketching scenes from looking out on the water. I've been thinking of buying a Ham operators set. I would use it simply as a hobby, though. If I do get one, maybe I can teach it to our kids some day.

Part of our plan after getting out of town was to act like normal people and not flaunt our wealth. Another part was to get married and settle in a nice area and blend in with everyone else. With what I still had from my original bank roll, we bought what we needed. We deposited a lot of the money from the suitcases in a bank close by and are living quite comfortably. We did get one of those fancy lockers at the bus station in Blister Cove for the rest of the bagged money. We get some out and make deposits into the bank from it monthly. Well over three quarters of the banded money is still in the beach bag with the dolphin on it. Right now, we have decided to just leave it there and use it as needed. Brenda thinks that putting all of it in the bank at once would draw too much attention. I agreed. Maybe after the baby gets here we will try to address that situation further.

We have talked briefly about returning to Haven City and buying Mrs. Miller's store from her. It would be a great investment and we probably should, but need to talk it through in depth before doing so. With kids in our daily life now, Brenda would need to stay at home and I would have to operate the shop. I don't know anything about running a business, but figure I could learn. If Brenda ran it, questions would be raised about what I do and why I don't need to work. I could find a job doing something, I suppose, but I really don't want to at this point.

Not too long after we got this place, I read in the paper that the leader of the once famous Speakeasy Gang, Mrs. Nora Jenkins, passed away and her niece, Molly Joiner, was arrested and sentenced to 25 years in prison. There was no mention of how they were found out. The story mentioned the late Frank Epperson as an accomplice, but there wasn't a thing about me in there. Hundreds of thousands of dollars were recovered in two banks in London, Ontario, Canada where they lived. Who was repaid (if anyone) was not mentioned. I wondered what they do with the money in those types of cases.

I used to look over my shoulder quite often for an FBI car to come up the driveway to get me. It would be great to see Agent Walt Ballard if he's still in the Bureau. Not that I would want to see him for the purpose of getting arrested, but to give him some flak about what I telephoned him about would be kind of neat. I have since taken for granted that my involvement in all of the robberies has been dropped and the case is closed. I hope I'm right in my assumption. I like it here and can hopefully live out the rest of my life here and raise a family that will become someone someday. At least they will get a better start than their parents got.

Today is a beautiful day at the beach and I'm enjoying the sunshine with my family. It's something that we try to do often. I love them both and love bouncing the little one on my knee. I remember wishing to have a little one to sit on my knee and that hope has come true. Soon, there will be one more.

"Isn't that right, Junior?" I said to my son.

The End

Would you like to see your manuscript become a book?

If you are interested in becoming a PublishAmerica author, please submit your manuscript for possible publication to us at:

acquisitions@publishamerica.com

You may also mail in your manuscript to:

**PublishAmerica
PO Box 151
Frederick, MD 21705**

We also offer free graphics for Children's Picture Books!

www.publishamerica.com